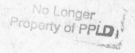

Praise for

the darkness gathers

"Tough but tender—a harrowing ride in the company of Lydia Strong, one of my favorite new characters, by one of my favorite new writers."
—Lee Child, *New York Times* bestselling author

"Once in a while a mystery novel appears that has everything you want and more: gutsy, complicated characters, a rocket-paced story that hardly gives you time to catch your breath, and twists and turns you never see coming. This is that novel. . . . *The Darkness Gathers* is flat-out terrific."
—Margaret Coel, *New York Times* bestselling author

"Fast-paced mystery . . . the tension is palpable."
—*Albuquerque Journal*

"Taut and suspenseful."
—*Cleveland Plain Dealer*

"Miscione appeared on the thriller scene a year ago with the widely acclaimed *Angel Fire* and should garner equally enthusiastic reviews for her second . . . it soars."
—*St. Petersburg Times*

"The author, who lives in Clearwater, has a thorough understanding of the vagaries of South Florida. And Miscione delivers some action-packed scenes, especially a few creepy nights in Manhattan and a chilling visit to Albania."
—*Sun-Sentinel*

lisa unger

writing as
Lisa Miscione

the darkness gathers

a novel

broadway paperbacks
new york

BROADWAY

Copyright © 2003 by Lisa Miscione
Preface copyright © 2011 by Lisa Unger
Excerpt from *Twice* copyright © 2004 by Lisa Miscione

All rights reserved.
Published in the United States by Broadway Paperbacks, an imprint of the Crown Publishing Group, a division of Random House, Inc., New York.

www.crownpublishing.com

Broadway Paperbacks and its logo, a letter B bisected on the diagonal, are trademarks of Random House, Inc.

Originally published in hardcover in slightly different form in the United States by St. Martin's Press, New York, in 2003 and subsequently in paperback by St. Martin's Press, New York, in 2004.

Library of Congress Cataloging-in-Publication Data
Miscione, Lisa.
The darkness gathers / Lisa Miscione.—1st ed.
        p.   cm.
1. Teenage girls—Crimes against—Fiction. 2. Women journalists—Fiction.
3. Missing persons—Fiction. 4. Crime writing—Fiction. 5. Miami (Fla.)—
Fiction. 6. Kidnapping—Fiction. I. Title.
        PS3613.I83 D3   2003
        813'.6—dc21   2002024527

ISBN 978-0-307-95311-7
eISBN 978-0-307-95312-4

Printed in the United States of America

Cover design by Mumtaz Mustafa
Cover photography by Jen Kiaba/Trevillion Images

10 9 8 7 6 5 4 3 2 1

First Broadway Paperbacks Edition

Preface
by Lisa Unger

I was nineteen years old when I first met Lydia Strong. I was living in the East Village, dating a New York City police officer, and attending Eugene Lang College, the undergraduate school of the New School for Social Research. I was sitting in a car, under the elevated section of the "1" line in the Bronx, waiting—for what I can't remember. But in my mind that day, I kept seeing this woman running past a church. She was in New Mexico. And all I knew about her was that she was a damaged person, someone in great pain. Running, for her, was salve, religion, and drug. That was Lydia.

I pulled a napkin and a pen from the glove compartment and started writing the book that would become *Angel Fire*. It took me ten years to write that novel, mostly because the years between age nineteen and twenty-nine were, for me, years of hard work and tumultuous change. But also because during that time, I let my dreams of becoming a writer languish a bit. Lydia was faithful; she waited.

In spite of a first-rate education, a career in publishing, and a strong desire to write fiction, I didn't know much of anything when I was writing my first novel. I don't think you *can* really know anything about writing a novel until you've actually written one. (And then you go to school again when you sit down to write your second, and your third, and so on.) All I knew during that time was that I was truly fascinated by this woman occupying a place in my imagination, and I was deeply intrigued by her very dark appetites. I was enthralled by her past, by the mysteries in her present, and why she wouldn't let herself love the man who loved her. There were lots of questions about Lydia Strong, and I was never happier over those ten years than when I was trying to answer them.

I was fortunate that the first novel I ever wrote was accepted by my (wonderful, brilliant) agent Elaine Markson, and that she fairly quickly brokered a deal for *Angel Fire* and my second, then unwritten, novel *The Darkness Gathers*. I spent the next few years with Lydia Strong and the very colorful cast of characters who populated her life. And I enjoyed every dark, harrowing, and complicated moment with them as I went on to write *Twice,* and then *Smoke.*

I followed Lydia from New Mexico, to New York City, to Albania, to Miami, and back. We trekked through the abandoned subway tunnels under Manhattan, to a compound in the backwoods of Florida, to a mysterious church in the Bronx, to a fictional town called Haunted. It was a total thrill ride, and I wrote like my fingers were on fire.

I am delighted that these early novels, which I published under my maiden name, Lisa Miscione, have found a new life on the shelves and a new home with the stellar team at Broadway Paperbacks. And, of course, I am thrilled that they've found their way into your hands. I know a lot of authors wish their early books would just disappear, because they've come so far as writers since they first began their careers. And I understand that, because we would all go back and rewrite everything if we could.

But I have a special place in my heart for these flawed, sometimes funny, complicated characters and their wild, action-packed stories. I still think about them, and I feel tremendous tenderness for even the most twisted and deranged among them. The writing of each book was pure pleasure. I hope that you enjoy your time with them as much as I have. And, thanks, as always, for reading.

part one

The offing was barred by a black bank of clouds, and the tranquil waterway leading to the uttermost ends of the earth flowed somber under an overcast sky— seemed to lead to the heart of an immense darkness.

—Joseph Conrad
Heart of Darkness

chapter one

The voice on the tape was thin and quavering. Lydia Strong had to rewind the tape and turn up the volume. In the background, she could hear the wet whisper of cars passing on rain-slick roads and, once, the loud, sharp blast of a semi's air horn.

"It's Tatiana," the message began, followed by a nervous little noise that was somewhere between a giggle and a sob. "Are you there . . . please? I can't believe she's doing this to me." The girl inhaled unevenly, holding tears back from her voice. She went on in another language, something throaty and harsh, Eastern European–sounding. Then she switched back to English. "I'm not supposed to call anyone. I don't have much time. I'm somewhere in—" The connection was broken.

The package had been sitting beige and innocuous in the pile of mail that had collected in Lydia's office during the two weeks she had been gone. The small, soft envelope mailed to Lydia care of her publisher and forwarded was just one item in a mound of mail she had received from what Jeffrey Mark called her "fan club." Prisoners, families of murder victims, aspiring serial killers, and miscellaneous psychotics drawn to her because of the books and articles she wrote about heinous crimes and the people who committed them. Winning a Pulitzer Prize and solving a few cases along the way as a consultant with the private investigation firm of Mark, Hanley and Striker, Lydia had become an icon of hope, it seemed, for the world's most desperate and its most sick and twisted.

She was about to toss the envelope into the trash with the rest of the letters, but when she lifted the pile, the Jiffy, heavier than the other items, fell to the floor with a dull thud and the slightest rattle. She looked at the package for a second, then reached down to pick it up. There was no return address, though it had been postmarked from Miami more than three weeks earlier. Written in capital letters in the lower-right-hand corner was an urgent plea: "PLEASE READ ME!"

She observed the moment where she could choose to open the package or choose to throw it away, never the wiser to its contents and the impact it might have on her life. But something about the smallness of it, the innocence of its soft beige form and the slight rattle that indicated to her a tape cassette piqued her curiosity, lit a tiny jolt of electricity inside her.

Lydia extracted a pair of surgical gloves, a letter opener, and a pair of tweezers from her desk drawer. She opened the package with the letter opener, careful not to disturb the seal, then removed a tape cassette and a handwritten note with the tweezers. The note was written with big loopy letters in a faltering cursive hand.

Dear Miss Strong,
You are a good woman of strength and honor. And you must help Tatiana Quinn and all the other girls who are in need of rescue. There are too many who are already past helping. But if you begin with Tatiana, you may be able to save so many more. I cannot tell you who I am or how I know this, or we will die. But I beg you to come to Miami and see for yourself. Nothing is as it seems here, but I know that you will see the truth and make it right. I pray that you will.

It was like a thousand other letters she had received over the years, and she felt the familiar wash of anxiety, resentment, and curiosity that generally overwhelmed her when someone asked for her help. But there was something different about this letter. Maybe it was the child's desperate voice, or the earnest tone of the letter, or maybe it was the implication that Lydia was *responsible* for the lives of the young girls supposedly in danger . . . and the fact that part of her believed that. Or maybe it was the haunting memory of Shawna Fox. But whatever it was, she didn't crumple the letter or destroy the tape. She just sat staring at the youthful handwriting, with its loopy letters full of hope.

Lydia leaned her head back against the black leather chair, closed her eyes, and released a long, slow breath. She felt two weeks of fatigue pulling at her muscles and her eyelids, even as the excitement of "the buzz" made her heart race a little. Images danced through her head: a girl alone on a street corner, huddled in a phone booth, staring nervously around her; the crowds that had gathered at Lydia's book signings during the media tour she had just conducted to promote *Blind Faith;* a murderer's face as she straddled him in a burning church, her gun inside his mouth; Jeffrey's smiling eyes. The tape player by her computer gave off a blank hiss for a few moments before she noticed and reached over to click it off. As she picked up the phone, she heard the elevator door that opened into their apartment. She realized that she was still wearing her jacket, still had her bag slung over her shoulder.

"Lydia?"

She jumped eagerly from her chair, moved quickly from her office, and walked across the bleached hardwood floor of the foyer and into the tight embrace of Jeffrey's arms.

"Hey, you," she said, leaning back to look at his face. His brown hair was damp from the light rain outside, and she caught the slightest scent of his cologne.

"God, I missed you," he said, kissing her, tasting her.

"Umm, me, too," she answered. She was amazed by the exuberance she felt, the sheer excitement of seeing his face and feeling his body.

"How did it go?" he asked, taking her bag and helping her off with her coat.

"You know, the usual. Inane interviews, packed book signings, bad hotel rooms. I'm never doing another book tour. It's torture."

"I've heard that before," he said, rolling his eyes. "You love it."

She smiled at his knowledge of her. "I didn't love being away from you," she replied.

They walked from the foyer to the kitchen, where they embraced again, Lydia looking over his shoulder at the view out their window. She missed the view of the Sangre de Cristo Mountains from her Santa Fe home, but nothing excited her like the New York City skyline at night. The possibilities were endless. She had to wonder what was happening behind each lighted window. She knew it was *all* happening—love, death, sex, drug abuse, loneliness, happiness, despair, even murder. But these days, it was what was happening in her own kitchen that excited her most of all. The buzz she had felt before Jeffrey came home, listening to the tape, had almost disappeared from her mind. Almost.

Jeffrey had coined the term *the buzz,* inventing a word for Lydia's unique ability to perceive what others did not—her ability to know when something was wrong, or not what it seemed, or needed investigating. Sometimes the truth left only a footprint in the sand, a scent on the wind. And Lydia had an uncanny ability to detect the most fleeting clues. Listening to the girl's voice on the tape, she'd felt it. She got a lot of crazy mail, a lot of false leads, a lot of desperate pleas. But listening to that tape, she'd heard the unmistakable pitch of fear, of need. A year ago, she would already have been researching. She'd have been on the Internet, looking for articles on a missing girl named Tatiana Quinn in Miami. But instead, she was now immersing herself in the happiness of being home with Jeffrey.

In their friendship, they'd been apart more than they'd been together. They met when she was just fifteen years old. At that time, he was an FBI agent working a serial-murder case; her mother was the thirteenth victim of the killer he hunted, Jed McIntyre. There had been a bond between Lydia and Jeffrey since the first night they met, a bond that had grown stronger over the years. Her mentor, her colleague, her friend—he had been all these things to her. And then last year, as together they worked a serial-murder case in Santa Fe, they had finally surrendered to the feelings that had always been just beneath the surface.

When they'd captured the killer, and Lydia had healed from her injuries, they'd returned to New York City. Lydia had turned in her manuscript and then, instead of jumping right into a new case, she had, maybe for the first time, relaxed as she waited for her book to be published. She took up yoga at a trendy East Village studio where Willem Dafoe studied. She went to Washington Square Park and watched the chess bums play their speed rounds, and wrote poetry. She searched for gourmet recipes on epicurious.com and cooked elaborate meals for herself and Jeffrey. She did not scan national newspapers and the Internet for new story ideas, waiting for something to seize her. She went for walks, talked on the phone, and visited with her grandparents in Sleepy Hollow, realizing she'd seriously neglected them over the last few years. She did not discuss with Jeffrey the cases he was working on with his private investigation firm, Mark, Hanley and Striker, Inc., for which she worked as part-time consultant. She was surprised to find one day, as she strolled down Fifth Avenue, looking in shop windows, that she had never been happier.

The thoughts that had obsessed her since the death of her mother were echoes of another life. It wasn't as though they had disappeared entirely, but she found she wasn't as driven to know what motivated killers, how their minds worked. She didn't feel any longer that she was somehow responsible for caging all the evil in the world like some hopeless superhero. She remembered her life before Santa Fe as feeling like she was running on a treadmill, full speed, but never getting further from what haunted her and never getting any closer to what she imagined might be the cure. She had finally given herself permission to turn it off and stand on solid ground. She now experienced moments of true inner peace.

On the other hand, old habits die hard. And, truth be told, in spite of her happiness, she *had* been getting a *bit* restless and was excited when the book tour began. But after a few days on the road, the hectic schedule, the sleeping away from Jeffrey, the forced re-membrance of the events in Santa Fe started to wear on her . . . and she just couldn't wait for it to be over. She had to laugh. She had always despised dependence in herself. Now she welcomed it, as she did all the new things she was discovering, all the emotions she had suppressed for so long. Happiness, sorrow, fear, longing, joy, and, most of all, of course, love were powerful forces within her, remind-ing her for the first time since her mother had died that she was alive. As if she had killed herself emotionally because she blamed herself for her mother's death and then resurrected herself, as well.

Now she sat with her elbows leaning on the glass kitchen table, legs folded beneath her, watching Jeffrey make her a cup of tea. She had always loved to watch him in the kitchen, all broad shoulders, chiseled jaw, and big hands—occupied not with guns and fistfights but pot holders and teakettles.

"We haven't been apart like this since we've been together," he said, sitting next to her. He placed a steaming cup of chamomile and Grand Marnier in front of her, and the smell was heaven.

"I know. It was torture. I've never had a *home* before that I missed when I was away. Every place, even the house in Santa Fe, which I loved, was just somewhere I kept my things," she said, looking into the cup, tracing the rim with her finger. "But this place . . . our home. I hated being away from it. I hated sleeping without you."

"Let's not make a habit of it." He placed a warm hand on the back of her neck and began working the tension he found there.

"Deal."

She looked around the kitchen, lighted by the orange glow of three pendant lamps hanging over the black granite island, the terra-cotta tile floor, the bleached wood cabinets with their stainless-steel fixtures. It was a warm and cozy room, ground zero for all conversation. Like everything in the apartment, they had designed it together, paying attention to every detail of the home they would share. They'd gotten rid of most of their old furniture and belongings, keeping only what meant most to them.

"New beginnings demand new objects," Lydia had declared. And Jeffrey had agreed. He'd never developed attachments to things anyway. He'd never had much of a home life, so he'd never spent much time on the East Village apartment he'd owned since he left the FBI. He'd started his private investigation firm from there, sleeping on a pullout couch in the back bedroom. Now the firm of Mark, Hanley and Striker employed over a hundred people and filled a suite of offices on the top floor of a high-rise on West Fifty-seventh Street. But his apartment had remained almost empty of furniture. He found the only possessions that meant anything to him were his mother's engagement ring, his father's old service revolver, and a closet full of designer clothes.

Lydia's apartment on Central Park West had looked like it belonged on the cover of *House Beautiful*: sleek, modern, impeccably decorated, but, Jeffrey thought, totally cold and impersonal. "You live in someone's *idea* of the most gorgeous New York apartment," he'd commented once. She'd sold it as is, furniture and all, to some software designer just months before the dot bomb. Jeffrey had sold his apartment, too, throwing in the pullout couch and rickety kitchen table and chairs. They'd both made a killing and then bought a three-bedroom duplex on Great Jones Street, downtown.

A metal door with three locks opened from the street into a

plain white elevator bank. A real Old New York industrial elevator with heavy metal doors and hinged grating lifted directly into the two-thousand-square-foot space. By New York standards, it was palatial. The cost was exorbitant, of course, as it was New York City ultrachic, shabby-cool. But Lydia had declared it home the minute they'd stepped off the elevator and onto the bleached wood floors. The private roof garden, which was at least a story higher than most of the other downtown buildings, sealed the deal. From the garden, they could see the whole city. At night, it was laid out around them like a blanket of stars, which was a good thing, since you rarely can see any actual stars in New York City.

Now it was home, the place in the world they shared. But it had seemed empty, a shell of itself when she was gone. Lydia was his home, Jeffrey had realized while she was traveling. He'd had her all to himself since Santa Fe and he'd grown used to that. But he had sensed her restlessness even before she left on the book tour, and he knew she would be getting back to work soon. In fact, he knew the second he had walked into the apartment and saw her come out of her office with her coat still on that something had caught her interest. It made him sad and tender for her, but he knew her well enough to know that he had to let her go in that way if he was to share her life at all.

"So, what were you doing when I came in?"

"Oh," she said, standing, "come with me. I want you to hear something."

"That's what I was afraid of," he said with a small laugh.

"It might be nothing."

"But first . . ." he said, pulling her into his lap and pressing his mouth to hers.

"Yes . . ." she answered, "first things first." She led him upstairs to their bedroom.

chapter two

It was quiet on Great Jones Street at 3:00 A.M. Lydia hadn't heard any screaming, singing, or horn blares in at least an hour as she lay listening to rain tap at the windows and to Jeffrey's soft, steady breath. Usually, she was history as soon as her head hit the pillow, sound in a deep black sleep that was difficult to disturb. And God help the person who did. But tonight, she was restless, sleep uncooperative. Realizing she was fighting a losing battle, she untangled herself from Jeffrey and slipped out from beneath the down comforter. Jeffrey turned with a sigh as she grabbed his black knit cotton sweater from the floor and put it on. She stood in front of the window for a second, the sill coming to just above her knee. Streetlights bathed the gritty neighborhood in an amber glow; three cabs sped down Lafayette as if they were racing one another. A man in a black coat strolled along, oblivious of the rain, in spite of the fact that he was soaked, water dripping down his face like tears. Maybe he had just given up, was so wet that rushing for shelter had grown pointless.

She padded down the spiral staircase that led from their second-floor bedroom directly into the living room. She didn't turn on any lights as she went into the kitchen and opened the stainless-steel refrigerator door. She wasn't hungry, but looking for food was just something to do. Jeffrey was so healthy—fruit, vegetables, some deviled eggs, carrot juice, skim milk, protein bars. She opened the freezer and saw a big cold bottle of Ketel One vodka. "Yum," she said, removing it. She got a lowball glass from the cabinet above the kitchen island, filled it with ice, and poured herself a double. She headed into her office. Because, of course, that's where she had been headed all along.

She listened to the tape again as she booted up her computer, sipping slowly on her vodka. "It's Tatiana. Are you there . . . please?"

"Who are you, Tatiana Quinn?" she whispered, her fingers dancing across the keyboard.

She logged on to her very powerful search engine and entered the name. Lydia waited, feeling the effect of the straight vodka right away, as she hadn't eaten since a late lunch and hadn't had a drink in weeks. The sound of the girl's voice on the tape—the call obviously made from a pay phone—young, vulnerable, got Lydia in the gut in a way she didn't appreciate. Ever since Shawna Fox, Lydia had developed a soft spot for lost or broken teenage girls.

A list of articles in order of their most recent appearance in newspapers filled her computer screen. She scrolled down to the earliest article, appearing in the *Miami Herald* on September 15. Its headline read DAUGHTER OF PROMINENT MIAMI BUSINESSMAN MISSING. The accompanying picture featured a small woman with her face buried in the shoulder of a very handsome gray-haired gentleman wearing an expensive suit and an expression of stoic grief; they were standing on the steps of a police precinct. There was something about the photograph that struck Lydia as odd. She stared at it for a second and realized that it was the art quality of the news photo, how focused the camera was on the man and women in the center of a moving crowd of police and bystanders. It communicated grief and grace under pressure, the chaos of the moment. It was beautiful. In fact, it was so perfect, it could have been staged by a publicist.

The article reported that fifteen-year-old Tatiana Quinn, who had emigrated to the United States with her mother from Albania in

1997, had disappeared from her bedroom sometime after midnight on September 13. Her backpack, the $160 dollars she had in her jewelry box, and her favorite clothes were also missing, leading police to the conclusion that she had run away. The article also revealed that Tatiana was Nathan Quinn's stepdaughter and not his biological daughter, the child from the first marriage of Jenna Quinn, the sobbing woman in the picture, according to the caption. The Quinns offered $1 million for information leading to Tatiana's safe return. That's a lot of money to throw around, thought Lydia as she continued to scroll through the articles. As the weeks wore on, the articles grew shorter; one reported that a Greyhound driver had been questioned regarding his claim that he had seen Tatiana on a bus bound for New York City; another reported that the Quinns had hired a private detective to find their daughter. The last article, written on October 17, was a feature on missing girls, the terrifying statistics on their fates, and a mention of Tatiana, "who has not been heard from and may never be." Looks like Tatiana has ceased to be of interest to the media, thought Lydia. Not even two months after her disappearance, and Tatiana had already become a past tense, a sad picture on the news, a mystery that leaves an ache when you read about her in the paper.

None of the articles mentioned the tape, which meant that no one knew about it, or that no one had told the police about it. The tape that Lydia had been sent, if it was in fact Tatiana Quinn's voice on it, would have been a big break, a compelling lead in the case of a missing child. So either the parents didn't know about it or, less likely, didn't care. But it just didn't make sense. If someone were truly concerned with helping Tatiana, why wouldn't he or she give the tape directly to the police?

People didn't throw a million dollars around for show. And grieving, terrified parents *with* a million dollars to throw around surely would have arranged for a phone tap in the event that the child called in a frightened moment. So did that mean Tatiana had left that message for someone else? There was definitely something strange going on.

"Lydia, it's four-thirty in the morning," said Jeffrey softly behind her.

"I know," she answered, not even looking up, "I couldn't sleep."

"What are you doing?" he asked, looking over her shoulder at the screen. Lydia had zoomed in on a picture of Tatiana's face. She was exquisite for a fifteen-year-old child—full waves of jet-black hair and fathomless blue-green eyes, high cheekbones, and fragile features. She was a Lolita, with that sexy, coquettish smile that didn't reach her eyes. Something about that look reminded Lydia of those beauty pageant children, their little-girl bodies in sparkling bodysuits, posing, provocatively, with no idea *what* they were provoking, looking like some disturbing combination of baby doll and whore. There was a vacancy to Tatiana's gaze, a look of wishing she was somewhere else.

"This is what I wanted you to hear," Lydia said as she rewound and played the tape again. She handed him the letter, which he had to squint to read in the dim light without his glasses. He sunk into the sienna leather couch across from her desk and put his feet up on the mahogany table, which had once been the door of an eighteenth-century Spanish castle. Lydia's office, which had been more or less transplanted from her home in Santa Fe, took up the greatest square footage on the first floor. The south wall faced Great Jones Street and was comprised largely of four ten-foot windows. The east wall was covered by floor-to-ceiling bookcases, containing the intellectual clutter of books she had read and all she had written in her career.

"What's that language she's speaking?" Jeffrey asked.

"I'm assuming it's Albanian. I have no idea what she's saying, though."

"So what have you found so far?" he asked.

She told him what she had read on the Internet.

"Something doesn't seem quite right," she said.

"Oh?"

"Well, a fifteen-year-old rich girl disappears. There's a flurry of media coverage; the parents offer a million-dollar reward for her return; weeks go by and attention peters out. Another little girl lost to the street, another statistic. Not really *that* out of the ordinary, except for the million. But then there's this tape, which is not mentioned anywhere. It's a big lead in an investigation that certainly shouldn't have been closed yet, especially when the parents are rich, prominent people. Desperate parents would run to the police and to the media with that kind of thing. But it doesn't look like they did. So that means to me that they didn't know about it. And who would send it to me? Why wouldn't they have gone to the police?"

"Maybe it's a crank. Maybe it's not Tatiana at all on that tape."

"But why? If someone went to all the trouble of setting up a crank call, why wouldn't they use it to try to get the million? Why would they send the tape to me? How would that help them?"

"Maybe they think it will seem more like a legitimate lead coming from you," Jeffrey offered, though it was a bit of reach.

"But it was sent anonymously."

"That's true. I've heard that name before . . . Nathan Quinn. Who is he?"

Lydia entered his name into the search engine. A list of over 150 articles in the last year alone appeared on her screen. She scrolled through and read the headlines aloud to Jeffrey.

"Let's see . . . 'Nathan Quinn donates one point five million to NEA'; that's five hundred thousand more than he offered for the safe return of his stepdaughter. Interesting . . . 'Nathan Quinn wins Ernst & Young Entrepreneur of the Year Award . . . importing/exporting business'; 'Venture Capitalist Nathan Quinn: Hero to Albanian Refugees.' The list goes on. Sounds like your general, all-around man-of-the-year type."

Jeffrey had come to stand behind her. "He gets a lot of media coverage. I guess that's why his name sounds familiar. But I could have sworn I'd heard it somewhere else."

"Maybe someone in your firm was talking about the case. Here's his picture. Does he look familiar?"

"Not really. But look at that jaw. He belongs on the hundred-dollar bill or something."

Nathan Quinn had a bearing that communicated power, and this was apparent even in the grainy Internet photographs they were looking at. He seemed to stand at least a few inches taller than most of the people around him; his shoulders were square, his smile cool and permanent, his taste in clothes impeccable. He was positively regal.

"Maybe someone is trying to ruin him?" Jeffrey suggested.

"Well, then why not go to the police? Or the media?"

"Well, you are *kind of* the media."

"Not the immediate, news-at-eleven kind of media."

She started tapping her pen on the desktop, a gesture that she had picked up from Jeffrey years earlier.

"The buzz?" he asked.

"Big-time."

"So? . . . What?"

She swiveled around to look at him. She cocked her head to the side and gave Jeffrey a gorgeous megawatt smile.

"You know," she said after a moment. "We've been working so hard, haven't we?"

"Well, not really. It's been a little slow. . . ."

"We have. And, honestly, Jeffrey, you are looking a little pale. The winter weather must be getting to you."

"It's only the end of October."

"I think we need a vacation."

"A vacation?"

"Yes, absolutely."

"Let me guess."

"I hear Miami is beautiful this time of year."

chapter three

Because the world generally yielded to his whims, it was rare that he lost his temper. But when he did, there were casualties. He inhaled deeply and closed his eyes, trying to quell the rising anger. He looked up at the sweating man in faded, ill-fitting jeans and distressed-leather jacket who stood across from him.

"I just don't understand how this can be possible," he said quietly, but with a benevolent smile on his handsome face, as if he was *trying* to understand.

"I'm telling you, sir. There's no trace of her," the man responded, backing away a step, edging toward the door. He seemed to sense his client's growing agitation and to understand how dangerous that was, though there were no outward indications of trouble.

"It is a myth that people just disappear, Mr. Parker."

"People disappear every day."

"It's not so," he responded, rising and walking around his large desk. "People are *made* to disappear. Or families lack the resources or the inclination to find the missing. But that is not the case here. Is it, Mr. Parker?"

"No, sir," the private detective answered, feeling dwarfed by the other man's sheer size. His hands looked like bear claws, large, menacing, effortlessly deadly.

"So, then, what is it, Mr. Parker? May I call you Steve? What is it, then, Steve? When a girl of Tatiana's considerable beauty—I mean truly stunning, remarkable beauty—walks the street, people notice. It is hard for me to understand how you, with your considerable investigative skills, could not have found one of those people."

"Sir, my associates and I have scoured Miami. Ridden the same Greyhound bus she supposedly took to New York. I have spent days in Port Authority talking to Greyhound employees, the homeless, and commuters. No one has ever seen her or heard of the bus driver who supposedly spotted her. I have been to places in that city that you don't even want to know exist. And no one, not one person, showed even a glimmer of recognition. Tatiana is gone, Mr. Quinn. You are only going to find her when she wants to be found. I'm sorry."

"You're sorry," Nathan Quinn repeated tonelessly. He turned his back on Stephen Parker and returned to the high-backed leather chair behind his large desk. He picked up a picture of Tatiana that he kept on his desk in a Waterford crystal frame. The sight of her face filled him with rage. If the lush office with its redwood desk, leather chairs, plush sofas, and recessed lighting hadn't been so dimly lighted, Stephen Parker might not have mistaken the look on Nathan Quinn's face for profound grief.

"Yes, sir, I'm sorry."

The door behind Parker opened and two men, even larger than Nathan Quinn, men who apparently had some steroids with their orange juice in the morning, entered quietly and closed the door behind them. Both of them were bald and wore black suits and collarless white shirts. They stood on either side of the door like a set of threatening bookends. Parker wondered how they had been summoned, then realized with dismay that he had checked his weapon in the secured atrium through which he had had to pass to enter Quinn's office. *Fuck,* he thought.

"Would you like a drink, Steve?"

"Um, no thanks, Mr. Quinn. I should be going. I just want you to know that I'm not going to charge you for my work. I didn't help you. So, if you'll just cover my expenses, we'll call it even."

Parker tried to quell the rising tide of panic he felt inside. After all, there was no reason to fear Nathan Quinn—he was just a man looking for his daughter. Parker had done his best but hadn't been able to help him. It wasn't as though Quinn was some thug, some mobster who was going to do him in just because he'd stumbled on some delicate information. Nathan Quinn was a respected businessman. He told himself all of these things, but it didn't stop his heart from beating like timpani or alleviate the dryness in his mouth. Logic told him one thing, but his instincts were saying quite another.

"No, Steve," he said quietly. "That wouldn't be right. I'm sure you did everything you could. If you stop and see my secretary at the office tomorrow, she'll have a check for you in the amount we initially discussed. Minus the bonus, of course, which I promised only if she was returned to me safe and sound."

"Of course," Parker said with alacrity. He felt a wash of relief that Nathan Quinn had acknowledged that there would be a to-morrow after all. But he wasn't going to feel 100 percent better until the meeting was over and he was still in one piece. "As for the other information that surfaced during my investigation," Parker added, just to be sure they understood each other, "well, that will be our little secret."

There was a moment where Nathan Quinn stared blackly at Stephen Parker, but then his grim expression turned into a cordial smile.

"I'd expect nothing less from a professional of your caliber, Mr. Parker," said Nathan Quinn, grinning complicitly.

The private detective returned the grin, then looked behind him at the men who stood by the door, arms crossed and faces expressionless.

"I should be going," Parker repeated, the discomfort he had felt not entirely dissipated.

"Yes, of course." Quinn rose and offered his hand, which Parker took. Quinn's grip was predictably crushing. When Parker was released, he rushed out the door, slamming it behind him.

Nathan Quinn was silent for a moment, watching the black lacquer doors as if waiting for Parker to return. Then he walked over to the bar and poured himself a glass of gin.

chapter four

Jeffrey was asleep beside Lydia on the flight to Miami, the result of his taking Tylenol PM and two shots of Jack Daniel's before getting on the plane. Bottled bravery, because Jeffrey was terrified of airplanes. His breathing was heavy, and his head was on her shoulder, one hand palm-up on her thigh. She kissed his forehead, glad he was sleeping instead of fidgeting and nervous, which, in turn, would make her fidgety and nervous. The first-class cabin was dark and nearly empty, except for a few other passengers. A young businessman sat on the aisle across from her, tapping furiously on his laptop. An older Asian woman, wearing a black silk tunic and a remarkable jade fu lion on prayer beads around her neck, had the kind of ageless beauty and silken hair of Asian women that Lydia had always admired. The other passengers were just dark, silent forms around her.

Too edgy to read or sleep, Lydia's thoughts turned again to Tatiana. A girl possessing such luminous beauty is in for all kinds of trouble in her life, thought Lydia. Average women, plagued with self-doubt about their bodies, battling negative self-images, constantly comparing themselves unfavorably to media images of beauty, would likely look on someone like Tatiana Quinn with a jealousy bordering on hatred, even though she was only fifteen. What they didn't know, what they could never know, was that physical beauty was no recipe for happiness. A certain kind of man would desire her, but feel inadequate and hate her for it, and perhaps become abusive. Another kind would never approach her at all, assuming that she was too good for him. Women would be falsely nice but secretly hate her. People worship that kind of physical perfection but despise it at the same time, aspire to it endlessly but can't bear to see it in others, a reminder of their own imperfections.

For some reason, Lydia kept thinking about the Gretchen Corley murder, a high-profile case on which she and Jeffrey had consulted briefly. Her mother, Kristen, had entered Gretchen in beauty pageants from the time she was old enough to walk, just as Kristen, a loser in the Miss America pageant, had been before her.

Lydia's personal theory about Gretchen Corley had been that her mother had murdered her, though no arrests had ever been made. The case was still unsolved. Lydia believed that Kristen had groomed Gretchen all her short life to be the little coquette that she was, all the while hating her for the youth and beauty that underscored Kristen's inevitable trek toward old age. And that Kristen had one day discovered her husband was molesting their daughter.

Instead of feeling a murderous rage toward *him* and the violation he had committed against their daughter, she must have been jealous toward the little girl, who, even at her young age, was more beautiful than Kristen had ever been. That in her heart, Kristen probably believed that her daughter had stolen her husband. A narcissist would be compelled to eliminate the threat. Lydia wondered if something like that could be at play with Tatiana.

Lydia believed that women like Kristen Corley, who admire their own beauty and believe it is the only valuable thing about them, were generally in for big trouble when they approached middle age, particularly if they were emotionally unstable to begin with. When outer beauty fades, all that remains is the self. Vain, beautiful women often lack self-esteem because they never explore their inner gifts. They only know themselves by the reflection in the mirror. Not that it is really their fault. No one teaches them otherwise. Lydia had always been grateful to her mother for teaching her better.

"Don't try to skate by on your looks, Lydia. They don't last. Use your brain." This was one of Marion's most annoying admonishments. When Lydia asked Marion, "Do you think I'm beautiful?" her mother answered, "You *are* beautiful . . . inside and out. But inside is what counts; outside is just icing." So, though Lydia considered herself a *little* vain, loving beautiful clothes and expensive cosmetics and maybe checking her reflection a little more often than Marion would have thought necessary, she knew the pursuit of perfection was a losing battle, one that could claim heavy casualties. Even your very sanity.

Tatiana was beautiful in a dangerous way. Lydia could see that from her pictures. It didn't necessarily mean anything in reference to her disappearance. What was her relationship to her mother, to her stepfather? Had her beauty caused her mother to be jealous, her stepfather to be overly solicitous? Had she been afraid in her home, thinking the streets were safer? Or had her beauty attracted someone who had seduced or abducted her, making it look as though she had run away?

So far, the Miami police had been unresponsive. She'd left two messages for the detective working the case, whose name she'd found in the articles on the Internet, a Detective Manuel Ignacio. The papers had called him "the Saint of Lost Children," a twenty-five-year veteran with an uncanny track record for finding missing kids in the first forty-eight hours. Those were the critical hours. Statistics showed that if a missing child was not found in that time frame, the chances of ever finding her alive decreased exponentially for every hour that passed.

Lydia had left a message, saying that she had a potential lead in the case but not mentioning specifically the tape cassette and note that she carried in her bag. But she imagined that with a million-dollar reward in the mix, Detective Ignacio spent a lot of time sifting through messages, most of which were probably false leads, costing countless lost man-hours. She'd left her cellular phone number, hoping he'd get back to her before she and Jeffrey showed up at the police station.

Jeffrey shifted next to her, trying to get comfortable in his sleep. She knew he would wake up with a sore neck and in a hazy bad mood.

"It would be nice if you could bring a case into this firm that actually made us some money," he'd complained as they were packing to go on their "vacation." Though she knew he didn't really care. The firm of Mark, Hanley and Striker took on enough high-paying cases—insurance fraud, rich husbands checking up on cheating wives, some government work, which Lydia wasn't 100 percent clear on and knew she wasn't supposed to be—that the partners could afford to back Lydia's hunches. Technically, she was employed by the firm as an investigative consultant. They called her in on cases they thought she could help with; she had access to their resources and manpower; the publicity from her books kept business coming into the firm. It was a very beneficial relationship for everyone.

Sometimes she got the feeling that Jacob Hanley resented her a bit, though. He certainly hadn't been happy about the trip to Miami. In fact, he seemed to go a little pale when they delivered the news. "What do you guys think you are going to find that the Miami police didn't find?" he'd asked when they'd stopped by the firm on their way out of town.

"I don't know. We're just going to check it out. Lydia has the buzz."

In response to that, Jacob, who had followed them from the lobby into Jeffrey's office and was slouching in the chair across from Jeffrey's desk, had practically snorted. "That's great," he said sullenly, with a dramatic throwing up of hands. "Do what you want."

"Don't worry about it, Hanley. It's more like a vacation than anything."

He made that snuffling noise with nose and throat again. "That's what you said when you went to Santa Fe last year."

Lydia had felt her temper flare a little bit at that. But she bit her tongue, which was never easy for her. Jeffrey and Hanley had been friends since West Point. So she had never offered her opinion that Hanley had always seemed like deadweight to her and that Jeffrey and Christian Striker had done most of the work in building the firm to what it was.

"And?" Jeffrey said, a little more anger in his eyes and tone than Lydia had expected.

"And you both practically got yourselves killed," Hanley responded, shifting his manner from that of annoyance to one of concern, a kind of tonal backpedaling. After the awkward pause that passed between them, Jacob raised his hands in a mock gesture of surrender. "I'm just saying, don't get yourselves into any trouble."

"Thanks for the advice," Jeffrey said. She could see from her position across the large office, sitting on the plush beige couch with the rust chenille pillows that she had picked out at Crate & Barrel, that Jeffrey was really annoyed. His jaw was clenched and he avoided looking at Hanley. "Anything else?"

"Just stay in touch. Let us know if we can help," he said, with his verbal tail between his legs.

Jeffrey didn't respond, and after a moment, Hanley got up and left. Lydia just sat on the couch as Jeffrey shoved files into the drawers and sifted through a stack of pink phone messages. She didn't say anything because she knew that his annoyance needed a target. And she didn't want to be it.

"And I *will* be snagging some beach time while we're in Miami," he said. "I don't want to wind up tailing people, sneaking around alleys, getting into shoot-outs, like we usually do."

She didn't argue. "Okay, okay. What's going on with you two?"

"Nothing. He's just . . . Forget it."

She didn't press it, knowing he'd tell her his thoughts once he'd sorted them out. But the conversation had had an odd effect on her, too. Sitting next to their suitcases, four hours before the quick flight to Miami, she had wanted to go home. For a second, she wished she'd never opened the brown envelope and had never even had the chance to get the buzz.

The fact was that she didn't want to be sneaking around alleys and getting into gunfights, *either*. Two years ago, she wouldn't have given a little investigational jaunt like this one a second thought. She would have been *hoping* to crack something big. But these days, she didn't feel overly inclined to put their lives in danger. Not for the first time since she'd put the serial killer in Santa Fe in a coma that he lay in to this day, she thought, Maybe I'm losing my edge. The things that had always thrilled her, had always driven her were suddenly not as appealing as the thought of being home with Jeffrey by the fire. God, what a *girl* I am all of a sudden, she had thought, disgusted. Maybe I should take up macramé. Even though she wasn't even sure what macramé was.

"Why are you frowning?" Jeffrey had asked.

"I'm not."

"You are. What are you thinking?"

"I'm thinking, Let's go. What are you doing?"

"I'm just sending an E-mail to Christian and Craig, asking them to do some checking around here. One of the articles you found mentioned that someone had seen Tatiana on a bus to New York City."

"Cool. Are you ready?"

"Yep. What's your hurry? Flight isn't for another four hours."

"I'm just anxious."

He walked over to her, took her hands, and pulled her up gently from the couch. He kissed her forehead and pulled her into his arms. She breathed deeply, feeling his closeness, smelling the familiar scent of his skin. "Don't worry," he said. "We'll find out what happened to her."

"I know," she said, feeling a little guilty because she wasn't sure that was the source of her anxiety. "Let's get a quick drink first."

They had stopped at the Irish bar on the corner, where Jeff ordered two shots of whiskey and two Tylenol PM tablets and Lydia had a Ketel One martini. Then they took a cab, where, in the drizzly gray of the Friday-afternoon rush hour, they crawled to JFK in a sea of honking horns and screaming cabdrivers. Jeff was half-asleep as they boarded the plane in the last moments before the door closed, almost exactly twenty-four hours since Lydia had first heard Tatiana's frightened voice.

The soft *ping* of the airplane intercom interrupted Lydia's thoughts. The pilot's practiced voice sounded muffled to Lydia because her ears always felt blocked when she flew. "We have begun our initial descent into the Miami area. The weather is a perfect seventy-five degrees. We will be pulling into the gate a few minutes earlier than expected this evening. Arrival time will be ten-fifteen P.M. We ask you to remain seated with your seat belts on and your trays in the upright position for the duration of the flight. Attendants, prepare for landing. We hope you enjoy your stay in Miami or wherever your final destination may be."

chapter five

Everything about this case had been weird. And it looked like it was about to get weirder. Detective Manuel Ignacio scribbled Lydia Strong's cellular phone number onto his scratch pad and saved her message on his voice mail. A thin ray of hope shone through the fog of six weeks of fatigue. He looked at the scratched face of his leather-band Timex and saw that it was 10:15. He sighed and put his head down in his hands; his wife was going to kill him. He was supposed to have been home by eight o'clock and he hadn't even called.

The children's division of the Missing Persons Department was quiet; somebody's screen saver made simulated ocean noises, and he could hear the desk sergeant's phone ringing endlessly down the hall. Everyone else on the team had gone home hours ago. It wasn't that they had given up on Tatiana; it was just that they knew the realities. Six weeks into an investigation like this, with no leads, no sightings, no legitimate tips—it didn't look good. Honestly, they would have called the case cold unofficially weeks ago if it hadn't been for Nathan Quinn breathing down the necks of the mayor and the chief of police, who, in turn, were breathing down his neck. Detective Ignacio knew that he was going to become the scapegoat on this if he didn't turn up something.

From the first night, when he had been called to the Quinns' home, he'd had a bad feeling. Sometimes it was like that with missing children for Ignacio: Sometimes he just knew he was going to find them safe and in one piece, and sometimes he could feel that they were gone for good—fallen prey to drugs, or abducted by someone with unspeakable desires—that their parents would forever be haunted by what *might* have happened to them. Sometimes he knew that he would end up recovering a body from a ditch, from the bottom of a lake. In this case, he didn't have any solid feeling like that. Just a nebulous feeling that things weren't going to go well.

When he'd arrived at the Quinn home, the first thing he heard was a woman crying—there was something haunting about the sound of it, something resigned and despondent. It was not the desperate, enraged cry of a woman who had just discovered her child was missing. He'd heard that sound so many times, there was something primal about it, something that made him shiver. But there was hope in it, a fierce need to believe that everything would turn out all right. The sound he heard when he stepped into the magnificent foyer was the cry of grief, total and inconsolable. The first thing he *saw* was the surveillance camera at the front door. Before he had a chance to be briefed by the uniformed officer who was first on the scene, Nathan Quinn had rushed to greet him.

"She's gone," he blurted out. "You have to find her."

Something about the way he said it, about the look in Quinn's eyes, gave the detective a sick chill. There was a petulant anger in his tone, a white rage in his eyes. But then the giant man broke down, sobbing, and Ignacio decided it had just been grief and fear. But he kept coming back to that moment in his thoughts.

The glorious Mission-style mansion was more opulent than Detective Ignacio had ever seen; the marble floors alone had probably cost more than he made in a year. Jenna Quinn hadn't risen to greet him when he'd walked up the dramatic staircase, down a wide hallway lined with expensive-looking art, and entered Tatiana's bedroom. She hadn't looked at him with hopeful eyes, as most parents did when he arrived to find their lost children. She had stopped crying, but her eyes were pink and swollen, and she sat on her daughter's bed, holding a tattered stuffed Snoopy.

He put his hand on her shoulder and said, "It's going to be all right, Mrs. Quinn." She jumped a little, but she didn't respond. She didn't have the vacant stare of someone slipping into shock, however; she was alert and, Detective Ignacio thought, uneasy.

Tatiana Quinn's bedroom was the dream of every teenage girl. The king-size bed on which Jenna sat was covered in the pink-and-white Laura Ashley sheets his own daughter had wanted but couldn't have because they were too expensive. The matching wallpaper was almost hidden by posters of the Backstreet Boys, 'NSYNC, and other teen idols, ones the detective recognized but couldn't name. A Sony Viao computer sat on top of a white desk, her school books and notepads were in a neat pile, and a deflated red backpack with stickers and buttons all over it hung from the chair. A huge entertainment center held a big-screen television, DVD player, and CD player, with tiny high-powered Bose speakers sitting on top. Her DVD collection ranged from *Snow White* and *101 Dalmatians* to *Crouching Tiger, Hidden Dragon* and *Chocolat*. The walk-in closet was bigger than his daughter's entire bedroom, stuffed with more clothes than he had seen outside a department store and a shoe collection that would have made Imelda Marcos blush.

He had a sense of her from the things in her room: a little girl, on the verge of being a young woman and not sure which she was more comfortable with yet—like all teenagers. As he looked at the Quinns sitting on their daughter's bed, Nathan with his arm around Jenna, whispering something in her ear, he thought, What could take a young girl from a home like this? Whatever it was, it had to be pretty bad—either she'd been abducted, taken against her will, or there was a drug problem, a bad boyfriend. Or maybe there was something even worse going on behind these expensive doors.

With the help of Jenna Quinn, who seemed to come alive again, they determined that also missing were Tatiana's small suitcase, a few of her favorite outfits, her Walkman and favorite CDs, and the $160 she had kept in her jewelry box. The surveillance camera had been turned off at 9:00 P.M., an hour after the Quinns had left to go to a party at the home of the late Gianni Versace, just minutes away. And that was pretty much it. No foreign fingerprints in the home, no sign of struggle or forced entry, no strange noises heard by the neighbors. No one had seen Tatiana leave the house.

The million-dollar reward had been more of a hindrance than a help in the investigation. In the first few days after the Quinns' impassioned plea on the five and eleven o'clock news, the phone rang off the hook. Thousands of man-hours were wasted following up on false tips. But then a couple of weeks into the investigation, a Greyhound bus driver had come forward to say someone meeting Tatiana's description had ridden the 12:05 bus from Miami to New York City the night she disappeared. He had come into the station, given a statement and his contact information to one of the detectives on Ignacio's team. The team was infused with hope again. But the next day, when Ignacio called to follow up, the contact information turned out to be false, and Greyhound denied having an employee by that name. It had already run in the paper; with all the heat on them, they never revealed to the press that they had been duped. For the life of him, he couldn't figure out why someone would do that.

But there were a lot of things about this case he couldn't figure out. Like why, when he started looking into some of Nathan Quinn's business dealings, the police chief himself called to assure Ignacio that he was barking up the wrong tree—and to stop barking, or else. And why had the maid, Valentina Fitore, who generally spent the night when the Quinns went out, gone home early instead? Who had turned off the surveillance camera, since Tatiana supposedly did not know how to operate it? And now, the call from Lydia Strong. So far, the national media had not shown any real interest, specifically because it *did* look as if Tatiana had run away and not been abducted. How had someone like Lydia Strong gotten interested? What information did she have? She said she was staying at the Delano Hotel in South Beach but wouldn't be in until late.

He dialed the cellular number he had scribbled down. Her voice mail picked up.

"Ms. Strong, this is Detective Ignacio, returning your call. I'm anxious to speak with you and hear what you have to say. You can reach me here tomorrow morning. Or if you get this message tonight, don't hesitate to try me on my cell phone." He left the number and hung up. He thought to call his wife but decided it was better just to go home. If he called, she'd bitch at him now and then again when he got home. If he just went home, she'd only have one opportunity to give him hell. He took his suit jacket from the back of the chair he had been sitting on and put it on, noticing that he had some catsup on the sleeve. He shut down his computer, turned off the metal desk lamp, and headed out the door.

chapter six

It was nearly ten when they checked into the glamorous Delano Hotel on Collins Avenue in South Beach. Lydia loved the luxurious Ian Schrager hotels for their chic atmosphere and exquisite service. Jeffrey thought everyone who worked there was falsely obsequious, and it made him uncomfortable. It didn't matter to him where they stayed, as long as the bed was comfortable. And on that detail, they both agreed—it was just that he couldn't believe how much it cost for a truly comfortable bed. The bellman escorted them through the billowing white curtains that towered above them from the twenty-foot ceiling and draped elegantly to the floor, past the dramatically arranged eclectic pieces of antique furniture. A white chaise longue was accented with a faux fur throw, white lilies were glam in their crystal vases atop veined marble surfaces, and each thick column that lined the long hallway hid a cozy sitting area.

The bellman, dressed in matching white shorts and polo shirt, towed their luggage down the very white, very long hallway to their room.

"Who's paying for this?" Jeffrey asked as the bellman left with a five-dollar tip from Lydia.

"Jacob Hanley," Lydia answered, smiling as she opened the French doors that led to the balcony. The sound and smell of the ocean swept into the room and billowed the white gauze curtains. He walked out onto the balcony with her and wrapped her in his arms from behind. The palm trees beneath them were illuminated by a glowing amber light, and the fronds rustled in the wind, which seemed to be picking up. And the infinity pool glowed a bright sky blue. In the distance, the sounds of the perpetual party that was South Beach drifted on the night air. A heavy bass from some punk's too-loud car stereo reverberated like a heartbeat; shrieks that could be delight or terror echoed like the cries of seagulls. Somewhere glass shattered, and a car alarm sounded in protest. The night was in full swing.

"You feel like going out for a drink?" she asked, sounding hopeful. The ten-year difference in their ages generally manifested itself at around this hour, when he was ready for bed and she was ready to go out dancing.

"Sure," he answered, casting a longing glance at the plush king-size bed behind them. "Let's go."

She picked up her big Furla black leather bag.

"You don't need that," he said.

"I never go anywhere without it, Jeffrey. You know that. It has my notebook, all my addresses. . . ." she said.

"Well, I'm not going to wind up carrying it," he said, knowing of course that he would if she wanted him to.

Ocean Drive was a parade of supermodels, drag queens, body-builders, and dumpy tourists looking around in awe of the scene. Each person was more gorgeous, more boisterous than the last. Surrounded by outrageous outfits, big hair, and loud voices, Lydia always thought of South Beach as the bastard child of the East Village and Mardi Gras on ecstasy. She was fascinated by the endless circus of fabulous, vacuous people . . . narcissism at its exuberant best. Passing a seemingly endless array of restaurants with hostesses beckoning them in, they finally settled on an Art Deco Mexican restaurant with a mariachi band singing love ballads. They slid into a plush velvet sofa that faced the street and ordered margaritas on the rocks with salt.

Jeffrey's cell phone beeped and he pulled it from his pants pocket.

"Craig sent an E-mail," he said.

Lydia always called Craig "the Brain" behind his back. He stood a full head taller than Jeffrey but looked as thin as one of his thighs. He was forever clad in hugely baggy jeans, a white T-shirt under a flannel shirt, and a pair of Doc Martens, and his pockets were always full of electronic devices—cell phone, pager, Palm Pilot, all manner of thin black beeping, ringing toys. A pair of round wire spectacles, nearly hidden by a shock of bleached-blond hair, framed blue-green eyes. Craig called himself "a cybernavigator," though his title at Jeffrey's firm was information specialist. He specialized in knowledge of all computer research tools; before being recruited for Mark, Striker and Hanley, he'd been an infamous hacker wanted by the FBI. He was eighteen when he was arrested and could have faced more than a little time in federal prison, but, luckily for him, Jacob Hanley was his uncle. All former FBI agents, with more connections between them than a motherboard, the team at Mark, Striker and Hanley had been able to get Craig a deal. He worked for the firm, kept his act together, and reported to a probation officer for the next three years.

Now, more or less plugged into the Internet and the Bureau systems, semilegally, twenty-four seven, Craig could gather almost any piece of information needed at any time of the day or night. Lydia wondered when he slept, and she joked that one day Jeffrey would go to Craig's office and find that he had become a disembodied voice, sucked into the computers like some character in a William Gibson novel.

"He says that he and Christian will start looking into things in New York for us tomorrow. He also says that he hopes we find Tatiana, because she's 'hot.'"

"Hey," said Lydia, "what happened to his crush on me?"

"Youth is fickle," Jeffrey replied.

"Hmm."

"He also says that his uncle Jacob is pissed that we're gone. Or at least that's what I translated from 'My uncle is way freaking that you guys bailed. What's up his hole, yo?'"

"Well, it's a good thing that it's *your* firm and he has *nothing* to say about what you do."

"Exactly."

She waited for him to explain the obvious ill feelings between him and Hanley, but he didn't. A hunky Latino waiter with black hair longer and more lustrous than Lydia's and smoldering brown eyes brought two huge margaritas. Lydia immediately started sipping. It was tart and very potent. Just the way she liked it.

"So what's the plan?"

"Well, Detective Ignacio called back. I think rather than return his call, we should pop in on him in the morning. Take the tape, see where it fits, and find out what his thoughts are. He was eager to hear what we have, but he sounded just beaten-down tired. So maybe he wants some help."

"What are you thinking about all of this? What are you expecting to find?"

The mariachi players, who had paused to smoke cigarettes and drink shots of tequila at the bar, took up their instruments again and began another ballad.

"I don't know. It just feels like more than a simple runaway case to me. Something about that letter struck a chord. Maybe I'm wrong."

He didn't say anything for a second, just took a slug of his drink, then grimaced at the tartness of it. She could tell he was debating whether or not to say what was on his mind, and she waited for him to make his decision, munching on chips from the basket between them.

"This is not about Shawna Fox, is it?" he asked finally. "This is not about you wanting to save her in Tatiana?"

She didn't deny it. Shawna had never had a chance. It had been too late for her even before Lydia and Jeffrey had taken on the case that would eventually bring her killer to justice. Shawna had been finding her way after years in abusive foster homes, when a madman had robbed her of her life. Too many young girls in the world met an ugly and unjust fate in one way or another. Maybe Tatiana could still be saved. Maybe there was hope for her and the other girls alluded to in the letter. But it wasn't just about that. It was the buzz drawing her into this case. The feeling that she couldn't deny or resist.

"If Tatiana had been easy to find, someone would have found her. If everything was as it should be, then I wouldn't have received that tape," she said, leaning closer to him, feeling her passion for her work ignite in the way she was used to. "This is what we do, isn't it, you and me? Look where no one else looks? Follow our instincts to the truth? Isn't it why we do this work?"

"No, that's what *you* do," he answered, smiling, feeling the electricity of her excitement. "*I'm* along to keep you grounded in reality, to analyze the facts."

"We make a good team."

"The best."

They raised their glasses to each other. He paused and looked away from her for a moment. "Which reminds me," he said softly, raising his eyes to meet hers, "I was thinking while you were away. . . ."

"Oh?"

"About us."

"What about us?" she asked. He watched her shift uncomfortably, start smoothing out the white cloth napkin on the table in front of her, staring at it intently. Everything about the moment was wrong, and he knew it. It was absolutely the wrong time and the wrong place to be having this conversation. But he'd been turning the question around in his mind since the night she'd left on her book tour. And now that they were together, under the full moon, the smell of the ocean heavy in the air, it was as if he couldn't hold it in another second, like if he waited one more hour or one more day, it would be too late.

"About the future," he said.

"Why worry about the future when the present is perfect?" she answered too quickly, folding the napkin into a neat triangle.

"I'm not worried about it," he said, shrugging off the lie. "I'm just wondering what you want."

She stopped looking at the napkin and turned her gaze on him. He always felt that look in his loins, the intensity of her eyes, the cool beauty of her face.

"I want you. I want us. Forever. You know that."

Love was not a strong-enough word for the way Lydia felt about Jeffrey. "Love" was hearts and flowers, candy and champagne. The feeling that she had in her heart for Jeffrey was riot and hurricane, fire and thunder. She would do anything for him, would adore and remain forever loyal to him all the days of her life. But the conversation, a perfectly natural one for two people who lived and owned property together, was giving Lydia chills. She didn't like to think about the future, or talk about it. As if assuming that there was a future was like tempting the gods to prove you wrong. She had spent so long resisting her love for Jeffrey because she was terrified of the grief she would feel if anything were to happen to him, knowing that she would disappear into blackness. It was a natural fear for someone who had lost her mother to a serial killer, who had been abandoned by her father at an early age, she thought. As if anything about that was natural. The way she had come to deal with it was by just being grateful for every day together, not worrying about tomorrow.

The mariachi band continued playing, their melodic voices filling the room and imbuing their conversation with a kind of maudlin energy it didn't deserve. The room was dim and warm.

Red velvet booths lined the walls, and low-hanging lamps were suspended over each table. The shade of each lamp was a different color, one cobalt, another jade, still another a flame orange. The tables were kidney-shaped and covered with fringed white tablecloths. The smell of tobacco wafted over from the next table and its scent, along with the stress Lydia was feeling as a result of their conversation, made her long powerfully for a cigarette, though it had been over a year since she'd last smoked.

Jeffrey could sense her pulling away from him. He knew the thought of marriage terrified her. "It promises something that can't be promised. People change and life is cruel. It's like tempting fate," she'd said before they were involved romantically. He hadn't really brought it up since. He internally kicked himself for his shitty timing. It was a conversation to have at home. But it was a conversation he needed to have with her. He wanted them to be a family, legally. He wanted them to *have* a family.

"Okay," he said, letting her off the hook suddenly, "it's a deal. You're stuck with me forever."

"That's it?"

"For now," he answered.

She watched him as he looked at the people passing outside the window. She hoped that she hadn't hurt him and that he understood. They sat in a comfortable silence for a bit, sipping their drinks. The effect of the tequila started to make Lydia tired, and she leaned into Jeffrey, who dropped his arm from the ledge behind her and placed it across her shoulders.

"You want to head back?" he asked her, and was answered by a small yawn.

"We need the check," he said as the young waiter approached.

"Your bill has been taken care of, sir."

Jeffrey frowned. "What do you mean? By whom?"

The waiter turned around to look at the bar and shook his beautiful head. "He's gone."

"What did he look like?" asked Lydia.

"He was big—not muscular, but strong," he said, then held his arms out to mimic a big belly. "He carried a lot of weight around his middle. Bald. Wore a black suit. I've never seen him before."

"What did he say?"

"He had a thick accent, maybe Eastern European or something. He had a shot of Grey Goose, pointed to you, and said to cover the tab and keep the change. He handed me a hundred dollars."

"He didn't use our names?" Jeffrey asked.

"No, sir."

"Thanks," Lydia said, grabbing her bag from the seat beside her and sliding out of the booth. They left the restaurant hand in hand as the mariachi band kept playing. The music followed them out onto the street and into the sea of people who were parading down Ocean Drive. The ocean yawned in a big black space to their right, and the giant palms across the street swayed in the breeze.

"That's weird," Lydia said, leaning into Jeffrey, observing cars and people on the street around them, wondering who was watching them. She pulled her bag close to her, suddenly feeling exposed.

"Only the people in my office know we're in Miami," said Jeffrey, thinking aloud.

"And Detective Ignacio," she answered, considering the possibilities. They pushed their way through the crowd, not moving quickly enough to be conspicuous, but not meandering, either. He draped his arm across her shoulder and pulled her in closer.

"Did you bring your gun?

She hesitated. "It's in my suitcase," she said, slipping her hand into the bag. "You?"

"Ditto."

"Maybe we're being paranoid," she said, glancing casually around her but making a point not to look behind. "Maybe it was just a really nice guy who gets off on random acts of kindness."

"Nobody's that nice."

"Cynic."

Jeffrey looked straight ahead and slowed their pace a bit. He scanned the area ahead of them, looking for someone matching the description the bartender had given. He saw at least three men in the crowd around them who fit the bill.

"Maybe the person trailing us in the black Mercedes is just making sure we get home safely," he said after a moment.

"Do you have eyes in the back of your head?" asked Lydia, knowing not to turn around and look, though that was her instinct.

"No, but I can see the reflection in the side-view mirrors on the parked cars."

"Very clever."

"Just keep walking."

They walked a block and made a quick left while the Mercedes was caught in traffic at the light, then hopped in a cab that was sitting on the corner.

"Make a U-turn, go back up this street, and then take the scenic route to the Delano," Jeffrey ordered the cabbie. Lydia knew if she had given an order like that, she would have gotten an argument. But no one argued with Jeffrey—except for Lydia, of course. He had some kind of natural authority to his tone that people responded to automatically. Jeffrey kept an eye on the side-view mirror, and when he was sure they hadn't been followed, he told the cab to head straight to the hotel.

They hustled through the lobby and took the elevator to their floor. When they reached their room, the door was ajar.

"Shit," Jeffrey said, thinking that the gun in his suitcase had probably just been stolen.

Lydia handed him the Glock she had in her bag.

"I thought you said it was in your suitcase."

She shrugged. "I didn't want you to think I was planning on getting into any gunfights."

"Stay here."

He pushed the door open and edged into the room. Lydia followed him. The room was empty and the bed had been turned down. A tiny box of Godiva chocolates sat innocently on each pillow. The small bedside lights had been turned on, casting a soothing pink light; soft classical music was being piped into the room from somewhere. But their suitcases sat open on their bed, looking as if they'd been neatly unpacked and repacked.

"This is the most considerate room ransacking I've ever seen," said Jeffrey as he walked over to the suitcases.

"That's how they do it at five-star hotels."

He removed a black leather box from his and opened the clasps. His Glock remained where he had left it, polished and disassembled. "I don't believe it," he said.

He looked through her suitcase. "Did they get the tape?" he asked. He turned, to see her removing the Jiffy envelope in its plastic evidence Baggie from her bag with a smile.

"I never go anywhere without my bag of tricks."

"Nice work, Felix."

chapter seven

It was pretty obvious that the whole thing had been carefully orchestrated. Paying their bill had been a kind of greeting. Following them had been a message. And entering their room but not actually removing anything had been a warning. We know you're here, we know why, and we don't like it. But who "they" were and how "they" could have known that Lydia and Jeffrey were in Miami and staying at the Delano remained a mystery. Jeffrey's office knew. And Detective Ignacio knew.

"If the police wanted to harass us, they would have been less subtle. Because they can be," said Jeffrey. "They would have shown up here, made a scene about the weapons, seized the tape. There wouldn't have been any guesswork."

"Well, that means then that either the detective's phone is not secure or mine isn't."

"Right. But who was listening, and why?"

"They were pretty showy about it. Trying to scare us off?"

"Then they clearly don't know you very well."

"Because now I'm hotter than ever to find out what's going on."

"You're hotter than ever. That's for sure," he said, drawing her down onto the bed.

They hadn't bothered to call the police, knowing that there was nothing they could have or would have done anyway. Jeffrey had locked the door and placed the chair in front of it, checked the room for bugs. It would require some *Mission Impossible*–style moves for someone to get onto the balcony. Glocks were loaded on the bedside tables. They felt safe enough for the night.

He traced her cheekbones with his finger and looked into her storm-cloud gray eyes, moved a lock of her blue-black hair off her face. She smiled into his eyes, and he felt it move him inside. When it was like this with them, when they were close, the future didn't matter to him anymore. Those moments were so powerful, so right, everything else seemed distant and unimportant.

Her body was lean and strong beneath him; he could feel her tautly muscled thighs entwining with his. He took in the scent of her skin, feeling her small, warm hands lightly take hold of his back. Just being close to her in this way felt like making love, with no space between them, their softest breaths as loud as the ocean.

chapter eight

He was sweating, though the air-conditioning was blowing as cold as it got in his black Porsche Boxster. At nearly 1:00 A.M., Alligator Alley was as dark and quiet as a grave. He opened her up. The car was so hot, so fast, it was a shame that it had to be driven even close to the speed limit. He felt calmer as he watched the speedometer climb toward one hundred miles per hour, the dials glowing neon blue and red in the darkness. He gripped the leather steering wheel with one hand, his other hand resting on the gearshift as if it were the knee of his lover. He was about to push it even further, but he lost his nerve, slowing to eighty-five miles an hour.

"Slow the fuck down, Sasa," growled Boris in his heavily accented English. "If we get pulled over . . ."

"If we get pulled over? What? What, Boris? What have we got?"

Boris glared at him for a minute and then looked away, staring out the window into the darkness, turning the back of his shaved head to Sasa. Sasa took more crap from Boris than from anyone. Nobody else would dare to talk to him the way Boris did. Because Boris was older, because he was Sasa's father's cousin, because Boris was generally right, Sasa let him speak his mind. But even Boris knew the line, and he was fucking close. Especially tonight, when Sasa was tense and tired, going someplace he didn't want to go.

He couldn't wait to get out of the Everglades and be back in South Beach. All that quiet, all that dark, all the bodies floating gray and bloated out there that no one would ever find—it made him edgy. He thought of the thousand pairs of dead eyes staring sightless, the wrinkled, rotting skin, the blood spilling into swamp water. He turned the radio on but picked up only static. He was glad he had brought someone with him on this trip. Even if it was only Boris.

"Hey, Boris, you take it in, eh? Give me a break tonight?" he said, looking over at the older man, whose huge frame seemed even larger in the small interior of the sports car. He had to cross his arms uncomfortably in front of him to fit his broad shoulders into the car.

"Fuck off, Sasa." But there was no conviction in it, maybe a little sadness, maybe a little fear. Nobody wanted to go in, not even the tough guys like Boris.

Boris smelled of vodka and body odor. With his moist baby-doll eyes edged in girlishly long lashes and the black canyons of fatigue, the pasty-white skin of neglected health, and a permanent five-o'clock shadow on his multiple chins, Boris always looked to Sasa like a malevolent Pillsbury Doughboy. Instead of giggling, if you poked him in the belly, he'd blow your head off.

Boris sat shaking his head at his own thoughts, coughing a hacking cough that was usual for him when he was upset. "He only wants you," Boris said finally, his voice raspy with phlegm. "They'll only see you. Otherwise, you wouldn't be here at all." Sasa said nothing. It was true, and they both knew it.

He was relieved when they pulled off the highway and onto the dark road that brought them closer to the end of this errand. He could see the lights of a house ahead of him, though there were still miles to go. It was that dark and that isolated. There were a million gleaming stars above them, and the only noise was the Boxster sounding like a jet engine in the stillness.

At the gate, a man wearing a cheap gray suit, a wrinkled navy tie, and sunglasses with a wire hanging from his ear put a hand out for Sasa to stop. His breath rolled in like a foul fog as Sasa lowered the window. "Sasa Fitore," he said before the man could ask. As the man repeated his name into the Nextel phone he pulled from a pocket, Sasa squashed the urge to put a bullet in his brain. He hated people who tried to exert authority over him. And he really hated people who wore sunglasses at night.

The man stepped aside, the gate swung open, and the Boxster glided up a long, winding drive edged on either side by thick foliage. Boris emitted a light snore, and Sasa elbowed him hard as they approached the house. Boris sat up straight and put his hand inside his jacket, looking instantly alert and deadly. They approached the stately home dominated by white columns and large bay windows. Landscaped artfully with lighted palms, it was grander and far more isolated than the Snug Island house and thus far better suited to his client's needs this evening. There was no hint as to what went on inside.

Sasa pulled up and found a spot to leave the car. There were more than twenty black sedans and limousines parked in front of him. Some of the chauffeurs stood outside their vehicles, smoking cigarettes or chatting with one another. Sasa counted three diplomatic and two government plates just at first glance as he stepped out of the car.

He jogged up the steep flight of stairs. He rang the bell and was admitted by a butler in a leather bondage mask. Sasa kept his head down as he was escorted through the house—he didn't want to see anyone he shouldn't. He heard a drunken cackle come from somewhere behind him. Somewhere deeper in the house, he heard a keening wail that could have been pleasure or pain—or both.

The butler opened the heavy wood door at the end of the hallway by its brass handle. Inside, the client was fondling the large artificial breasts of a tall, gorgeous woman, whose face Sasa had seen before but couldn't place. She was a striking redhead, her skin like snow. Her mouth was as red and wet as cherry candy, and she pouted at Sasa in a pretty, nasty way, which made him stir inside. She straddled Sasa's client on the sofa, though he was fully dressed. He was touching her when Sasa entered, and the woman did not move to cover herself. Sasa tried not to stare.

"You're late," Nathan Quinn said simply, gently pushing the woman from him and turning toward Sasa.

"Yes," Sasa replied, "we had to make an important stop along the way." He didn't offer an apology. They both knew who had whom by the balls, in spite of the way it seemed.

"I see. But you have it, of course."

"Of course," he answered, pulling the DVD from the inside breast pocket of his thin leather blazer. He walked forward and handed the black jewel case to the client, whose large hands made it look like a playing card. The man stared at it for a moment, a wolfish expression taking over his already-intimidating face. A low growl escaped from his throat. And then he turned that look on Sasa, who struggled not to back up toward the door. "Will you stay and watch tonight?"

"No, thank you," Sasa said, his regretful smile not in the least sincere.

And at that, he seemed to disappear from Quinn's consciousness. Quinn extended his hand to the woman, and they walked from the study. As they walked past Sasa, he noticed she still had not closed the top of her vampish red Lycra dress. The butler had stood waiting to escort Sasa back, and he did so now, closing the door behind him. Halfway down the stairs, Sasa heard a cheer erupt from the house. Show time.

He lighted a cigarette with his sterling Zippo and walked to his car. He was sweating again; it was too hot for the leather jacket he wore. Boris had managed to extract himself from the vehicle and was leaning against the hood.

"Z'all right?"

Sasa nodded. Boris looked away. Sasa got in his car and waited for Boris to remove his enormous ass from the hood and get in. As soon as he had closed the door, Sasa pulled down the drive fast, his tires squealing as he went.

chapter nine

The opulent home of Nathan and Jenna Quinn was located on Snug Island, an enclave of exclusive waterfront properties near South Beach, a jewel nestled in giant palms. It was a peaceful and beautiful neighborhood, whispering fronds and wind chimes the only sounds, the scents of saltwater and newly cut grass heavy in the air. The tranquillity and beauty were so striking in contrast to their sometimes gritty and harsh neighborhood at home that Lydia found herself trying to remember for a moment why she and Jeffrey stayed in New York City. She figured their duplex apartment, about a quarter of the size of the grandly opulent homes they passed—if she was being generous in her estimate—had cost about as much. Oh, well, I guess that's the price you pay to live in the center of the universe, she thought.

It was coming on noon, and Lydia's stomach was starting to rumble as they pulled up the steep drive edged in stout palms in their rented black Jeep Grand Cherokee. They followed Detective Manuel Ignacio in his maroon Taurus, which looked as if it had seen better days, even though it was well maintained. The same could be said of the detective. A handsome man, who looked to be approaching fifty, he had the slightest hint of blue fatigue under his eyes and just the shadow of stubble on his jaw, though it was early in the day. But he was neatly, if not expensively, dressed in a starched white shirt, navy tie, and charcoal gray suit, only the slightest paunch hanging over his belt. His graying black hair was neatly cut and precisely combed. He had the look of a man who worked hard and did his job well, but the stress of the case was obviously taking its toll. Burnout was right around the corner for this detective.

When the detective had arrived at the precinct that morning just after 8:00 A.M., carrying a cup of Starbucks coffee and a copy of the *Miami Herald,* he found Lydia and Jeffrey waiting outside his office. Lydia was used to being treated like an interloper when she tried to insinuate herself into a case. But the detective had seemed glad to see them, greeting them both with an enthusiastic handshake and offering them coffee. He welcomed them into his office, which was neater and more organized than the office of any cop she had ever met in her life.

"Military?" she asked him.

"Marines," he answered, not seeming to wonder why she had made the observation. "My father, too. I had to bounce a quarter on my bed from the time I was old enough to make it myself. The guys make fun of me, but people don't realize how much time it wastes if you're disorganized. And when you are talking about missing children, there's no time to waste. Every minute, they're further away from being found."

Lydia nodded and seated herself in an orange faux-leather and chrome chair, noting the coordinating gold shag carpet and wood-paneled walls. *Very seventies.*

"So six, almost seven weeks into the Tatiana Quinn case, and what are you thinking? Are you going to find her?"

"I have to say I honestly don't know. Usually by now, I would say, No way. But something keeps me going—and not just the fact that Nathan Quinn pulls some big puppet strings in this department. Something else. Keeps me up nights."

He ran down the details of the case for Lydia and Jeffrey, starting from the first night, the false leads due to the million-dollar reward, and then the mysterious bus driver. He seemed to become more tired as he went on. Lydia and Jeffrey paid close attention, following along on the board the detective had set up to track all the events, leads, and tips his team had explored, hoping their fresh eyes and ears might pick up on something that the team had missed. But Lydia wasn't optimistic, having already determined that Detective Ignacio wasn't a man to miss the smallest detail. She sensed his dedication to his work in his welcome. Most cops worried about somebody stealing their thunder, being the one to break the case. They held things back from Lydia, not wanting her to think of something they hadn't. But Detective Ignacio, she could tell, was hoping she would. He cared about Tatiana more than he did about his own glory, and that was refreshing to see.

"You said you had something for me, Ms. Strong," he said when he had finished. "Believe me, I could use a break."

She put the evidence bag on his desk. "Do you have a cassette player?" she asked.

He pulled a beat-up old RadioShack tape player out of his desk. Lydia hesitated.

"It's not fancy, but it works."

"I'm sure. But this is the only copy I have of the tape I'm about to give to you, and if the machine shreds it, we've lost the only lead you might have."

"Good point. Come with me."

He led them down a gray-carpeted hallway, past glass-walled offices, through some cubes, and into an impressive audiovisual room. They walked past rows of top-of-the-line computers, carrels holding television monitors with video and DVD players, and finally reached a glass-enclosed room that held a number of cassette and CD players. Headphones hung from hooks along the wall. The detective closed the door behind them, and they each pulled up a chair.

"Well, you can't say that the Miami Police Department isn't in step with the times," commented Jeffrey.

"We have our problems, but that's not one of them," answered the detective. He looked at Jeffrey a second and then said, "Were you at one time an FBI agent, Mr. Mark?"

"I was. I left the Bureau to start my own private investigation firm, Mark, Hanley and Striker, Inc."

"I've heard of it, of course. You know, they still teach that case of yours at Quantico. I had the privilege to attend the class they give for interested local detectives. That's quite a thing to have your first case be one of the highest-profile serial-murder cases of the century."

"Well, I can't take credit for solving the case. It was really Lydia," Jeffrey said, glancing at her uneasily. He was relieved to see that she didn't have that glazed-over look in her eyes that she usually got when this conversation came up, that look that said she'd checked out emotionally.

"That's right," said the detective after an embarrassed pause. "Ms. Strong, I'm sorry to have brought that up."

"It's all right," she said. And Jeffrey could tell that it was. She had been dealing with the memory of her mother's murder much more easily since the Angel Fire case. "Call me Lydia."

"Call me Manny. And that case last year," said Ignacio, as if thinking aloud, "that was both of you, as well."

"Again, it was mostly Lydia."

"We make a good team," Lydia said, smiling—something she did a lot more of these days.

She took the tape out of the evidence bag with tweezers and managed to get it into the machine without touching it. She pressed the play button, and Tatiana's voice filled the room. They were quiet as they listened to the frightened girl, and Lydia thought she saw Detective Ignacio mist up a bit. He rewound the tape and listened to it a second time.

"What's she saying there? Is it Albanian?"

"It must be," said Lydia. "And this," she said after he had

pressed the stop button with a sigh. She handed him the note that had arrived with the tape, and he read it.

"It could have been the maid, Valentina Fitore, who sent this to you," he said after a moment. "Her English is a little shaky, and I've had the feeling she's been hiding something all along. But when I questioned her, I got nothing. You know, the tactics that you use to get information out of U.S. citizens don't always work with people from countries like Albania, places that are controlled by organized crime. The American police look like Boy Scouts; our prisons look like Club Med compared to the hell they've seen in the Balkans. I got the sense she wanted to talk but was more afraid of something else than she was of me. When did you receive this?"

"I got it in the mail the day before yesterday. It was forwarded to me from my publisher. The postmark on the envelope is October first. You can hold on to it, if you want. Have it analyzed."

"Absolutely. Prints, DNA, hair, fibers, handwriting analysis—the whole shebang. But let's make a dub of this tape and take it over to Jenna Quinn and see what type of reaction we get out of her. Or maybe this isn't even Tatiana. Just another dead end." He leaned back in his chair and looked at the stucco ceiling. Then he pulled a blank tape from a box on the table and put it in the cassette player, next to the original. A high-pitched squeal emitted from the machine as he dubbed the tape.

"If Valentina doesn't speak much English," said Lydia, "she couldn't have written this note."

"That's true." He shrugged. "Maybe someone helped her."

"Will I be able to talk to Valentina?" asked Lydia when the machine had quieted down.

"You'll probably be better off talking to her when she's not at the Quinns'."

"Why's that?"

"Because she's terrified of them."

"Do you think they had something to do with Tatiana's disappearance, Detective?"

He shook his head slowly, raising his thick eyebrows. She noticed him running his fingers under the edge of the table.

"I just don't know," he said. But something in his eyes gave Lydia a different answer. She didn't press him. "So," he said, "what's your interest in this case? Are you in this for the long haul, or are you just satisfying your curiosity? 'Cause I wouldn't resist the help if you're planning to come on board."

Jeffrey shot Lydia a warning glance, then said, "Let's just say we are considering the possibility."

"Good enough," said Ignacio, rising. "I can use all the help I can get. You'll come along to the Quinn residence?"

"Sure," Jeffrey replied.

"What type of research have you done on the Quinns?" asked Lydia when they'd left the audiovisual room and were back in his office, where he grabbed his car keys.

"It's been pretty extensive," he said as he scribbled something on a piece of paper and slid it across the desk at her. It read "Not here."

Lydia and Jeffrey exchanged a glance and she nodded.

"We had an encounter last night, Detective. A kind of unfriendly greeting."

"Really," said the detective, looking at his phone and then his watch. "We should get moving—only two hours before Jenna Quinn's weekly manicure appointment. You can tell me about it on the way."

Outside, the detective sat in the backseat of their Jeep for a few minutes as Jeffrey relayed the details of their encounter the night before. In turn, the detective told them how his research on Nathan Quinn had been cut short. "Maybe I'm being paranoid, but I feel like *I'm* under surveillance. You know, on the one hand, it's like the brass is on top of me to solve this case. And on the other, they're trying to keep me from finding out what really happened to this girl," he said, the frustration he'd been reining in at the precinct showing now.

"Well, maybe we can help each other, Detective," said Lydia.

He smiled grimly, nodding his head, and reached for the door. "Just don't disappear on me like the private detective that Nathan Quinn hired. One minute, this guy is all over me, following up leads, traveling to New York after that Greyhound driver thing; the next thing, he's gone. Stopped returning my phone calls a couple days ago. He just dropped the case. Left a message finally night before last saying it was a dead end and he had better things to do."

"That's weird," said Lydia. "Did you follow up?"

"No," he said with a cheerless chuckle. "I have too much on my plate to chase after Stephen Parker, PI."

He left the Jeep and then led the way to the Quinns' in his Taurus. On the way over, Lydia called Craig in New York.

"One more thing to add to your search," she said to him. "Find out what you can on Nathan Quinn, his connections, associations, et cetera. Any shady business dealings. You know the drill."

"You got it," he said. She could already hear the soft tapping of his fingers dancing across the keyboard.

"Is your uncle still freaking?"

"He's not even here today."

"Yeah? Where's he at?"

"I don't know," he said, sighing. "Don't care as long he's off my back."

"Jacob's not in today," Lydia reported to Jeffrey after she had hung up with Craig.

"His wife . . . Myra's been having some problems. Jacob's been vague."

"Health problems?"

"I think so."

The conversation ended when they made a left off the highway and onto the bridge that led to Snug Island. The ocean waters of the Intracoastal Waterway glimmered on either side of them, and Lydia rolled down the window to take in the salt air.

A nervous, wide-eyed Valentina Fitore barely contained a gasp as she opened the door and saw Lydia standing between the two men. The small woman, who looked to be approaching sixty, had the shadow of prettiness on her face. She still might have been an attractive woman, but Lydia could see years of hard living, sadness, and struggle in her tired eyes and wrinkled skin. Bending over in physical labor had left her in a permanent slouch, and her hands were cracked and dry. But there was something delicate and lady-like about her, something that made Lydia want to reach out and comfort her. She wore an English maid's uniform—black skirt and blouse, an apron of ruffled white cotton. Someone's idea of what the maid should wear, thought Lydia, someone vain and controlling.

"Good morning, Valentina," the detective said kindly. "Is Mrs. Quinn at home?" His tone indicated that he already knew the answer.

"Yes, I'll see. Please wait," she said haltingly, trying to shut the door and have them wait on the stoop.

"It's awfully hot, Mrs. Fitore. Do you mind if we wait in the foyer?" the detective asked gently but firmly, pushing his way into the house.

"Oh . . ." she said. She stepped back, appearing confused and unsure of herself.

"Do you know who this is, Mrs. Fitore?" asked the detective, pointing to Lydia.

The maid put her head down and said firmly, "No. No."

"Okay," Ignacio said quietly, patting her shoulder lightly. "Go get Mrs. Quinn. Tell her it's important that she see us immediately."

Twenty minutes passed as the three stood in the round foyer. Lydia paced a bit while Jeffrey and Detective Ignacio chatted quietly about the detective's visit to Quantico. She circled the glass and wrought-iron table that sat in the center of the room, stopping to look at a replica of *David* that stood in a small portico above a fountain on the wall at the base of the stairs. She glanced up the dramatic staircase, which made her think of the one in Tara in *Gone With the Wind.* She half-expected to see a woman in a sweeping ball gown come dancing down to greet them. An enormous crystal chandelier hung from the ceiling. For all the opulence of the foyer, there was no elegance to it. Each object was chosen to communicate wealth, but each competed with the others—the antebellum luxury of the staircase, the Renaissance grandeur of the *David.* Expensive but tacky. The objects people chose to decorate their homes communicated as much about them as the words they chose to construct their sentences. Whoever had decorated this room wanted people to know immediately upon entering that the Quinns had more money than God.

"Hello!" Detective Ignacio yelled suddenly, making Lydia jump, then laugh a little. She liked him. "Hello, Mrs. Quinn! Detective Ignacio here. I need to speak with you." The maid rushed out from the hallway, frowning, her finger to her lips.

"Shh, Detective. Just a minute. Mrs. Quinn come in just a minute."

"What kind of woman takes twenty minutes to come to the door when a detective arrives to tell her that he has a lead in her missing daughter's case?" Lydia whispered to Jeffrey.

Jenna Quinn appeared at the top of the stairs. Radiant in a pink Chanel suit and black patent-leather pumps, her hair expensively frosted and pulled into a French twist, nails and makeup impeccable, Jenna put on the perfect mask of breathless apology upon reaching them. But Lydia could see that it did not reach her eyes, which were as cold and as soulless as stone.

"I'm so sorry, Detective. I was in the shower. Please come in.

Sit down," she said, leading them into the library, which was to the right of the foyer, and indicating a leather sofa and chairs.

She was in the shower, but she took the time to dry and put her hair into a twist, apply makeup, choose the Rolex, a diamond bracelet and matching earrings, Lydia was thinking as the detective introduced her and Jeffrey to Jenna. Jenna gave Lydia a weak fingertip handshake, which was one of Lydia's major pet peeves. Meant, she assumed, to communicate a dainty femininity, it instead communicated guarded pettiness and a passive-aggressive personality.

Jenna batted her eyelashes a bit and smiled shyly at Jeffrey as she offered him her fingertips. Jeffrey greeted her the same way he greeted everyone, with respect but distance, and a smattering of suspicion. Lydia loved that Jeffrey was impervious to manipulation. When he had no noticeable reaction to her subtle flirtation, Jenna turned her attention back to the detective.

"Do you have news about my daughter, Detective?" she asked, widening her eyes in a look that Lydia suspected was a bad impression of hope. She then seated herself behind an enormous mahogany desk across the room. On either side of the desk sat two onyx statues of greyhounds, their musculature carefully sculpted, their teeth bared.

The ceilings must have been twenty feet high. A gigantic brass and frosted glass chandelier hung down from the center of a compass that had been painted on the ceiling. A narrow staircase wound up one wall to a catwalk and a full story of bookshelves stocked with what looked to be hundreds of leather-bound editions.

"Possibly," the detective replied, getting up and moving toward the desk, closing the distance she had placed between them. As he removed the tape from his pocket, Lydia noticed for the first time that he held the tape player she had seen in his office in the crook of his arm, concealed under his suit jacket. "Miss Strong received this tape in the mail. It was sent by an anonymous party. I wanted to play this for you and see if you can offer us some insight."

"I'd be happy to." She smiled up at him and shifted in her chair. Lydia was having trouble figuring Jenna Quinn out. She was putting on a show, probably the same lady-of-the-manor one she put on every day. Lydia could see by the way her eyes darted about, and by the way she kept smoothing her skirt, that she was nervous, uncomfortable. But the true essence of her personality was buried under a carefully constructed facade. Maybe even Jenna didn't know the real woman under the shell of cosmetics and expensive clothes.

The detective placed his RadioShack tape player on the desk. All three of them had their eyes on her as the tape played. Jenna sat as still and perfectly coiffed as a mannequin. When the tape ended, there was an expectant silence.

"That's not my daughter," said Jenna finally.

"Are you sure, Mrs. Quinn?"

"I think I know the sound of my own child's voice, Detective," she answered primly. She turned a cold gaze on Lydia, who matched it and was gratified to see Jenna shrink back just slightly before she asked, "Where did you get this tape?"

"When she speaks in Albanian, what's she saying?" asked the detective, ignoring her question.

"It's hard to understand," said Jenna, looking at the floor. "I don't know."

"Come on, Mrs. Quinn. Give us a break," he said, his tone more coaxing than exasperated.

She was silent for a second. And then she said, "The girl talks of her mother. She says her mother is weak and foolish, always pulled this way and that by the men, always believing their lies."

"That's harsh," said the detective, wincing dramatically. "Any truth to that, Mrs. Quinn?"

"As I said, that's not my daughter. I am just translating the words of this strange girl for you, as you asked," she said, indignant. "Where did that tape come from?"

"The detective told you that I received it in the mail from an anonymous party," said Lydia from her perch on the couch.

"We thought it might have come from your answering machine, Mrs. Quinn."

"We don't have an answering machine. We have voice mail. There is a tap and a trace on our phone. If Tatiana called here, your men would have heard it. Isn't that so, Detective?"

"Well, who else might she have called if she needed help?"

"How should I know?" she snapped, her Eastern European accent insinuating itself more strongly now. "Don't you see? Tatiana hated me and she hated her stepfather. She kept everything from us . . . her thoughts, her feelings, her friends. She ran away, and she won't come back until she wants something."

There was something oddly desperate in Jenna's outburst. For a second, Lydia saw a flicker of honest emotion in Jenna's cold blue eyes.

"Have you lost hope, Mrs. Quinn?" Lydia asked, trying to understand the woman in front of her. "Is that why you are so angry?"

"I lost hope a long time ago, Ms. Strong. In everything. Is there anything else?"

"This note," said the detective, handing it to her. "What can you tell us about this?"

Her face remained expressionless as she read the note, but Lydia saw her chest rise and fall slightly and thought she detected a shake in her hand.

"This means nothing to me," she said, her voice angry and bitter. "Another false lead, Detective. If there's nothing else, I'd like you to leave."

"Do you recognize the handwriting, Mrs. Quinn?" the detective pressed, impervious to her growing agitation.

"No," she said, not looking at the note again.

"I'd like to look at Tatiana's room," Lydia said.

"Unless you have a warrant, absolutely not. Detective, do I need to call my lawyer?"

"Ms. Strong and Mr. Mark are trying to help you, Mrs. Quinn. They came here of their own accord to help us solve this case. They are trying to find your daughter."

"Tatiana doesn't want to be found, Detective. No one has hurt or abducted her. She has run away and destroyed us both, even though we did everything for her, gave her everything a child could need or ask for." She turned from them and gazed at the ceiling, tracing the bottom of her eyes with a tissue, careful not to smear her eyeliner. Lydia smelled a whiff of self-dramatization.

"Well, Mr. Quinn is not inclined to give up. And neither am I," said the detective. Jenna Quinn did not respond for a moment. She sat small and rigid behind the desk, her eyes staring at a point on the ceiling. Then she rose.

"Perhaps you would do better to bring this matter to Mr. Quinn, then. If there's nothing else, I have an appointment."

With that, she walked out of the library and across the marble foyer and opened the front door. She stood and waited there as the three of them rose and followed her path.

"Mrs. Quinn, if you change your mind about cooperating with Ms. Strong and Mr. Mark, give me a call."

"Or me," said Lydia, handing her a card.

"Thank you," she said, chillingly polite.

She slammed the door behind them.

"That went well," said Jeffrey, speaking up for the first time.

The detective smiled. "In all of this, I've never seen her get so upset. I've never seen that side of her before."

"What do you think it means?"

"I think it means we're onto something."

chapter ten

Lydia, Jeffrey, and Detective Ignacio sat in a Cuban restaurant about five minutes from the residence of Valentina Fitore, sipping *café con leche* and eating pungent *ropa vieja,* yellow rice, and black beans. The tiny, plain restaurant, which had been barely noticeable from the street, was made glorious by the rich aromas of coffee and seasoned pork. A woman with a bright, toothless smile, her hair in a net, had greeted the detective at the door with an enthusiastic hug and, with an expansive sweep of her arm, invited them in. *"Venga, venga. Siéntate,"* she said happily. They took their choice of the three bright red wooden tables with four matching chairs at each and sat by the window. The detective ordered in Spanish for the three of them, and the woman limped into the kitchen, visible through an open doorway, and cooked the food herself. Though the tender strips of flank steak looked and smelled delectable and Lydia had been starving just awhile ago, she pushed the food around on her plate. She'd lost her appetite and didn't speak as the detective recounted for them the story of the missing Greyhound bus driver. She knew she should be listening to the details, but she couldn't concentrate.

The ghosts that had rested were stirring within Lydia now. A dark feeling had crept over her after leaving the Quinn residence, and though she tried to shake it, she felt it settling into her bones like a chill that portends the flu. She had grown quiet as she tried to put words to what she had felt in the Quinn home, as she tried to make sense of the malevolence and fear she had felt radiating from the walls. Jenna Quinn had confused Lydia. Usually, a person's essence was clear to her within seconds of the first greeting. People emitted an energy that either meshed or clashed, that attracted or repelled. But Jenna Quinn was either so guarded or so practiced in the art of deception that Lydia had no clear idea who she was or what her real agenda might be. She knew who Jenna wanted everyone to think she was—Mrs. Quinn, the immaculately groomed, grieving, betrayed mother; the sad, beautiful wife. But there was a flicker of something real under the facade. Lydia had caught a glimpse of it, but she couldn't tell what it was. It annoyed her that Jenna hadn't given herself away.

People subconsciously telegraphed the truth in their speech and in their gestures. Lydia had learned long ago that the furtive gesture, the thing left unsaid, the shifting glance spoke volumes. It was her gift to intuit the truth even when it was hidden, even when it escaped the notice of others. She'd had this ability all her life but had really only acknowledged it after the murder of her mother.

Two days before Marion Strong was killed, Lydia saw her murderer in a supermarket parking lot. Lydia was waiting for her mother in the car while Marion ran into the A&P to get a quart of milk. Sitting in her mother's old Buick, the fifteen-year-old Lydia punched the hard plastic keys on the AM/FM radio, checking each preset station for acceptable listening. Suddenly, she felt the hairs rise on the back of her neck. She felt heat start at the base of her skull and move at a quickfire pace down her spine. A hollow of fear opened in her belly. She turned around and looked out the rear windshield.

The car's side windows were open and the already cool fall air seemed to chill and the darkening of the sky quickened. The man stood with his legs a little more than shoulder width apart, one hand in the pocket of his denim jacket, the other resting on the side-view mirror of his red-and-white car, which reminded Lydia of the car in *Starsky and Hutch.* His flaming red hair was curly and disheveled, blowing into his eyes. She remembered that he did not move to keep it off his face. He just stared and rocked lightly back onto his heels and then forward onto the balls of his feet. Seeing him standing beside his car, his gaze locked on her, made her senses tingle. She detected malice in his unyielding stare, perversion in the way he began to caress the side-view mirror when their eyes met. She reached over to lock the doors and roll up the windows without taking her eyes off of him.

When her mother returned to the car, Lydia pointed the man out to her. He just stood there smiling. Marion tried to tell her it was nothing. But Lydia could see her mother was afraid by the hurried way she threw the milk into the backseat and the way she fumbled to put the key in the ignition. They drove off, and the man pulled out after them. But when Marion made a quick turn, he did not pursue them. They laughed; the threat, real or imagined, was gone. But Lydia would look back at that moment as the point at which she could have saved her mother's life. She had written down the license plate number with blue eyeliner on the back of a note a friend had passed to her in class. That information had led to the apprehension of Jed McIntyre, serial murderer of thirteen single mothers in the area around Nyack, New York. But only after he had killed Marion Strong, leaving her where Lydia would find her beaten and violated as she returned home from school.

She knew now, of course, that even if they had reported the incident in the parking lot to the police, they wouldn't have been able to do anything. But when she got that feeling, the feeling she and Jeffrey had come to know as "the buzz," she had never been able to walk away from it again, wondering always who else would die if she did.

She looked at Jeffrey, Detective Ignacio droning on in the periphery of her consciousness. Jeffrey had finished his meal and had started working on hers. She heard her blood rushing in her ears and she pushed down a feeling of anxiety that welled inside her. She hadn't felt like this in so long, not since Santa Fe, when she started to believe there was a serial killer at the beginning of a rampage. It was more complicated now, though. When the buzz had hit her before, she jumped into action. It gave her purpose. Every time, she was infused with hope, as if she had been given another chance to save her mother. She had risked her life, and Jeffrey's, without a second thought. And every time, after a case was solved and the book written, she was left with an emptiness that accompanied the inevitable knowledge that her mother was still dead, still murdered. Now that she had come to recognize this about herself in her healing over the last year, she wasn't sure if she had ever been motivated to help anyone but herself. Perhaps her whole career had been a hopelessly inadequate attempt to save her mother, to alleviate her own guilt. What did that make her? she wondered.

"What do you think, Lydia?" asked Jeffrey, breaking into her thoughts.

"Did anyone actually go to the address?" she asked in response. She *had* been listening, but with only about half a percent of her brain. They had been talking about the false address the fake bus driver had left.

"We looked it up. The street doesn't exist."

"Sounds to me like someone was trying to throw you off her track."

"We weren't *on* her track."

"Are you sure? What lead were you working on when that came up?"

"That's what I'm saying," he said, sipping his *café con leche*. "The case had grown cold even then. There were no leads."

"Well then, maybe someone was trying to get you going again. Maybe Nathan Quinn was trying to light a fire under you."

"So he hired someone to come in and feed us a false lead, then disappear?"

Lydia shrugged. "Stranger things have happened. It would have been a stupid thing to do, but maybe he was desperate."

"Did the security camera at the precinct get a picture of him?" asked Jeffrey.

"Yeah. It's not a very good picture, almost as though he turned away on purpose. But you know we have that new face-recognition software, put it on security cameras all over the place. If the guy had a mug shot on record, it would have popped up."

"What did he look like?"

"Big guy, heavy, strong-looking. He had a shaved head. He said he was from the former Yugoslavia, Macedonia—one of those places."

"Sounds like the same description the bartender gave us of the guy who paid our bill," said Jeffrey. "Let's take a picture over to that guy after we see Valentina Fitore."

"Who interviewed him?" asked Lydia.

"This rookie we got on the team, Charlie Sutton. He should've really checked the guy out while he was still there. He was just excited to have the lead. He blew it."

"Well, how did you pursue this tip?" asked Jeffrey.

"We got in touch with the NYPD; they put a team on it up there. We spent a couple of days at the bus station here, walking around with her picture. Interviewed ticket clerks, bus drivers, homeless people who lie around the station. Stephen Parker, the PI Quinn hired, flew up to New York, went to Port Authority, did the same thing. Another waste of manpower, with no results," he said, seeming to deflate as he spoke. "I had even more heat on me than ever from that point. It looked like my fuckup, like I had let a lead slip through my fingers. It got the media all revved up again, but then they lost interest."

"So maybe that was it. A stunt to get the media involved again. To keep the story in the paper."

"Maybe," the detective said without much enthusiasm. Lydia could tell he was burning out on the case. He'd been through all these mental acrobatics already and he was tired. She didn't blame him.

"So who was she, Detective?" Lydia asked, hoping that making him think about Tatiana would get him fueled up again. "Was she the type of girl who runs away? Did she have a boyfriend? Who were her friends at school? Did you find a journal? Read her E-mail?"

He smiled a little and met Lydia's eyes.

"Sometimes I forget about her, you know? She's become this abstraction, what with all the other stuff going on in this case. It's like she exists in the shadow of Nathan Quinn's desire to find her."

Lydia nodded, having sensed this already.

"She didn't have many friends. She was beautiful, you know. Something like that isolates a kid. Kids are even pettier, crueler, and more jealous than adults, because they haven't learned to hide it yet. I think she was shy, too. The kids I spoke to at her school said she didn't speak up much in class, didn't socialize during gym and lunch. I got the sense they thought of her as a snob, even though they all seemed pretty snobby to me," he said.

"She was an average student, not great, but not a problem child. She worked hard, but she seemed to have problems concentrating, according to her teachers. I didn't find a journal. She didn't have E-mail . . . probably the only kid in the world who doesn't. Her parents didn't allow that and didn't let her have a phone in her room, not even an extension phone." He paused, seeming to drift for a minute. He took a sip of his coffee, then wiped his mouth with his napkin.

"She had all these things, you know . . . all these clothes, makeup, CDs, but I just had the sense of unhappiness in the room. My kid, she doesn't have half the stuff, but when you walk into her room, it's like . . . happy girl clutter, everything messy, stickers and sparkles all over the place. It's almost as if you can hear her giggling, dreaming, gossiping . . . like it echoes in that *stuff*. With Tatiana's room, it seemed as though everything was for show, like a picture in a book. She was someone's idea of the perfect teenager. But there was another layer that no one saw, that no one was allowed to see. I'm no closer to knowing what goes on in that house than I was the first night. For people who seem so perfect, no one seems all that happy. It's like that house is a soundstage, like their whole life is a soundstage. But God only knows what happens when the camera is off."

"Whoever sent me that tape knows. Could it have been sent by anyone other than Valentina?"

"If she had a close friend or a boyfriend, no one knows about it. I think she spent time with Valentina's daughter Marianna, who's nearly eighteen. But that was more of a baby-sitter thing, when Valentina couldn't stay."

The detective massaged his temples. "But something keeps me from giving up inside. You know, I could just be going through the motions, thinking that she was gone for good but persisting because the men upstairs won't say die. But remember that movie *Poltergeist*, where they could hear that little girl's voice but she's just out of their reach. That's how I feel about Tatiana."

They were all quiet, and a siren wailed down the street outside the restaurant. Lydia leaned back in her chair and looked out into the street, where a young woman was reprimanding a child at the crosswalk and a teenage boy was skulking with a skateboard under his arm. The sky was painting itself shades of gray behind thick, high piles of darkening cumulous clouds.

"So why don't you two go take the picture to the bartender and let me go talk to Valentina by myself?" said Lydia finally. "She's scared of you, Detective. But if she sent the tape to me, maybe I'll be able to convince her to talk. She might feel less intimidated if I go alone."

She could tell Jeffrey didn't like the idea very much, but he nodded his agreement. He had too much respect for her to act like her protective boyfriend in front of other law-enforcement people, knowing that it undermined her in a male-dominated profession. They got the check from their elderly Cuban waitress, who patted Detective Ignacio on the cheek.

"*Gracias, mi amor,*" he said, kissing her hand. She trotted away, giggling like a schoolgirl.

"Come here often?" asked Lydia, snagging the bill from his hand.

"My first time. I just have a thing for old Cuban ladies," he said, smiling.

Lydia called Craig from the Jeep after Jeffrey and Detective Ignacio headed back to the precinct to pick up the surveillance picture so they could show it to the waiter at the Mexican restaurant. The detective had promised to get Lydia and Jeffrey in to see Nathan Quinn as soon as possible. And Lydia wanted to be armed with as much information as she could get.

Though she could hear the threatening rumble of thunder in the distance, the storm that had seemed imminent was biding its time, hanging around, making the air thick with humidity. Lydia was parked across the street from Valentina Fitore's Fort Lauderdale home, waiting for her to return from her work at the Quinns'. According to the detective, she generally arrived home at around six o'clock.

A modest yellow-and-white ranch house, surrounded by neat hedges and blooming hibiscus trees, it was one of five different models Lydia had observed driving through the subdivision. Property in Fort Lauderdale wasn't cheap, and the upper-middle-class subdivision didn't seem a likely choice for the family maid, not to mention an immigrant from Albania, unless she was paid very, very well. The black Porsche Boxster that sat in the driveway was somewhat conspicuous among the late-model Toyotas and Volkswagens that were parked in front of some of the other houses. She wondered whom the car belonged to and why Valentina wasn't home yet from work. It was almost 6:30.

"What do you have for me?" she asked Craig.

"Let's see," he said with a sigh. "There's no way to describe Nathan Quinn, other than he is an American blue blood. The heir to the fortune his father, Reginald Quinn, made in real estate, he went to Groton, then on to Yale, which he graduated in 1963. From there, he went into international banking at Chase Manhattan. He got his MBA from Columbia University. And after working at Chase for nearly fifteen years, he spread his wings and opened his own company, Quinn Enterprises."

"What do they do?"

"As far as I can tell, they are a venture-capitalist firm. They loan money to entrepreneurs, struggling countries, whatever they deem to be an appropriate risk. And then they either make a huge percentage on their shares when the enterprise succeeds or take ownership when it fails. It's hard to tell, though. It's a privately held company. They're clean with the IRS. They made nearly a billion dollars in the nineties. But the weird thing is, they pulled out of their dot-com companies a few months before everything started to crash. Meaning they didn't lose their shirts like a lot of people."

"Interesting."

"It gets more interesting."

"Do tell."

She watched as a handsome, well-dressed young man left the Fitore residence. At first glance, he looked like a thinner, more modern James Dean, with slicked-back darkish blond hair. He walked with a casual slump and the smooth, confident gait of a young punk who thinks he's a man. She could also tell by the way his expensive jacket hung at the inseam that he was carrying a gun—a very big gun.

"Jenna and Tatiana Quinn and the maid, Valentina Fitore, are all Albanian, right? Quinn Enterprises was heavily invested in the Albanian government—if you can call it that—that took the reins right after the fall of communism. You know about that? The whole pyramid scheme that basically destroyed the country's entire economy?"

"Um, no."

Craig had a way of making Lydia feel like the most uninformed human being on the planet. Even though she read more than most people and studied newspapers religiously, he always seemed to have more information than seemed possible for someone so young.

"When the Communist regime ended in Albania," he explained patiently, "chaos ensued, leaving the country ripe for the takeover of organized crime. It was already the poorest country in Europe, but things got even worse in 1997. An investment opportunity, into which hundreds of thousands of Albanian citizens had sunk their life savings, was revealed as fraudulent. The government had, according to critics, colluded in the scheme. Riots ensued when the investors realized that their money was gone forever."

"Wow . . . that's fucked-up."

"Well, Nathan Quinn made a lot of money on that, too."

"How?"

"I'm not clear on that. I just tripped over the information. I was entering the names of the companies in which Quinn Enterprises had invested, which I got from the IRS database, into a search engine—"

"Craig," she interrupted, "you hacked into the IRS? Please don't tell me these things. Jeffrey would kill us both."

"Okay, I mean got from my 'contact' at the IRS. One of these companies was called American Equities. I got a list of articles about the crash. Turns out that Quinn Enterprises funded the company that destroyed the Albanian economy. The president of AE, an alleged boss in the Albanian mob, a John Gotti–type character over there named Radovan Mladic, killed himself. Quinn walked away from the whole thing without a financial blemish. In fact, nearly a hundred million dollars richer, according to the IRS."

"That has to be illegal somehow? Aren't there laws?" asked Lydia.

"Not for some of us, apparently," he replied with a smug laugh.

Lydia found herself wondering if Craig was talking about Quinn or about himself. She couldn't imagine how he was hacking into government computers without getting caught. And she didn't want to know.

She watched the young man get into the Porsche and back up out of the driveway. He pulled up right next to the Jeep, but because of the black tinted windows on her vehicle and the fact that she slouched down in her seat, he didn't notice her inside. He flicked on the interior light and was intent on his own reflection in the rearview mirror as he paused for a second while he smoothed out his already-perfect hair. He had the bluest eyes Lydia had ever seen. Then he gunned the engine, barked second, and was gone.

"That's all I've got for now. I'm still digging."

"Thanks, Craig."

She hung up the phone and looked at the black tire marks the Porsche had left in the road. She didn't have time to wonder who the young man was, because then a black stretch limousine pulled up to the curb. She had to assume it was the Quinns' driver, because Valentina Fitore climbed out, still in her maid's uniform. She walked around to the driver, who hadn't made a move to get out and open the door for her. They exchanged what looked to be a few friendly words, and then he drove off, leaving Valentina standing in the street.

Lydia climbed out of her Jeep and walked around the front of the vehicle.

"Mrs. Fitore," she called.

Valentina looked as if she had been expecting Lydia, and she regarded her with some combination of sad resignation and fear. She backed away a little, glancing uneasily around her.

"Mrs. Fitore," Lydia said gently, leaning on the hood. "We need to talk."

"I can't speak to you, Miss Strong. I make a horrible mistake." she said. Her words were clear and her accent heavy. She had forced her mouth into a hard line, and she frowned, deep lines creasing her brow. Lydia could see in Valentina the stress of a lifetime of struggle and fighting to protect herself.

"Please, Valentina. I want to help Tatiana," she said, appealing to the emotions that must have been present to inspire her to send the letter and tape, if she had, in fact, done so. Lydia could see in Valentina's eyes the battle being waged between conscience and fear.

Then she saw the older woman's expression soften, and Valentina took a step toward Lydia. But when she opened her mouth, her words were drowned by a screeching of tires that sounded like a human scream. Time seemed to slow and warp as a black Mercedes sedan with heavily tinted windows closed in on them like a storm. In one moment, Valentina stood before Lydia. In the next, she was struck hard by the metal grill with a sickening crack. She was mercilessly pushed by the car fender as Lydia watched, helpless, astonished. An inhuman sound that was despair and anger escaped Lydia's throat as she, unthinking, ran after the Mercedes. When it stopped, Lydia froze, and for an eternal moment the street seemed to hold its breath. A flock of small green parrots screeched overhead as they fled from the tree they'd been perched in. Then the driver slammed the car into reverse, Lydia directly in its path. She managed to leap to the side of the road and crawl behind the Jeep. Her gun was still inside the vehicle, sitting uselessly on the bottom of her bag on the backseat. She struggled toward the back door, watching the wheels of the Mercedes from beneath her car as it continued its path, backing down the street, then sped off. She lay still for a moment, gasping for breath; then she pulled herself from the ground. People had started to come from their houses.

"Are you all right?" a frightened voice called.

"Call an ambulance," a more frightened voice answered, and Lydia realized it was her own voice. She ran toward Valentina, who lay on the road, a crumbled pile of herself in a spreading pool of blood. Her dead eyes registered horrified surprise, her lips slightly parted.

"Oh God," whispered Lydia, assailed by guilt and regret as she knelt beside the woman, Valentina's blood soaking into the knees of Lydia's jeans. "Oh God. What's happening here?"

chapter eleven

He felt a shock of fear when he saw her sitting with her head in her hands and the knees of her jeans soaked through with blood. She sat alone in a glass-walled interrogation room. Her heels resting on the metal chair legs, her elbows on her thighs, she moved her fingers across her forehead in circles, as if rubbing away the sight she had just witnessed. He was reminded what a small woman she was, just under five six, weighing in at 120 pounds, give or take. He always thought of her as strong and powerful, the energy of her personality taking up much more space than her physical frame. He remembered the first time he'd seen her, perched on the stoop of her mother's house in Sleepy Hollow, sinking into grief, terrified and traumatized. He hadn't thought of that night in so long.

Jeffrey and Detective Ignacio had raced back to the station house when the call came over the police radio. And the ride had been an eternity, even knowing that Valentina was the sole casualty at the scene. He'd had an instinct that Lydia should not make that trip alone, but he had kept his mouth shut, knowing that she would have given him shit for being overprotective. She easily could have been killed. It would be awhile before he could forgive himself for that.

She raised her eyes, saw him approaching, and gave him a weak smile. He hoped she would jump up and run to him, but she didn't. He could see as he strode toward her that she had pulled the shades down in her eyes. She had taken on the coldness that she used to protect herself in moments like this. And he hated it. Hated that she'd had cause to learn how to do that in her life, and hated that she was in a position where she needed to again. Their last year together had been so peaceful, free from murder and mayhem. He was starting to think that they needed a career change.

"Are you all right?" he asked when he entered the room. She rose and let herself be taken into his arms, where she clung to him for a second.

"I'm okay. Valentina Fitore is dead," she said, moving away from him and sitting down again. Jeffrey and Detective Ignacio took seats at the table.

"What happened?"

"One second, we were standing on the street. The next second, a black Mercedes came out of nowhere and just mowed her down. It was unbelievable. I never saw it coming."

"They're calling it a hit-and-run," said the detective.

"It was no accident—whoever was driving that car aimed for her and raced off after he'd finished the job. It was a hit, no doubt about it."

"Did you give your statement?"

She nodded. "I told them what I saw."

"And why you were there?" asked the detective, wondering how much damage control he was going to have to do with his superiors.

"More or less. I said it was for an interview, based on a correspondence I had received from Mrs. Fitore. In my capacity as a writer, of course."

The detective smiled.

"Did you get a chance to talk to her? Did she say anything to you before she died?"

"She never had a chance."

Lydia tried not to replay the moment in her mind over and over. But her brain was stuck in some sort of sick loop. Repeatedly, she saw Valentina lifted away by the Mercedes's fender, heard the horrifying crack at impact, saw her lifeless eyes. But sitting there waiting for Jeffrey and the detective, she'd had a chance to consider a few other things, as well. Who suspected that Valentina had information she shouldn't have, and how did that person know that Lydia would be there waiting to speak to her about it? How did Valentina afford to live in a neighborhood like that on a maid's salary? And why wasn't that a detail that seemed suspicious to Ignacio? Who was the young man driving the Porsche?

She looked over at the detective, who had his head down, one hand on his forehead, and was tapping his right index finger lightly on the table. He's kept something from you, her inner voice warned as goose bumps raised on her arms. There's another piece to the puzzle that he didn't reveal.

She slid in closer to him. "I was thinking, Detective," she said slowly, "that's an awfully nice house for a maid. And another interesting thing I observed . . . I saw a young man leaving in a Boxster."

The tapping finger stilled, but Detective Ignacio didn't raise his eyes to hers.

"What's going on, Detective? I get the sense that there's more to Valentina Fitore than you let on."

The detective looked a little embarrassed. She watched as a flush of red crept up from beneath his collar and painted his cheeks.

"Valentina lives with her daughter. Marianna is just a kid, like I told you. A sophomore in college this year," he said, delaying what came next. "But Valentina's brother, Sasa, spends a lot of time at the house. Sasa . . . he's a real bad man in the Albanian Mafia. On a pretty high level, from what I understand. Anyway, that's somebody else's problem."

"The feds?" asked Jeffrey.

"Yeah. And they're pretty uptight about the whole thing. When this whole Tatiana thing came down, they more or less told us to back off the Fitores. They didn't want us fucking up their investigation. I guess I was sort of hoping that maybe there wasn't a connection between Sasa Fitore and Tatiana's disappearance. I guess I was wrong." He shook his head.

"That's why you let Lydia go there alone? Because you knew you would get shit for going where you had been told to step off?" asked Jeffrey.

The detective looked down at the table. "I'm sorry, Lydia. I never imagined I was putting you in any danger. Not like that."

"I know," she said. She didn't blame him for being desperate and taking his opportunity for a back door into the Fitore house. But Jeffrey did.

"I'd never even heard of the Albanian Mafia until all this came down," he said, looking at Lydia but avoiding Jeffrey's eyes. "Apparently, they flew onto the FBI's radar in 1994. The feds call them YACS—Yugoslavians, Albanians, Croats, and Serbs, though they mostly consist of Albanians. They pulled a bunch of heists—ATMs, cell phones . . . small-time stuff but big money. They were superorganized, skilled paramilitary shit, planning for every contingency . . . even getting arrested. And when someone got caught, he never talked. Like I said, the American police and prison systems look like Club Med to some of these guys. The FBI spent years spinning their wheels. Then things started to escalate after 1997. The feds started to believe that they were into all kinds of shit—drugs, prostitution, slavery. And they're vicious—they make the Italians look like a bunch of Campfire Girls. They don't have a code. . . . Women and children are fair game. They don't have "families" and "bosses" like the Cosa Nostra. So they've been harder to pin down. I am guessing that now the feds have something on Sasa and they don't want it fucked up, even at the expense of a little girl's life."

Jeffrey knew better than anyone that the FBI could be like a dog with a bone—it was part of the reason he'd left the Bureau. When it came to an end result, they worried more about media scandal than they did about human casualties, more about making the collar at any cost.

"I'm sure we can expect a visit sometime soon," said Jeffrey.

"I'll bet you're right. And I have a few questions for them, too," Lydia responded. She paused a second and then leaned toward Detective Ignacio. "If we're going to help you find Tatiana, Detective, you're going to have to be honest with us from this point forward. No more surprises."

Jeffrey didn't say anything, but his cool expression and folded hands said he wasn't happy about anything that was going on.

"You have my word," the detective said, raising his hands and giving a little laugh. Jeffrey thought he looked too relieved, as if he'd gotten away with something.

"What's he into, Manny?" said Jeffrey.

"Who? Sasa?" he asked.

Jeffrey just looked at him.

"I don't know for sure," he said. "A prostitution thing, you know, pimping, I'd imagine."

Lydia noticed the blush creeping back up from his collar. Jeffrey shook his head. "No, that's not big enough for all of this intrigue," he said.

"Listen, I really *don't* know for sure," he said earnestly. He paused a second, as if trying to figure out how to say it. "But I heard that it involves films." He sounded as if the words tasted bitter on his tongue. "Bad stuff. You know, bondage porn that ends with murder."

"You're talking about snuff films?" asked Lydia, incredulous.

The detective nodded. His answer hung in the air between them, the implications expanding in each of their minds. Lydia's mind went back to the letter she'd received: "And you must help Tatiana Quinn and all the other girls who are in need of rescue. There are too many who are already past helping."

"And even with this knowledge, you were able to convince

yourself that there was no connection between Sasa Fitore and the fact that a young girl is missing?" asked Lydia, trying and failing to keep the judgment out of her voice.

His face darkened a bit. "Like I said, I've been warned to step off. I have to follow the rules here or I'll lose my career. I'm not a free agent like the two of you. I lose my job and my kid doesn't go to college, my wife doesn't get medication for her diabetes. Do you understand that?"

She did understand. She understood that this was the reason he'd been so happy to have their help, because they were going to be able to follow leads that he couldn't, take the kind of risks that he wasn't willing or able to take for Tatiana.

"Do you think that whoever killed Valentina did it because she knew something and someone didn't want her to talk? Or could it have been a message to Sasa?"

"I don't know," said the detective. "I just don't know."

"It's a pretty big coincidence that Valentina got hit just a couple of hours after we took that tape and note to Jenna Quinn," observed Jeffrey.

Lydia nodded, taking the information in and wondering if they had gotten Valentina killed. And if so, what did that tell them about Jenna Quinn?

"What about the bartender?" asked Lydia, remembering the errand Manny and Jeff had been on when Valentina was killed.

"When we walked in the door of the restaurant, that pretty-boy bartender looked like he was going to wet himself. He pretended he didn't remember me," said Jeffrey. "Eventually, fifty dollars jogged his memory about the event. But when we showed him the picture from the surveillance photo, he said he couldn't be sure if it was the same man who had bought our drinks. Said it was possible but that he wasn't a hundred percent sure."

"He was lying," said Detective Ignacio. "Someone got to him. I thought he was going to pass out when we showed him the picture."

Jeffrey nodded his agreement and then turned to Lydia with a frown. "If we're done here, I'm taking you back to the hotel. You need some rest." Jeffrey's tone suggested that argument was futile, the kind of hard flatness he got to his voice when he was covering worry or fear with anger. And she was tired, so she rose to comply.

"Look, Lydia, I'm sorry about not telling you everything. I never imagined you could get hurt," the detective said, offering his hand, which she took.

"I understand, Manny. I really do."

Jeffrey was conspicuously silent, and the detective gave him a rueful look.

"Manny, when do you think you can get us in with Nathan Quinn?" asked Lydia as she and Jeffrey reached the door.

"I'll call you at the Delano tomorrow and tell you when. Don't bother just showing up at his office. No one sees Nathan Quinn without an appointment."

chapter twelve

The ocean whispered and a child laughed. A gull screeched overhead, and the breeze flipped pages of a magazine Lydia had been reading before she dozed off, startling her back to semiwakefulness. She looked around her and saw the beach through amber-colored glasses and was aware of a certain unreality the afternoon had taken on, as if she were peering into another dimension through the glass of a genie's bottle. The pall that she had been carrying around with her since Valentina was murdered two days before was starting to lift. Jeffrey's towel was empty, wrinkled, and pressed into the sand where he had lain a few moments ago . . . or was it longer? Next to her, the laptop was closed. She looked around her and didn't see him, then sat up in the low beach chair and reached for her bottle of water. It was warm, but she drank it anyway. Jeffrey had gotten his beach time after all, as they waited for their audience tomorrow with Nathan Quinn.

She fought a swell of anxiety as her eyes scanned the beach again, searching for Jeffrey's familiar form among the crowd of strangers. The Art Deco buildings across Ocean Drive stood pink, lavender, yellow, and white, solid and pretty among the giant palms and endless parade of strollers, shoppers, and restaurantgoers. In the distance, towering condominium buildings stood grand and elegant against the jewel blue sky. The scene around her was a picture postcard, but all she could imagine was how quickly things could go bad, how the sky could darken, the wind pick up, how people might start to run. She could imagine the happy chatter of their voices turning to alarm, the music coming from boom boxes, drowned out by a violent clap of thunder. She pushed her imaginings away; she hadn't allowed her mind to conjure images like that for a long time.

It was as if seeing Valentina murdered had released old fears within her. Demons she thought she'd wrestled and defeated had come back to call. A little vodka—no, a lot of vodka, and a lot of sleep had helped to fade the image of Valentina being struck by the Mercedes. But it was as if the direct exposure to violence had left her vulnerable again to the old feelings of guilt and fear that she had suffered since the death of her mother. She'd thought she was free of the feelings that had kept her denying her love for Jeffrey for so long. Free of the fear of losing someone else. She hadn't said anything, but every time Jeffrey had left her sight, she had half-believed she would never see him again. She hated it. She hated feeling weak and vulnerable and scared.

But stronger than her fear was the buzz that had been coursing through her veins like a drug since they'd left the precinct. She had spent most of the day before scanning the Internet, confirming the information she had received from Craig and trying to find something more specifically damning on Nathan Quinn. But it seemed like everything printed about the man was a virtual valentine. No publication had anything bad to say about him or about any of his companies. The newspapers and local reports carried brief mentions of the "hit-and-run" that had claimed Valentina Fitore's life, but it was made to sound like an accident. They said her body was to be shipped back to Albania for burial but that a memorial service was to be held at an Albanian center in Miami on Friday. There was no mention at all that she was the Quinns' maid. It seemed as if someone didn't want people to know that Valentina had been murdered and that she was connected to the disappearance of Tatiana. It made her wonder how far-fetched it was to imagine that someone was controlling the media coverage of the event. And if similar forces were at play in the case of Tatiana, controlling the investigation of her disappearance.

The morning after the murder, Detective Ignacio had called to tell Lydia and Jeffrey that the two of them had an appointment with Nathan Quinn on Tuesday at noon. "The feds have taken over the Valentina Fitore investigation," explained Detective Ignacio over the phone. "I told them what we know. I told them about the tape and the letter and how you were there to talk about Tatiana. They kind of humored me. It was like 'Yeah, good work, Detective. Go home.' And they said they would contact you. I have to be honest—this is the most fucked-up investigation I've ever been a part of. Someone doesn't want connections made."

But the FBI hadn't contacted her. Lydia actually went so far as to get the name of the head agent on the case, someone named Anton Bentley, and called him herself. But he hadn't returned her call.

The sun was heading toward the horizon, and the umbrella that shaded Lydia from its rays would have to be moved if it was going to protect them until sunset. But as she was about to get up to adjust it, Jeffrey returned with two margaritas. He handed them to her, moved the umbrella to block the setting sun, and sat beside her. He put a cool hand on her hot skin, shiny and slick with sunscreen; she handed him back one of the drinks.

A dark quiet had come over her after the murder she had witnessed, and he remembered the days when she used to pull away from him when she was afraid or sad. Some of the taut stress he had seen in her face when he had picked her up from the police station had faded, finally, after nearly two days. He had wanted them to leave Miami that next morning. But she wouldn't hear of it. She was sure now that the disappearance of Tatiana was tied into something really big, really ugly. And getting her to leave would be nearly impossible. He was inclined to agree with her; the machinations of some sinister force were clear to him, too, even without the benefit of Lydia's intuitions. But it made him want to take Lydia and return to New York, back to the quiet life they had lived over the last year. He felt homesick for that, afraid that they might not get back to it for a long time.

"You're looking better," he said. She was beautiful in her red Moschino bikini, her pale skin growing gold from the sun. Her thick black hair was swept up in a French twist and held in place with a black jade hair clip.

"I'm feeling better," she said, and smiled without much conviction.

"It's nice here . . . on the beach," he said. "I could get used to this."

Neither of them said anything for a moment.

"So," she said, "who do you think killed Valentina Fitore?"

He thought on it for a second. They hadn't discussed the incident yet. He hadn't pressed it, knowing that she was still processing what had happened and trying to cast the horror of it from her soul before she could analyze it with her brain.

"Someone who was uncomfortable with what she knew and what she might tell you."

"Someone who doesn't want us to find out where Tatiana is? Or what happened to her?"

"That implies that Valentina knew."

"Maybe she did."

"If she knew, then why wouldn't she have just written that in the letter, instead of being so cryptic? Or delivered an anonymous tip to the police?"

"So if she didn't know, then why would someone kill her?"

"Maybe because she didn't know what she knew."

"Huh?"

"I mean, maybe she had information that she didn't understand the significance of, but that you might have. Or that the police or the FBI might have. Maybe her murder had less to do with Tatiana and more to do with Sasa. Less to do with the disappearance of a little girl and more to do with Sasa's involvements."

Lydia considered this, turning over the possibilities in her head. She stabbed at her margarita with the straw, then removed it from the plastic cup and began to chew on its end. Jeffrey knew it would only be a matter of days before she bought a pack of cigarettes, though she hadn't smoked in over a year.

"Or both," she said finally.

Jeffrey nodded his head thoughtfully. "Or both," he agreed.

"So we have a missing girl," she said, thinking aloud, "widely believed to be a runaway, even by her own mother. We have a maid, sister of a suspected mobster, who probably sent me that tape and letter implying that there was more to Tatiana's disappearance than meets the eye. And who was then murdered for a reason still unclear to us. Since we've arrived, we've been followed, had our hotel room broken into and our bags searched, albeit respectfully. Detective Ignacio is at the end of his rope, feels he is being watched. There is pressure on him to solve Tatiana's case, but the powers that be are limiting his area of investigation. And we have a parallel FBI investigation into Sasa Fitore and the Albanian mob, as well as a rumored snuff ring that interferes with, rather than facilitates, the search for Tatiana."

The towering cumulous clouds over the ocean displayed a Technicolor light show of fuchsia, lavender, and tangerine as the sun crept toward the horizon. The temperature had dropped, but the humidity still raised sweat on Jeffrey's brow. He was lying on his tight stomach, leaning on his elbows. He wore a baggy pair of navy blue Ralph Lauren bathing trunks and nothing else. From where she sat just above him, she could see the scar left by a bullet he had taken through his right shoulder. She reached over and touched it with fingers cool and moist from the sweating plastic cup she held. He took hold of her hand and rolled over onto his back, displaying his enviable abs and pecs, which were becoming just a bit softer as he approached his forty-second birthday. He kissed her fingers.

"And we have Nathan Quinn," she continued, "heir to a real estate fortune, Yale-educated, entrepreneur, philanthropist. I found an article relating to the Albanian pyramid scheme that Quinn Enterprises had a hand in, at least as far as giving VC money to the company responsible. He called it a 'bad investment,' though he made nearly a hundred million dollars. And he wound up starting a foundation to help Albanian refugees in America. He *spun* it. He turned himself into a hero," she said with a laugh, moving off her chair and sitting next to Jeffrey. "An entire country was destroyed because of one of his ventures and he came up smelling like a rose. Someone, somewhere, has to be pissed about that."

Jeffrey sighed, watching the colors in the sky grow darker . . . lavender to deep purple, tangerine to flame.

"Or maybe Nathan Quinn is what he seems," he said. "No more guilty for the Albanian thing than any investor unwittingly involved in a bad deal. Maybe Tatiana *did* run away, a spoiled rich kid who didn't get cable in her bedroom and had a hissy. Maybe Valentina was hit by one of Sasa's enemies. Maybe there's nothing here and we should just go home, get married, and start a family. You can write mystery novels. Make up the bad stuff and leave the real crime to someone else, let it poison and destroy someone else's life. And we'll just live happily ever after off the proceeds of your books."

She looked at him with a sudden bright smile and laughing eyes. She reached out and pinched him hard on the thigh, then leaned in and kissed him on the mouth. She was back. He was afraid he'd lost her a bit after the trauma of watching Valentina die. But she'd bounced back stronger. She was stronger and healthier emotionally than she'd been a year ago, and he was relieved to see that.

"Yeah, right," she said with a glimmer of uncertainty in her eyes. "Imagine that."

Both of them knew he was only half-kidding.

chapter thirteen

Detective Manny Ignacio should have headed home hours ago, but he couldn't face it. He just couldn't end another day with nothing to show for it. So when he'd pulled out of the precinct parking lot, instead of turning right and going to his wife and daughter, where he belonged, he turned left. The maroon interior of his Taurus was filthy: dust on the dash, crumbs wedged into the crevices of the parking brake, a spot of chocolate on the passenger's seat, a cigarette burn on the floor. It still smelled vaguely of smoke, though he'd quit over a year ago.

He'd quit because his daughter had asked him to. Clarabell, his little pal—he'd called her that ever since she was born. She wasn't a beautiful girl in the frightening way that Tatiana was, and part of him had always been glad for that. Too much responsibility goes along with that for a little girl. For her parents, too. She was pretty, though, in a fleshy, innocent way, with round green eyes and full pink lips. And she was her father's daughter, knew just how to turn him around inside. Knew that she was the light and love of his every day. He was proud, because he knew that kind of love from her father gave a girl confidence, made her strong. She was smart and knew what she was worth, and no man would ever be able to tell her differently, because her father had showed her how she deserved to be treated. Just by loving her and loving her mother and never making a secret of it, he had given her that. Not that either one of them was very happy with him right now, feeling neglected since he'd been working the Tatiana Quinn case. He'd make it up to them. He always did.

He pulled into the parking lot of Jonah's, a bar owned by a retired cop and frequented by a clientele made up of 90 percent cops. He didn't generally find himself in places like this. He was a family man and believed his free time belonged to his wife, daughter, and his parents, not to a bunch of his drunken comrades in arms. But tonight, he had a fierce need for a tequila shot with a Corona chaser. He had a case of the mean reds, where he was so angry and frustrated with this case and every ugly thing about it that he didn't want to take that kind of energy into his home. He needed to wind down a bit, have just one drink.

He was washed in the smell of smoke and the sound of laughter when he pulled open the bar's door. The bar was only moderately crowded, with plenty of empty tables. At first glance, he saw at least five familiar faces. He lifted a hand in general greeting but took a seat alone at the bar. His reflection in the mirror looked even more beaten down and tired than he felt, if that was possible. He had always prided himself on being a relatively handsome man, one who looked younger than his years. But fifty wasn't looking good on him tonight. He thought it might be time for a trip to Puerto Rico, away from the crush of Miami and into the quiet of the place he'd known as a boy. Just a few more weeks and he would put in for the time, take Clarabell out of school for a week. The three of them needed the time together anyway.

Even though he didn't come here to Jonah's often, he knew Trisha, the big-breasted, bleach-blond bartender. Her hair looked like spun gold, soft and fluid, and her blue eyes were wise and kind, turned up just bit at her temple, like a cat's.

"Hey, there," she said cordially, although giving him a concerned once-over. "It's been a while, Manny. Everything all right?"

"Can't complain," he answered with a smile he hoped was more convincing than it felt.

"What can I get you?"

"A shot of Patrón and a Corona chaser, with lime."

She gave a nod and turned to fill his order. He watched her for a second to make sure she took the bottle of Patrón from the top shelf; he didn't want well tequila. He already had a headache. As he took his eyes away from her, he scanned the reflection in the mirror, checking out the people behind him—mostly men, straddling their seats the wrong way, as if sitting in a chair properly wasn't masculine enough. Most of the men wore their weapons in plain view, even though they were off duty, having removed their jackets in the warmth of the bar. They felt safe surrounded by their own. Maybe that's why he'd come tonight.

Trisha brought him his drinks, along with an extra slice of lime and a saltshaker. He noticed that her nails had a perfect French manicure; he liked a woman who took care of herself. It couldn't be easy to keep nails like that when working behind the bar. He licked the web between his thumb and his forefinger and sprinkled salt there, then licked it off. Then he shot the tequila, followed it by sucking on the lime slice, and then washed it all down with the Corona. He felt a rush of heat as some of the tension left his shoulders and neck. He closed his eyes a second, and when he opened them again, he saw two figures in the mirror, one tall and lean, with light slicked-back hair; one just a bit shorter and broader, with a bald head. They were making their way into the dim hallway that led to the men's room in the back. He noticed that one or two of the cops behind him had followed the men he saw in the mirror with their eyes. Even in the brief second he'd seen them, he knew they weren't cops. Something about the big guy.

He sucked down the last of his Corona and sat a second, trying to figure out what was bothering him about the men he'd seen, why he felt a sudden unease. Finally, he rose, left a ten-dollar bill on the bar, and walked toward the back. As he rounded the corner, the sound from the barroom was cut in half. He unsnapped the holster on the Glock at his waist and took off the safety, then made his way toward the men's room. He pushed the door open slowly and was greeted by the aroma of urine. He stood there a second and regarded the empty urinals, listening to a toilet run and watching water drip from a faucet. He could see his own reflection in the mirror and recognized his game face, his "Don't fuck with me" face.

He paused a minute and took a breath before entering and letting the door close behind him. Bending down toward the filthy tiled floor, he saw two pairs of black-booted feet standing side by side in one of the stalls. He removed his gun from the holster and stepped toward the stall. He stood waiting, trying to control his labored breathing and the adrenaline he felt begin to pump. After a second, the leaner man stepped out of the stall first, followed by the stockier man. Manny saw an earring and a deep scar on the face of the big guy, saw a Rolex and a Sig in the hand of the leaner guy. In his other hand, he held what looked like a Polaroid.

"Gay bar's down the street, girls," said Manny. The big guy moved forward but was stopped by a hand to his chest. In that moment, Manny recognized him as the man from the surveillance photo, the alleged Greyhound bus driver.

"I've been looking everywhere for you," Manny said, leveling the Glock. "Let's go have a talk back at the station."

"Let's not," said the leaner man, his voice low, hard. Manny noted the same slight accent that he heard in Jenna Quinn's voice. His eyes were blue and heavily lidded, and in them Manny saw malice and amusement. He wore a black wool gabardine suit that was clearly tailored to his body. A royal blue shirt that picked up the color of his eyes was open at the chest, exposing golden hair and the edge of a tattoo that Manny couldn't quite make out. But Manny knew the man he was looking at. It was Sasa Fitore.

Manny regarded him and his 9-mm Sig-Sauer for a moment,

then reached out for the photograph Sasa held out to him with his free hand, his curiosity getting the better of him. He kept the gun pointed at Sasa as he glanced at the photograph.

He felt fear constrict his throat as he recognized his daughter, Clarabell, sound asleep in her bed, holding tightly the stuffed blue Grover doll she'd had since she was two. Manny had tucked his little girl into bed last night, so he remembered that she had been wearing pink cotton pajamas with big white sheep on them that, from a distance, looked like clouds, the same pajamas she wore in the photograph. He looked up at Sasa, whose face was dominated by a wide grin.

chapter fourteen

Most women never realize that charm is a choice. A more effective technique than force in manipulating people and situations, it is, in fact, the primary choice of skilled predators. Bred to be conscious of how their behavior affects others, bred to be acquiescent and to ignore their own instincts, many women would rather be dead than be rude to someone charming. And often that's the choice they unwittingly make. Nathan Quinn was a very charming man. But Lydia Strong was not impressed. And she had no problem being rude. But at the moment, she was on her best behavior, taking in his show with the same riveted attention she paid to a Charlie Manson interview.

From the moment Lydia and Jeffrey entered his office building, a not-so-subtle power struggle had commenced. They were greeted by guards in the lobby of the high-rise building that housed Quinn Enterprises. Escorted with the utmost courtesy, they were ushered under a giant globe that hung suspended from the towering ceiling, nearly filling the lobby, making everyone passing through seem the size of an ant. Emblazoned across the world was the company name, each letter the size of a Volkswagen.

"Excuse me, Lois," Jeffrey whispered, "are these the offices of the *Daily Planet*?"

"Could be, Superman."

"That's Clark to you."

"I didn't hear you complaining last night."

"'It's a bird, it's a plane . . . .'"

"That's enough, Jeffrey."

Jeffrey counted four surveillance cameras as they approached the elevators. The doors slid open silently without being beckoned, and Lydia and Jeffrey stepped in, flanked by the uniformed security guards. The walls were comprised of smoky black mirrors, and there was only one button above the keypad into which one of the guards entered a code. The elevator rose swiftly and smoothly. When the doors opened, they entered an elegant lobby walled entirely in glass. The Atlantic Ocean was visible to the east, and the rest of the windows provided a panoramic view of the Miami area. A stunning redheaded rose looked up at them from behind a black lacquer desk. Lydia tried not to stare at her enormous breasts, though they were obviously on display for just that purpose, protruding from a low-cut red silk blouse worn beneath her suit jacket.

"Follow me, please," she said, smiling cordially but coldly.

They followed her, still flanked by the security guards. As the woman sashayed her generous ass, Lydia watched and thought, smiling to herself, that someone playing the rumba should be following her around. She noticed Jeffrey noticing, as well. The woman took them to a small waiting area furnished with a bar, two leather sofas, a low glass cocktail table, and a mirrored wall. Then she left without a word.

"Will you surrender your weapons, please?" asked one of the security guards as he shut the door behind them.

Lydia and Jeffrey looked at each other.

"Of course, they'll be returned to you when you leave."

Jeffrey was reluctant. As a law-enforcement officer, he would never even have considered it. In fact, this was the very reason why Detective Ignacio had declined to join them on their visit to Nathan Quinn. He'd already been through this whole dance and wasn't up for it again. But Jeffrey had not been willing to leave the hotel without the Glock, due to the events of the last few days.

"I'm afraid we cannot allow you to see Mr. Quinn until you have surrendered your weapons."

"We'll give you our magazines," said Jeffrey.

"And the cartridge in the chamber, please."

"Of course."

And so it was settled. But the whole incident put Jeffrey on edge. Why would a businessman, even one of Quinn's stature, have such tight security? What was he afraid of? Lydia and Jeffrey seated themselves on one of the sofas and said nothing as they waited for nearly half an hour. They were both aware of the surveillance camera in the corner, the mirrored wall, and the probability of a listening device. So Lydia flipped through the dull, dense pages of *The Economist,* while Jeffrey sat stone-faced, staring at the wall, occasionally looking at his watch. After glancing at his watch for the fifth time, he said, "Five more minutes and we're leaving."

She just nodded. She knew it was a manipulation tactic to keep people waiting for this long. It was fully forty-five minutes after their scheduled appointment. Nathan Quinn was attempting to communicate that his time was more valuable than either of theirs, he knew it, and he wanted to make sure they knew it, too; he was not intimidated or impressed by either of them; and they would see him on his terms or not at all.

As if on cue, when Jeffrey rose to leave, the redheaded receptionist returned, looking cool and sultry. "Mr. Quinn will see you now."

"How good of him," said Lydia, not even bothering to keep the sarcasm out of her voice.

The receptionist, who stood a head taller than Lydia, gave her a pinched look through the lenses of her ultrachic glasses and said, "Mr. Quinn is a very busy man."

Lydia didn't respond, and they were escorted down a long hallway. As they approached the double doors at the end of the hall, the lighting seemed to dim, though Lydia thought it might have been her imagination. The doors, made of a rich dark wood, were elaborately carved with what looked like some type of forest scene, though it was hard to see because the lighting was low and the receptionist opened them by pewter handles shaped like gargoyle claws as soon as they arrived.

Quinn got up from behind a mammoth desk. An imposing man, standing over six feet tall and radiating an aura of power. Lydia would not have been surprised if he had thrown his head back and roared upon their entering his lair. But then he did surprise her.

"Ms. Strong, Mr. Mark," he said, moving toward them with his hand outstretched. She noticed on his right ring finger a large gold insignia ring with Greek letters and a scroll covering what looked to be a sword, but he withdrew his hand quickly and she couldn't get a closer look. "You can't imagine how much hope it's given me to hear my daughter's voice. Detective Ignacio sent a copy of the tape over to me yesterday. It's been such a nightmare."

He was fairly gushing. Lydia tried to keep the skepticism she felt from showing on her face. He walked them over to plush sofas, a guiding hand on Lydia's arm, and stood across from them. He wore an expression of anguish, leaning toward them as if intending to plead for their help. Lydia glanced at Jeffrey, who wore the poker face she had always admired.

Quinn turned his gaze on Lydia and locked eyes with her. She imagined that many women swooned in the power of his gaze, under the influence of his charm. But she could sense a manipulating energy that instantly brought guards up inside her. Like a predator, he seemed to sense it. He turned up the volume on his personality.

"So you *do* believe that the voice on the tape was Tatiana's," Lydia said.

"Without a doubt."

"Because your wife felt differently," she said, narrowing her eyes a bit, not sure whom to believe or why either of them would benefit from lying.

"She was mistaken," he said quickly.

"If that was Tatiana, then what do you make of what she said about her mother?" asked Lydia. "What do you think she meant when she said, 'I can't believe she's doing this to me.'"

"Adolescent girls and their mothers are always at odds, Ms. Strong," he said with an understanding smile, as though Tatiana had simply broken curfew. "Who knows what injustice Tatiana believes her mother and I have perpetrated against her.

"I am a huge fan of your books, Ms. Strong," he went on, ignoring Jeffrey entirely. "I can't believe I didn't think to call you myself. Together, I know you and I can solve this. I really don't feel that the police have done everything they can. I think they gave up on her when they concluded, unofficially of course, that she ran away. But now we have renewed hope. Can I offer you some coffee, a soda maybe?"

"No, thank you," said Lydia. But he seemed not to have even heard her, seemed to have forgotten that he had even asked a question.

She looked around the office, which reminded her of the library in his home, with everything about it designed to intimidate a visitor. With the high ceilings and enormous plush pieces of furniture, one couldn't help but feel dwarfed. The furniture was soft, so Lydia had sunk into the cushion when she sat, while the giant Quinn stood, towering over them. Jeffrey, she noticed, sat on the edge of the couch. She pushed herself up and did the same.

"When I met Jenna," Quinn said, "I had everything a man could want. More money than most people ever dream of, a successful career. I had never even thought about a family. But when Tatiana and Jenna came into my life, I realized all I had been missing. Suddenly, I was a husband and a father. I felt truly blessed. It was a difficult transition for her, certainly. To come from poverty and suddenly to have everything a little girl could want. But with love, she adapted. She was a beautiful child, growing into a stunning woman. Intelligent, warm, unspoiled, in spite of the fact that I spoiled her a little. And now . . . this. She's gone. I don't know if she ran away. I don't know if someone,"—he seemed to choke on the word and all its implications—"abducted her. She sounded so afraid on that tape. All I know is that I want her back and that I will stop at nothing until we have found her."

He sat down on the arm of one of the chairs and lowered his eyes, maybe suddenly conscious of how desperate he seemed to deliver his speech. Lydia watched him a moment and then glanced around the office. There was a large well-lighted portrait of Nathan, Jenna, and Tatiana on the wall above him. Nathan reclined in a large wing-backed chair, his legs crossed, while Jenna stood behind him and to the right, her hand resting on his shoulder. Tatiana sat at his feet, her legs tucked to the side, her hands folded in her lap. They all smiled woodenly.

"Mrs. Quinn gave us the impression that Tatiana was a very unhappy girl and that there was a lot of tension among the three of you," said Lydia, deciding not to pull any punches and see what happened when people didn't follow in the direction Nathan Quinn led them. She thought she saw his face darken for a fraction of a second, but then he chuckled a little.

"My wife, of course, is distraught. Like I said, most teenage daughters and their mothers go through a rough patch. Of course they fought. Jenna feels betrayed because she believes that Tatiana ran away."

"And what do you believe?"

"I don't know. I just want her found. Whether she was abducted or whether she ran away, she's *somewhere*. I have to believe that with the proper amount of motivation and the right amount of resources, she will be found. I have both."

"I'm sorry to say this, Mr. Quinn," said Lydia, "but there's no way to know when that message was left. Have you considered the possibility that Tatiana is dead?"

Jeffrey turned his head to look at Lydia. It was a horrible thing to say, and he knew that she was baiting Quinn, looking for him to react in some unguarded, unplanned way so that she could have a better sense of what she was dealing with. But it was a harsh tactic, even for her. And she didn't get what she was looking for. His answer was quick and cool.

"No. Because that's *failure,* Ms. Strong," he said, shifting his body forward on the chair arm and engaging her eyes like some kind of freaky motivational speaker. "And failure is not an option here. Are you going to help me, or are we all wasting our time?"

She took a moment before she answered, watching as a muscle twitched in Quinn's jaw. "I'm going to help Tatiana, if I can."

"You'll be amply rewarded," he said with a satisfied smile.

"I'm not interested in money. That's not why I came here."

He seemed not to understand her and cocked his head, narrowing his eyes. "Then why?"

"Because someone wrote to me and asked for my help. Did you read the note that came with the tape?"

"Yes," he said, holding her eyes. "And I'm in the dark about that aspect of it."

Lydia nodded. "No ideas? No thoughts at all?"

His face darkened again and he said, "Do you think I had something to do with Tatiana disappearing? You think that note was sent by someone with insight into what goes on in my personal life? That I have some deep dark secret?"

"I know that I watched the person I suspected of sending them, your maid, Valentina, murdered before my eyes. I know that we have been followed and had our hotel room broken into."

"And you think I'm involved?" he asked with a condescending smile, as if she were a child suggesting that the world was flat.

"I don't have any opinion right now," she said, lying. She leaned forward a bit, holding his steely gaze. "All we care about is finding Tatiana."

"Well, we have that in common, then."

"Do you have enemies, Mr. Quinn? People who want to hurt you?" asked Jeffrey, speaking up for the first time. He had grown uncomfortable with the energy between Lydia and Quinn; it was as if they were engaged in some type of mental duel.

"You don't get where I am without making enemies," he said, smiling. "But luckily, they are professional enemies."

"Is that why your personal security is so tight?"

Quinn's smile twitched a bit. "You can never be too careful, Mr. Mark."

"I imagine that's true," said Lydia thoughtfully. "I'm curious, though. When whole economies collapse due to one of your business ventures, there must be some personal as well as professional hurt feelings, though. I mean, lives were destroyed. Families were destroyed."

Quinn sighed and shook his head. He was going for the Atlas look, weight of the world and all that. For a split second, he made Lydia think of O. J. Simpson, that practiced look of innocence, so convincing that he believed it himself.

"What most people don't realize," he said slowly, sadly, with just a dash of condescension, "is that in high finance, as in war, there can be casualties . . . human casualties. The Albanian government gambled on their future. American Equities took advantage of their naïveté. I was nothing more than an investor, and, I'm ashamed to say, ignorant to what American Equities was involved in. Anyway, I fail to see what this has to do with Tatiana."

"How did you meet Jenna?"

"Excuse me?"

"Your wife, she's from Albania, isn't she?"

"Yes. . . ."

"So, how did you meet her? I imagine it must have been during one of your visits to Albania during the time American Equities was involved over there."

It was a wild guess, but she could see from the look on his face that she'd hit one out of the park. And Lydia was grinning inside because she could see that Nathan Quinn hadn't been prepared for this line of questioning. But she already had a sense of him and knew it wouldn't be so easy to get under his skin.

"That's irrelevant," he said stiffly.

The buzz was like static in her ears; she could hear it and feel its vibrations in her fingertips. Nathan Quinn rose and turned his back to Lydia and Jeffrey as he went to the bar and poured himself an inch of amber liquid from a crystal decanter. He sipped from it as he turned around to face them. But he did not return to his seat; instead, he paced the length of his desk slowly.

"If you must know, Ms. Strong, my wife was a prostitute when I met her," he said, tossing back the drink. "She had no choice after her husband died. Her family had forsaken her because she had married a man they disapproved of. She was alone with a small daughter, and there was only one way to survive. Of course, she was a marked woman in that society, but I fell in love with her. I saved her and Tatiana from that life. You should have seen how they lived."

Neither Lydia nor Jeffrey said a word, just watched him pace. He lowered his head and his voice was soft.

"Of course, you can imagine why I wouldn't want anyone to know that. I've never told anyone. For Jenna's sake more than mine. She's very ashamed of her past," he said, sitting opposite them again and looking at each of them in the eye. "I tell you because I want you to know that I have nothing to hide. And I want your help in finding my daughter, even if that means, for a time, that you'll suspect me."

Lydia suppressed the urge to applaud. It was a masterful

performance. He actually looked as though he might weep. Lydia didn't know what Quinn's agenda was or what he had to do with Tatiana's disappearance, but she knew he couldn't be trusted and she didn't believe a word he said.

"Thank you for sharing that with us," she said sweetly. "If we are to find Tatiana, your honesty will be very important. We'll do our best to make sure that aspect of the case remains between us."

"Do more than your best, Ms. Strong," he said, a note of menace sneaking into his careful symphony. "It would destroy my wife."

"Of course," said Lydia, her favorite noncommittal response to commands she had no intention of obeying.

"There was something in your statement about the night of Tatiana's disappearance that I wonder if you could clear up for us," said Jeffrey.

"What's that?"

"The surveillance camera was turned off. But you said that Tatiana didn't know how to operate the equipment."

"Yes," he said enthusiastically. "That's one of the things that makes me believe that Tatiana didn't run off on her own."

"Well, who does know how to operate it?"

"My wife and I."

"So you activated the alarm when you left for the evening. And came home to find it deactivated?"

"Yes."

"And you're positive that Tatiana didn't know how to turn it off."

"Yes."

"What about Valentina?"

"No. Valentina couldn't even operate the DVD player. She was uncomfortable with technology."

"How did she come to work for you?" asked Lydia.

"She was referred to me by a woman who administers the Albanian refugee grant that I established. My wife and Tatiana liked her, felt comfortable with her, so we hired her. She's been like a part of our family. We'll miss her very much," he said without emotion, looking at his watch. Lydia sensed that they were about to come to the end of their interview.

"You must have paid her well," Lydia said, pressing on.

"We paid her nearly fifty thousand dollars a year. She had a child to support. She was technically an employee of Quinn Enterprises."

"That's good money for a maid," said Lydia. "But not enough to pay for the house she lived in."

"I wouldn't know anything about that. She was the help; I didn't inquire into her personal life."

"Did you know her family?"

"Marianna, her daughter, watched Tatiana occasionally when Valentina couldn't stay. I never really spoke with her, except to say hello."

"What about Sasa Fitore, Valentina's brother? Did you know him?" she asked, watching his eyes very carefully.

But they revealed nothing, and his smile didn't waver a bit. "As I said, she was the help. We didn't associate with her family."

Nathan walked behind his desk, then sat and removed a large leather binder from a drawer in the center. He looked over at Lydia and Jeffrey, who had risen.

"I want to put the two of you on retainer to find my daughter. Name your price," he said, uncapping a black fountain pen.

"We're not the help, Mr. Quinn," said Lydia with a cool smile before Jeffrey could speak. "We don't want your money."

"Nobody works for free, Ms. Strong," he said, looking up from his checkbook with a smug smile and narrowed eyes. "What's your angle?"

"Like I said, we're just interested in finding Tatiana. You can be assured that we'll use everything in our power to do that."

"And then you'll write about the case."

"Maybe."

"So you get paid later, then." His smile widened in victory.

She shrugged. She'd never really thought of it that way.

"At the end of the day, we all want to get paid, Ms. Strong," he said.

She could see that he was annoyed that their investigation couldn't be bought and was trying to get a rise out of her. She didn't respond, refusing to give him the satisfaction of a verbal battle, refusing to defend or explain herself to the likes of Nathan Quinn. She just gave him her best pitying smile.

"We'll be in touch," she said as they walked out the door. She did her best to swagger out with confidence, Jeffrey at her side. But she would have been more comfortable turning her back on a black bear.

"God forbid," Jeffrey whispered after he had closed the door behind them, "we should make any money for this shit."

Lydia glared at him as the sexy receptionist ran up the hall toward them, apparently unprepared for any movement in the office not choreographed by Nathan Quinn. She escorted them back to the waiting area, where the guards returned the cartridges for their guns and walked them to the elevator.

"You would take money from that psychopath?" she whispered after the doors closed and they were alone.

"No," he admitted grudgingly.

As they walked beneath the mammoth globe, Lydia's cell phone rang. She hurriedly dug it out of her bag.

"Hello? . . . When? . . . All right, we're on our way."

"What's up?" Jeffrey asked.

"Stephen Parker's dead."

"Who's that?"

She paused, dropping the phone back in her bag and turning her eyes to Jeffrey.

"The last private investigator on Nathan Quinn's payroll."

chapter fifteen

The inscription on Stephen Parker's Presidential Rolex read: *Yours until the end of time.* According to the medical examiner, time had ended for Parker nearly four days ago. His ex-wife, who had given him the watch during their marriage, had called time about three years earlier. But when he didn't show for their son's fifth birthday party, she reported him missing.

"I just thought the guy was blowing me off. I should have looked into it."

Detective Ignacio had been self-flagellating since he got an E-mail from his buddy in Homicide. Parker had been on the adult missing persons list for two days, but nobody there had connected his name with the Tatiana case; no one had brought it up to the detective. Why would they? Parker hadn't been a big player in the case, as far as the detective was concerned. Until now.

"Nobody communicates in that fucking place," said the detective, more annoyed at himself than anyone.

"So what happened?" Lydia asked for the third time since they'd sat down at an isolated table at the back of the Delano's restaurant. The doors to the veranda stood open and the breeze billowed the gauzy white drapes that hung from the ceiling. Lydia could see their reflection in the etched mirror screen that stood behind the bar. Detective Ignacio looked as though he'd wilted a bit since they saw him last; his shirt was wrinkled and his tie loose. The jacket he wore had a tiny grease stain on the lapel. He looked more exhausted than the last time Lydia had seen him, and there was something off about his energy. He was edgy, fidgety; he was making Lydia nervous.

"Parker's a single guy, works alone," he said, drinking from a glass of ice water a waitress had placed on the table. "Looks like he'd been missing for about four days; that's when he stopped picking up messages from his voice mail anyway. According to the Missing Persons Department—missing adults are handled in a division separate from that for missing children—his ex-wife came in a few days ago and filed a report. Said he missed his son's birthday party and that as bad a husband as he had been, he was a great dad. Wouldn't have missed it unless something was very wrong. He wasn't at home, wasn't at the office. The guys in Missing Persons took the report, went to his house, made a few calls. They didn't exactly bend over backward. He's an adult male, so it was a pretty low-priority case."

"So where did they find his body?" asked Jeffrey.

"They didn't find his *body*, exactly. They found his arm."

Lydia grimaced and leaned back from the table. She removed her washed-silk navy blue Calvin Klein blazer and placed it over her lap. She was suddenly feeling overly warm.

"How did they know it was *his* arm?" asked Jeffrey.

"The watch. His wife had mentioned that he always wore this watch, when she went down to the morgue with the detective she had reported him missing to—you know, to make sure Parker wasn't one of the John Does there."

"I hate to ask," said Lydia, "but where did they find his arm?"

"An alligator hunter found it in the belly of an eleven-foot male. Partially digested."

"Shut up."

"I'm serious."

"Jesus," she said.

"I thought alligators were endangered. Who hunts alligators?" asked Jeffrey.

"Hey, this is Florida. We're lousy with alligators. There's a season for hunting them. This was the first week this fall. Their skins bring in about twenty-five dollars a foot. So a couple of guys were hunting gators. They caught one, skinned it, got curious, opened its belly, and got a big surprise. We're lucky they called the police."

"No shit. That watch is worth about twelve grand," commented Jeffrey.

Lydia felt a wave of nausea so severe that she sat up and nearly bolted for the rest room she'd noticed on her way in. But it passed as quickly as it came and she sat quietly, bracing herself for another bout. She felt slightly feverish, though her hands were cold and clammy.

"You all right, Lydia?" asked Jeffrey when he saw the color had drained from her face.

"I'm fine," she said.

"You're not going squeamish on me, are you?"

"Don't be ridiculous."

Lydia had been exposed to plenty of gruesome sights and recounted horrors in her life. She had never been made ill by any of them. The wave of nausea was purely physical, and she started to think about what she had eaten during the day. But aside from coffee and a croissant, she'd had nothing. Maybe I just need to eat something, she thought.

"So what happened to him, then?" asked Lydia, trying to ignore her stomach.

"It's hard to say. But I'd guess someone killed him and dumped his body in the Everglades, and some alligators got an easy dinner."

"Maybe it was an accident," Jeffrey suggested, "an episode of *Crocodile Hunter* gone wrong."

"His ex-wife said he wasn't a hunter," the detective answered, not picking up the joke and appearing distracted. "Besides, you probably wouldn't be wearing a Presidential Rolex if you were hunting gators."

"When did you first meet him?"

"Quinn hired him about seven days into the investigation. I was glad to have him, especially since everywhere I turned, there was a wall in my face. I figured if Quinn had hired him, maybe people wouldn't be so quick to tell him where and where not to look. But he didn't seem to be getting anywhere. And after about three weeks, when he got back from New York, he started to seem desperate. He came into my office one night late, closed the door, and asked me what I knew about Sasa Fitore. At that point, I didn't even know about him. Some detective, right? He seemed scared that night, now that I think of it. But I was fucking tired and I had too much on my plate to worry about Parker's issues. He left my office. And it was then that I started looking into Fitore's record. He's got a couple of charges—pimping, possession, crap like that. Never did any time, though. I swear it was an hour after I'd pulled his file when the feds showed up in my office. They told me to back off, not to mention Sasa Fitore to anyone in the context of my investigation or they'd have my job. Or worse, have me arrested on obstruction. Said if Sasa Fitore had anything to do with Tatiana, they'd figure it out in the course of their investigation and let me know. I walked away. What else could I do? I figured Stephen Parker had done the same."

"Was Quinn his only client?"

"I'm trying to find out who else he was working for at the time."

"I'm guessing that Nathan Quinn paid him enough that he didn't have to take on any other jobs," said Lydia, "and I don't think Quinn is the type of client who likes to share."

"You're probably right."

"It's interesting how many people on Quinn's payroll seem to be turning up dead lately," said Jeffrey.

"See?" said Lydia.

"What?" asked Detective Ignacio.

Lydia recounted for him the details of their visit to Quinn Enterprises, including his offer to pay them for their investigation.

"So what did you walk out of there thinking?" asked the detective, jingling the ice in his class.

"That I wanted to get as far away from Nathan Quinn as fast as I could."

The detective paused and looked at Lydia and Jeffrey. He looked some combination of disappointed and hopeful. "Does that mean you're going to walk away from this?"

Lydia and Jeffrey looked at each other. An exchange of words between them wasn't necessary. She knew he wanted to leave Miami and he knew that there was no way that was going to happen.

"No way," said Lydia. "We're going to find out what happened to Tatiana and we're going to take Nathan Quinn down in the process."

"Whoa," Jeffrey and Detective Ignacio said simultaneously.

"We don't know that Nathan Quinn has done anything wrong," said Jeffrey, lowering his voice and looking around the restaurant.

"Give me a break. That guy is as dirty as they come."

"You think he's involved with his stepdaughter's disappearance? How?" asked the detective, leaning closer to her.

"I didn't say that. I don't think he knows where Tatiana is. It's why he wants her back so badly—rather, *how* he wants her back so badly—that puts me on edge. There's desperation without emotion, a desire without love to the way he talks about her. Like a junkie looking for a fix. It's ugly. . . . There's something ugly about it. I don't believe he knows where she is, but I bet he's a big part of why she's gone. Whether she ran away or was abducted. He's definitely involved and he knows more than he shared with us, but I don't think he knows where she is. Otherwise, he wouldn't be riding everyone so hard."

"Yeah," said Manny. "Leave no stone unturned unless it involves his 'business affairs.'"

His sarcasm hung in the air like cigarette smoke. "What did Stephen Parker find out about Sasa Fitore and how did it connect to Nathan Quinn?" Jeffrey asked, thinking aloud. Then he turned to the detective. "How did that conversation between the two of you end?"

"I don't remember," Detective Ignacio said softly.

"You don't remember?" asked Lydia.

The detective didn't say anything, just shook his head and looked down at the table.

"Lydia," said the detective after a moment, "you need to be careful."

"Careful about what?"

"It's just that Nathan Quinn is connected to organizations that . . . you know, control things in the world. People like him can make life dangerous for people who piss them off."

Lydia was lost. She wasn't sure how the conversation had taken this turn.

"What are you talking about, Manny?"

"Listen. You guys were here for a couple of hours. They found you, followed you, and broke into your hotel room. Valentina is dead because they knew she was about to talk to you. Stephen Parker is dead. I was stopped by my superior officers from looking into Quinn's business dealings. I mean," he said with a shrug, glancing behind him, "think about it."

"*They?* Who's 'they'? You sound like a conspiracy theorist," said Lydia with an uncertain laugh. She regarded the man for a second, wondering why he suddenly seemed afraid that she and Jeffrey were about to drag him in deeper than he was willing to go. He'd been so eager for their help when they arrived. Had been concerned enough about the investigation that he let Lydia follow a lead he knew might be dangerous for all of them to pursue. He met her eyes, and she thought for a second that she saw fear in them.

"I have a family, Lydia," he said finally, softly, offering an excuse against an accusation that hadn't been made.

Lydia looked at him coolly, cocked her head to the side, and smiled a little.

"Someone got to you, didn't they, Manny?"

He looked away from her, shame softening his handsome features, his bottom lip trembling almost imperceptibly. He folded his hands and sighed.

"No, it's not like that. It's just that I have to focus on Tatiana. Just on finding her or what happened to her," he said, stumbling over his words as if they didn't fit comfortably in his mouth.

"There's a piece missing from your puzzle, Detective. And without it, you'll never have the full picture. You'll never find Tatiana."

He nodded and lowered his voice to a whisper. "I'm afraid that's a price I'm going to have to be willing to pay. I have a little girl, too."

The detective stood up and straightened his tie, as if trying to hold on to his dignity in an unbearable situation. He looked beaten. Lydia opened her mouth to speak, but he held up his hand. She could see in his tired eyes that he had weighed his options and the consequences in his mind and made his decision.

"The FBI will be in touch with you by tomorrow, Lydia, regarding what you saw at the Fitore residence. I spoke with them today and have been told I'm to have no part in that investigation. Let me know what you decide to do."

"What's going on, Detective?" Jeffrey asked, moving to get up. "We can help you."

"No, you can't. Don't overestimate your power to handle this. Take my advice and go back to New York. Forget you ever heard about Nathan Quinn and Sasa Fitore. And hope they forget they ever heard of you."

He left them then, striding confidently from the restaurant, not looking behind him. He looked short and shabbily dressed in the context of the beautifully decorated room. For a second, neither of them spoke, just looked after the detective, mouths slightly open, brows knitted.

"So I suppose there's no chance we're going to take his advice and walk away," said Jeffrey.

"Over my dead body."

"That's what I'm afraid of."

"Oh, come on. You, too? I didn't think you scared so easy," she said with a teasing smile, trying to lighten the mood.

"I didn't use to," he said, reaching for her hand. "But I've got . . . I think *we've* got more to live for now, don't we? I don't want to sound like a pussy, but I've never been happier than I have in the last year with you. I don't want to lose that. Do you?"

She didn't say anything, his words echoing her own recent thoughts about what she was and wasn't willing to put on the line anymore.

"I wouldn't risk our lives, either. Not anymore. I think Detective Ignacio is overestimating Nathan Quinn."

"Lydia, two people connected with this case are dead already."

"And what about Tatiana?"

"She might be dead, too. You said so yourself."

"But what if she isn't and we are the only two people who have a chance of finding and helping her?"

"It's Detective Ignacio's job to find Tatiana."

"But he *won't* find her because he's too afraid to follow the path that might lead to her," she said, an old feeling of desperation creeping up on her. The image of a frightened girl huddling in a phone booth somewhere, thin and cold, hair soaked with rain, played in Lydia's head. She'd been too late for Shawna, but something told her that Tatiana was still within her reach.

The restaurant was getting more crowded, the sound of laughter and conversation starting to fill the room. She looked around at the people gathering for happy hour, smartly dressed, ordering chic cocktails. She envied them, suddenly, lives that seemed so *normal,* so safe to her. Her life hadn't been normal since she was fifteen years old. Since then, it had been populated with monsters. *You bring it on yourself. You invite them in,* she chastised herself.

"All right, let's think about this for a minute," said Jeffrey. "Is this still about finding Tatiana for you? Or is it about Nathan Quinn now? Is he the villain of the year? The next bad guy on your list?"

"Maybe both."

He exhaled sharply. "I don't have to remind you that we have no proof that he's done anything wrong."

"I'm not often wrong about things like this, Jeffrey."

It was true. In all the years he'd known her, she'd almost never had an instinct that failed them. This time, he had an instinct, too: to get himself and Lydia as far away from this case as possible. The detective's warning resonated with Jeffrey. In his years as an FBI agent, he had come to realize that there are men in the world who have all the control. Control over governments, over most of the world's money and resources, over the media. He had felt their influence as an FBI agent, much in the way Detective Ignacio was feeling it—investigations manipulated, evidence and witnesses disappearing. It was just something that he had come to accept—that behind the events of the world were puppet masters like Nathan Quinn. And if you got caught up in their game, chose to play on the wrong team, you got crushed like meat in a grinder.

He flagged down the perky blond waitress who'd been hovering and ordered two martinis for them.

"A couple of years after the Jed McIntyre case, when Jacob Hanley and I were partners, we ran into something like this," he said suddenly, as if he had been holding it back.

"You never told me about it."

"You were still just a kid, then. And I haven't thought about it in awhile."

"What happened?"

"There was a girl found dead in Tompkins Square Park. That

was back in the mid-eighties, when the East Village was in real bad shape and Tompkins Square was a place strictly for junkies and homeless people. She was the daughter of a very wealthy executive at Chase Manhattan Bank. She was a junior at Chapin . . . a gorgeous, brilliant debutante, real New York society. Anyway, a homeless man found her. She'd been raped and strangled to death."

"I vaguely remember that, now that you mention it."

"We were brought in on the case because this girl was the fifth to have gone missing in the past year who fit a particular profile: all society girls from various prep schools around the city . . . all pretty, busty, long dark hair. Anyway, long story short, all the evidence came back to this kid. He was a member of a hugely powerful political family, had just graduated from Yale, was about to head to Columbia Law. To look at him, he was every parent's wet dream. But I swear to God, I saw a demon in this kid's eyes. So we went after him.

"But every time we got close, something happened. One judge took four hours to issue us a search warrant for his parents' Upper West Side penthouse. When we got there, the whole family and their very powerful attorney were waiting for us. Someone had tipped them off. We found a pair of girl's panties in his gym locker at the New York Health and Racket Club. But they were lost somehow after we had taken them into evidence. The media started hammering us, writing articles about how we were harassing an innocent boy, trying to pin something on him, when the girls' bodies hadn't even been found, except that one. This was before DNA evidence was as widely used as it is now—it was still like science fiction back then.

"Next thing we know, NYPD had arrested the homeless man who found the girl in Tompkins Square Park. The FBI got kicked off the investigation altogether. The police all of a sudden found the bodies in an abandoned building in Alphabet City. And the case was closed."

"But you didn't think the homeless guy was responsible."

"He definitely wasn't the guy. First of all, he was a diagnosed paranoid schizophrenic . . . so far gone that he was totally delusional, barely operating in reality. Which satisfied the public perception that he was the type of person who would have committed this kind of crime, but, in actuality, his mental state eliminated him as a possibility. He just didn't have the mental organization to pull off an abduction, a rape, and a murder and then hide the bodies. Plus, why would he have reported the last girl he found in the park? He certainly didn't have opportunity or proximity to these girls. It was ludicrous really. But the media was on board with it. Certainly this crazy homeless man was a better villain than a bright young law student with a brilliant future," Jeffrey said, disgust and anger filtering into his words.

"So what did you do?"

"Jacob and I protested to our supervisor. We were told in no uncertain terms to stand down. They didn't give us any explanation; they didn't even really try to convince us that we were wrong. They just issued the order to walk away, go back to D.C. for our next assignment, and that was what we were expected to do. There was just this sense that it was bigger than we were, a sort of implied threat that if we made waves, we could kiss our careers good-bye."

"And you let it go?"

"Not exactly. I called this woman I knew who worked at the *New York Times,* Sarah Winter. She was young and ambitious, looking to make a name for herself. I figured an exposé like this would appeal to her. I met her for a drink at Telephone Bar on Second Avenue and I told her the story."

He paused as the waitress delivered their drinks and thanked her. Jeffrey raised his glass to Lydia, who lifted hers in response. "Where was Jake in all of this?" she asked.

"He was ready to walk away. After the meeting with our supervisor, this real old-school bastard named Leon McCord, who later died of colon cancer, Jacob was really nervous. So I didn't tell him about the reporter. I just went on my own."

"You're killing me here. What happened?"

Lydia felt another, milder wave of nausea. She suppressed it but pushed her drink away.

"The next day, it just all resolved itself so neatly, it was surreal. The homeless man—his name was George . . . George Hewlett—managed somehow to hang himself in his cell. And, get this, there were layoffs at the *Times*. Guess who was one of the unlucky reporters to find herself out of job?"

"You're kidding."

"No . . . and that was it. There was no battle left to fight. I mean, it was perfect. If George or Sarah had been murdered, say, or even if Sarah alone had been fired, or if George's case had made it to trial . . . well, it would have been like a John Grisham novel—lone FBI agent bucking the secret establishment, exposing an evil conspiracy. But, instead, it just disappeared."

"Whatever happened to Sarah?"

"I don't know. I never knew her personally. I called over to the *Times,* and someone told me that there had been layoffs and that her job had been eliminated. I tried to find her phone number but was never able to locate her. I've never seen her byline anywhere."

"So what's your point?"

"Just that there are people behind the scenes who call the shots, you know. They can make inconvenient scenarios—and people—disappear."

"You're afraid that we're becoming one of those inconveniences."

"I'd say it's a fair bet. Who knows what Stephen Parker stumbled upon—he's dead. Or what Valentina knew—she's dead. Or what Manny was close to finding—someone warned him off. Usually when these things start happening, it indicates that someone is invested in having secrets kept. If we keep nosing around . . ."

"They might be finding pieces of us in alligators all over Florida?"

Jeffrey shrugged. "*Something* spooked Detective Ignacio. He doesn't seem like the skittish type. It would have to be something or someone pretty powerful to call that dog off."

Lydia nodded. "He *did* seem afraid, like he thought he had to make a choice between his family and going after Nathan Quinn . . . and possibly Tatiana's safe return."

Jeffrey couldn't blame him. There was nothing more important to him than Lydia. He would choose her life over his own or anyone else's, if it came to that.

"Can you walk away from this? When a girl's life hangs in the balance and two people are already dead?"

"If I thought staying our course meant risking our lives, then yes. What about you, Lydia? Can you walk away?"

Lydia folded her arms and leaned over the table a bit. She searched his face and saw tiny lines she hadn't noticed before around his hazel eyes, realized he hadn't shaved that morning. She slipped her foot from her shoe, slid it under the table, and traced his calf with the tip of her toe. Her nausea had subsided, replaced with the familiar feeling of electricity in her blood. The thought of powerful forces conspiring to keep secrets was irresistible to her.

"Just twenty-four more hours."

"For what?"

"To dig around a bit and see what we find. If nothing pops by this time tomorrow night, then we are fated to go home to our new, happy, quiet life. And I'll seriously consider a career as a novelist," she said, smiling. When the buzz was at its hottest, she felt like she was ten feet tall and bulletproof.

"And if something 'pops'? What then?" he asked, meeting her storm-cloud eyes and reaching for her fingers with one hand, rubbing her small forearm with the other.

But they weren't invincible. The boundary of their skin was weak, their beating hearts delicate and fallible. And she could feel that they stood at the bottom of a dark mountain.

His hands were hot on her, pulling her into the safety and comfort of his aura. But she could not shake the images in her mind: the girl in the phone booth, Shawna Fox's green eyes, Jed McIntyre in the parking lot, rocking back and forth as if the chaos of his thoughts kept him in constant motion.

She searched for a witty one-liner to make him laugh, to pull him into her buzz. But she couldn't think of anything. So she just hung her head a bit and looked down at his hand on her arm, touched his strong fingers.

"I'm not sure," she admitted. "I just don't know."

chapter sixteen

Lydia Strong had written in her book *With a Vengeance* that Jed McIntyre had been trying to create a "brethren of misery" when he murdered thirteen single working mothers in upstate New York. Jed McIntyre had been impressed that someone finally understood him so well. He hadn't really even known it at the time, but he eventually acknowledged that he had wanted other people to suffer the way he had suffered when his father murdered his mother, slit her throat with a dull cleaver in her own kitchen. He wanted someone else in the world to understand his loneliness, grief, and isolation. But of course it ran so much deeper—or, rather, so much higher—than that. It's not as though one makes a conscious decision to become a serial murderer. It's more like you feel so bad, so ugly, so broken inside all day, doing the things that other people do. Then somehow, maybe accidentally, or maybe because you read something or see something on the television, you discover something that makes you feel less bad all the time. For some people, it's drugs and alcohol; for some people, it's food; and for him, it was murder. But still he was touched, really moved that Lydia had taken the time to get to know him. It made him want to be a better man for her. But of course that wasn't possible.

He had known already, from the first moment he saw her, that Lydia was special. Her delicate, ephemeral beauty, her intelligent gray eyes, these would have changed the game for him had he been allowed to continue playing. He remembered how their eyes had met in the parking lot of the A&P that twilight more than sixteen years ago. She had felt him, felt his intentions, seen into his dark, twisted soul; he had watched the knowledge drain the color from her face, watched her small hand dart out to lock the car doors, then roll up the windows. But then she turned to look at him with some combination of curiosity, defiance, and fear. He'd had to smile; she melted something within him. He should have known she'd be the one to lead to his arrest. He'd been so careless that night, he almost deserved to get caught. She'd distracted him and made him forget himself.

He barely dared to think of her, except for once a month, when he wrote her a letter. When he thought of her, not even the medication could quell the desires that rose in him. Not that the pills really worked anyway; they really only dulled the twisting, aching, burning inside him. It was like he existed behind an opaque Plexiglas screen, barely recognizable, his voice unintelligible, even to himself. But it was good to have the meds as long as he was in this place; otherwise, he'd surely go insane.

He caught sight of himself in the two-way mirror. His Day-Glo orange jumper was most unflattering, a terrible color for a fair-skinned redhead, making him look even paler and more washed-out than he normally did. And it certainly did nothing to show off the body he'd been so carefully cultivating over his years here. It took discipline, real mental discipline, to work out when you were so heavily medicated. But it was a kind of release. He took great satisfaction in his hard, lean, muscular body, with cuts that would make Arnold blush like a little girl. If he'd been soft and paunchy when they'd brought him in here, he was a machine now. He looked down at his sinewy wrists and at the cuffs there, which matched the shackles on his ankles. He hated them; they made him look so common, like a thug or a gangster. But he had a feeling he wouldn't be wearing them for long.

He looked across the long Formica table at the man who sat as far away from him as possible. He reminded Jed of one of those dream-team lawyers, the self-righteous swagger, the intimidating frown of disdain. He knew enough about the trappings of wealth to identify the gentleman's three-thousand-dollar suit, his weekend-in-the-Caribbean tan, his manicured fingernails, his thick, glittering Tag Heuer watch. His silver-white hair seemed to glow against his tanned face; his blue eyes glittered like gems, bright and hard and cold. R. Alexander Harriman, Esq., used the kind of state-appointed attorneys who had represented Jed at his previous release review hearings to clean out his colon.

After his last hearing, two years ago, Jed had resigned himself to a lifetime behind bars. As he walked into the review, he had been sure that he had sufficiently duped the shrinks into believing that he had found Jesus and that his "mental illness" was under control with medication. He was sure that he would be sent to some halfway house, where escape would be possible. But when he'd walked in the door to appear before the committee, he'd seen former Special Agent Jeffrey Mark sitting at the table, in front of him the stack of letters Jed had monthly sent to Lydia Strong. He couldn't believe that thirteen years later, Agent Mark still had a hard-on for him. But then as Jeffrey Mark spoke passionately to the board against Jed's release, Jed realized that Agent Mark had a hard-on for Lydia Strong. Well, well, even the good guys were not above lusting after fifteen-year-old girls. When the parole board denied him, Jeffrey Mark had smiled. Mark, that smug, self-righteous bastard, leaned forward in his chair and said, before he could be stopped, "I'll be here every single time you come up for review, you sick fuck."

But that was before R. Alexander Harriman, Esq., had appeared in the visitors' room like an avenging angel—well, really more like Satan in some clever guise, bargaining for Jed's soul. Little did R. Alexander Harriman, Esq., and his mysterious client realize that they were getting the short end of that stick.

They'd been sitting in the cold, harshly lighted room for nearly an hour, and Harriman hadn't said one word to him, but Jed occasionally caught him sneaking a glance, a look of disgust and apprehension on his face. They both startled when the door opened quickly and the guard entered.

"The Review Board is assembled, Mr. Harriman, and will see you and your client now," said a bulky, fuzzy-headed young Samoan man, leaning down to unshackle Jed's chains from the table. Another guard stood at the door.

The attorney leaned toward Jed and said in a fierce whisper, "There will be no fucking with me or my client, Mr. McIntyre. I want you to understand that. You will be back in here so fast, it will make your teeth rattle. And there will be no second chances. You'll rot in here until you die, and then you'll rot in hell. Are we clear?" His words were like hammers and about as hard to swallow, but Jed held his tongue and turned on as much obsequious charm as he could muster without gagging. Frankly, he'd suck the old man's dick if it would get him out of the New York State Facility for the Criminally Insane.

"Of course, Mr. Harriman. Thank you."

Jed was rewarded for his good behavior when he walked into the institutional room where the board had assembled. Of the ten people seated, Jeffrey Mark was not among them, nor was there a single attending psychiatrist who had treated him over the last sixteen years. In fact, he'd never seen any of them before in his life.

chapter seventeen

The day started gray and dismal, large black clouds looming over the beach. The sun was just making its debut as she left Jeffrey warm and wrapped up in the comforter like a burrito, heading out to run for the first time in weeks. Running was like a religion for Lydia, a kind of prayer. Today, her body was forced to do contrition, make penance for weeks of inactivity. But she took an animalistic pleasure in being reduced to her muscles and her lungs, in the endorphins coursing through her blood. After the first mile along the damp shoreline with the smell of the ocean and the cries of seagulls filling her senses, she settled into her pace. Her mind was clear, and she could think about what their next move should be.

The pieces of this puzzle didn't quite seem to fit together; everything about it was just a little off, including how Lydia and Jeffrey had become involved. Since their conversation the night before, she'd started to wonder if they *had* stumbled onto something that they weren't equipped to handle . . . and if maybe it would be better for them just to walk away before that became impossible. But the only way she would be able to live with that would be if she knew for a fact that she was risking their lives to find Tatiana Quinn; if she knew beyond a doubt that all the veiled threats, the stalking black Mercedes, and the menacing Nathan Quinn were not just smoke and mirrors, some magician's trick to scare them away.

She picked up her pace and slowed her breathing, heading for a jetty, where she planned to turn around. The beach was nearly empty, and thunder rumbled somewhere off in the distance, the waves large and white-capped. An old woman in a romantic floppy straw hat and red-and-white polka-dotted bathing suit smiled as Lydia blew past her. A skinny kid in white bathing trunks threw a Frisbee to a black Labrador, who ran off with it, forcing the boy to chase him and tackle him in order to get it back; it was a game they both seemed to enjoy, running and splashing up water. The dog's barking and the boy's laughter carried toward her on the wind.

She watched their game as she drew closer to them. She watched them so intently, struck by the innocent happiness of their play, that she failed to notice at first the two figures who walked into her path. When she registered that they had stopped directly in front of her, weren't gazing at the ocean but at her approach, she stopped. Her fanny pack, strapped tightly at her waist, held her Glock, and she unzipped it.

Two men, one black, one white, started walking toward her. The white guy wore pressed jeans and heavy Timberland boots, a light navy blue Windbreaker over a white T-shirt. His head looked like almost a perfect square. It was huge, even atop his massive shoulders. He was missing a neck but made up for it with a giant chin. The black guy was longer, leaner, wearing a charcoal Henley, a cotton barn jacket, a pair of impeccably pressed chinos, and black Bruno Magli shoes. He had small, tight dreadlocks pulled back loosely. She could see their heavy weapons. The white guy wore his on a shoulder holster; the black guy had his at his waist. As they got closer, she looked around her. The beach was suddenly deserted; a few drops of rain fell from the sky.

She had two options. The first and most attractive option was to turn and run. But she could see that they were both much taller than she and in good shape, which meant that no matter how fast she was, they'd be faster in a straight sprint, simply because they had longer legs. The other option was to shoot the black guy first, because he wore his gun at his waist, and then clip the white guy while he was still struggling with that pesky shoulder holster.

But as they drew close enough for her to see their eyes, she zipped the Glock back into its pouch. Their smug bearing, the way Big Head had his hands in his pockets, the way Dreads never took his eyes off the pouch at her waist made her realize they were feds. She felt a little shaky as the adrenaline drained from her system, leaving a slight residue of anger.

"Have a permit for that weapon, Ms. Strong?"

Oh, so it's going to be like that.

"I don't suppose you could have come to the lobby and called my room. Do they teach Stalk and Surprise One Oh One on your first or second day at Quantico?"

"I'm Special Agent Negron," said Big Head, ignoring her smart-ass comment but looking as though he was sucking on lemons, "and this is my partner, Special Agent Bentley. We would like to talk to you about your visit with Valentina Fitore."

She took the identification he handed to her, scrutinized it, making a show of comparing his face to the face on the card in its leather envelope.

"It was a short visit," she said finally.

"So we heard. Can we go somewhere to talk?"

"Absolutely. You can meet me and my partner back at the hotel in half an hour."

She turned her back on them and jogged toward the hotel. She didn't appreciate being bullied by FBI agents; she would talk to them on her terms, or they could chase her and arrest her. Which they did not.

Back at the hotel, the agents came up to Lydia and Jeffrey's room. Lydia ordered coffee and pastries from room service, and after introductions, the four of them sat in the room's comfortable sitting area. The two agents sat on the couch, Jeffrey in the plush white chair facing them, Lydia perched on the arm of the same chair. Lydia told them about the tape and letter she had received, about her visit to Valentina's home and how she had watched the Mercedes run her down.

"You told the police that there was no license plate on the car," said Negron, tapping notes into his Palm Pilot.

"That's right."

"Are you sure?"

"Of course I'm sure," she said. She'd been frightened and shocked, but she'd had the presence of mind to look for a plate.

"And you're positive that this couldn't have been an accident?"

"What about the scenario that I'm describing isn't getting through?" said Lydia. "Someone purposely *mowed her down*. There was no mistaking it."

"And who knew you were going to see her that evening?"

"That I know of? Jeffrey, Detective Manuel Ignacio, and our office back in New York," she answered. "Possibly you, if you've had Detective Ignacio's phone tapped."

"Why did you go to see her?" asked Negron, narrowing his eyes but not responding to her comment.

"Because I suspected that she had information on the disappearance of Tatiana Quinn that she was afraid to reveal. I wanted to convince her to confide in me."

"But she died before she was able to do that? Or did she tell you anything?"

"She never had a chance."

"Why did you assume that she was the one to have sent you the note and the tape?"

"It seemed like a logical conclusion to draw. She was in the house all the time and was close to the family."

"Well, there's a wrinkle in your theory, Ms. Strong, because Valentina was illiterate."

Lydia frowned. That *was* a wrinkle. But it might also be good news; because if someone helped her to write the note, then that person could be found.

"How would you know that? That she's illiterate."

"How we get our information is not your concern," Negron answered primly. "How would a relatively recent immigrant know who you were? You're not exactly a household name. Why would she choose you and not, say, the police?"

"I can't answer that, Special Agent Negron. But I would like to remind you that I haven't done anything wrong, and I don't appreciate your attitude. I am a private citizen and I had a private correspondence with someone who clearly was in need of my help. I had every right to pursue that. I'm just sorry our encounter led to her murder."

"Ms. Strong," said Special Agent Bentley, speaking up for the first time and revealing himself with a soft-spoken air of authority as the senior partner, "Valentina Fitore was the sister of Sasa Fitore, who, as you unfortunately already know, is currently under investigation by the FBI for his alleged participation in organized criminal activities. He is also part of a larger classified investigation. Because of this, I am not prepared to share any information or theories with you. I will tell you, however, that your investigation is complicating ours."

"I don't see how," she answered.

"It doesn't matter whether you see how or not," he said curtly. "I'm just telling you that you are barking up the wrong tree. Trust me when I tell you that you will get no closer to Tatiana by taking a path that crosses ours."

Jeffrey could see that Lydia was about to blow a gasket, so he placed a hand on her arm and leaned forward toward the agents.

"What do you want from us, guys? I'm sure you have done your homework enough to know who we are, the connections we have, the fact that my firm is run by former FBI men and still works with the Bureau. We're here; we're in this. Let's try to help each other."

"See, that's the thing," Negron said unpleasantly. "We don't need your help. And if you want to help yourselves, you'll stay out of our way."

Bentley cast a disapproving look at Negron and said, "What my partner means is that the situation we are working here is very sensitive. If you fuck it up, trust me, it's going to be bad for everyone. Now, please, just step off."

The agents rose together. And Agent Negron said, "We'll be in touch if we have any more questions."

They opened the door and surprised the blond baby-faced room-service waiter, who appeared just to have been about to knock.

"You won't stay for breakfast?" asked Lydia sweetly. Bentley gave her a look and brushed past the waiter, Negron following behind. Lydia signed for the food and closed the door.

"We're not very popular, are we?" said Lydia, unwrapping the basket of fresh hot pastries and choosing a raspberry Danish. The sweet sugar frosting, flaky pastry, and tart raspberry filling melted in her mouth and instantly nullified the healthy feeling she'd had after her run.

"It does seem that every time we turn around, someone is encouraging us to mind our own business."

"Which generally means that there's a good reason not to."

Three pastries and a cup of coffee later, they were in the Jeep and on their way to Valentina Fitore's memorial service. The light rain that had fallen in the morning had done nothing to diminish the stifling humidity, though the cloud cover was still thick, blocking the rays of the sun.

Jeffrey eyed the other parked cars, wondering which of them held the FBI surveillance team. He decided it was probably the white van on the corner. He hoped they wouldn't get arrested today as they continued to poke around an investigation they had been encouraged to abandon. That would really set Jacob off, if he had to send the lawyers down to Florida. Jeffrey hadn't even discussed with Lydia the problems he was having with Jacob. Last night would have been a good time to bring it up, but he still wasn't 100 percent sure what was going on. Better to wait until he was positive.

Jacob, Jeffrey, and Christian Striker had started the firm nearly seven years ago. All former FBI men, they'd grown tired of the politics of the Bureau, tired of the paranoia about public perception of the organization, and decided they'd be more effective investigators on their own. They'd been hugely successful, in large part due to Lydia, her contributions as a consultant, and the publicity that surrounded the books she wrote on some of their cases. Jeffrey had been pushing to make her a partner in the firm. Christian was totally onboard. But Jacob was fighting it, confirming Jeffrey's long-held suspicion that Jacob had some kind of personal problem with Lydia.

"She drains this firm of money," he complained to Jeffrey.

"That's bullshit," Jeffrey snapped. Though her investigations did tend to be expensive, the publicity she received brought in more high-paying clients than they ever would have garnered on their own. Before the Cheerleader Murder case, Lydia's first with the firm, they'd been doing insurance fraud and working freelance with the FBI and NYPD on cold cases and cases that were too messy for agencies whose people had to follow rules. The cash flow had been steady, although low. They never turned a profit until Lydia got involved. Recently, Jeffrey had asked to see the books, something he had never had any interest in before, leaving the money business of the firm to Jacob. But it had been nearly a month since Jeffrey had started asking, and every time, Jacob gave him some kind of runaround. When Jeffrey tried to log on to the firm's computer to check it himself, tired of waiting for Jacob, he found that he needed a password to access the accounting program he didn't have.

That was the day Lydia came home from her book tour. Since they were off to Miami the next day, he hadn't had a chance to talk to Christian about it. And he wasn't ready to confront Jacob.

Jeffrey's conversation with Lydia last night brought back a memory that he hadn't shined a light on in years. A memory that he had chosen to omit in retelling the story to Lydia. It was not like him to sweep things into his subconscious. And he was beginning to question the trust he'd had in Jacob all these years. It hurt him more than it made him angry to think . . . . Well, he wasn't sure what to think. He just knew something wasn't right. He could figure it out when they got back to New York, which he hoped would be tonight.

The center, a small nondescript building painted a cheerful yellow and white, sat on a dusty side street, without much else surrounding it. There was a shoe-repair shop with a cracked window and a CLOSED sign on the door. The sign looked like it had been there for a while. A larger building that looked like a warehouse lacked identifying signage. An empty lot, where weeds and patchy grass had taken over and a few cars were parked, dominated the rest of the street. There was an understated sign over the door that read ALBANIAN CENTER in English, below which were some words in another language, which Lydia brilliantly deduced to be Albanian. Next to the door was a bulletin board behind a glass case containing a picture of Valentina, the date and the time of the service, and a few paragraphs in Albanian. It seemed like a meager memorial for a life to Lydia, who thought, You live a hurricane of emotions, dreams, experiences, hardships; you raise children. Your life seems so important, your problems so consuming, your successes so thrilling. And in the end, your picture winds up on a bulletin board, your life reduced to a snapshot and some kind words on a piece of paper. She could hear a powerful voice speaking through the closed wooden doors. They moved inside quietly and found a dim spot at the back of the room, but off to the side, so that they could see faces.

The room was plain—freshly polished wood floors and newly painted white walls. Rows of theater seats faced a simple stage area, where a larger copy of the picture of Valentina from the bulletin board sat atop an easel and was surrounded by bouquets of carnations. A large man in a bad suit and worse toupee stood at a podium, speaking loudly in Albanian, his eyes occasionally tearing. The rows were sprinkled with people, some fidgeting in their seats, someone coughing, someone weeping.

Lydia's eyes scanned the room. She saw Sasa Fitore sitting in the front row, his arm around the slumped shoulders of a woman with long red hair and pale skin, her face hidden as she wept into her hands. Lydia assumed it was Marianna, whom she and Jeffrey had decided was a good bet on who had helped Valentina write the note. Sasa's eyes were red and had dark smudges underneath, but his face was expressionless, except for his mouth, which was drawn into a tight line.

The two rows behind Marianna and Sasa were nearly shoulder-to-shoulder with a motley group of men. Wearing ill-fitting black suits in various shapes and sizes, they almost all sat stone-faced, their arms crossed. The one closest to Lydia had a scar that ran from his eye down his neck, disappearing into his shirt collar.

"Rough crowd," Jeffrey whispered.

"They must be his crew," Lydia whispered back, and Jeffrey nodded in agreement.

There didn't seem to be a religious tone to the service at all, and Lydia remembered that religion had been outlawed in Albania by dictator Enver Hoxna in 1967 and that even after the Communist regime fell, people had been slow to practice again. Valentina had likely been raised a Muslim, but chances were that Marianna didn't have any religious affiliation. Lydia thought of her own mother, a devout Catholic, and only vaguely remembered her service and funeral through a fog of grief. But she did remember the horrible empty hole in her heart, the crippling fear and sadness that had assailed her as she watched her mother's coffin lowered into the ground. The urge to scream, which she'd choked back, the thought of her mother alone in the cold earth breaking her in half. Lydia shook her head as if to rattle the memories from it, and Jeffrey put his hand on her arm, knowing instinctively where her thoughts had taken her.

Of course, they weren't actually here to pay their respects. In Lydia's experience, things often shook loose at weddings and funerals. Emotions ran high; people broke down. Not that it was a reliable or appropriate place to gather information, but sometimes you learned things just the same . . . merely by observing people's reactions, their connections to one another. Marianna and Sasa looked about right to her, though Sasa looked a bit stiff, as though he was conscious of eyes on him, as if he was watching his back. Marianna grieved with abandon, not concerned with appearances. The men behind him had the look of soldiers, watchful and protective, grim. The rest of the mourners gathered looked solemn but not as though they were personally grieving; Lydia assumed they were neighbors and fellow immigrants, present out of respect. If this had been a different kind of murder, they would be looking for suspects in the crowd. But as it was, they were just looking for the direction in which to take their next step.

The man speaking at the podium stepped down off the stage and offered his hand to Marianna, who, when she stood, was a full head taller than Lydia expected. With skin the color of cream and green eyes that rivaled oceans and gems in their color, in their depth and glimmering facets, Marianna was a radiant beauty. Her hair, as orange as wires, was as thick and straight as unraveled bolts of velvet, and she moved with the grace and bearing of a dancer. She had the kind of beauty that brought men to their knees and women to plastic surgeons.

"My mother," said Marianna in English, "put everyone before herself. She never thought of her own needs, only those of others."

For a moment, Marianna seemed to be looking directly at Lydia with a kind of fire, a kind of anger in her eyes. It occurred to Lydia that Marianna might blame her for her mother's death. But when, with as much subtlety as possible, Lydia took a step back so that she could glance behind her without making a show of it, she followed Marianna's eyes to a small woman who seemed to hide in the shadows. She wore a simple black sleeveless dress, accented with an elegant strand of pearls. The brim on a tightly woven black straw hat and the thick black sunglasses she wore partially obscured her face, but it only took Lydia a second to recognize Jenna Quinn. Lydia tugged on Jeffrey's sleeve, and he nodded his head once to acknowledge that he had already seen Jenna.

Marianna continued her eulogy now in Albanian, her tone shifting between sadness and anger. She had looked at Jenna only that once; the rest of the time, she kept her eyes down, trying to control the quiver in her voice. Lydia felt sad for her. She was so young; she still needed her mother. Coming on thirty-two, some days Lydia still needed hers. When Lydia's mother had been alive, it was a daily battle over hair and clothes, makeup and boys, homework and television; it was probably the same for Marianna. But when her mother was gone, Lydia's childhood departed, as well. Part of her realized that she'd never be anyone else's baby, that she'd never share that intimate bond, no matter how much it felt like a shackle sometimes, with anyone else. Lydia wondered what had happened to that bond between Jenna and Tatiana, if it had ever existed, if it still did, and what could sunder it. Lydia watched Jenna out of the corner of her eye and was surprised to see her raise a Kleenex and dab underneath her glasses. There's more to this than you imagine, said Lydia's inner voice. When she looked again, Jenna Quinn was gone.

As the service ended, the men behind Sasa and Marianna surrounded the man and his niece, then whisked them out of the center, but not before Marianna and Lydia exchanged a glance. Lydia was quick to follow them out and saw Marianna and two of the men get into a limousine, which pulled away slowly. Lydia and Jeffrey hung back in the vestibule of the building, just inside the door, as the other mourners filed out.

Another black stretch limo pulled up; Sasa said a few words to the men who stood around him, tossing the man with the scar on his neck a set of keys. The man jogged off out of sight, and a few seconds later, the Porsche Boxster pulled around the corner and took off with a screech of tires, eliciting a shout from Sasa and laughter from the men. The limousine still waited as the remaining men piled into two black Land Rovers. The rear window of the limo rolled down, and a delicate hand emerged with a lighted cigarette. Sasa took the cigarette and dragged on it, reaching his other hand into the window as if he were stroking someone's cheek, and a smile bloomed on his face. He dropped the cigarette into the street and opened the door. He stepped inside, seating himself opposite the woman. The same slender hand reached out to close the door, but not before Lydia caught a glimpse of the black brim of her hat. The limo followed one of the Land Rovers and was tailed by the other as they pulled away.

"Interesting," said Jeffrey.

"Very."

"I can't talk to you, Lydia. Don't put me in this position."

"What's the connection, Manny? Just tell me that."

He'd agreed to meet them at the Cuban place where they'd eaten before, but now he looked like he regretted it. "I thought you said that you had information for me."

"You don't call that information? Did you know that Sasa Fitore and Jenna Quinn were connected?"

"Listen . . . I only came to tell you that the Tatiana Quinn investigation is closed. She's officially been declared a runaway."

"Then why are you even here? Why didn't you tell me that on the phone?"

The detective just shrugged. He cared, and she could see it in him. He was still curious; it was killing him to walk away from a case that he knew was far from closed. But she could also see his resolve in the way his jaw was set, in the way he couldn't look either of them in the eye. Lydia just shook her head. She couldn't believe the change in him. She was disappointed, and when he looked at her, he saw it. He got up to leave.

"I don't know why I came. It was a mistake."

"What about Stephen Parker? Did you learn anything more that could help us from that?" asked Jeffrey, grasping at straws.

"Yeah. Keep your head out of the gator's mouth."

Jeffrey laughed without any humor, nodded, and took a sip of his *café con leche*.

"I hope you can sleep at night, Manny," Lydia said quietly, but loudly enough that he could hear her where he stood at the door. It was a shitty thing to say; she knew he had no choice, but she was angry and frustrated. He turned and looked at her, his hand on the wall, as if he had to steady himself. He sighed.

"If there's one thing I've learned over the years—Stephen Parker knew it, too—its not money but the *love* of money that's the root of all evil. Look at the money; see where that takes you," he said, and pushed the door open, causing a little bell to jingle. The sound of cars passing on wet streets carried into the restaurant.

"What?" Lydia asked.

"You heard me," he said, and the door closed behind him.

Lydia and Jeffrey looked at each other.

"So, you're the big-time PI," Lydia said. "What do you make of that?"

"Craig said that Nathan Quinn's business dealings were clean, as far as he could tell?"

"That's what he said."

He thought a second, staring into the golden sugar gathered at the bottom of his cup, swirling it as though trying to divine tea leaves.

"What about Jenna's assets?"

"People from Albania don't have assets. It's the poorest country in Europe. She was a prostitute, to boot."

"So says Nathan Quinn."

She raised her eyebrows. "Good point."

"Do we have any way of finding out who she was before she married Quinn?"

"If they were married in the United States, Craig will be able to find their marriage license and get her maiden name. That would be a good start. I'll have him check with INS, too."

From a pay phone in the lobby of the Delano Hotel, Lydia called Craig and made him go outside and call her back from a pay phone on the street.

"You're going all *Sopranos* on me," said Craig when he finally rang back.

"There's a lot of weird shit going on. Humor me."

She told him what she wanted him to do.

"Once I have her name, what do you want me to look for?"

"Banking records, anything suspicious in her name—big withdrawals or deposits, personal accounts at offshore banks. Can you do that?"

He snorted his disdain. "Of course. How do you want me to reach you?"

"I'll call you in a few hours."

"I thought you guys were coming back tonight."

"Possibly. We'll see."

She hung up the phone and rested her head on the cool plastic of the receiver for a second before turning and walking toward the bar, where Jeffrey waited. They had booked themselves on a flight leaving Miami at 8:10 that night. She had promised Jeffrey the previous night that if nothing popped by five o'clock, they'd pack and leave. It was just past two o'clock now. The connection between Jenna and Sasa was interesting, but it hadn't brought them any closer to finding Tatiana. Not yet anyway.

She felt a twinge in her lower abdomen as she climbed onto the stool next to Jeffrey's, reminding her that she had felt lousy since the attack of nausea the night before. She'd just been ignoring it . . . mind over illness. Jeffrey didn't turn to look at her as she sat. His energy was off, his aura was dim, and he seemed tired. She counted on his good humor and strong spirit to balance out her obsessive-compulsive streak, her tendency toward depression. She realized suddenly that she wasn't sure how to make him feel better when he was down.

"So let's break this thing down and try to decide what our involvement should be," he said.

He slid his drink off the cocktail napkin and pulled a Mont Blanc pen from his pocket. It reminded her of the pen that she had found back in New Mexico, a serial killer's sick gift. She shivered as Jeffrey scribbled on the napkin.

"We have Tatiana, missing now two months. Valentina murdered. Stephen Parker murdered. Jenna Quinn fraternizing with a known mobster, also, coincidentally or not, the brother of her maid. Detective Ignacio, we're imagining, threatened to the point that he wants nothing to do with us or the case he's been sweating blood over for the last eight weeks. Who threatened him, we don't know. Tatiana has been officially declared a runaway by the police.

Feds crawling all over the place, claiming that our investigation is impeding theirs. And Nathan Quinn, one scary, powerful man."

The result of his napkin scribbling looked like the work of a Cubist on acid.

"Let's not forget about Sasa Fitore," he continued. "Who is he? What is his connection to all of this?"

"What a mess," said Lydia, feeling overwhelmed suddenly by all the elements of the case and how nothing seemed to fit, how there was no picture forming in the puzzle pieces.

"It stinks. This is too much fallout for the disappearance of one girl. You're right: There's definitely something ugly and dangerous swimming in the water. Tatiana is just the dorsal fin that broke the surface."

"Very poetic," she said, smiling. When he didn't smile back, she placed a hand on his shoulder. "What's up? I'm supposed to be the moody, distant one, haunted by the investigation. You're supposed to be Mr. Just the Facts Ma'am, emotionally disinterested, the rock. We had our whole shtick worked out."

He smiled, swiveled toward her on the stool, and placed a gentle hand on her leg. "I'm fine. Just beat. I want to head back to New York tonight. But I don't feel right about leaving yet, and I know you don't, either."

She ordered a club soda from the bartender, hoping to soothe her restless stomach, and nibbled on some peanuts, enjoying their salty, greasy flavor.

"You're the most important thing in my life," she said quietly, not looking at him. "I trust you more than anyone. So if you tell me your instincts are screaming for us to leave and we're staying because you know I want to, then we're out of here."

She meant it, though she knew he would never make her walk away from her work. But she would if he asked her to. Maybe she would come to resent it in time, but she'd do anything for him. Maybe that's why it worked so well with them—because both of them would lay their lives down for the other, but neither would ever ask it.

He looked at her, waiting for her to lift her eyes. She was force, electric, uncontainable. If you got on her bad side, he couldn't think of a person who stood a chance. But it was the tender places within her that had always brought him to his knees inside himself. He was moved, as he always was, by her depth and by her strength. He was amused by how she never ceased to surprise him. He put his hand on her shoulder and she turned her gaze on him and smiled. "Okay?" she asked.

"Okay," he answered. "One more day."

"Ms. Strong?" The maître d' approached them. An older man with graying hair, laughing ice blue eyes, and weathered skin, he had the air of a retired sea captain, in spite of his tuxedo and impeccable manicure.

"Yes?"

"You have a phone call. Would you like to take it at the bar?"

She nodded and he produced a cordless handset. She thought it must be Craig, though it was fast even for him to have come up with anything. She felt Jeffrey's curious eyes on her.

"Hello?"

"Is this Lydia Strong?"

"Who's asking?"

"I have information for you."

It was the voice of a young woman. She was whispering, and Lydia could hear music and raised, exuberant voices in the background. Lydia could hear the edge of fear and uncertainty and knew immediately she wasn't dealing with a criminal. But she did have to wonder how the fuck everyone and their mother knew she and Jeffrey were staying at the Delano. As private investigators, they were going to have to learn in the future how to move about with a little more stealth.

"Relating to what?"

"Tatiana."

"All right. What do you want?"

"I just need to see you. Alone."

"When and where?"

"At the G-Spot . . . it's a club on South Beach. Tonight after midnight. . . . I'll find you."

Bodies sweated and heaved, Crystal Method throbbed over the speakers, and a powerful strobe light cast the dance floor in a sickening flicker. The cacophony of raised voices shouting over the music added another layer to the dull roar. Lydia thought she was too old by about five years to be a patron of the G-Spot as she shoved her way through the crowd, looking for a woman she had never seen before.

The day had started out badly and looked about to get worse as Lydia shoved her way in toward the bar. Even in college, this type of atmosphere had never appealed to her; the loud music, crushing bodies, leering eyes had always filled her with a low-grade panic, a kind of psychological claustrophobia. As if the energy, a kind of yearning, grinding pulse, was too big, too dangerous to be contained within the walls and the alcohol- and drug-induced exuberance could quickly turn to brutality, to riot. She had always thought of clubs like this, with their mammoth open spaces and warehouse ceilings, their dark corners and deafening music, as a natural habitat for predators. They lurked here, waiting for victims: women too young, innocent, drunk, or high to recognize danger even as they sat in its crosshairs.

After shouting to the bald, excessively pierced and tattooed bartender that she wanted a martini, Lydia looked at her watch and saw that it was nearly midnight. They would probably have been in bed at home already if they had taken the flight they were booked on from Miami to New York earlier that evening. But instead, they were still here, Jeffrey back at the hotel, fuming, and Lydia fighting off the crush of people apparently desperate enough to riot for cocktails. When the bartender brought her the drink, Lydia handed him a twenty, yelled at him to keep the change, and pushed her way back from the bar. He smiled at her, and she saw a glimmer of silver on the tip of his tongue. Lydia distrusted people who pierced themselves in tender places.

She spied a quiet corner through the smoke as a gorgeous black couple—she all legs and cheekbones, lavender contact lenses; he with impossibly defined muscles, slicked-back hair, too much cologne—got up to dance and left vacant seats. She sat on the plush red velvet chair, which allowed her to face out at the club and be seen by people who entered. Her cocktail was terrible, obviously the cheapest-possible well vodka and not the Ketel One she'd ordered. She drank it, even though she knew a searing headache would be the price she'd pay for the calming effect it was having. She reached into the small velvet clutch she carried and removed the pack of Dunhill cigarettes she had purchased in the hotel lobby on her way here. If Jeffrey was trailing her, which was a safe bet, he was going to bitch endlessly. Lydia hadn't smoked in over a year but, without a pang of guilt, she opened the pack, withdrew a cigarette, and lighted it with a tiny black lighter. It tasted good, very good, as she drew the smoke into her lungs like a long-lost lover into an embrace. Smoking was like that for her, like an abusive relationship that she didn't leave for years because the sex was so good. She knew it would kill her someday, but when it was good, it was so good, she couldn't have imagined living without it. And even after it was over, she always remembered the pleasure, always toyed in her mind with the idea of going back.

She caught her reflection in a mirrored wall. Her jet-black hair was slicked back and pulled into a tight ponytail at the base of her neck. The only makeup she wore was a deep red matte shade of lipstick from MAC. A Jean Paul Gaultier tight black choker-collar halter was low enough to show a little cleavage and hugged her hips over a pair of narrow black leather pants. A shamefully expensive pair of black midcalf boots looked fabulous but hurt like hell. Her reflection in the mirror as she sat waiting reminded her of the old days—days thankfully gone. The days before she had admitted to being in love with Jeffrey for most of her adult life. She'd had more meaningless, probably dangerous, one-night stands than a season of *Sex and the City*. It was a part of her life that she and Jeffrey never discussed. She wondered if it would make a difference if he knew that she'd only been trying to find a substitute for him. She decided it was a gamble she wasn't willing to take. Besides, he'd never asked her how many men she'd been with before him. And it wasn't information she was about to volunteer.

Somehow above the din of the club, she heard her cell phone chirp. As she reached into her bag, her fingers brushed the cool metal of her Glock. Jeffrey's mobile number glowed on the phone's digital display.

"Yes?"

"Did she show up yet?"

"No."

"How long are you going to wait?"

"A little while. Where are you?"

"Back at the hotel."

"Liar."

"Give me a break. You didn't seriously expect me to wait in our room while you ran off in the middle of the night to meet some mystery woman . . . at the G-Spot, of all places. I can't believe you're smoking."

"Just like a private *dick*," she said. "Always following me around." As a card-carrying feminist, whatever that was, she felt compelled to complain about his overprotective streak, but she was secretly glad he always covered her back. Besides, she would have followed him, too.

"She wanted me to come alone, Jeffrey," she explained, as if talking to a stubborn toddler.

"Do you see me?"

She looked around the room. "No."

"Then you're as alone as you're going to get as long as I'm alive."

"My hero."

"I'll be here if you need me."

"In my country, a beautiful woman like you would never sit alone for long. But here"—he gestured magnificently—"these American men are too afraid to approach you. I am not afraid."

"They're afraid for a reason," Lydia said, glaring at him. She'd been waiting over an hour and was starting to lose her patience. But she was flattered. She *had* been striving for the unapproachable look and was starting to doubt herself. He was the third man she'd had to fend off, and she was sick of being polite.

He laughed and sat down opposite her with the ease of someone who was welcome. He was smarm personified, and all the expensive clothes and jewelry in the world weren't going to change that for him. With his slicked-back hair, a maroon silk shirt open to his hairy navel, copious gold chains, and tight black jeans, he looked like Tony Montana's dopey twin.

"Listen," she said, leaning so close to him that she could smell his cologne, "get the fuck away from me. Right now."

His eyes widened in surprise and his broad smile twitched. He gave a little chuckle and looked around self-consciously, then back at her. He struggled to maintain his suave demeanor, and the smile crept back. He was a trooper; she had to give him that.

"I'm serious," she added, hoping to dispel any doubt he might be entertaining. He got up.

"American bitch," he said as he walked off. She just rolled her eyes, took another Dunhill from the pack, and lighted it. She wouldn't wait much longer.

chapter eighteen

The crowds seemed to part for Marianna Fitore; she was a goddess in a swank cherry red dress that she wore like a bad attitude. It
clung to her hips and breasts and shot dramatically over her right
shoulder, danced around her tight thighs. She swept past Lydia,
lightly touching her arm as she went. Lydia stood and followed
her through the crowd and down a flight of stairs, then along a
tiny hallway that led to a dimly lighted room. Lydia could hear the
music from upstairs pulsing through the floor, but this room was
subdued. Reeking of pot, cigarette smoke, and Lydia didn't even
want to imagine what else, the room was a maze of velvet couches.
Melding forms lounged and moaned, groping at one another.
Candles melted on endless ledges on the walls and on the floor, casting strange shadows. Lydia lost sight of Marianna for a moment in
the darkness and she stopped, not sure whether to continue forward
or go back. She was feeling suddenly vulnerable, and she began to
question the wisdom of following the girl down here. She wondered
if Jeffrey was somewhere close behind.

"Ms. Strong, I'm here," Marianna whispered, and pulled her
down onto a plush seat. Lydia could barely see the girl's face, but she
could see the nervousness in her eyes.

"You were at my mother's service today," she said.

"Yes, I was. I'm sorry for your loss."

The girl nodded, and it was a moment before she could speak

again as she tried to control herself. "I do not want my mother to have died for nothing. She took a great risk in contacting you, and she paid the price."

"So she did send the package."

"With my help, yes. I thought it was a mistake. And so it was. But it was the right thing to do. Too many girls are in danger—not just Tatiana. For so many, it's already too late."

"What do you mean?"

The girl sighed and leaned back, wrapping her arms around herself. Her eyes grew wide and her bottom lip quivered. "If you haven't seen with your own eyes what goes on in this world, you would never believe it."

Lydia said nothing, just placed a hand on the girl's knee. Marianna reached into a sequined bag that she carried and removed a black DVD case.

"My country has been destroyed. And the people left there are like vultures feeding off the carrion of our dead culture. They would sell their daughters for the American dollar, not caring what their fate might be."

Lydia wasn't sure she understood, but she took the case from Marianna and put it in her clutch.

"I stole that from my uncle so that you can see what I'm talking about. If he knows I have betrayed him, I will die," she said simply.

"What is it?"

"It is the truth of the world."

Now that Lydia's eyes had acclimated to the darkness, she could see Marianna's face better. The glassy look in Marianna's eyes told Lydia that she was high.

"What do you mean by that?"

"There are men, men like Nathan Quinn, who run the world, you know, with their money. But they are not good men; they are devils with ravenous appetites, hungry only for human flesh. It is a secret society of powerful, powerful men. If you turn on CNN, you'll see the faces they wear for the world. When you play that DVD, you'll see them as they truly are."

Listening to Marianna, a chill had come over Lydia. She tried to block out the low moans and quiet laughter from the forms reclining on the couches around them. Other forms moved in the darkness like wraiths. Lydia hoped that Jeffrey was one of them.

"Why have you given this to me, Marianna? If girls are in danger, like you claimed in your note, why not go to the police or to the FBI?"

Marianna turned suddenly cold eyes on Lydia and shook her head. "Americans are like children sometimes, children who think that Santa Claus brings them their many gifts. Don't you hear me?" She was becoming frantic, her beauty growing sharp and mean, her soft features growing brittle, her voice rising an octave. "They own the police, the FBI, the CIA."

"Okay, take it easy," Lydia said gently, placing her hand on Marianna's bare white shoulder, where she could feel the tensed muscles. "You'll have to forgive me," Lydia said, humoring her, "I haven't seen the things you have."

Marianna seemed to deflate. She slumped back against the wall, smoothed her hair away from her face with both hands, and let out a shuddering sigh.

"I'm sorry, Ms. Strong," she said, her shoulder relaxing under Lydia's grip. Her eyes were suddenly wide and moist, the eyes of a little girl, her mascara starting to run a bit. Lydia could feel the girl trembling.

"It's all right. Call me Lydia."

"We saw you on television. . . . I don't remember what program. And my mother said, 'There is a woman of strength and honor. She can help us.' That is why she sent you the note and the tape."

"Where did that tape come from?"

"From our machine, a few days after Tatiana disappeared."

"And you didn't tell the police because you thought they couldn't be trusted? Not even Detective Ignacio?"

She nodded, mascara trailing down her cheek, a thin black line leading to the corner of her mouth. She didn't bother to wipe it away.

"And why didn't you tell Jenna Quinn? Why couldn't you have trusted Tatiana's own mother?"

"We did tell her," Marianna answered. "She said it wasn't our business. We couldn't understand . . ."

Lydia could see that something had distracted the girl; her eyes started to shift and she sat up on the couch, sliding forward. "I've already told you too much," she said in a desperate whisper, her eyes focusing on something beyond Lydia.

"I can't help you or anyone if I don't have all the information I need," Lydia said, grabbing her wrist, trying to keep connected to her before she floated away. "What is Sasa's connection to Nathan and Jenna Quinn?"

She hesitated as her eyes searched the room, then took a deep breath and seemed to relax a little. "Nathan Quinn is his . . . his contact, his client. Sasa and Jenna are lovers."

Lydia had already suspected that just from the touch she'd witnessed between Sasa and Jenna at the memorial service. But for a second, she didn't understand what Sasa could have that Quinn would want to buy. Then she remembered what Detective Ignacio had told them about Sasa Fitore. "What do you mean, 'his client'?"

Marianna nodded toward Lydia's purse, where she'd slipped the DVD. "You'll see." Then suddenly she grew fierce. "He is my uncle, but he's a demon. Do you understand? *Somebody* has to stop him."

Then Marianna got up suddenly and backed away toward the door. Lydia could see Marianna's chest heaving like a dancer's after a performance. The girl was panicking, and Lydia scanned the room to find the source of her fear. She felt her own heart start to race.

"Marianna, please. There's still too much I don't understand. You need to tell me about the films."

"I'll call you."

In a flash of red, she disappeared into the darkness. Lydia followed her through the black velvet curtain and saw the hem of Marianna's dress turn the corner leading to the staircase. The sound of music and the crowd upstairs grew louder as Lydia jogged up the long, narrow flight. At the top, she pushed herself through a throng of bodies, catching sight of Marianna's bright orange hair. The music seemed to grow louder still, and Lydia's heart was pounding as she followed Marianna onto the dance floor. Progress was slow, and she lost sight of the girl in the mass of people moving to the heavy techno beat. The strobe light came on again, accenting a high siren of music, turning the dancers into ghosts of themselves, pale and horrible, their movements stuttered and menacing.

Though the music raged, a stunned silence fell after the first gunshot. Then after the second, people on the dance floor began to scream and run, panic setting in, Lydia caught in the thick of it. She was pushed along in the crowd as the music stopped and the lights came up. A third gunshot rang out and Lydia pushed her way against the crowd of people fleeing blindly for cover. As the crowd cleared, Lydia saw her. She had fallen, her dress and long hair splayed about her, the dance floor lighted beneath her. When Lydia got to her, she was still alive, the red of her dress soaked black with a spreading stain over her heart, her delicate white shoulder marred by a tiny, perfectly circular entry wound. Lydia sat next to her, touched a hand to her forehead.

"It's all right," Marianna said. "Nothing was ever as I thought it would be anyway."

"You're fine, baby. You're going to be fine," said Lydia, looking into her eyes with a reassuring smile.

"The girls . . . they never have a chance," she whispered, and closed her eyes. She looked like a sleeping angel.

It was at that moment that Lydia felt the cool metal at the base of her skull.

"Don't turn around," a deep voice growled in an accent that was becoming familiar.

Lydia sat still, not even removing her hand from Marianna's forehead.

"We've been more than tolerant. This is your last opportunity to walk away. There won't be another warning."

Lydia almost wept with relief when she heard Jeffrey's voice. "This is your last opportunity to walk away, you fat fuck. Drop your weapon."

There was a cool, low chuckle from behind her, and in the next second, the club seemed to explode with shouts and sirens as the police pulled up and burst in the doors from the street. She felt the nose of the gun drop from her skull, and when she turned, the man was fleeing. All she could see was the back of his bald head.

"Are you okay?" asked Jeffrey, dropping to his knees and taking her face in his hands as the police swarmed around them. She nodded and tried unsuccessfully to hold back the sob of anger and fear and sadness that had welled up within her.

chapter nineteen

"Is the body count so high everywhere you go, Ms. Strong?" asked Agent Negron in the back of an FBI surveillance van that smelled like stale coffee, cigarettes, and body odor. He leaned toward her, his face wrenched into an angry frown, his breath smelling of garlic. Lydia didn't feel like answering him, or really saying much of anything, so she sat sullenly on a small swivel chair with her arms crossed, twisting herself back and forth slowly.

Agent Bentley sat with his head in his hands, his shoulders slumped. "I can't fucking believe this," he muttered.

"What the fuck is going on, Special Agents?" asked Jeffrey. Lydia could see how angry he was from the muscle twitching in his jaw. He was sweating in the overwarm van, which was cramped with too many bodies, and his forehead was drawn into a harsh scowl. Lydia thought he looked pretty intimidating. And while Negron seemed to cringe just a little, Bentley raised his head and matched Jeffrey's angry glare.

"What's going on," he said, looking tired, "is that someone just killed a girl here. A girl who was at great personal risk, a key element in our investigation. Now, thanks to you and your partner, we are pretty much fucked."

"Well, we didn't kill her," said Jeffrey. "We came here because she called us."

"After we asked you to back off," said Bentley, lowering his voice to almost a whisper. He looked truly sad, his eyes rimmed with red and his mouth turned down at the corners. Lydia felt bad for him suddenly. Not to mention guilty. They *had* fucked up his investigation, one he'd probably been working on for months. And Marianna was dead.

"We don't work for you, Special Agent," Jeffrey said.

"I have a hard time believing that Marianna was cooperating with the FBI," said Lydia, a thought occurring to her.

"And why is that so hard for you to believe?" asked Bentley.

"Because she had nothing but disdain and distrust for your agency."

"Marianna had a three-hundred-dollar-a-day habit. She was a troubled young girl," said Bentley. "Are you going to believe what I'm telling you, Lydia, or some cokehead?"

Lydia felt confused. She wasn't sure what reason Marianna would have had to lie to her . . . or why she would have risked her life to do so. On the other hand, she wasn't sure why Bentley would lie, either. But her gut told her to put her money on the "cokehead."

"She told me that Nathan Quinn was a client of Sasa Fitore's snuff-film operation."

"Give me a break," said Bentley. "Did you take some ecstasy while you were hanging out at the G-Spot? Snuff doesn't exist; it's an urban legend. I had you figured for smarter than that." His tone was harsh and sarcastic, but she could see in the narrowing of his eyes and how he leaned away from her that she had touched some kind of nerve.

"And she told me that Sasa Fitore and Jenna Quinn were lovers."

"That's bullshit. You got bad information from a messed-up girl."

"If she was so messed up, so unreliable, what was she doing for you?"

He blinked slowly and looked at Lydia with dark brown eyes that revealed nothing. He was silent for a second, her words hanging in the air between them. I win, thought Lydia.

"Look," he said, softening, changing tack. "I know you guys are looking for Tatiana. And I respect that. I have a daughter, too. And believe me, I hope that the little girl is all right. But I need you to *trust* me here, Lydia. You need to back away and leave me to do my job. Sasa Fitore has *nothing* to do with Tatiana Quinn."

"How do you know that?"

"I'm going to say it one more time," said Bentley. "This is your last warning."

"I've been hearing that a lot tonight."

He sighed and looked away from her, rubbing his eyes. She could sense his frustration with her. He was hiding something, but she couldn't imagine why or what. She just couldn't bring herself to believe that there was no connection between the two cases, as much as she wanted to. The buzz told her they were on the right trail; if they weren't, there wouldn't be so many people trying to get them to back off.

"What else did she tell you?" he asked, his tone quiet, exasperated.

She gave him a rundown of their conversation. She did not reveal that she had the DVD in her bag, which she had managed to hold on to during everything. She really had no choice but to repeat the things that Marianna had said, and eventually she would probably turn the film over to them as well, but not before she had a chance to look at it herself. If she gave it to them now, she might never know what was on it.

Meanwhile, she struggled to put out of her mind the fact that she was partly responsible for two deaths in four days' time, that she had watched two women die in front of her. Just another reminder that people die in horrible ways every day and that there was nothing she could do about it. The hunt for Tatiana had already cost in flesh and blood, and the bill hadn't even been totaled yet. Lydia felt numb.

"There's no reason to be afraid."

A nervous giggle sounded offscreen. Then came the heavily accented words of a young girl, her fear palpable: "I don't want to take my clothes off. You never said that."

"Why not? You're not ashamed of your body, are you? You're beautiful. You're so beautiful." The man's voice was deep and soothing, gently coaxing.

"I'm not."

"Oh, you are. Come here."

The camera was trained on a bed of red satin pillows. The voices had been offscreen, but finally a man whose face had been blanked out in postproduction led a young girl dressed in an elaborate red lace bustier with matching panties and garter into focus. He held her hand gently as she positioned herself on the cushions. She was thin and pale and had limp blond hair and a sweet, full face. Too young for the lingerie she wore, barely filling it.

"Now lie back."

She did as she was told. "You are going to be the most famous Victoria's Secret model ever. When this issue comes out, your career is going to skyrocket."

"Skyrocket, yes," she repeated softly.

"You'll have lots of money, live in a beautiful house."

"With a pool?"

"Anything you want," he said, the slightest hint of impatience creeping into the practiced veneer of his smooth and seductive voice. "You just have to do what I say. Now close your eyes and get comfortable."

The girl stared uneasily at the camera, or the man behind it, seeming to detect the change in his tone, but she closed her eyes.

"Now, touch yourself."

She opened her eyes a bit, then started to touch one of her thighs tentatively.

"Not there," he snapped.

"Where, Sasa?" she asked, genuinely confused, fear starting to warp the features of her face.

Lydia paused the DVD. "Did you hear that?" Jeffrey nodded, then restarted it.

It was then that two large men in leather masks stepped into view, one on either side of the girl. The girl's face dissolved into tears as she scrambled to all fours and began crawling away. A tiny yelp escaped her as she was pulled back by one of the men, naked except for tight black briefs.

Lydia reached out to pause the DVD player on her laptop and the image, in all its horror, froze on the screen, dominated by the girl's terrified face. Lydia lowered her head into her hands. The blood rushed in her ears, and anxiety made her throat dry and tight. Jeffrey had turned away from the screen, as well.

"We have to watch it," Lydia said after a minute, and pressed the play icon on her computer screen.

One of the men produced a syringe and stuck it into the girl's arm, causing her to shriek. It was the last sound she made for a while. She went limp after a moment but was still conscious, moving her limbs slowly, slapping weakly at the men as they raped her repeatedly. She was like a half-conscious rag doll, trapped in misery and horror, unable to fight as they moaned and roared over her. Then she started to cry, deep, rasping sobs that would have been screams if she'd had any strength. When the men had each ejaculated on her small body, her cheap negligee ripped and lying next to her, they waited, pacing.

"Wait until she's a little more lively," said another voice from offscreen. They hadn't heard this voice before on the tape, but they recognized it.

"Let's get a fresh one," came a muffled suggestion from behind one of the masks.

"You only paid for one, gentlemen," said the voice sternly. "And there are other patrons waiting their turn this evening."

"But this one didn't have enough fight in her," complained the masked figure.

"If you want to discuss this, let's turn off the camera."

The screen went blue for a minute, and Lydia was hopeful that it was over. But in a second, a horrible wail, the sound of unspeakable pain and terror, jarred Lydia and Jeffrey, both of them jumping. One of the men held what looked like a Taser gun and was sticking the girl with it as she tried to crawl away from him on the floor. The screen fluttered and then suddenly the girl was back on the bed, her arms and legs spread wide and tied to posts that hadn't been there before. She had stopped screaming, and her head lolled back and forth as she mumbled something in another language that had the measured rhythm of a prayer or a nursery rhyme.

Lydia put her head back in her hands, unable to watch as the men proceeded to burn her with cigarettes. The screaming started again, this time weaker, more desperate wails.

Jeffrey distracted himself by examining the men, looking for identifying marks. Both of them wore matching thick gold rings on their right hands, though he couldn't make out the insignia, and they both wore gold wedding bands on their left. The heavier man had a tattoo on his left forearm that had been blacked out in postproduction. The thinner man, with a mass of gray hair on his chest, had a large black mole on his right shoulder blade. Jeffrey had ceased to *see* the video, despite paying attention to every detail. It was a skill he had learned when he'd hunted a child murderer in New York, the case that had ended on a darkened rooftop in the Bronx, with Jeffrey taking the only bullet of his career. The crime scenes had been heart-wrenching, little boys murdered and violated in ways he chose to block from the personal memory of his life. But professionally, he remembered every detail. You had to be like that in this business; otherwise, the demons ate your life whole.

He looked over at Lydia, who had raised her head from her hands and wore an expression of horror. In the light of the screen, her face was pale, and dark circles shadowed her eyes.

"Wait," she said, reaching over to the laptop and pausing it. "Look at their right hands."

"The rings? I noticed them."

"Is that the same ring Nathan Quinn was wearing?"

"It's hard to tell," said Jeffrey, reaching over to freeze the image and zooming in on one of the rings. The image was fuzzy and the features of the ring hard to distinguish.

"I wouldn't rule it out," said Jeffrey.

"I think it is. . . . Look," she said, putting her finger on the screen. "You can see the scroll and the letters, and the shape of the sword."

"It could be," said Jeff, zooming out and pressing play.

When the DVD started again, the screaming grew louder. They watched as the heavier man opened the girl's tiny body with a serrated knife. Jeffrey managed to turn it off again quickly, but not before the blood began to rush from the wound.

Lydia got up and ran to the bathroom, her two-day battle with nausea finally lost. When she returned, her eyes were red and she sat on the chair across from the bed. They locked eyes.

"What the fuck was that?" asked Lydia, coughing weakly.

"That was one of the snuff films Detective Ignacio was talking about. He was right," said Jeffrey.

"Was it real?" asked Lydia. "Could it have been fake?"

"It looked real. I've never seen anything like that. The camera work was pretty unsophisticated; the angle never shifted. It felt real."

Even when Manny had suggested the possibility after Valentina had been killed, Jeffrey hadn't quite believed it. The FBI had always denied that snuff films were real, just as Agent Bentley had said earlier, had always claimed that there was no market for them, that no one had ever actually seen one, and that there was no way to distribute them without someone getting caught. There was little question that what they had just seen was real. Furthermore, Jeffrey realized that the market was a closed one. The target group was not just the people who wanted to *see* snuff but also the men who wanted to *make* snuff. Maybe that was why it had been impossible to prove, until now. Suddenly, what Marianna had told Lydia didn't seem so far-fetched.

And now that they had seen the film, there was no turning back.

"Is that what happened to Tatiana?" Lydia asked, thinking aloud.

"I don't know. I don't think so."

"Why not?"

"Because that voice, the second offscreen voice, the one doing the negotiating?"

"It was Nathan Quinn."

"I'd bet money on it."

"And the other voice, the director—the girl called him Sasa."

"Sasa Fitore."

"So Sasa Fitore is making films with Nathan Quinn. Arranging for Quinn's wealthy contacts to get into the act?" asked Lydia.

"And then probably arranging for closed viewings of the DVD for the men who'd rather watch than do the deed," said Jeffrey.

"Meanwhile, Sasa Fitore is fucking Jenna Quinn on the side."

"Things could get very messy."

"And we're still no closer to finding out what happened to Tatiana."

Lydia went over to the minibar and extracted two tiny bottles of Absolut and two of Perrier. She poured them each a cocktail, then stepped out onto the balcony. She took the salt air into her lungs. The large yellow moon hung over the rolling ocean in a sky brilliant with stars; the palms fluttered lazily in the slight breeze. Nature, as usual, was oblivious to evil. She chose to take that as a sign, a sign that while man was prone to evil acts, the universe was good; that there was a benevolent God, hoping for the best even in the darkest moments, balancing sin with miracle, and demons with angels.

Jeffrey walked out and placed an arm around her shoulder; she moved into him, wrapping her arms around his waist. She looked up at him and he kissed her gently. They had reached their threshold that evening for witnessing human suffering. But tomorrow was a new day.

part two

But the darkness pulls in everything:
shapes and fires, animals and myself,
how easily it gathers them!
powers and people—

—RAINER MARIA RILKE

She had made such a mess of her life. And it wasn't the first time or even the second. Nothing had happened the way they promised her it would. She was ashamed of herself for ever believing that it would be different. No one had ever been honest with her except for Radovan, and he was gone. She felt small and cold inside.

The room was dim, candles burning down low on the dresser, and the hour late—or early, depending on how you looked at it. She could hear him breathing deeply, sound asleep. How he slept at night, she didn't know, with all that blood on his hands. She wasn't nearly as guilty, and yet she hadn't slept in months. His heart was a black, dead place, and she hadn't seen that until it was too late. Wasn't that always the way with men—they seemed like a savior until they had you bound and gagged. Then the mask came off and you were stuck with a monster.

She slid out from beneath the cotton and down covers of the king-size bed and walked over to the mirror above the French wood dresser. Lighted from below by the candles, she looked like a hag, with deep black circles and wrinkles etched around her eyes and mouth, the skin loose and pasty. The candlelight illuminated the stray wisps of her hair, and she fought back tears. Her beauty was one of her only commodities, and it was fading fast. Not that, if she was honest with herself, it had ever proved much of an asset. For her or for Tatiana. Beauty had always been her biggest problem.

That and a weak heart. But Tatiana was strong, unlike her mother. She wouldn't grow up to be the pawn in the ugly, dirty games of men. If Jenna could get the two of them out of this new mess she'd gotten them into, there would be no more men. They'd make it on their own somewhere. Women did that in the world; it wasn't like Albania, where you were little more than a whore and a maid your whole life. They'd have plenty of money when the deal was done. Somehow, they'd make it right, where the money had come from; somehow they would find a way to remove the stain. She pushed the thoughts from her head. It was better not to think on it, on what she had become to save her daughter and herself.

"What are you doing?" he said from the bed, his voice sleepy and impatient.

"I can't sleep," she said, her voice taking on the soft and apologetic tone she always used with him. It was the voice her mother had used with her father.

"You worry too much," he said. "You don't trust me?"

"Of course I do, darling," she said, walking over to him and placing a hand on his face. He grabbed her wrist.

"But?"

"It's just that I wonder whom *we* can trust." He released her arm and she sat down on the bed beside him. He touched her breast beneath the cream silk nightgown she wore, and she tried not to shrink away.

"That's what you don't understand." His voice took on the smug and condescending tone so typical of men like him. "We don't have to trust anyone, because we're in control of all of this. We have what everyone wants."

"What do we have, Sasa?"

"Information."

She was starting to suspect that Sasa Fitore was an idiot. She nodded. "You're right, of course," she said sweetly. "But that detective. He found out about your association with Nathan. And now the other two. What if they find out about American Equities and American Beauty?"

"I told you. You worry too much. The detective won't be sharing any more information with anyone."

"You didn't . . ."

"Don't worry about what I did and didn't do," he said, getting angry now. He sat up on his elbows, his blue eyes blazing and his blond hair falling onto his forehead. He had the Byzantine double-headed eagle of the Albanian flag tattooed in black on his chest.

His cell phone rang on the dresser, and she got up quickly to get it for him, eager to have an excuse to move away from him. Since first Valentina had been killed and then tonight Marianna, she could barely stand to have his hands on her. He hadn't grieved a moment or shed a tear for his sister or his niece. "They betrayed us," he'd said to her. And in that statement was an explicit warning to her. She was more afraid of him now than she'd ever been of Nathan Quinn. At least, she thought, they didn't betray themselves.

"What?" he said into the phone. "All right."

"Listen," he said to her as he got out of bed and hung up the phone. "You just handle your end of this and I'll handle mine. In the end, everyone will be fucked except for you and me. And we'll be laughing about this in Rio, yes?"

He took her face in his hands and she nodded, feeling tiny and powerless with him so close and so strong.

"Good," he said, kissing her on the forehead like a child. "Now, go home before you're missed."

"Nathan's in New York, looking for Tatiana."

Sasa laughed at how well that element of everything had worked out. They'd confused the hell out of the police by sending Boris, having him pretend to be a Greyhound bus driver, and now every free moment Nathan Quinn had, he went to New York to look for his precious Tatiana. As if only *he* could find her in that sea of junkies and prostitutes. If only Nathan knew how much the girl hated him. All the money and all the powerful men he had at his disposal weren't going to change that for him. Not that the little bitch cared much for Sasa, either. He'd seen the way she looked at him when she thought he didn't see. If he didn't know better, he'd think there was murder in her eyes sometimes.

"Where are you going?" she asked as he pulled on a pair of Calvin Klein jeans and a black ribbed sweater. He checked out his impressive physique in the mirror as he dressed, liking the way the candlelight accentuated the cuts of his muscles.

"I have one more thing to take care of before we leave," he said, pulling on a pair of work boots.

She hurried to get dressed so that she could leave with him. She didn't want to be alone in the house where Valentina and Marianna had lived. She couldn't bear to face their ghosts alone.

chapter twenty-one

Cities that weren't New York always seemed like they were faking it. When you were in New York, whether it was the elegance of Park Avenue, the seedy cool of the East Village, the ultrachic shops and cafés in Soho, there was no mistaking where you were. The smells: the sweet warm scent of honey-roasted nuts and pretzels from the street vendors' carts, the acrid stink of urine in the subway on a hot day. The sounds: the cacophony of car horns, the wail of sirens, homeless people arguing with their loud, slurred voices. The stately buildings: the elegance of Grand Central, the Deco Chrysler Building, even the run-down, abandoned structures of Alphabet City were distinguishable from any other place on earth. When Lydia visited another city, she always felt like she was waiting for it to reveal a personality, some little quirk of individuality that identified its character. But in America, she was almost always disappointed. Even San Francisco, which most New Yorkers agreed was acceptable, just seemed like a loosely connected group of passably cool neighborhoods.

Lydia had heard people describe Miami as New York City on the beach. But from what she'd seen, most of the city possessed the hard edge of the urban condition but little of the sophistication. South Beach was a party, no doubt, and the beach was gorgeous, but the rest of the area was a collection of opulent burbs scattered about but separate from the massive highways passing through run-down neighborhoods with poorly kept streets. Parts of it just looked neglected to Lydia. But there was definitely no shortage of good coffee. Which was hugely important. Especially at 4:30 A.M., as she and Jeffrey sat in their rented Jeep outside the Fitore residence.

Sleep is like a cat. It doesn't come when it's called, only when it wants to. It didn't want anything from Lydia and Jeffrey as they had lain wide-eyed in the darkness, staring at the ceiling fan, an eerie glow from the yellow moon washing the room.

"The detail that continues to bother me is the surveillance camera," Jeffrey said suddenly after an hour of silence in which they'd both tried to sleep and failed.

"That's the detail that continues to bother you?" said Lydia, still struggling with the images that played over and over in her mind: Valentina hitting the grill of the Mercedes; Marianna dying on the dance floor of the G-Spot; the nameless pale wisp of a girl being repeatedly raped by men in black leather masks. Every time Lydia closed her eyes, she was assailed by these images. She had seen too much death in her life. She wondered, not for the first time, if she was some kind of cosmic magnet for mayhem, if it was her fate, and not just her choice, to chase the evil of the world and bear witness to its deeds.

"There were no fingerprints on the inside touch pad; it had been wiped clean. The outside pad had only Nathan Quinn's fingerprints on it, which means that it had also been wiped clean before the Quinns came home. So that means that someone came in from the outside, from the front door. Otherwise, they wouldn't have bothered wiping down the outside pad and doorknob."

"Okay . . ."

"But the camera would have had to have been turned off from the inside; otherwise, it would have captured at least a second of the person entering the house, or the intruder would have worn a mask, or spray-painted the lens in order to avoid being identified later."

"So whoever entered wanted it to *look* like Tatiana had run away? Which rules out a kidnapping for ransom, or for some threat to the Quinns."

"But they didn't realize that Tatiana didn't know how to operate the camera. Or it was just a detail they overlooked."

"Or she did know how. *Somebody* turned off the camera from the inside of the house and then let the intruder in."

"Maybe she wasn't alone in the house."

"But no one else entered after the Quinns left that night. The security system was armed, and there were cameras all over the property, not just on the front door."

"Right, but it was only armed when the Quinns left. What if someone entered the house *before* they left."

"Valentina left early that night, but we never found out why."

"Maybe so that Jenna had time to let someone in."

"Sasa."

"Maybe." Jeffrey shrugged. "But the question is, Why? Why would Jenna arrange for the abduction of her own daughter? And why would Sasa participate?"

Lydia remembered Sasa at his sister's memorial service. She recalled the way he had reached his hand into the open car window as if caressing someone's cheek. Another strand tangled in the knot of this investigation.

"How are we going to find out the answers to these questions when everyone who will talk to us ends up dead, and everyone else tells us to walk away?" Lydia asked the ceiling fan.

"Maybe we just need to be a little more subtle. Let's take a ride."

Craig didn't seem in the least surprised or sleepy when he answered the phone at 4:00 A.M. He was not, however, happy that Lydia again asked him to go to the street and call her back from a pay phone, but he did it anyway. She sat in the Jeep, parked directly next to the phone, close enough to reach it from the driver's seat, and watched

Jeffrey through the plate-glass window of the twenty-four-hour Kinko's. He leaned over the counter, smiling and saying something to the young Hispanic girl who worked the desk, and Lydia saw her smile back. Lydia watched as the girl reached into the drawer and pulled out a set of keys. "Okay, come on," Lydia read on her lips. The girl led Jeffrey over to the darkened computer center and took a seat. A few seconds later, one of the screens turned blue. She got up and Jeffrey sat down. From where Lydia sat, she could see the back of his head. He was burning the DVD they had watched, then would put the copy in a FedEx envelope to be mailed back to the office in New York, same business-day delivery. They both agreed they needed a copy sent away in case anything happened to them. They also agreed, after what they had seen yesterday, that neither one of them was willing to walk away, no matter what the cost. There were just some things that could not be ignored; some things the very knowledge of which changed the world for the worse. And neither one of them was willing to live in that world until they had changed it back to the way it should be. She was edgy and suddenly tired, of course, now that sleep was nowhere in her future. Lydia sat there, zoning out on the orange-and-green glowing gauges on the dash. She was reasonably sure they hadn't been followed. She glanced around her and lighted a cigarette, trying to keep it out the window. She looked for the black Mercedes, carrying menacing Eastern European men with guns. When the phone in the booth rang, she jumped, feeling a burst of adrenaline.

"This is the last time I'm doing this. It's fucking freezing out here," said Craig on the other end of the line. She could hear the street noise behind him.

"I know, I know. What's up?"

He paused. "I think it's big. But I'll just give you the facts; you make the connections. The first thing is that Nathan Quinn is supposedly a power player on the Council."

"What's that?"

"Well, ostensibly, it's an organization of world leaders in government, business, science, the media, what have you. They get together to talk about global issues. It's *supposedly* this kind of benevolent forum for great minds to discuss and decide the pressing issues of the world."

"But . . . ?"

"There *are* some conspiracy theorists who believe that these men control the fate of the free world, that they are the Establishment with a capital *E*. That all the governments of the world are their pawns, and that the decisions that are reached during their very secret meetings affect global policy—everything from who goes to war with whom, who imports or exports what, which economies collapse or flourish."

A blossom of dread opened in her stomach as Marianna's words come back to her in a flood: "There are men who run the world . . . devils with ravenous appetites. . . . When you play that DVD, you'll see them as they truly are."

"Oh God," she said.

"When I hacked into the CIA database, because, you know, they have files on all those guys—I mean, a source I have told me that all of Quinn's CIA files are sealed. They are megaclassified, like basically only the president will ever have access to anything in there. And maybe not even him."

She'd heard about organizations like the Council, sort of in the periphery of her consciousness, but she'd never really given much thought to the idea of a secret society of powerful men controlling the world. She had always been too busy with real and immediate demons, those brandishing weapons or living in her head. But it did make a sick kind of sense, and she felt her stomach lurch. She thought about how she and Jeffrey had been followed, how their bags had been searched. She thought about how Detective Ignacio felt that he was being watched and how he had been "asked" to stop his queries into Nathan Quinn's business dealings. How Valentina and Marianna had been murdered before her eyes. A darkness gathered over the events, casting them in a shadow of malice. If all the separate elements of the case were really the machinations of one entity, then they might be wrestling a giant, and she wondered for the first time if they had a chance in hell of coming out on top. And whether Tatiana would be crushed in the struggle.

She sighed heavily into the phone.

"There's more," said Craig after giving her a moment to digest the information.

"Okay," she said, snapping back. "What else . . . what did you find out about Jenna Quinn?"

"Nathan and Jenna Quinn were married at the end of 1997. Her last name at the time was Mladic."

"As in Radovan Mladic?" asked Lydia, remembering the name of the mob boss who Craig said owned American Equities.

"The same; she was married to him. In fact, she was and still is the co-owner of American Equities."

"The company still exists?"

"It still exists in Albania, but I have no idea what it does. Nobody seems to, not the International Business Network for World e-Commerce and Industry or the International Trade Commission. It's listed in the IBN as an importing/exporting company. But there is no information regarding the product. It's almost like they're hiding in plain sight."

"Is there an address or phone number in Albania?"

"Yeah. But no Web site. Do you have a pen?"

She pulled her giant leather day planner, worn and overstuffed with receipts, notes, and addresses, from her bag and a yellow Post-it fluttered to the floor of the Jeep like a butterfly.

"Go ahead," she said, prepared to write the information down.

"What about Nathan Quinn? Does he hold an interest in the company?" she asked after he had given her the information.

"If he does, it's not on his books. The next time you see Nathan

Quinn, you should tell him that Quinn Enterprises needs some work on their fire wall. And that their CFO's password is *IQUIT*."

"What about her assets?"

"Well, Jenna *Quinn* doesn't have two nickels to rub together. She and Tatiana are both U.S. citizens, which, if you know anything about immigration, takes years and years for most people, even if they're married to an American. But in the Quinns' case, the sea of red tape seems to have parted. Must be one of the perks of being a member of the Council. They were both citizens by the end of 1998. Jenna Quinn doesn't even have a credit rating. Jenna *Mladic*, on the other hand . . ." He paused dramatically.

"What?"

"I don't have figures—it's hard to get that information from other countries without accounts and passwords, even for me. But she has accounts at a bank in Albania and, so far, one other in the Cayman Islands. Active accounts, with regular deposits and withdrawals. That much I know."

She remembered what Detective Ignacio had said about seeing where the money led them, and she wondered if he had followed it this far or further. And what—or whom—he had found at the end of the trail that had frightened him.

"I didn't think they had banks in Albania after the crash."

"Well, it's what international bankers like to call an 'emerging' market."

"What does that mean?"

"It means that other foreign companies or governments will establish banks in struggling economies, ostensibly as a kind of foreign aid, to issue small business loans, grant credit to bolster a weak economy."

"But it also allows them control over who gets the money and what kind of businesses emerge?"

"Exactly."

"Sounds very 'conspiracy theory,' doesn't it? Wealthy investors, members of the Council, like Quinn, pump money into a Third World economy, investing heavily in the most promising business ventures, and in a generation, if all goes well, you own the ruling class of that country. If things go badly, like they did in Albania, you just walk away."

"It's no shit. This stuff is in play every single day, and most people are fast asleep, dreaming about working hard and making it big someday, thinking they live in a democracy. But really there are these shadowy figures controlling the money—who gets the small business loan, who gets the VC money. It can be spooky if you think about it."

"So do we know who established the bank?"

"Not yet."

"Where are her deposits coming from?"

"I don't know. All I know is that they come into the bank on the last Friday of every month. I do know that the bank is located in the same Albanian town as American Equities, a town called Vlorë."

"Are they wire transfers, or is someone coming in and depositing physical money into the account?"

"No idea. If it was an American bank, I could hack in, no problem. At least as far as getting account activity. But these Eastern European banks are funky; some of them aren't even on-line. . . . It's amazing. I'll keep trying, but I can't promise you anything. Maybe if I can get some hot Albanian chick on the phone who digs me, I'll get further," he said, and she could hear a smile creeping into his voice.

"Work it, tiger," she replied, charmed by his boyishness, as always, and for a second losing the heaviness that had settled in her heart and behind her eyes. "What about before Jenna married Mladic?"

"Don't know. Again, they don't keep the same kinds of records there as they do here. God bless America, the land of information technology. Otherwise, I'm a fish out of water."

She watched Jeffrey walk across the parking lot toward the Jeep. He was tall, broad-shouldered, and powerful and had a confident stride. He was her hero in a black cotton T-shirt, faded blue button-fly Levi's, and black motorcycle boots. Just looking at him sometimes infused her with confidence; with him on her team, she could face anything and win. She smiled, turning back to her conversation with Craig. "We're sending something to you. Keep it safe. Don't show anyone. Don't even open the package."

"No problem," he said with a yawn. "That's all I have for you, Lydia. And I'm fucking freezing, so I'm gonna go."

"Good work. We'll see you soon."

"Lydia?"

"Yeah."

"Be careful."

"You bet."

Jeffrey always settled in at a stakeout better than Lydia. He seemed to sink into the driver's seat, become one with the upholstery, his eyes opened only halfway but seeing everything. He was utterly calm, totally focused, perfectly still, and could stay that way for hours. Lydia fidgeted, scanning through radio stations, flipping through the pages of the Jeep Grand Cherokee driver's manual. They had the windows cracked for some air, but the engine was turned off, which meant that the humidity was raising sweat on her forehead and the back of her neck. They didn't speak. That was the other thing: Jeffrey didn't believe in speaking during stakeouts. Conversation diffused focus, might be overheard, was a waste of energy that needed to be concentrated on watching. This was one of the ways in which Jeffrey and Lydia differed in their investigative talents. Jeffrey got off on gathering evidence, following clues and leads, trailing suspects. He liked the hard, the cold, the what you could see, the trail of evidence that led to an undeniable truth. Lydia knew that the truth might leave only a scent on the wind, a footprint in the sand; it was her gift to follow energy, to intuit the volumes spoken by the furtive gesture, the thing left unsaid.

But the energy in this case was confused, shooting at her from a thousand different directions, its source unclear. She sensed multiple agendas from everyone—Nathan and Jenna Quinn, Special Agents Negron and Bentley. Marianna was high; how much of what she'd said was reliable? Lydia believed that Valentina might have told the truth if she'd had a chance. Lydia looked at the road. They were parked just feet from where Valentina's life had ended. She thought in the glimmer of sunrise that she could see the stain of her blood on the asphalt, but maybe it was just the shadows of the trees.

She mimicked Jeffrey, leaning back against the headrest, folding her arms across her chest. She measured her breathing and focused on the front door of the Fitore home.

She felt the now-familiar nausea creep back up on her, and felt a finger of pain poke her abdomen.

She was about to break Jeffrey's rule of speaking during the stakeout when he sat up suddenly. The garage door opened a second later, and the Boxster roared out, followed by a white Mercedes. The Mercedes turned left and rolled past them, and as it did, Lydia saw Jenna Quinn at the wheel. "Well, well," said Lydia.

"Which one should we follow?" asked Jeff.

"The Boxster, definitely."

They trailed behind about a hundred feet, letting a black Toyota with a Garfield suctioned to the rear windshield and a red Geo with vanity plates that read KISS ME pass in front of them. The Boxster moved slowly, obeying the thirty-five-mile-an-hour speed limit on the quiet residential street, then sped up as he turned onto Sunrise Boulevard. Though the sun had just debuted over the horizon, there were plenty of cars making their way onto I-95 South, enough so they didn't stand out as they followed Sasa up the ramp. It was still dark enough that most cars had on their headlights, which gave them a bit of an advantage. But a glance in the rearview mirror was all it took for Jeffrey to realize that they were not alone. A bright yellow Ryder truck trailed four cars back, the same one he had seen parked on Sasa's block.

They headed south on the highway under high concrete overpasses that twisted around one another and reminded Lydia of the skyways on *The Jetsons,* that sort of fifties vision of what the future might look like. As they drove, the affluent suburbs and brightly colored minimalls featuring Chi-Chi's and Big K's fell away, replaced by flat gray buildings and small run-down houses. Sasa exited the highway, and they followed. Jeffrey looked in the rearview mirror and no longer saw the Ryder truck behind them. But somehow, that didn't make him feel any better; he was on edge as they drove through what looked to be the worst neighborhood in Miami. They passed burned-out buildings with darkened figures hovering in doorways; a thin prostitute preened and strutted on a corner, her red hair matted and filthy, the lines on her arms barely concealed by a tattered black shirt, her smile forced and desperate. Lydia tried to keep the pity off her face as they drove past her. A young pregnant woman in blue overalls walked slowly down the street, wheeling a shopping cart and smoking a cigarette. Most of the shops and restaurants were gated, not open yet, except for a coffee shop and a newspaper stand. Lydia noted that the liquor store was also open for business. They moved deeper into the neighborhood, trying to stay as far back as possible without losing Sasa. When he finally slowed and parked the car in front of what looked to be an abandoned building on a deserted block, they slowed and pulled over before turning the corner. Lydia removed her gun from her bag, shoved the bag in the backseat and the gun at her waist. If she had learned anything over the last few days, it was to keep the gun where she could reach it in a hurry. She flashed for a moment on the last time she had fired her Glock; she could still smell the smoke and see the madman's eyes, hear him struggle to breathe with a broken nose and the Glock in his mouth. She shuddered inside, as if someone had walked over her grave.

They got out of the Jeep, and Lydia looked at it as though they might never see it again, though there was no sign of life on the street, and the only sound was that of the cars speeding down the highway off in the distance.

"Stay close and no hotdogging," warned Jeffrey.

"'Hotdogging'?" said Lydia with a glare. "I really resent that you—"

He lifted a finger to his mouth, a gesture that Lydia found unspeakably annoying and condescending. But she held her tongue, inwardly vowing to make him pay later. She wore tight black jeans and a loose black Ralph Lauren motocross shirt over the gun at her waist. The metal was hard and cold, the muzzle poking her uncomfortably in the belly, but it felt good to be reminded it was there. Her well-loved Calvin Klein motorcycle ankle boots were made of soft black leather and had tough, flexible soles, good for fighting—and running, if it came to that.

As they walked toward the Boxster, now parked and empty, the neighborhood reminded her of Manhattan's meatpacking district at night because of its look of abandoned industry, grimy, with too many doorways and dark places for someone to hide. A rat skittered in front of her feet, and if she hadn't been a native New Yorker, she might have shrieked. She might have anyway, had she not been more concerned with the attention she would draw. Jeffrey looked back at her as the gigantic rat made its way down the street. "New York rats kick the asses of Miami rats," he whispered with a smile. She hoped he was right.

They walked up a short, narrow flight of concrete steps to a faded red metal door that was ajar. In fact, it looked as though it had been pried open with a crowbar more than once in the past. It was scratched and dented, but the lock looked new. Since it was the only door in sight, Jeffrey considered it a good bet that Sasa had entered there. But still, there was something about the whole scenario that had him tense and watching their backs. The Ryder truck was nowhere to be seen, and Jeffrey wondered whether it had been following them after all.

"This is a little too easy," whispered Lydia, echoing his feelings.

He nodded but pushed the door open slowly. It led to a long, dark staircase. They exchanged a look, Jeffrey shrugged, and they began to climb, guns drawn. They kept their backs partially to the wall, Lydia keeping one eye behind them, and crept along the side of the stairs, hoping to minimize creaking. They both heard the muffled voice of an angry man above them behind a closed door. The closer they got, the less light carried from the open door beneath them. It was almost pitch-black by the time they reached the top.

"She leaves for Albania tomorrow," the voice said behind the closed door. It was the voice they'd heard on the DVD—no doubt about it, given the way Lydia's stomach hollowed out at the sound of it. "We need to be in Vlorë by tomorrow and ready to roll. There's no time to waste. Once he finds out what we've done, there won't be a place in the world we can run to. But by Monday, American Equities and American Beauty won't even exist anymore. . . . We won't exist. And Nathan Quinn will be left holding his dick."

There was a pause and then the man said, "Okay," exhaling heavily. They heard him hang up the phone, and then silence again. Jeffrey flicked the safety off his Glock, preparing for Sasa to burst through the door. Lydia and Jeffrey looked at each other, barely able to make out each other's faces in the dark. But they heard him walk off over hardwood floors and a door slam, then quiet. They waited a minute before moving in slowly.

Lydia suppressed a groan as she recognized the room from the DVD they had watched. It was a huge loft space with high opaque windows, dirty wood floors, and gray walls. Supporting columns stood like soldiers in the dim light. She noticed the bed, which had been stripped of its red satin sheets and pillows, sat atop a number of overlapping tarps, in front of a white screen. She didn't want to walk over to inspect the area, but she did anyway. Everything smelled of bleach, as though it had been scoured. She wondered how much death and horror this room had seen, trying not to hear the screams echoing off the walls, worming their way into the floorboards, living in the stale air.

Before she knew what was happening, Jeffrey grabbed her from behind and pulled her over in back of the screen behind the bed. In a few seconds, she heard footsteps; a door opened and closed. She often wondered how Jeffrey always heard things a few seconds before she did. She figured it was because she was always inside her own head, making connections, feeling energies. He was always paying attention to the physical, the external, watching the road signs. They stood still, occupying one space as he stood behind her, pressed against the wall, holding her around the waist. Their breathing was shallow as someone paced back and forth. She hated not being able to see. But the door slammed again. They heard a lock turn, footfalls down the stairs, and they stood still for a few seconds in the silence. Then they heard the Boxster's engine rev to life downstairs.

Lydia slowly peered around the screen and saw that the room was empty.

"I know where we are. I know what this is," she whispered.

He nodded, "This is the room from the video."

"Yeah," she agreed. "The Miami offices of American Equities."

chapter twenty-two

The different elements of their investigation seemed strange and disjointed; each facet made the picture less clear, the light more diffuse. Each lead seemed, in fact, to take them *away* from Tatiana. But after her conversation with Craig, a form began to appear through the fog for Lydia. Jeffrey raised his eyebrows at what she said and seemed to process the possibilities, still staying quiet because he wasn't sure where they were or if they were alone. He walked over to the other door, which led, it turned out, to an office.

The room smelled of stale cigarette smoke. Furnished with a metal and faux-wood desk and accompanying swivel chair, a three-drawer filing cabinet, and a green plastic chair that reminded Lydia of high school cafeterias, it was the most generic of offices. Sitting on the desk were a blank blotter, a pen cup holding several orange Bic pens, a digital clock, and a halogen lamp beside a decorative box of tissues. It struck Lydia as odd that men who raped and murdered young women might find need for something as clean and innocent as a Kleenex.

Lydia sat down at the desk while Jeffrey stood at the door, leaving it open a crack, peering out into the other room. Since there was no door other than the one through which they'd entered, if someone came up the staircase, they were going to have to talk or shoot their way out.

"What makes you say it's the Equities office?" asked Jeffrey, still keeping his voice low.

"I don't know," she said slowly, running her fingers under the surface of the desk, looking for bugs. She didn't have much hope that a snuff-film production company would keep good records, but she started rifling through drawers. "There's no computer and no telephone," commented Lydia.

"And no camera equipment out in the other room."

The desk drawers were empty, so Lydia moved over to the filing cabinet. Oddly, the drawers were all opened slightly and filled with files.

She smiled at her luck. But then as she started flipping through the file folders, her smile faded. Each folder, marked with a white tab hand-scrawled with a woman's name, contained a badly shot picture of a naked woman. Attempting to look sexy and seductive, they instead looked cheap and used, afraid. Along with the photos in each file were vital statistics, copies of their passports, all from Albania, and what looked to be a printout from a Web site page. It featured a poor-quality scan of the photo, the vital statistics, likes and dislikes, and the girl's name, different from the one on the file, changed to names like Candy, Brandy, Brittany. The company name at the top of the Web page read: AMERICAN BEAUTY, below which was a disclaimer about American Beauty being a modeling agency and that there was no implication intended that these girls would perform any service other than modeling. She noticed that some of the files had been reused; one name had been scratched out and written over with another. She had an idea of what had happened to the others before their files had been recycled. Lydia noted that there was no phone number to call and that the Web address was not printed anywhere.

"Jeffrey, you have to see this," she said. He left the door reluctantly, walked behind her, and looked over her shoulder.

"Grab one of those folders and let's get out of here," he said, returning to his post.

"Wait a minute."

"Hurry up, Lydia. We've been here too long already."

She flipped through the files, looking for a picture of the girl they had watched murdered on the DVD last night, or, worse, for a picture of Tatiana, but she found neither. She took a random folder, laid it on the floor, and opened the next drawer. There she found some stationery with the American Beauty letterhead lying in a box on the bottom. It took a second before she noticed the small print on the bottom that read: "A subsidiary of American Equities." She grabbed a sheet. "Jackpot," she said, opening the final drawer. Inside was an At-A-Glance date book. She opened it and flipped through the pages. On the first Saturday of each month, someone had written "Vlorë" and a time, "Italy" and a time, a number ranging from forty to seventy, and a dollar figure. Lydia had no idea what she was looking at, but she knew it was important. She grabbed everything and moved to the door.

"Let's get out of here," she said, feeling a sharp edge of excitement and a nervous energy that told her it was time to go.

"Do you smell that?" asked Jeffrey, shoving the file and date book under his shirt and into the waistband of his jeans as they walked toward the door through which they had entered the loft space. Lydia sniffed.

"It smells like . . ."

"Gasoline."

A puddle began to spread from the crack under the door and they heard heavy footsteps retreating quickly down the staircase outside. And in the same second that flames licked in from under the door in a hot whisper, Jeffrey pulled them out of the way.

"Shit," he said as they looked around them for a way out. They ran to the other end of the space, heading toward a large, heavy opaque window that looked as though it hadn't been opened in a decade. They each took a handle and tried to lift it, but it had been painted shut.

"Stand back," Jeffrey said as he aimed his gun at the glass. In three shots, it had completely shattered, leaving sharp teeth of glass in the edges and revealing a five-foot drop onto a tin roof beneath. As Jeffrey hopped up on the sill and kicked out the rest of the glass on the bottom of the frame, he caught sight of the rear end of the Boxster, followed by the Ryder truck, both speeding up the street. The flames were spreading across the room in what appeared to be a straight line and were licking at the door to the office where they had just been. Jeffrey reached a hand down to Lydia and helped pull her up on the sill and then hopped down to the tin roof outside.

"Be careful. Don't cut yourself," he said just as a stalactite of glass sliced through her shirt and tore a gash in her shoulder. Her adrenaline pumping, she barely felt it, but she saw the blood trail out from under her cuff and run down the back of her white hand. They stuck close to a wall to the right of the window and edged down the slight slope, smoke billowing out the window behind them. In front of her, Jeffrey held out his arm to keep her back. "Let me make sure there's no one on the street before we jump down."

"Jump down?"

"Maybe I could just whistle for the Jeep and it'll come galloping over to the rescue."

"Just like Knight Rider."

"Exactly."

Jeffrey scanned the block. Unless someone was hiding in a doorway or behind a Dumpster, which seemed highly possible, he saw no one. They had no choice but to go for it and hope someone wasn't waiting for them when they hit the ground. He would kick himself later for walking into such an obvious trap, but right now he just wanted to get them out alive. "I'm going to go down first," he said. "Watch the street. Make sure no one shoots me in the back while I'm dangling from the gutter."

"Great," Lydia replied, sarcasm being her weapon against mortal fear. She drew her gun and gazed uneasily back and forth up the deserted street, looking for moving shadows, remembering that she was a lousy shot. When she heard Jeffrey's feet hit the ground, she lay down on her belly and peered over the side.

"Just turn around, drop your feet over the side, and lower yourself down, holding on to the gutter. Keep your knees soft when you land," he said, looking around him.

"Okay, Mr. One Hundred Pull-ups a Day."

She lowered herself slowly, muscles burning, her arms starting to shake almost immediately. When she felt his fingertips brush her thighs, she tried to lower herself a little farther but lost her strength and fell the rest of the way, tumbling on top of Jeffrey. He bore the impact of her weight with a groan as they hit the ground hard.

"That went well," he croaked. They both stood and dusted themselves off, breathing heavily, Lydia coughing from the smoke and the effort. They could see the flames through the window he had shot out above them. And when they heard sirens wailing in the distance, they bolted for the Jeep.

chapter twenty-three

The back of the limousine was cold and the company was even colder. Mr. Harriman was revolted by and a little afraid of Jed, and Jed could sense it. And to be honest, he was a little insulted by the lawyer's attitude. He had conducted himself with professionalism during their entire encounter. He certainly was smarter than to bite the hand that feeds. Still, when Jed had climbed into the back of the limo and extended his hand to Harriman, the man looked at Jed as if he were offering a pile of excrement.

"Let's not pretend we're friends, shall we?" he'd said, glaring over the small gold rims of his spectacles.

They had left a beautiful set of clothes for him at the hospital to change into upon his release. Very nice faded blue jeans from the Gap, a warm navy cotton turtleneck with coordinating plaid flannel shirt, a brand-new pair of Timberland work boots and wool socks, and an oxide gray REI parka with a detachable fleece lining. And there was a large duffel bag of new clothes waiting for him in the limo, as well as a case containing more sophisticated surveillance equipment than he'd ever seen—high-powered binoculars and telescope, night-vision goggles, and some other items, including a large hunting knife. He hadn't been able to identify everything in the quick glance he'd been offered as Harriman ran down the catalog of items to be left with him.

"My client believes in giving his employees the freedom of their . . . uh . . . talents," said Harriman. "So naturally, we leave you to your own devices. Lining your duffel bag, in addition to the new clothes, you'll find one hundred thousand dollars in small unmarked bills. When this money is gone, you're on your own, so I suggest you make it last. Obviously, I have not revealed to you my true name or the name of my client . . . so don't come looking for me. I'll remind you again that if you even think about attempting to find me . . . well, I'm sure you can imagine the type of power and connections it took to have you released. Do not imagine that those powers cannot be used to your very grave detriment, Mr. McIntyre."

They had pulled into a parking garage in the city during this conversation and come to rest next to a black Land Rover. "This vehicle," said Harriman, pointing to the Rover, "belongs to you now, Mr. McIntyre. You'll find all the necessary paperwork, including a Pennsylvania driver's license in the glove box. There is also a Social Security card. Both documents are in the name of Martin Monroe. Martin Monroe's record is clean and his résumé, which is fully verifiable and which closely resembles your own, will allow you to find work at some point in the future. Do you have any questions, Mr. McIntyre?"

Jed was impressed, really impressed. "Why?" he asked, his engineer's brain really wanting to know. "Why would anybody do this?"

"Let's just say my client has some macabre whims. And the resources to indulge them."

chapter twenty-four

The desk clerk at the Delano looked at Lydia and Jeffrey with disdain as the two of them, dirty and trailing about as much dust as Afghan refugees, walked through the elegant lobby. Feeling shaken and angry, she sneered at the concierge, who raised a curious and condescending eyebrow at their disheveled appearance. Waiting for the elevators to arrive, Lydia smoothed out her hair pointlessly in the mirrored doors, then turned to the side to inspect the cut on her arm.

"That'll leave a nice scar if we don't get it stitched," said Jeffrey, leaning in to take a look.

"It's not that deep," she said, but it stung when he touched it, and she flinched.

"We'll stop by the emergency room on the way to the airport."

"We don't have time."

"You're right," said Agent Bentley to her reflection as he came up behind them, accompanied by his trusty sidekick, Agent Negron. When the elevator opened, the two FBI agents pushed Lydia and Jeffrey in before them.

"Ms. Strong, Mr. Mark, you have two choices," said Agent Bentley, apparently having trouble keeping his temper. He was clenching his big white teeth and speaking through them. "Either you will cooperate and accept our escort back to the airport, where you will catch the first flight to New York, or we will arrest you for knowingly interfering with a federal investigation, which has led to the destruction of evidence."

Lydia looked at him with an expression of mock sheepishness. Jeffrey said, "I don't know what you're talking about."

"You know full well what I am talking about," said Agent Bentley, reaching behind him and pressing the stop button on the elevator. It groaned to a halt, and Lydia felt a hollow of fear open in her belly. In the distance, an alarm bell began to clang, adding an aura of panic to the moment. Lydia looked Agent Bentley in the eyes and didn't like what she saw there—or, rather, what she didn't see there. He was a man on the edge, someone who had been pushed to the limits of what he could endure. His eyes were red-rimmed, and a muscle in his jaw twitched. Lydia moved in close to Jeffrey and grabbed his wrist.

"We're leaving," said Lydia. "Just let us get our bags and we're out of here. Nothing and no one is worth this much hassle. We were trying to help. Maybe we were a little pushy about it. But we're done here. Someone else can worry about Tatiana Quinn."

Agent Bentley looked at her with some combination of skepticism and relief. "No fucking around," he said, half-questioning, half-threatening.

"No fucking around," she answered. "We're on a two o'clock flight to New York. You can call the airline and check it out for yourself."

Bentley reached behind him and the elevator started its ascent with a jolt. A voice came crackling loudly over the speaker, "Everyone all right up there?"

"It's moving now," said Bentley, sounding carefree as he spoke into the intercom. "You better check it out when it lets us off, though."

"Will do. Sorry about that, sir."

"No problem."

The doors opened on Lydia and Jeffrey's floor, and the four of them filed out.

"I'm sure you won't object to our sticking around and making sure you get to the airport safely, what with all the misadventure you two seem to get yourselves involved in," said Bentley with mock courtesy.

"Suit yourself," replied Jeffrey as he pushed open the door to their room.

Within fifteen minutes, they had packed their bags, while Bentley and Negron sat on the couch like a couple of sour gargoyles. Within thirty, they were in their Jeep on the way to the airport, the FBI escort close behind. Exhausted and bruised, they had every intention of returning to New York. Because they could only get a flight to Tirana, Albania, from JFK. Tomorrow.

True to their word, Agents Negron and Bentley had graciously escorted them to the Miami Airport, were so kind as to wait while they dropped off their rental car, and then drove them to the terminal. There, Negron ate some Goobers and read the latest issue of *Hot Rod*, while Bentley seemed content to sit and glare at Lydia and Jeffrey until they walked up the gangway to their flight. As she smiled and waved to them obnoxiously through the portal window of the airplane, Negron gave her the finger from behind the tinted plate glass.

"I'm so glad I don't work for the fucking Bureau anymore," said Jeffrey, exhaling through his nose sharply.

"I think they're glad, too."

They sat staring straight ahead for a moment. Jeffrey hadn't had time to work himself into a state before getting on the plane . . . and hadn't had time to get a drink. So when Lydia felt him start to fidget as the plane began to taxi down the runway, she fished through her bag until she found her bottle of Tylenol PM, as well as a tiny bottle of Absolut Citron that she had taken from the minibar for just this purpose. She handed them to him.

"Thank you, Doctor," he said. She held his hand, which had suddenly gone cold, and smiled at him. It constantly amazed her that he was so afraid to fly, when he was so fearless about everything else. She figured it was a control issue. He'd probably be less afraid if he was actually *flying* the jet.

"Can I have that stuff from the office?" she asked.

He lifted his shirt and handed her the file folder and date book, both all wrinkled and warm. She put the folder in her lap and smoothed it out with both hands, then opened the date book and flipped through the pages.

"What is this?" she asked, thinking aloud.

"It looks like some kind of schedule," he answered, leaning in and putting a hand on her thigh. "Pickup and drop-off times."

"Yeah, but picking up and dropping off what? And these dollar figures? Is that how much the cargo is worth?"

He shook his head slowly, frowning. "Well, I guess we'll find out."

"If we can find the spot. All we know is that it's in a city called Vlorë."

"We'll find it."

"You know," she said, putting the date book down on her lap. "I guess I always thought of evil as being random in nature. I guess I never thought of it as so organized, backed by money and power. I never thought of it as making plans and keeping schedules."

"What about the Nazis? They were organized. The entire government was evil."

"If you believe Marianna, *our* entire government is evil."

"I don't know about that. Maybe there are evil men with evil agendas manipulating certain aspects of the government, but I don't believe that it's evil at the core. Americans are the good guys in the world order."

She shrugged. "I don't know what to believe." She paused for a second, then said, "What happened there? I mean, was it a coincidence that we were there when someone torched the place? Is that why Sasa went there? To get rid of evidence? Or did someone follow us there with the intention of erasing the evidence and us along with it?"

"I don't know," he said, remembering the Ryder truck and wondering who had been behind the wheel of that vehicle.

The plane started to race down the runway, and Jeffrey visibly stiffened. She smiled sympathetically and placed a hand on his cheek.

"You just shot our way out of a burning building less than four hours ago. But you're afraid to fly?" she teased, trying to distract him a little.

"I know," he said, shutting his eyes, his breathing shallow.

She held his hand tightly as the wheels left the ground, and in a matter of seconds, the airport was a miniature village behind them. She imagined Dreads and Big Head the size of ants. What was their agenda? she wondered.

"And where does Jenna Quinn fit into this?" she said over the high-pitched whir of the landing gear retreating into the belly of the plane. "If she is the owner of American Equities, does that mean that she's involved in this company American Beauty? Does that mean that she's involved with the snuff films?"

She thought again of the DVD, the original sitting in the bottom of her bag, the copy on its way to New York. What kinds of people were responsible for something like that? Who did you have to be to make a film like that, or to get off on watching one? Someone like Nathan Quinn, so consumed with his own power that other people seemed so far beneath him as to be less than trash? People who consider themselves so far above the laws of society

and morality that anything goes when it comes to their sexual pleasure? And was all of this somehow the key to what had happened to
Tatiana? She remembered again what Detective Ignacio had said to
her about the money. Well, they were going to follow it and Sasa all
the way to Albania. She shuddered, remembering Sasa Fitore's voice
on the tape, how cold it was, how he lied to and manipulated that
girl and watched as she died in horror and agony. She felt her face
flush with anger. Nathan Quinn and Sasa Fitore were neck and neck
for bad guy of the month.

When Jeffrey started to doze off, the Tylenol PM and shot of
Absolut kicking in, Lydia pulled down her tray table and plugged
her laptop into the modem jack, which would, of course, cost about
a thousand dollars a second. When the machine booted up, she
logged on to her search engine and entered the city name Vlorë. She
waited while the slow connection loaded. It only took five minutes
of scanning through the links before she came across a transcript of
a news segment on the ABC Web site that answered a few of her
questions; some articles from the BBC on-line filled in some more
of the blanks.

Once an important fishing and trading port located on the
Adriatic coast of southwestern Albania, Vlorë had in recent years
been exporting something far more lucrative—young women and
girls. Just seventy miles by boat from the coast of Italy, Vlorë, with
its corrupt police and ineffectual government, had evolved into the
epicenter of the country's smuggling industry. Lured from their
families with promises of rich husbands, modeling careers, or just
abducted and subdued by torture and violence, the girls were smuggled in high-powered speedboats to the Italian coast, where they
were sold to pimps or issued new passports and smuggled into other
countries, including the United States. According to the ABC tele-
cast, a young virgin could bring as much as ten thousand dollars. The
beleaguered Italian border guards claimed to be able to stop only a
fraction of the illegal immigrants. Loose estimates suggested that

there were about thirty thousand Albanian prostitutes in Europe alone, nearly 1 percent of the entire population of Albania. The girls became, for all intents and purposes, sex slaves . . . trapped, hopeless. Unable to escape, but even if they managed to, they could never go home again. A woman who had been raped in Albania would be murdered by her father and brothers, blamed for the violence perpetrated against her. They were lost women, invisible to the world.

Lydia had written an article for *Vanity Fair* years back about a similar trade conducted by the Russian mob. She thought then that she had made a difference; she realized now that she hadn't even scratched the surface. And for a moment, Lydia felt a wave of gratitude to have been born an American woman in the twentieth century. She closed her eyes and saw the faces of millions of women throughout the world without rights, living lives dictated by terror and oppression, beaten, tortured, sold into sexual slavery, and murdered. Afghanistan, Africa, Albania, and the former Yugoslavia, poverty stricken, war torn, morality and humanity running a distant second to survival at any cost.

Lydia thought of Marianna and the fear she'd seen in her beautiful young eyes. She'd said, "My country has been destroyed. And the people left there are like vultures feeding off the carrion of our dead culture. They would sell their daughters for the American dollar, not caring what their fate might be."

Lydia had been blind not to recognize instantly that schedule for what it was. Or maybe she just hadn't wanted to acknowledge it; in her heart, as the reality dawned on her, she wasn't really surprised. After all, she had seen it years before under a different guise. Lydia had just left the *Washington Post* to strike out on her own, to work on more in-depth pieces and try her hand at writing the book that turned out to be *With a Vengeance*. She still had a voice mailbox at the *Post,* though, because so many leads came to her there. Working late one night on her book and reaching a creative lull, she checked her messages at the paper. There was a call from a young woman named Felice. Thinking of her now, she was reminded of Marianna. Though Felice had been plain and small, older by a few years than Marianna, her tiny arms bruised with track marks, she had shared Marianna's distrust of the police and the FBI. Felice was from Russia, forced to be a prostitute, she claimed, an indentured servant to the pimp who had lured her from her neighborhood, promising her the life of a rich American model, a beautiful home in California for her family. She had been given heroin against her will, she said, and was now addicted and walking the streets. And she was not the only one. She had kept quiet because she was terrified of her pimp, of the American police, but also because she had the dimmest glimmer of hope that one day she would work off her "debt" and be free. It was a carrot her pimp had dangled when he was not beating her or forcing her to take drugs. But then, young women Felice knew began to disappear, turning up dead in rivers and alleys. She knew that she could be next at any time and that she had to do something before she died. Lydia had been compassionate but skeptical; she took the address where Felice claimed the girls were kept. After an investigation that led Lydia and Jeffrey from D.C. to New York to Minneapolis to Chicago, her article resulted in a sting that took down an international prostitution ring. Unfortunately, Felice died of an overdose just days after she had been freed from her captors and accepted into a rehab program at a clinic.

But if Marianna was right, this was even worse. And what they'd seen—the haunting, evil images on the DVD—indicated that she was. It had to be stopped by any means necessary. And Sasa Fitore had to be made to pay.

Lydia saw the faces of these women—Tatiana, Marianna, Felice, even Shawna, the pretty young victims of an ugly, indifferent world, like millions of others. But Tatiana was not lost—yet. Lydia could feel it, could almost touch her. And in finding and saving her, Lydia could strike a blow for all the cheated, murdered, lost women and little girls. The electric buzz made her restless, and desperate for a cigarette. She nudged Jeffrey awake to show him what she had found.

In the crowded, ugly airport Lydia and Jeffrey crushed their way through the usual mob of passengers, both of them getting jostled and pushed because they were too exhausted to be aggressive enough to make it out of JFK in under forty-five minutes. It entailed pushing your way off the plane while people struggled with the overhead compartments, then rushing down the gangway, making a half jog through the long hallways and escalators, volleying for the prime spot at the baggage claim, right near the mouth that puked tacky, dirty luggage. You had to have your ticket ready in case you were actually stopped by the people supposedly checking exiting luggage, then race for the taxi line. But tonight, they just allowed themselves to be scooted along by the crowd. Lydia was surprised and endlessly grateful to be approached by a limousine driver at the baggage claim.

He wore a driver's uniform complete with a cap and jacket bearing an emblem and held a sign reading MARK/STRONG in black Magic Marker. His other hand rested on a luggage cart, and Lydia thought he was a mirage, seen through the blurred vision of her fatigue.

"Who sent you?" asked Jeffrey, suspiciously eyeing the frighteningly thin, acne-scarred man with thinning hair and a beak nose. He looked nervous and shifty as Jeffrey insisted that he call his dispatcher to find out who had sent him.

A small old woman with a cane bodychecked Lydia aside to reach for her embroidered suitcase, yelling, "Excuse me, excuse me" with a disproportionate amount of desperation and annoyance. When the luggage passed her by anyway, the woman let out a disappointed cry. Lydia rushed after the soft heavy bag with leather handles that the woman had reached for, grabbed it, and hauled it back to her. She snatched it from Lydia as if Lydia had been trying to steal it. She nodded in a gesture of grudging thanks, her eyes narrowed in a frown, as if trying to figure out Lydia's angle, then she hobbled off. Lydia fantasized for a moment about having knocked the old lady over with her luggage, instead of handing it to her. "I've fallen and I can't get up," she would have cried miserably. "Bitch," Lydia muttered, sincerely hoping that the limo had not been ordered by one of the various people who seemed to want her and Jeffrey out of the way, because she was exhausted and really wanted to avoid the taxi line at JFK.

"Jacob sent the limo," said Jeffrey, taking the luggage from her and piling it on the cart the chauffeur was pushing.

"How uncharacteristically considerate of him."

"And he's waiting in it to ride with us."

"Great," she said with a sigh.

"My lady, your lecture mobile awaits," he said with a flourish of his hand.

Out on the sidewalk, Lydia's thin leather jacket, T-shirt, and lightweight rayon pants were no match for the slicing chill in the fall air or the pinprick drizzle that wasn't quite snow but would be if the temperature dropped another degree. She pulled the jacket tightly around her, folding her arms and pushing in close to Jeffrey as they waited for the limousine driver to pull the car around.

"Did you have a nice vacation?" Jacob asked, looking at Jeffrey and ignoring Lydia entirely as they climbed into the car and sat opposite him.

"Not really," replied Jeffrey sullenly, acting like a teenager in a black mood.

"That's what I heard."

The air was thick among the three of them, and Lydia thought Jacob seemed pale and drawn, wrapped in a heavy navy peacoat, a black turtleneck sticking out from beneath it. He was a handsome man sometimes when the light hit him right and he smiled. But not tonight. Tonight, he was angry, and anger didn't become him. His cheekbones jutted out of his thin face, and his mouth was set, eyes narrow, nostrils flared.

"And what did you hear exactly, Jacob?" asked Jeffrey.

"I think we should drop Lydia off so that you and I can talk. Alone."

Lydia bristled but said nothing.

"Whatever you have to say can be said in front of Lydia."

"I'm afraid I don't feel that way."

"I don't give a fuck how you feel, Jacob," replied Jeffrey, exploding in anger and leaning forward. "She's my partner."

"Really. I was under the impression that *I* was your partner, Jeff. Remember Mark, Hanley and Striker, Inc.? She is not a partner in this firm, and we have firm business to discuss."

"As far as I'm concerned, she's more a partner than you are lately."

Here we go, thought Lydia, looking out the window as the driver merged into the heavy traffic on the Van Wyck. A field of headlights glowed in the silvery drizzle; horns honked halfheartedly. She could tell by Jeffrey's tone and expression that he had been holding ill feeling for Jacob inside, and she didn't understand why he'd never discussed it with her.

"Just what the fuck is that supposed to mean?"

Jeffrey looked away from Jacob and shook his head. "On second thought, maybe you're right. Maybe we do need to talk alone."

"I hate to be a third wheel. Would you boys like me to get out and walk?"

Nobody laughed at her joke. "Jesus, what is going on between you two?"

Neither man answered, Jeffrey looking out the window, Jacob looking at Lydia with something that looked an awful lot like distrust and anger. She glared right back at him. He was out of shape; she could definitely take him.

"You pissed a lot of people off in Miami," he said, pointing at Lydia.

She shrugged. He pulled a folded piece of paper out of the inside lapel of his jacket and handed her a faxed copy of the bill at the Delano, totaling almost five thousand dollars for the days they had stayed there. "And you cost this firm a lot of money."

Jeffrey grabbed the bill from her hand. "This is not about Lydia and her spending habits. She brings more money into this firm in a year than you have in the last five. You *don't* run things, Jacob. Don't think I don't realize that you are hiding the books from me. I may not have the same business sense that you do, but I'm not an idiot."

"She's been planting ideas like that in your head. She's trying to manipulate you into making her a partner."

"You're some detective, Jacob. Always one step ahead of us all," said Lydia with tired sarcasm. She was waiting for him to slip and call her Yoko. She mentally checked out of the conversation, too angry to keep her mouth shut and too tired to get involved. Besides, she didn't have the faintest idea what either of them was talking about.

"Lydia doesn't know anything about that, Jacob," Jeffrey said quietly. "She's never said a word against you."

"Yeah, right," he said. "So for all the money you spent, all the people you pissed off, and for all the people who are in body bags as a result of your Miami 'vacation,' is there even a client? Has anyone hired you, paid you anything? Have you forgotten that we're running a business here?"

"There are more important things in this world than a paycheck, Jacob. The firm makes enough money that we can get involved in cases that don't pay us anything."

"Right, whenever Lydia gets the 'buzz.'"

"That's right, Jacob," Jeffrey said calmly. "Because there's usually a very good reason for it."

"Like this?" asked Jacob, removing the black DVD jewel case from his pocket.

"Where did you get that?"

"I made Craig turn it over to me, even though he didn't want to. You shouldn't encourage him to hide things from me, Jeff."

Lydia felt a stab of betrayal as she looked over and recognized the DVD. She wondered if Craig had told Jacob everything. But then she wondered why it should matter. They were supposed to be able to trust Jacob. He was supposed to be on their team. She looked over at him and noticed a tremor in his hand. Why does he feel like the enemy all of a sudden? she wondered.

"Did you watch it?" she asked him.

"Yes, I did. Though I wish to God I hadn't."

"There's a little girl missing, Jacob. Women are dying, being murdered for someone's sexual pleasure. Human beings are being trafficked, sold into slavery. Do you understand that?"

"Yes, Lydia. I understand that. It's been that way since the beginning of time."

She shook her head, as if to help his words sink in while shaking them off at the same time. "What are you talking about?"

"There has always been a master class. Men whose money and power allow them to buy and sell other, less powerful human beings to fill their needs. Whether the need is to build pyramids or tend cotton fields or satisfy their sexual urges, it really doesn't matter. It's all the same. It's always been this way. It's just generally better hidden than this, especially these days, with the media and the culture of political correctness being what it is."

He opened the case and took out the DVD while Jeffrey and Lydia looked at him, incredulous. He snapped it in two and threw the pieces out the window. A horn honked in protest of his littering.

"You can't stop it any more than you could single-handedly stop the drug trade. And if you try, you'll both be destroyed, and this firm will be destroyed along with you. I can't allow that. It means too much to me. You," he said, turning to Jeffrey, "mean too much to me."

There was silence for a moment as Jeffrey looked at Jacob's face in the dim light. He remembered clearly the days when he had loved Jacob, when they had been friends who trusted each other and counted on each other. The man sitting across from him had some-how become a stranger. Jeffrey realized that the only feeling he had in his heart for his college friend was indifference, and a smattering of distrust. He couldn't say when this had happened or why, but he suspected that his feelings for Jacob had begun to erode a night long ago in a dark New York City hotel room.

"I remember that night," said Jeffrey.

"What night?"

"In New York. The George Hewlett case."

Jacob paused a second, taking a breath before speaking. "I was able to stop you from destroying yourself then, Jeffrey. Over a homeless man, the ultimate failure of society, you would have ruined us all."

"Oh my God, Jacob," said Jeffrey sadly. "Who are you?"

The hand still shook, Lydia noticed. And Jacob lowered his eyes in what looked like shame.

"What are you guys talking about?"

"The story I told you in Miami, about George Hewlett. There was a little more to it." Jeff kept his eyes on Jacob as he spoke. "I went back to my hotel—you remember I was still stationed in D.C. at the time—after my meeting with Sarah. When I got there, the door was ajar. Jacob was there. It was so *weird;* he was just sitting there in the dark, like we were in some kind of bad spy movie. I said, 'Jake, what the fuck are you doing, man? You scared the shit out of me.'"

Jeff paused for a second, looking at Lydia. "I can't believe I never told you this. It's like I put it out of my mind."

"Anyway, Jacob says, 'Why did you do that, Jeff?' And he was scared, but a little angry, too. 'It's one thing for you to be a cowboy. But I have a wife and kids, man. Did you think about that? Do you have any idea what you're fucking with by doing what you just did?' I got really pissed, told him I couldn't believe his career was more important to him than the fact that an innocent man was probably going to get the death penalty for a crime he didn't commit. And he said, 'Not our careers, man. Our *lives*. These are people you do not fuck with. Don't you understand that?' And I'll never forget what he said, next. 'That homeless guy, his life was already wasted. You, me, my wife and unborn baby, our lives still mean something. I saved your ass tonight, Jeff. I won't be able to save it again if you don't drop this thing.' And then he left. I called after him, but he just turned around and gave me this sad shake of his head.

"I didn't know what to think at first when he left. It kind of half-felt like a joke. I tried to forget about it, convince myself that he was just being paranoid. I turned on the lights and television, made myself a drink from the minibar. But I started wondering how he knew where I had gone and what I had done. It's not as though he knew the woman I was with, so even if he was tailing me, it would have been hard for him to get close enough to me to hear without my recognizing him. Then *I* started to feel paranoid.

"But like I said, the next day it all went away."

Lydia looked at Jacob and saw someone she wasn't sure of. She had always known that Jacob disliked her, but she never imagined him to be anything but loyal to Jeffrey. He looked small and mean when she looked into his eyes.

"It wasn't so cloak-and-dagger as that, Jeff. I was just worried about losing our jobs," Jacob said with an unconvincing laugh.

"Of course. It was all in my imagination," said Jeff, looking out the window. Lydia couldn't read his expression.

"And what about Tatiana Quinn, Jacob?" asked Lydia. "Daughter of the rich and powerful Nathan Quinn. How much is her life worth? Is finding her going to ruin us all?"

"Tatiana is dead, Lydia."

The words felt like a punch in the stomach, and Lydia flinched.

"No, she isn't," she said reflexively.

"Yes, Lydia. She is. They found her body tonight. During the raid of a crack den on Tenth Street, they found her in a closet. Beaten beyond recognition, violated. One of the cops recognized her necklace from the description of what she'd worn when she ran away. The medical examiner identified her by the dental records they had on file. One of the dealers they picked up said she showed up a couple of weeks ago, had been prostituting herself for crack."

She waited for a wave of grief, but a feeling of disbelief lingered instead. A stubborn faith that Tatiana was still alive wrapped itself around Lydia's heart. But she nodded her head, pretending to accept the news, and stared out the window. Jeffrey placed a hand on her leg.

"How did you find out about it?" Jeffrey asked.

"Bad news travels fast."

"I want to see the body," said Lydia.

"She's already on her way back to Miami."

"That's impossible. The red tape alone would hold that up for days."

"The sea of red tape parts for the likes of Nathan Quinn," he said, echoing what Craig had said to her last night.

"That's right," she said with bitter sarcasm, "the master class."

They all sat in silence for what seemed like forever. Lydia rolled down the window a crack, letting in the whisper of tires on wet asphalt and a flutter of raindrops. The car pulled off the FDR at Houston Street. A squeegee man accosted the front windshield of the limo at the light, but the driver ignored him. Lydia pulled out a dollar and handed it to him through the window crack. She heard him yell "God bless you" as they moved on slick roads through Alphabet City and then further into the East Village, turning onto Lafayette and then onto Great Jones. The limo idled in front of the building.

"Jeff, let's go someplace and talk."

"Not tonight, Jacob. I'll meet you in the office tomorrow morning at nine. I want to see those books. No excuses."

"Fine. I was never trying to hide anything from you, man."

Jeff nodded, looking at him with cool eyes and a sad half smile. The driver opened the door for Lydia, holding an umbrella over her head, and walked her to the front door. He went back to help Jeffrey with the bags as Lydia opened the door to the elevator vestibule, which, she noticed, needed a coat of paint. Too bad they were heading to Eastern Europe tomorrow to thwart a sex slavery/snuff ring. How are you ever supposed to get anything done around the house? she wondered. If she were a member of the "master class" she wouldn't have to trouble herself with such worries. She punched their code into the keypad by the elevator and the door opened. She got in and held it as Jeffrey and the chauffeur came in with the bags.

"Everything's going to be okay," he said softly in her ear. She almost believed it.

"She's not dead, Jeffrey," she said as they walked into the apartment.

"Lydia . . ."

"She's not."

He didn't argue with her, knowing that it was pointless.

"Why didn't you tell me about Jacob?" she asked.

He put a finger to her lip. "No more talking tonight."

"But—"

He grabbed Lydia and pulled her into him, pressing his mouth to hers. He wanted, needed, to shut everything out but her. She wrapped her arms around his neck and felt herself being lifted a little in his embrace. His lips found the delicate lobe of her ear and moved down to the soft flesh of her neck. "Let's take a shower," he whispered in her ear.

"Umm," she replied, taking his hand and leading him upstairs.

They let the scalding water fill the bathroom with steam as Jeffrey peeled off her clothes. Plush throw rugs protected her bare feet from the cool stone tile floor as she kicked off her boots and let Jeffrey slide her pants down over her hips.

"I forgot about this," he said, lifting her ripped shirt off over her head and inspecting the cut on her arm.

"It's fine," she said, lying. Smiling, she reached to unbuckle his belt, unbutton his jeans. She lifted off his shirt and ran her hands along the soft skin and hard muscle of his chest, pressed her bare skin against his. It was good to think of nothing but the moment, to leave the evil outside the bathroom door and immerse herself in the hot water and in Jeffrey. The water burned and beat down on her skin in a pleasant way as she stepped over the ledge of the Jacuzzi tub. She loved hot, hot showers that left her skin red and tingling. He climbed in beside her and they stood for a second, looking at each other. He pushed her hair back from her eyes and water washed over them. He kissed her with the same desperate passion that he had the first time their lips had touched, and she melted into him, as unable to resist now as she had been back then. She felt him grow hard, and she ached inside. Each time they made love, it felt like they had been together for a lifetime already, it was so intimate, so loving, their knowledge of each other so complete. But every time it was different, too, new levels of pleasure, new shades of emotion. She groaned as he entered her, holding on to her back, pressing her against the tile. She wrapped a leg around him, her arms around his shoulders, her mouth on his neck.

They were only their bodies and their hearts; everything ugly and wrong they had known over the last few days was shady and indistinct behind the steam that filled the bathroom and fogged the mirrors.

Is it possible to love something as much as you hate it? Is it possible to be as turned on by something as you are repulsed by it? Lydia was thinking as Jeffrey rubbed Neosporin into the gash on her arm and then tenderly applied three butterfly bandages. It turned out to be about six inches long, but not as deep as it felt. White stars of pain danced before her eyes as Jeffrey nursed her wound.

"That should help it heal better," he said, kissing her on the forehead and leaning back on the mahogany headrest of the bed in their Great Jones loft. Their bedroom was lighted by a single white pillar candle, and Chopin intoned mournfully on the Bose CD alarm clock beside their bed, lulling her into an ever-blacker mood. She'd never been happier to see their beautiful duplex, or to climb onto their luxurious four-poster king-size bed, or to wrap herself in the velvet duvet, the pleasure of relief being one decibel away from orgasm. But it was to be a one-night reprieve, and then back into the lion's den. She lay back and let her tired body become one with the mattress. But when she closed her eyes, visions of the last few days visited her like Harpies shrieking their fury. She shuddered, opened her eyes, and met Jeffrey's warm gaze. His was the very face of comfort and security. She was constantly amazed that the same person who aroused in her such passion could make her feel so safe and calm, so peaceful with just one glance.

"It's going to be okay. We're going to be okay," he said for the second time that night, reaching over to shut off the Chopin. "That music is so depressing," he said.

He got up and walked over to the dresser and blew out the candle there. "Let's go to bed, okay?"

When he came back, he reached over and turned down the covers on her side of the bed. She scooted over, wearing black cotton panties and a matching camisole. He tucked her in and kissed her on the lips. "I love you," she said.

"I love you, too."

He got in bed beside her, and then there was a fifteen-second wrestling match for sheets, blankets, and comforter, which Lydia won, making Jeffrey snuggle in close to her to remain under the covers. "You're such a bed hog," he complained.

"Whatever," she said, enjoying the warmth of his body. No more than five minutes later, she heard his breathing grow deep and steady. She lay there with her eyes open, wide-awake, staring at the window where the amber glow from the streetlight leaked beneath the blinds, sleep slipping away like water through cupped fingers.

chapter twenty-five

The bruised and bluish body, thin and stiff on the metal gurney, was not his daughter. Did they think he did not know every inch of her, down to her delicate fingertips? The body before him was common and cheap, weak and discarded by life. Tatiana would never look like that—even in death. He closed his eyes and nearly lost consciousness in his relief in the airport cargo hold, where he'd insisted he be shown the body by the medical examiner, who greeted the plane with him. She was still alive. Of course. He had felt her even over the past few hours, during which he had known more fear and grief than he had in all his life. But who had gone to so much trouble to make him think otherwise? Who wanted him to believe that his daughter was dead?

He nodded his head to the medical examiner. "That's her," he said, choking.

"I'm sorry, Mr. Quinn, truly sorry for your loss."

He nodded, barely able to contain his joy, covering his mouth with his hand. He walked, head bent, through the crowd of police officers who had comprised his escort, back to the waiting limousine. His driver opened the door for him, and he climbed into the darkness, sank into the rich black leather, and let his head fall back and his eyes close. He'd come back from New York just hours before he got the call from the NYPD. He'd come back and found Jenna gone.

Tatiana was to have been the jewel in his crown, priceless, glorious, dazzling in her beauty. The first night he saw her, he'd known that she belonged to him. Her father's princess, dressed in a black velvet shift with patent-leather ballet slippers. She was still a little girl, but the fullness of womanhood was beginning to show itself in her hips and her tiny breasts. Even at thirteen, she was the envy of every woman in the room. He saw it in their stolen glances, in the shadow of self-consciousness that danced across their eyes as they compared their skin, their bodies, the luster in their hair to Tatiana's. Of course, there was no comparison. She was one of God's perfect creations.

She was a miniature of her mother, though Jenna's beauty had begun to fade even then. Jenna had already started to hate Tatiana in that jealous motherly way. But there was a fierce love there, too. He knew they were a package deal. And there was no length to which he would not have gone, no act too low to make them his. He'd proven that. In the end, Jenna and Tatiana had no choice but to come with him to America. They would have been killed if they had remained in Albania. Or worse . . . they would have been poor.

Jenna had actually proven herself a suitable mate, uninterested in his personal affairs, unemotional, and possessing a keen business sense. He'd allowed her to keep her interest in American Equities because she proved a valuable liaison when it came to the Albanians. Nathan wanted nothing to do with the ones who didn't speak English; he couldn't communicate with them anyway.

And Tatiana grew more stunning every day. It had been easy to turn her head with pretty things and pretty words. Even easier to turn her against Jenna in subtle ways, since an adolescent girl and her mother are natural enemies anyway. Jenna said no; Nathan said yes. Jenna and Tatiana argued; Nathan comforted. They grew closer. Everything was evolving as it was meant to between them. And didn't she know the power she had over him? Didn't she know that for her slightest smile, for that sweet, shy glance, he would move the earth for her?

But he didn't have the kind of control he'd thought he would. The way she threw herself into his arms when he arrived home from work, the way she lounged around in thin pajamas, or in her bikini by the pool . . . her creamy flesh, her fragrant hair. It was pleasure torture. He'd gotten careless.

Jenna had taken the limo to a charity auction, which he'd declined to attend, giving him an evening alone with Tatiana. He'd rented a movie for them to watch together, and Tatiana made microwave popcorn. She was luminous in a pink T-shirt with a tiny red heart embroidered between her breasts. He could see through her white pajama bottom to her red thong underwear. Her lustrous hair was pulled up into a twist, exposing the delicate skin and graceful lines of her neck. She moved in close to him on the couch and put her head on his lap, balancing the bowl of popcorn on her flat belly. She chattered innocently about something or other going on at school, but he couldn't hear her because of the blood rushing in his ears. He turned the light off and the movie on. In the darkness, with the light from the television dancing on the walls, he began to stroke her hair. It was an innocent gesture, except that his fingers were on fire, wanting more. He released her hair from the clip and it spilled across his lap. She seemed to move in closer, so he allowed himself to move his hand down over her arm. He did not see or hear a word of the movie in front of them, so full were his senses, so intense the ache in his loins. He was hard as rock, just centimeters from where her head rested on his thigh. He couldn't stop his hand from touching the exposed flesh of her belly where her T-shirt had ridden up. She didn't move or jump up or protest, but her whole body stiffened. In a heartbeat, she had gone from total trust and comfort to wariness. He removed his hand. After a moment, she sat up and slid casually to the other end of the couch. He didn't say a word, did not react in the least, as if it couldn't matter to him less. But the energy between them had shifted.

After a few more minutes, she said, "I think I'll go to bed."

"You don't want to watch the rest of the movie? Are you feeling all right?"

"I'm tired," she said quietly, not holding his eyes.

"Okay, sweetheart. Good night."

She didn't come over to kiss him on the cheek as she had every previous night; she just walked out of the room and up the grand staircase, looking fragile and small.

In the night, as he lay awake thinking of her sleeping in her bed, he heard her knock on her mother's bedroom door.

"Can I sleep with you?" he had heard Tatiana say from the doorjamb.

"Yes, darling. What's wrong?"

"Just a bad dream."

She seemed to forgive him a little over the next few days, but he never earned her total trust again. And then just a few weeks later, she was gone. He didn't think she had run away, but he couldn't be sure. Until now. He'd been so guilt-stricken that he'd never imagined someone had tried to steal his prize. Who would dare? he wondered. And why? With Jenna gone, the answer suddenly seemed so simple. He couldn't believe what a fool he was.

He considered Lydia Strong for a second and smiled. For a while, he'd believed her to be his one best hope of finding Tatiana. But then she made a mess, getting into places where she had no business, and he realized she had no better lead on Tatiana than he did. He was disappointed and angry. She hadn't been as easy to handle as Parker or Ignacio. But he'd gotten creative and arranged for an effective distraction. She'd have enough on her hands now to keep her out of his affairs. Meanwhile, he had to find a way to bring his baby home.

chapter twenty-six

The coffeepot gurgled and filled the kitchen with the warm, comforting aroma of brewing Hawaiian Kona as Lydia sat flipping through the pages of the *New York Times*. The morning light outside was bright and cold, the sky ice blue, the windows frosted and foggy. Jeffrey came down the stairs, dressed in gray chinos, black lug-sole oxfords, and a black ribbed sweater.

"You look good, baby," she said as he leaned in to kiss her. He smelled lightly of cologne and shaving cream. He nodded, preoccupied, and walked over to the coffeepot and poured them each a cup.

"Are you going to get us ready while I go talk to Jacob?"

"Sure. Jeffrey, why didn't you tell me what was going on with the two of you?"

"I don't know," he said, sitting down with a sigh. "It was like I couldn't get my head around it. He's been my friend for so long, I haven't been able to confront the person that he is because I keep remembering the person he was when we were young. But, first the books, and now remembering the whole George Hewlett thing . . . I don't feel like I can trust him anymore. Maybe I'm wrong, overreacting because we've had some tough days. I don't want to imagine that he was up to things behind my back. We had Christmas dinner with his family," he said, his eyebrows knitting into a frown.

"Follow your instincts, Jeffrey. If you feel that something's not right, it probably isn't."

She reached out for his hand.

"I'm sure it's nothing. He just hates *me*. Your wanting to bring me in as a partner probably just freaked him out. Which, by the way, is totally unnecessary."

"I just want you to be a part of the firm."

"I am a part of it."

"I mean legally. I want you to reap some of the benefits that you sow there."

"I already do, through your happiness and success."

"I just don't want things to be 'mine' and 'yours.' I want things to be 'ours.' Isn't that what you want?"

She cocked her head and looked at him. He stared at his coffee cup, seeming suddenly a little sad and younger than his forty-one years. She *had* hurt him that night in Miami.

"This life is ours, Jeffrey. There's nothing that we don't share," she said.

"I know that. I know," he said, standing up. He hadn't meant to start this, especially when he was minutes from walking out the door. She was beautiful in the morning light, wearing a simple white nightshirt, made gorgeous by the way it exposed her skin, revealed the outline of her body. She looked at him so earnestly, with a trace of worry in her eyes. She stood up and walked around the table, then wrapped her arms around his waist and placed her head on his chest. He held her tightly, placing his lips on her head. He wanted to say, I couldn't live a day without you. You are everything to me. I spent so long watching you run from me, waiting for you to come back. Now that you are with me, I couldn't bear to lose you again. But something kept him from saying it. As close as they were, he still felt the need to tread carefully on this subject with her. Talking about forever seemed to make her afraid. And he never wanted her to feel afraid. The night that he had been shot, just over two years ago now, they had stood on a precipice in their relationship. There had been a bond between them since the night they met, the night her mother was murdered. In the early years of their relationship, he had been a grown man and she just a young girl. He kept in touch with her after her mother's death through her grandparents, making a point to see them when he visited the New York area. When she moved to Washington, D.C., to attend Georgetown University, her grandfather asked Jeffrey to keep an eye on her, which he gladly did. Every Thursday, they would have dinner or go to the movies. He came to regard her as a young friend, though, even then, there was something beneath the surface—a kind of love, a desire to protect and shelter her.

Then one night, just before she graduated from college, she seemed to have transformed from a girl to a woman overnight. He realized that he was in love with her. But still he kept his distance, never wanting to violate the trust she had in him. He knew that she felt safe with him, and he never wanted that to change.

She began her career as a journalist with the *Washington Post*; they began working together on some cases, informally at first and then formally with the Cheerleader Murder case. When she struck out on her own to write *With a Vengeance,* the book about Jed McIntyre and the women he murdered, including her mother, Jeffrey worked with her on pulling together all the details of the case. She started traveling for other stories, and he, fed up with the Bureau, moved to New York to start his own firm. She eventually bought an apartment there to be close to him and to her grandparents. Sometimes they saw each other every day, sometimes not for weeks at a time. Until the night he was shot. She had told him much later that this was the night she was forced to confront the feelings she had been holding inside for about as long as he had. But still it was about a year later, in New Mexico, when they had both finally given in to each other.

Jeffrey had lived with the ache for Lydia for so long, tortured when she was close, and tortured when she was away. The loneliness of those years, in spite of a good number of flings and one-night stands, was difficult to look back on. To have a life with her finally was everything he had imagined it would be. He knew she felt the same way; they were kindred spirits, bound together by love, respect, trust, passion, and something more. Something that had existed when he first looked into her eyes fifteen years ago. Was it ridiculous and old-fashioned for him to want to marry her? "Marriage promises something that can't be promised. People change and life is cruel." He'd heard her say that so many times before they moved in together. She hadn't said it since, but was that the way she truly felt? That what held them together might someday fade and legal agreements would just make it more difficult to part? Is that why he *wanted* to make it legal? Then there was the matter of starting a family. Did she even want that? And how could they even consider it doing the kind of work that they did, risking their lives with regularity? If they had a child, they certainly wouldn't be getting on a plane to Albania that night. Was that a good or a bad thing? These were things they'd never touched, like the good china in a cabinet, too delicate for every day, saved for an occasion that never comes.

"We'll talk later, okay?" he said into her silky hair, drawing in the scent of lavender.

She walked him to the elevator as he pulled on his leather coat.

"Don't open the door for any Eastern European guys with guns," he said with a smile as the doors closed. She felt vaguely sad, as if she should call him back, hold him, and apologize—for what, she wasn't sure.

She walked back to the kitchen, poured herself another cup of coffee, and headed toward the stairs, but before she got there, she was assailed by another bout of nausea so powerful that she dropped the cup to the floor and barely made it to the downstairs toilet. She threw up coffee, the only thing in her stomach, and then dry-heaved for the next five minutes. Then she sat on the cold tiles of the bathroom floor, feeling weak and dizzy, resting her head against the bathtub, the nausea subsiding as quickly as it had come.

This is the second time you've hurled in forty-eight hours, bitched her crabby inner voice. What is going on with you? She had an idea that she hardly dared to face.

They were a cozy couple; even he had to admit that. Though what someone of Lydia Strong's intelligence could find to engage her in the muscle-bound, pretty-boy, ex-G-man was beyond him. Maybe she was entertained by his very large gun. It was a little disappointing, actually. He'd expected her to be more cerebral, preferably celibate, maybe on a subconscious level saving herself for him. She kept all his letters; he knew that much. She thought of him at least once a month. The thought made him feel all warm and fuzzy inside. Well, there'd be time to talk about all of that. When they were alone.

It was cold on his roof perch, even in the heavy parka, black wool hat, and leather gloves. But it was worth it for the view into their apartment. He would have thought they'd be more privacy-conscious. The upstairs had shades, but the downstairs was wide open. Peering through his high-powered binoculars, a thoughtful gift from his benefactor, he watched them walk to the elevator, saw him disappear as Lydia waved. Did she look a little sad?

He hurried from his spot, keeping low beneath the wall, then raced down the fire stairs that opened onto Lafayette, just in time to see Jeffrey Mark heading toward the subway station. The wind burned the skin on his face, but he felt alive for the first time in years.

Maybe it was because he had an awareness that he and Lydia were in danger, or maybe it was just that he'd spent so many years of tailing other people, but Jeffrey sensed he was being followed. He wondered briefly if he was being paranoid, but stopping suddenly at a newsstand to pick up a copy of the *Post,* he saw a tall dark figure in a thick parka and black hat move away from the crush of commuters heading down into the Astor Place subway stop, then slip into a doorway behind him.

"Now what?" he muttered to himself, handing some change to the vendor. He'd take the *Post* to the *Times* Lydia preferred any day. He stood there for a minute, flipping through the tabloid pages, trying to think what to do next, and then decided to head down the stairs to the train with the rest of the crowd. He needed to get to the West Side and had been heading to the N or the R train, but he didn't want to lead whoever was following him to the office. He folded the paper under his arm and jogged down the stairs, moving against the flow of people coming up. He walked to the end of the crowded platform, as the downtown number 4 train squealed into the station on the other side of the metal partitions. He heard the familiar tones announcing the train was about to depart and then heard the conductor yell angrily over the speaker, "Stand clear of the closing doors." He leaned over the tracks to look for the lights of the approaching uptown train but saw nothing. People continued to file down the stairs, the platform getting ever more crowded.

As he kept moving back, he saw a figure taller than the rest, wearing a black wool hat, pushing his way through the crowd. Jeffrey felt a surge of adrenaline and was conscious of the cool metal of the gun at his waist. Though shooting on a crowded subway platform was at best ill-advised.

"Come on, come on," he said under his breath, willing the train to come as the figure moved closer. Jeffrey craned his neck to try to see a face, but he couldn't make out anything in the crowd. Finally, he heard the squeal of metal on metal and saw the light in the tunnel as the silver train pulled into the station. A flow of people burst through the doors as soon as they opened and the people waiting fanned out around them, preparing to enter. Commuters, normally reasonably mild-mannered and polite people, pushed and shoved, cursed at and elbowed one another with increasing intensity as the tones sounded. Jeffrey kept his eyes on the black hat, biding his time, wondering if the man could see him through the crowd. He pretended to be waiting for the next train, leaning against one of the metal beams that stood like soldiers along the platform. He noticed the man in the parka, whom he could see better now that the crowd had cleared, do the same. Then, just before the doors closed, Jeffrey shoved his way onto the train, eliciting groans from those around him and a low "Motherfucker" from one of the other passengers. He was pressed between the metal door in front and soft flesh covered in winter coats behind. He could see the form still leaning against the beam on the platform, and Jeffrey smiled.

Until the train passed Jed McIntyre on the platform, grinning ghoulishly, lifting a gloved hand to wave at Jeffrey as the train carried him away.

"Lydia, are you all right?"

"Yes, I'm fine. What do you want?"

"I just wanted to apologize."

"Don't apologize to me, Jacob. Apologize to Jeffrey. He's on his way to the office right now."

"I wanted you to know that Nathan Quinn identified the body of Tatiana last night in Miami. I guess she ran away after all."

Lydia gripped the cordless phone and sat down on the plush chenille sofa in the living room. She'd been feeling a bit stronger before the phone rang; the nausea had passed, leaving a shaky fatigue in its wake.

"So that will be the end of this, then. Right, Lydia?"

Maybe Tatiana *was* dead. But no, it didn't feel right. She just couldn't accept it as the truth.

"You might be right, Jacob. There's nothing left to investigate."

"I'm serious, Lydia. It's time to call it quits with this. If not for your sake, then for Jeffrey's. It doesn't do any of us any good to be on the bad side of the FBI."

"Don't you ever get sick of this role? The skulking in the back of limos, darkened hotel rooms, issuing cryptic warnings? Because it's tired, Jacob."

She heard him sigh on the other end of the phone. "I should have known better than to try to reason with you. You don't give a shit about Jeff, do you? All you care about is your 'buzz.' And you don't care who gets hurt in the process of trying to satisfy your curiosity. Even someone you claim to love," he said.

The accusation stung like a slap in the face.

"You don't know me, Jacob. And you don't know what you're talking about."

"Don't I? I watched you lead that guy on for years, dragging him into all kinds of messes, knowing he was in love with you and using that," he said with venom.

"Is that what all of this is about? Some cliché about the friend feeling threatened by the girlfriend. Aren't we all too old for this?"

"If you think you're going to insinuate yourself into this firm and drag us all into your crazy adventures, you've got another thing coming. I won't allow it."

She felt a swell of indignation and anger. His accusations were unfair and dead wrong, but it hurt her somehow to learn that he thought of her this way. She quelled the urge to defend herself and her relationship with Jeffrey.

"You're out of line, Jacob," she said, her tone quiet, although her whole body was shaking with anger. "I would never do anything to hurt the firm or Jeffrey."

"Prove it. Tatiana's dead. Let her rest. Let us all rest, Lydia," he said, and hung up the phone.

As the line went dead, she had a flicker of self-doubt. Maybe Tatiana was just a runaway who had turned into a crack whore;

maybe the rest of it was too big for the two of them and she was leading them into a situation where they'd be crushed beneath the wheels of a machine that couldn't be stopped. Maybe she was moving forward without regard for Jeffrey, for the firm, for their life together. But in her heart, she knew it would be impossible for either of them to turn back now. Even if there might be good reason to.

She padded back over to the kitchen and poured herself a cup of coffee to replace the one that she'd shattered on the floor while bolting for the bathroom. She had already pushed the whole puking incident and what it might mean from her mind as she climbed the spiral staircase. The conversation with Jacob, however, was still ringing in her ears. She was going to break her tradition of hot showers only at night and cold showers in the morning. After all, they were headed to the Third World in a few hours; she had no idea when she might have hot water or decent water pressure again.

The bottom had fallen out of his stomach as Jeffrey pushed his way through the crowded car. There was not a thought in his mind; he was just an organism reacting to fear and anger. The train had slowed to an infuriating creep and then stopped altogether. People cursed at him as he shoved his way toward the door leading to the next car. Reaching it finally, he walked out and climbed over the gate, then dropped into the tunnel just as the train started moving again. It moved slowly at first and then rushed past him in a roaring river of silver and light as he pressed his body flat against the tunnel wall. When it passed, he started to run through the blackness toward the glow of the Astor Place station, which he could just barely see in the distance. It seemed to be miles ahead of him.

She sat on the bed, sipping the hot, strong coffee, waiting for the bathroom to fill with steam, half-listening to the happy chatter of the morning show hosts on the television. She pulled open all the upstairs shades, so the room was flooded with the morning light. Lydia relished these minutes of peace, like she relished the thought of the hot shower that awaited her, knowing that they might be her last for a while. She concentrated on her breathing for a moment, centering herself. She should have gone for a run, but she just didn't have it in her after the last few days. She reached for the remote and switched off the television, then turned on the radio.

"Roxanne, you don't have to put on the red light," she sang in unison with Sting as she walked into the steamy bathroom, closing the door behind her.

The people standing on the platform barely glanced at him as he lifted himself from the tracks. He ran across the tile floors and up the concrete steps, taking two at time. He was nearly breathless, every joint in his lower body screaming in pain as he ran back up Lafayette. He pulled his cellular phone out of his pocket and dialed their home number. "Please, God . . ." he whispered as the phone rang. "Please." The machine picked up, and he heard Lydia's voice as the simple message played: "We're unavailable. Leave a message."

"Lydia," he yelled, "pick up the fucking phone." But she didn't, and as he rounded the corner onto Great Jones Street, he could see that the door to their elevator vestibule was ajar.

He wondered how she'd react when she saw him. Would she collapse? Would she scream? Would she act all tough and smart-ass, pretend he wasn't the leading man in all of her worst nightmares? He couldn't wait to find out, couldn't wait to feel her writhing in his arms.

The upstairs, he noted, was as tastefully decorated as downstairs. He bet the king-size four-poster bed had seen some serious action. The look on Jeffrey Mark's face had been worth the risk he'd taken by following him to the subway; it was priceless: confusion, then disbelief, then horror, all within milliseconds as the train passed by. He laughed a deep, satisfying laugh. He took in all the details of the bedroom, the tousled sheets, the coffee cup on the nightstand, the suitcases standing by the closet door. There was a picture on the nightstand; he couldn't quite make out the image.

Jed McIntyre almost felt bad as he peered through his binoculars and saw Jeffrey burst into his bedroom. He was red in the face, his hair matted with sweat, his pants filthy with black dirt. Picking the street lock and leaving the door open in the elevator vestibule was a nice touch; it had probably sent the poor guy's terror meter off the charts. Yes, he did feel bad for Jeffrey. After all, they both loved the same woman. And only one of them could have her.

Lydia, wrapped in a plush pink towel, opened the bathroom door, releasing a plume of steam as Jeffrey came crashing through the door.

"Jesus Christ, Jeffrey," she yelled, "what are you doing? You scared the shit out of—" But the look on his face was enough to make her shut up and run over to him.

"What? Jeffrey, what's wrong?"

He dropped to his knees and wrapped his arms around her thighs, resting his head on her stomach. He was breathing heavily, and holding on to her as if he were about to drown.

"Oh, Jeffrey, what happened?" she said, dropping to her knees beside him. He looked down at her and took her face in his hands. She could hardly believe her ears when he said, "Jed McIntyre. I just saw Jed McIntyre. I thought . . . Oh God. Thank God." He kissed her mouth and held her as if she had returned from the grave.

chapter twenty-seven

Lydia had never questioned the existence of God—though she questioned whether most religions had anything to do with God at all. She had never asked herself the question "Is there a God?" But rather, "What must he think of us?"

It was not much of a faith. But it had always worked for her, had always helped her through the uncrossable spaces of her life. There was some force larger than she was, larger than the world she knew. Someday, it would all make sense.

Today was not that day. But she felt that it was important not to overreact. It was very, very important that she sit still on the bed while Jeffrey, red-faced, vein bulging on the side of his neck, roared at whomever he had called on the phone. But he was far away, behind a kind of emotional glass. She just sat staring out the window, smoothing out the covers on either side of her with the flat of her palms. You opened the door again. You can't be surprised when the monsters waiting outside walk in, she thought.

Nearly seventeen years after her mother, Marion, was murdered, Lydia remembered her only in snapshots. The moments she held in her mind were blurred and mysterious, underexposed and grainy. Older women on a crowded subway platform, their black hair streaked with gray, could begin a slide show before Lydia's eyes. A feverish memory of Marion leaning over her, concern wrinkling the corner of her eyes and drawing her mouth into a thin, tight line on the night that Lydia came down with chicken pox. Marion in round wire granny glasses, checking over Lydia's homework under the orange light of the imitation Tiffany lamp that hung over their kitchen table, her face a mask of studious concentration. The rarer moments when she laughed with abandon, how she would throw her head back, her hair loose from its tight bun, her eyes glistening. And she could hear her mother's voice inside her head. Of course, now it had mingled with her own voice and was sometimes indistinguishable from it. It was a strong and reliable combination. She often wondered if this voice was her mother's, speaking to her from the world beyond. Watching her, guiding her. But she could never be sure.

"She's with you, Lydia. She will always be with you," her grandmother had said over and over again since Marion's death.

But though Lydia could *see* her and *hear* her, she could never claim to have *felt* her. So many times she'd heard people who had lost loved ones say, "I can feel her inside me." But try as she had, she could never feel the essence of her mother hovering over her in the way she might have imagined, had desperately wanted to. She had always been disappointed by that, always felt cheated in that way, always jealous of people who claimed that they carried their dead parents with them in their hearts somehow.

There was a level of rage and fear in Jeffrey's voice that Lydia had never heard before, and it drew her from her thoughts to focus on him. Jeffrey rarely lost his temper. And it always frightened Lydia when he did. Because if Jeffrey couldn't control a situation, it generally meant that it couldn't be controlled.

He hung up the phone and looked at it for a second as if it were Jed McIntyre himself, hatred burning crimson on his cheeks. Then he picked the phone up and with deliberate intent ripped it from the wall and threw it out the bedroom door, where it then crashed down the spiral staircase. This seemed to spend him, and he sat deflated on the bed. Lydia slid over next to him and placed a hand on his shoulder.

"They released him. He didn't escape. They let him go."

"How is that possible? He wasn't scheduled to have another release hearing until 2005. The last time, that director told you that he had about as much chance of being released as Charlie Manson."

"I don't know. I can't get anyone to give me any answers."

"Are you sure it was him?" she asked pointlessly.

"I've never been more sure of anything."

The buzzer rang downstairs and both of them startled. Jeffrey pressed the intercom button next to the bedroom light switch. "Who the fuck is it?" he barked.

"It's Jacob. Can I come up? I heard the news and came right over."

Lydia and Jeffrey exchanged a look, both of them thinking the same thing: How could he have found out so fast?

"Listen, I don't want to be the one to say I told you so . . . but I told you so," Jacob said to Jeffrey, stripping off his overcoat. He sat down on the plush chenille sofa, leaning back comfortably. Jeffrey tried to remember that they were still friends, but a fresh gnawing distrust of Jacob made him short and impatient.

"What are you talking about now, Jacob?"

Jacob looked at Jeffrey as if he needed to ride to school on a special bus—with some combination of disgust and pity. "I'm talking about Jed McIntyre. You don't think this is a coincidence, do you?"

"You think this has something to do with Tatiana Quinn?"

"I think it has to do with Nathan Quinn."

"That's ridiculous."

"Why do you think that, Jacob?" asked Lydia, who had appeared at the top of the stairs above them. Her hair was still wet; she looked tiny in one of Jeffrey's gray Tommy Hilfiger sweatshirts and a pair of black leggings. She perched on the top step as if waiting to take flight. She hadn't told Jeffrey about their conversation and probably wouldn't. It would only make him angry, and it wouldn't change the fact that Jacob disliked and distrusted her . . . and vice versa. "What would he have to gain?"

"To keep you out of his affairs? As a distraction, to draw your attention from the investigation."

"That's pretty extreme. Wouldn't it have been easier just to have us killed?"

Jacob shrugged. He couldn't argue with that. "I'm not Nathan Quinn. I don't know how his mind works. But I do know that not many people could have orchestrated something like this."

"So why do you care about any of this, Jacob? I mean, what does any of it have to do with you?" asked Jeffrey.

"Because this is my firm, too, Jeff. Don't you think this firm's involvements affect me?" he asked, glancing at Lydia.

"To be honest with you, Jake," said Jeffrey, "I don't know what to think about you these days. I mean, look at this from my perspective. I've been asking you for months to see the books and you've been stalling. I tried to log on to our accounting program and found that I needed a password that I didn't have. Within a few hours of our landing in Miami, we were being followed. Someone was on top of every single move we made there, in spite of our only being in regular contact with the firm—namely, Craig—back in New York. Everyone we talked to is dead. Someone tried to set us on fire. You meet us at the airport with all these cryptic threats.

"Now, all of a sudden, Tatiana is supposedly dead . . . her body found in some New York City crack den . . . just another runaway. Case closed, kids. . . . Walk away. And suddenly I'm remembering the whole George Hewlett case, things from more than a decade ago."

"It's ancient history, Jeff," said Jacob.

Both Lydia and Jeffrey turned to stare at Jacob. He watched them both now from his seat across the wide room. Jeffrey got up and walked slowly over near the couch and sat in a chair facing Jacob.

"What happened that night, Jacob?"

"It was a hundred years ago. . . . I barely remember it," he said with a forced laugh. "I thought Lydia was the one in charge of the far-fetched scenarios."

He laughed again, more uncomfortable by the second with both of their eyes on him. "You guys are serious? What? You think I had anything to do with everything that's going on right now? What motivation would I have to hurt either one of you?"

A convincing look of resigned hurt shadowed his features, as he leaned forward and reached into the briefcase he'd brought with him. He removed a bound stack of papers.

"Jeff," he said, "here is a summary printout of the last five years of accounting and the password so that you can log on and see all the details. I want you to know that I have never deceived you. I have never betrayed you. I have only, always, looked out for you."

"What's going on, Jacob?" asked Jeffrey coolly, but there was sadness and uncertainty in his eyes.

The two men looked at each other, and Lydia could see a battle being waged within each of them. They were men who used to trust each other, rely on each other, but the currents of their lives had swept them so far apart somehow that they were practically strangers.

"Trust me when I tell you that literally nothing is what you think," said Jacob slowly and softly. He didn't look at either one of them, staring instead at some distant space between them. Lydia and Jeffrey both waited, looking at Jacob as he stood and pulled his coat back on.

"Nathan Quinn has grown very powerful, too powerful. Steps are being taken to change that."

"What do you mean?" asked Jeffrey.

"That's already more than you should know," he answered. "Just take my advice and stay out of this. Forget about Albania. Forget about Tatiana."

"Oh, for Christ's sake," Lydia shouted, "I am so sick of all this crap. I feel like I'm in a rerun of *The X-Files*."

"Let me put it in plain English. You fucked around with Nathan Quinn and now he's fucking around with you. It's gone too far now and it's beyond my powers to help either of you. I tried. Now, like I said before, you're on your own."

He stood up to leave.

Jeffrey frowned. "How do you know we're going to Albania?"

Jacob hesitated before saying, "If you don't want me to know your travel plans, then don't make your reservations via our Expedia account."

"I want you out, Jacob," said Jeffrey.

"I'm leaving."

"No, I mean out of the firm. You can't be trusted anymore. Name your price. I'll buy you out."

"Fuck you."

"Were you a part of this? A part of Jed McIntyre being released?"

He laughed with disdain. "Do you think I have that kind of power?"

"How did you know what happened? How did you get here so fast?"

"While you were ripping the director of the mental hospital a new asshole, he was sending me an E-mail to call you off. It wasn't his fault. It all happened above his head."

"I don't give a shit whose fault it was. Jed McIntyre's out there now and he's after Lydia."

"And now you have two psychos on your hands. That was some 'vacation' you took to Miami. Was Tatiana worth all of this?"

Jeffrey and Jacob were standing inches from each other; Lydia was bracing herself for the conflict to come to blows. But Jeffrey backed away, his fists clenching. When he spoke again, his tone was quiet but lethal.

"Get out, Jacob. Get the fuck out. And get a business lawyer, because I'm going to have you out on the street so fast, you won't know what hit you. That's my firm and don't you forget it."

"We'll see."

They were silent after Jacob had disappeared into the elevator. Lydia felt like their life was unraveling and she only had herself to blame. She wished that brown envelope had never dropped to the floor, that she'd never broken the seal. Was Tatiana worth all of this? Worth the reanimation of her worst nightmare?

"Next time," he said, sitting next to her on the couch, "I get to pick where we go on vacation."

chapter twenty-eight

Jeffrey was smart enough to know that Lydia had a few things about herself that she kept from him. It didn't bother him. He didn't need to be inside her skin, inside her head every second . . . as long as he knew he was in her heart. And of that, he was sure. He had a few things that he kept to himself as well, though they were strictly professional.

There was quite a bit, in fact, about the private investigation firm of Mark, Hanley and Striker that Lydia wasn't privy to. She knew, for example, that the firm worked on cases with the FBI and the NYPD. But she didn't know what those cases were and that people from the firm very often were brought in to go places where men carrying shields were not permitted to go. He'd shared a lot with her, probably some things that he shouldn't have, but not everything. Just as she had sources and contacts that she had never revealed, so did Jeffrey.

Sometimes the law imposed more shackles on its enforcers than it did on its offenders. Anyone on the job knew that. The price of living in a "free" society dictated that, as of a day ago, Jed McIntyre was a man who had served his debt to society. Obviously, something dirty, something evil had been behind his release. The police were not going to be of any help to them. But he knew someone who would.

He listened as Lydia moved around upstairs, packing for the trip they still had every intention of taking. He was surprised and relieved that she still wanted to go to Albania after hearing the news that Jed McIntyre was on the loose. A trip that had seemed pretty risky last night was probably the safest option for them right now. But Jed McIntyre could not be allowed to roam the streets.

He picked up the phone, keeping his eyes on the staircase, and dialed. Dax Chicago didn't so much answer the phone as groan into the receiver.

"Dax?"

"Yeah," he answered, his heavy Australian accent dragging the word out to three syllables.

"It's Jeff Mark."

"Wuzup, mate?"

"I have a job for you."

Lydia could hear Jeffrey talking on the phone downstairs, the authoritative rise and fall of his voice, his quick, hard sentences, and wondered to whom he was speaking. She had pulled down the shades again in the bedroom, conscious now of who might be watching her, and tried to shake the feeling that the happy life she and Jeffrey had constructed was shaking at its foundation and that she was to blame.

She wasn't exactly chastising herself; after all, she'd only done what she'd always done—followed her instincts, tried to help someone who had reached out to her. She wondered now if being herself meant that her life with Jeffrey would unravel, wondered how true a home they had made together. Or maybe she just wasn't meant to be happy and safe; maybe that wasn't her fate. Was she being forced to make a choice between the thing that drove her, her purpose, and their life together? No, that wasn't fair. She could have both. She wasn't sure she could live without either.

"Remind me again why we're doing this?" Jeffrey asked, walking into the room and startling her from her thoughts.

"We're looking for Tatiana Quinn," she answered, keeping her eyes lowered.

"That's why we're going to Albania?"

"Detective Ignacio said to go where the money led. The money is in Albania, so is American Equities, so is Sasa Fitore . . . so that's where we're going."

She walked back and forth between the closet and the bed, shoving clothes into two backpacks. He sat on the edge of the bed and watched her. She moved stiffly but quickly, as if she was in a hurry to go someplace she didn't want to be. She hadn't looked at him since she'd received the news about Jed McIntyre. Her face was pale, her eyes unreachable.

"So how do you want to play this?" he asked, more anger in his tone than he had intended. "Do you just want to pretend this isn't happening? Or are we going to pretend that it isn't having an effect on you, that you're too tough to care that the man who murdered your mother is on the loose and somewhere close by."

"Jeffrey . . ."

"What? I'm serious. I just want to know how I'm supposed to act."

"Jesus, give me a second to process it. I don't know how to feel," she snapped, shoving a sweater hard into one of the bags. "I never thought I'd have to deal with this. I thought he was going to be locked away forever. That's why I kept all those letters. Every month, it was like confirmation that he was locked away, that he could never reach me, that my nightmares were just that . . . nightmares. I need a little time to figure out how to handle this. Would you feel better if I broke down in your arms and begged you to protect me? You know me better than that, don't you?"

He lowered his head. She was right, of course. He was angry with her for not reacting in a way that would allow him to comfort her.

"I'm sorry, Lydia. I guess I just don't know what to do. I only want to fix this somehow."

She sat down next to him. "You don't have to fix everything, Jeffrey. We're a team. We'll handle this together. When we get back."

"It seems weird to be rushing off when we know Jed McIntyre is running around New York City."

"The farther away the better. Besides, if Jacob is right, and Nathan Quinn arranged Jed McIntyre's release to keep us from going to Albania, I'm certainly not willing to comply. Besides, what are we going to do? Wait around for Jed to come after me? There's no reason not to go."

He shuddered to hear her use his first name so casually, like he was an acquaintance they met for the occasional cocktail. It implied an intimacy in her mind, communicated that Jed McIntyre was in her thoughts more than he knew.

"Flawless logic, as usual."

"In the meantime, why don't you call one of your secret Rambo contacts and see if they can't get a handle on him?"

"What secret Rambo contacts?" he asked with a smile that managed to be at once innocent and sly.

chapter twenty-nine

"How do we know we can even trust this guy?" asked Jeffrey as they followed the rail-thin, shabbily dressed man through the nearly empty Rinas airport. Like most of the buildings in Albania, it had suffered from the 1997 riots and looting; it was run-down and filthy, reeking of urine. There were more people armed and in ragtag uniforms than there were travelers. They stood about smoking, machine guns draped casually over their shoulders. She wondered what laws they were willing to enforce with those guns in a relative state of anarchy.

"We definitely can't trust him," said Lydia. "But he'll have to do. There's no other way to get around."

Their guide had been the youngest of a crowd of men waiting at the baggage claim with signs that read DRIVER or GUIDE. His startling blue eyes and riot of red freckles gave him the look of innocence, and there was a sparkle there that communicated a depth and resourcefulness that appealed to Lydia. Lydia picked him on instinct from the throng of men vying for their American dollars.

"Can you take us to Vlorë?"

He'd looked temporarily taken aback. "Very far," he said. "Very dangerous."

"You take us there, stay with us, and then bring us back. We'll pay you in American dollars . . . fifty dollars a day."

Lydia knew that this was more than many Albanians saw in a month. His attitude changed considerably.

"Of course, of course . . . Vlorë beautiful place. This way, please." They followed him out of doors that were held open with garbage cans overflowing with rubbish. Lydia was surprised to see him open the door of a Mercedes sedan that looked in reasonable shape and get into the driver's seat. She remembered something she had read about most drivers in Albania having learned to operate a motor vehicle only since 1991; it had been illegal during Communist rule, and, as a result, there was now a high incidence of spectacular car wrecks. She said a silent prayer as their driver spun away from the terminal and roared out of the airport.

"What's your name?" asked Lydia, looking in vain for a seat belt and finding frayed stubs where they should have been. Inexplicably, the seat belts had been cut out of the car.

"Gabriel is my name, miss," he said. Then he added, "My English is good."

"Yes, it is. I'm Lydia, and this is Jeffrey."

"Why do you come here? To Albania?"

"I'm a writer. I'm doing an article."

"Oh," he said, impressed. "You write about Albania. Maybe someone will come to help us."

"I hope so," she said, and meant it.

It was dark, and the countryside between Tirana, Albania's capital, and Vlorë passed by in the shadow of clouds drifting in front of the moon, occasionally revealing abandoned villages, burned-out cars and tractors by the side of the road, and piles of garbage. Twice, Lydia heard the unmistakable sound of automatic-weapon fire. Albania looked like other Third World countries she had seen, but without the energy, without the hustle, as if it had given up. The road was less a road than it was a mass of churned gravel and dirt, and seemed to hinder rather than facilitate their forward progress.

According to the map she had, Vlorë was a little more than sixty miles from the airport, but she figured it would take two or maybe three hours to get there because of the bad condition of the road. After major delays in New York, a seemingly endless layover in Zurich, not to mention the slow line for a visa stamp upon arriving at Rinas airport, they were on their way to Vlorë significantly later than Lydia had hoped. The ride that stretched before them now seemed nothing short of interminable.

She wondered what would happen to them if the car broke down. That was the thing that always made Lydia the most uneasy about the Third World—the *what ifs*. In the United States, if something broke down or you found yourself in trouble, help was just a phone call away—police, hospitals, AAA. Here, if you got a flat tire or got into an accident, you were out of luck. She wondered what it must be like to live like that, always on the edge of disaster, no formal network of people and organizations created for the sole purpose of saving your ass. She hoped they wouldn't have to find out.

"The Communists never repaired the roads," said Gabriel in an apologetic tone. "They did not like for people to travel. They had helicopters. I am lucky to have this car. It's very strong."

"Where did you get it?" Jeffrey asked.

"After the Communists left, things were better for a while. We voted; there was a democracy. New things came from the West—cars, computers, televisions. But then after the collapse and the riots, things got very bad. Worse than communism. There was no fuel for cars, so people left them by the road. I found this one. When we got gasoline again, I became a taxi driver."

Lydia thought of what Marianna had said about Americans being like children, thinking Santa Claus leaves presents under the tree. The concept of the government collapsing, the country descending into chaos and anarchy, not being able to buy gasoline would be inconceivable to most people in the United States. It was amazing that half a day on an airplane had transported them to another universe.

Jeffrey held Lydia against him with one strong arm, bracing himself against being thrown around the car with the other. She occasionally slipped into a troubled doze, in spite of the totally worn-out shock absorbers and the rough ride. She wasn't sure how much time had passed as they rode in silence.

"It is good we are here," the driver said finally, pointing ahead to the lights of a city on the horizon. "Soon we run out of gas."

Since the collapse of the tentative economy in 1997 and the resultant riots and chaos, Albania, from all accounts, was a disaster area. Hermetically sealed from the rest of the world since 1944, then enduring the fall of communism, the rush of Western capitalism, and the subsequent crash, the country and its people had been devastated. What Lydia saw as they pulled into Vlorë was a city in ruin, barely functional. It was a city of ancient greatness and its past grandeur still echoed in its battered streets and uneven buildings, with their shot-out windows, angry graffiti, and bloody doorways. A dilapidated mosque with a crumbling minaret sagged on its frame; an old woman struggled up the remains of a sidewalk, a donkey trailing behind her. Lydia could smell the stench of an open sewer.

"I think you missed your calling," said Jeffrey. "You should have been a travel agent."

"Do you know somewhere we can stay?" she asked the driver, ignoring Jeffrey.

"Yes, yes. I will take you to the best hotel in Vlorë."

Lydia couldn't imagine what that meant.

The hotel lobby was dark except for the light coming from several candles placed throughout the space; a thin woman with limp blond hair sat behind the counter, staring at them without much interest as they entered. Gabriel approached her and said a few words to her in Albanian. She narrowed her eyes at him and answered in a dull monotone. Gabriel turned to Lydia and Jeffrey.

"There's no electricity for three days. No hot water."

"Why not?"

"There was a car accident. Someone crashed into one of the power lines. No one knows when there will be electricity again."

Some men sat around a table near a bar in the corner of the lobby, drinking what Lydia thought must be raki, the national drink—a kind of poor man's grappa. They were shabbily dressed, except for one young man who wore wire-rimmed glasses, a Western-style shirt, tailored pants, and what looked to be expensive shoes, from what Lydia could see in the dim light. They stared at Lydia and Jeffrey with a kind of suspicious, although not malicious, interest.

"It's fine," Lydia said to Gabriel, knowing that they were not going to find any place better and not wanting to drive around the city trying. "Get yourself a room, as well. We'll pay."

"No, no. My brother lives here. I will go to stay with him and come back for you in the morning."

Lydia nodded and he handed her a key. He held on to it for a second, and when she looked up at him, he said quietly, "Lock the door before you sleep and keep all your valuables in your pockets. You are never safe here."

"Thank you," she said, discreetly handing him five ten-dollar bills folded in half.

Lydia felt as though they had stepped back in time as the woman, dressed in what looked like a peasant costume—long, heavy woolen skirt and tunic covered by a soiled white apron—her hair in a loose bun, with strands escaping and glowing in the candlelight like spiderwebs, led them up a hallway by candlelight. She opened the door for Lydia and Jeffrey and Lydia handed her the fifteen dollars for the cost of the room—a fee she knew was exorbitantly inflated because they were Westerners. The woman left the candle with them and walked back down the hall without a word.

Lydia was glad they only had a candle for light, not wanting to examine the room too closely. A double bed sagged like a hammock in the middle of the room. A wooden chair looked sad and rickety beside a window where the moonlight shone through. The adjoining bathroom, a five-star luxury in a place like this, was passably clean, if she tried to ignore the faint odor.

"This is nice," said Jeffrey, sinking into the bed, not even bothering to take his clothes off.

"Don't get comfortable," she said.

"Why not?"

"We only have a couple of hours to find that pickup spot."

As medieval as their hotel had seemed, the Paradiso was as modern a nightclub as could be found in any major city in the world. As Lydia and Jeffrey had struck out onto the rutted streets, its neon sign had been like a beacon in the darkened city. Loud music was leaking out the door, which was guarded by two burly men with shaved heads and gold chains. A white SUV-cum-stretch limousine was parked out front. Women who were clearly prostitutes paraded up and down the block, passing in front of the crumbling, graffiti-riven concrete wall next to the club. They seemed extremely young to Lydia. One with bleach-blond hair and a hot pink Lycra dress had barely developed breasts and hips, but she blew a kiss to Jeffrey.

A twenty-dollar bill got Lydia and Jeffrey through the door. "Americans?" asked one of the beefy bouncers. Lydia nodded and the man smiled enthusiastically. "Welcome!"

The bar was lined with American and European brands of liquor and cigarettes. Lydia wasn't surprised that those companies had wasted no time in getting their products into the depressed country; with the First World becoming so health-conscious, they were always looking for new markets that cared more for escapist pleasure than long life. A heavy techno beat dominated the large space, which was crowded with people and filled with smoke. The dance floor heaved with bodies. Jeffrey ordered two straight Stolis from the bar, and they found a corner where they could watch the show.

On a stage above the dance floor, cheaply, scantily clad women gyrated listlessly. Occasionally, two or three of them would walk down a narrow flight of stairs on the side of the stage and move into the crowd, which was comprised almost entirely of men. More girls replaced them on the stage. Lydia then noticed that those who walked into the crowd would pair up with one of the men and disappear into the back of the club. After they had watched this ritual a number of times, Lydia and Jeffrey followed.

They trailed a thin young girl whose badly dyed black hair revealed at least an inch of sandy blond roots and a man so heavy that the floorboards creaked audibly beneath his feet and the back of whose head had three chins. He wore the most hideous-possible powder blue polyester suit. The dandruff on his shoulders glowed in the hallway's black light. Lydia tried to imagine a dollar figure that would make it all right to have physical contact with him, couldn't come up with one, and cringed as the man placed a heavily ringed hand on the girl's fragile neck. The hallway was narrow and seemed to go on forever before the couple disappeared ahead of them.

Lydia and Jeffrey were stopped by another bouncer at the velvet curtain through which the couple had passed. Lydia couldn't be sure whether it was a different man from the one at door or not, for they all looked so similar with their shaved heads and gold chains. But his attitude was far less welcoming. "Private," he growled. When Lydia handed him a fifty-dollar bill, he nodded to another bouncer, and they found themselves flanked and about to be escorted from the club.

Like a guardian angel, Gabriel appeared from behind one of the curtains and said a few magic words in Albanian, and the men seemed to relax. "They are my friends," he said in English. And then he looked at Lydia and Jeffrey. "I've been waiting for you." He led them away behind the curtain to a quiet table.

"Why have you come here?" he asked when they were seated, leaning in close to them. His breath was rank, and Lydia noticed that his teeth were brown and crooked. The face that had seemed sweet and boyish, peppered with freckles, was more hard-edged and tired, older than she had thought.

"Just looking for a good time," Lydia answered, not sure how well they could trust him.

"That's 'bullshit'—isn't that what the Americans say?" he said, curling his mouth into some expression halfway between smile and sneer.

She looked around and noted with slight distaste the couple they had followed into the lounge. The girl was engaged in a lack-luster lap dance, her hands caressing her companion's fat head, her eyes dull and staring off into the distance. Several other couples were engaged in the same activity. And Lydia noted that there was yet another velvet-curtained doorway at the far end of the room. She didn't have to wonder what happened if the men elected to be escorted through that doorway. Apparently at the Paradiso, there were levels of debauchery, pleasure for every budget.

"Why do you care what we're doing here?" asked Jeffrey.

"Maybe I can help you," he answered with a nonchalant shrug.

"Why would you want to help us?"

He flipped a Marlboro from a soft pack he removed from his pocket. He held the pack out to Lydia and she took one, ignoring a scowl from Jeffrey. Gabriel lighted it for her with the flourish of a silver Zippo. "I like your American dollars," he answered easily.

Lydia regarded him for second, trying to weigh what they had to lose by trusting him versus what he could tell them or show them that they might not be able to find out on their own. She decided the gamble might be worth the risk.

"Who owns this place?" she asked.

"The same people who own everything. The Mafia, as you call them. Not the Italians . . . the Albanian mob. They control the country now. There is no government here anymore. Even those in power are only puppets of the mob," he said. He had a peculiar way about him, at once grandiose and insecure, as though he were pretending to be a man he wasn't and lived in fear of being discovered.

"These women, where do they come from?"

"From the villages, mostly. They are simple, you know, not smart," he said, tapping his temple. "They think that they will have jobs as waitresses in the city, make money for their families. But then they become prostitutes."

"By force or by their own free will?"

"Who can say? Some claim it is by force, but how can you trust the word of a whore, eh? But once they've become whores, they can never go back to their families. Even if a woman is raped in Albania, she is considered dirty. She might even be killed by her husband or her brothers." He spoke without judgment. This was the world, as Gabriel knew it, and he didn't seem to have an opinion about it one way or the other. Lydia was sure they couldn't really trust him, but she figured as long as they had American dollars to give him, he'd tell her what she wanted to know, and take her where she wanted to go.

"Does the name Nathan Quinn mean anything to you?"

He shook his head slowly, seeming to mull it over. "No. I do not think I have heard that name."

"What about Radovan Mladic?"

A look of distaste crossed his face as he dredged mucus from the back of his throat and spit emphatically on the ground near Lydia's feet. "The ruin of this country is on the soul of that man."

He lighted another cigarette and said, "After the fall of communism, there was hope for the first time. Goods and money flowed in from the West. We were able to see television broadcasts, magazines from overseas," he said, gesticulating grandly while his eyes darted back and forth between Lydia and Jeffrey as if gauging their responses.

"We saw that the world was decades ahead of us. When businesses from Italy and Greece, and even the United States, started to come here, we thought, We will be rich like those from the West. American Equities was one of those companies. People all over the country invested the money they had.

"But Radovan Mladic was a criminal. He had always been a criminal . . . a pimp, as Americans say, and a dealer of guns and heroin. But no one seemed to care. . . . They just wanted to invest their money and become rich. They didn't even know what American Equities was or what kind of business they were doing; they were so naïve. American Equities stole the people's money. And then the riots came. Most of us still do not understand what really happened here. But we have never recovered."

"What happened to him?" Jeffrey asked.

"He was murdered, shot in the head."

"Murdered?" asked Lydia. "I thought he committed suicide."

"No. He was killed."

"By whom?"

"A lot of people take credit for it; no one knows for certain. They found his body after the building that housed American Equities was burned to the ground."

"What happened to his wife?" she asked, trying to get a handle on how accurate his information might be.

He shrugged. "I don't know. Someone said maybe she went to America."

Since they had seen Jenna Quinn at Valentina's service, a

thought had been turning somewhere in the back of Lydia's mind: Jenna Quinn was the missing piece to their investigation, and nothing made sense until Lydia factored her in as a player. But she still wasn't clear on the woman's motivations or how, why, and if she could be involved in her own daughter's disappearance.

Lydia looked at her watch, suddenly remembering what they had come for and what they needed to know.

"There's someplace I want you to take us, Gabriel," she said.

"Where?"

She leaned toward him and lowered her voice. "Where the boats come from Italy to take the girls overseas."

"I don't know what you're talking about," he said, suddenly cagey.

"Bullshit," she said, and smiled.

Gabriel looked around him in the dimly lighted room; he seemed to be considering his options. He'd turned skittish on her, and for a second she thought he would get up and bolt.

"Maybe," he said, lighting still another cigarette off the one he was about to extinguish, "for the right price."

It was nearly dawn by the time they saw what they had come to see. The sky had lightened from pitch to charcoal, the stars fading slowly, when in the distance they heard the low rumbling of a high-powered speedboat and saw the circle of a spotlight bouncing on its bow. Lydia, Jeffrey, and Gabriel crouched behind large rusted barrels, peering through the spaces between them to watch the dock just fifty yards away. The large boat pulled up slowly, its engine roaring, and then the engine cut out and the ship drifted into the dock. A man stood at the bow and another one at the stern. From a darkened boathouse, two men came running out to grab the lines. Their machine guns hung from straps slung across their chests.

"If they catch us here, they'll kill us all," said Gabriel solemnly.

Lydia nodded, wondering why a hundred dollars had convinced Gabriel to risk his life. Was the money worth so much? Or was his life worth that little?

"They take the girls from their villages, maybe from school or from a nightclub," he whispered, confirming what Lydia had read. "They tell them that they will be models, or maybe they are promised rich American husbands. Then they bring them here. It is only a few hours by boat to Italy, where they are sold to pimps. A pretty, young virgin is worth the most."

Two men emerged from the boat's cabin and walked to shore as three large military vans with flashing lights raced up to the water's edge. The dock stood at an isolated collection of piers surrounded by an abandoned warehouse. It had once probably been the hub of all the country's importing and exporting, Vlorë being Albania's largest port after Durrës. But all the buildings seemed to sag on their frames, the abandonment and neglect evident in the garbage strewn about, the graffiti covering the walls, and the eerie silence; the only sound was the Adriatic lapping against the seawalls. The air was heavy with the smell of salt and rotting fish.

"Have the police come?" Lydia whispered as she watched uniformed officers jump from the vehicles.

"Yes," said, Gabriel laughing mirthlessly. "They've come for their paychecks."

One by one, the girls filed out of the vans and formed a line, awaiting passage to Italy, believing that they were on their way to a better life. There had to be at least seventy of them. They were too far away and the light was too low for Lydia to see their faces, but she noticed how some of them held hands, how other groups of two or three seemed to cling together. They weren't bound or handcuffed, except by their own hopes and dreams. Most of them were being led to their deaths, and they didn't even know it.

"We have to do something," she said suddenly to Jeffrey.

"No," he said firmly, turning a stern gaze on her. "There are four men, by my count, with machine guns. Probably more below. We're outmanned and outgunned. We'll just get ourselves killed, and we're not going to help anyone tonight—or ever—if that happens."

"Don't be crazy," Gabriel said, putting a hand on her arm. "You are not in America. This is a country without heroes. Nobody wins here."

"Except for the criminals," whispered Lydia angrily.

"Not even them. Look at where they live. What does that money buy them? Venereal disease and an early grave from drink, drugs, cigarettes . . . or all three."

His logic was irrefutable, but she felt almost desperate with helplessness as she watched the men from the boat hand envelopes to each of the men in uniform. The police were selling girls into sexual slavery. They were powerless here, stupid even to have come. Jacob had been right after all. They weren't going to stop this any more than they were single-handedly going to end the drug trade. She realized that Jeffrey had a tight grip on her arm, as if he didn't trust her not to get up and run toward the boat.

They watched as the girls filed onto the boat, not one of them giving a backward glance to their homeland. The vans pulled silently away, disappearing behind the decrepit buildings as the first light of morning broke the sky in brilliant yellow. The boat engine came loudly to life as a white SUV limousine pulled up, tires spitting up gravel as it came to a stop. Lydia wondered if it was the same one they had seen in front of the club; she didn't imagine there were too many of them in Albania. The sky was shading to pink and orange, the moon still visible as a figure emerged from the boat and jumped off onto the dock. The boat roared across the water as the figure walked casually toward the limo. She recognized the gait even in the slight morning light. The elegant figure with the cool strut was Sasa Fitore.

chapter thirty

"It's going to be hard to follow him on these deserted roads," said Jeffrey, as the limousine pulled away and the sound of the boat engine faded off into the distance.

"We don't need to follow too closely," said Lydia. "I know where he's going."

"And how do you know that?" asked Jeffrey, looking at her as she removed a piece of paper from her pocket.

"This is the address of American Equities. Craig gave it to me." She handed the paper to Gabriel, who nodded but said nothing. "Do you know where it is?" she asked.

"I know," he said.

"Okay," said Lydia. "Take us there."

Gabriel walked toward the Mercedes, and Jeffrey held Lydia back by the arm. "This is a bad idea," he said softly.

"I have a feeling, Jeffrey, that when we follow Sasa, he's going to lead us directly to Tatiana."

"Yeah, well, I have a feeling he's going to lead us directly into a really big mess."

"We've been in messes before."

He could see that there was no arguing with her now. She had a desperate fire in her eyes, and she was pulling away from him, moving toward the car. He followed her.

"Let's go," she said to Gabriel.

"Why do you think we're going to find her here?" asked Jeffrey as the car made its way up a steep rocky hill and onto a road surrounded by trees. The road wound in such a way that a set of taillights could be seen in the distance.

"I've just been thinking about all the pieces and how they haven't seemed to fit together."

"What do you mean?"

"Well, how someone had to have been in the house the night Tatiana disappeared, for example. Someone turned off that camera. And the fact that Nathan Quinn was so desperate to find her, putting all this pressure on the police, and yet people at the top were keeping Detective Ignacio from looking into Quinn's business affairs. The detective knew that those connections would lead somewhere; that's why he told us to follow the money, but he dropped the case because he was afraid of something. How someone was ahead of every move we made in Miami, killing off the people who were trying to give us information. Then Jacob, with his whole cryptic warning shtick, telling us that Tatiana's body had been found. I mean, it's not just as if Tatiana is missing and can't be found. It's as if all these forces are at work trying to keep her from being found. Trying to *hide* her from something."

"Or someone."

"So I'm wondering who would be that motivated to hide and protect Tatiana. So motivated that they would be willing and able to go to these lengths to keep her hidden. And what could be so horrible, so powerful, that it would be necessary to do so? And only one thing makes sense to me."

"What's that?"

"Only a mother would go to such lengths to protect a child."

"Jenna Quinn? But what is she protecting Tatiana from?"

"Nathan Quinn."

"And what makes you think she's powerful enough to do all of this?"

"What if she had help from some powerful people with parallel interests?"

"I'm not following you."

"Something Jacob said stuck with me. Remember what he said about Nathan Quinn being out of control and how steps were being taken to change that? And then on the tape, Tatiana said, 'I can't believe *she's* doing this to me'?"

"Yeah, I remember that. . . ."

"Well, steps are being taken by whom? Maybe some of Nathan's powerful connections have turned against him. Maybe he's no longer playing by the rules of, say, the Council. They've lost control of him."

"And now they're trying to stop him?"

"And Jenna Quinn agreed to help them."

"Okay . . . but who are 'they'?"

"I think," said Gabriel, bringing the car to a sudden stop, "that you are about to find out."

They came from the trees like wraiths. There was no moving forward; the road was blocked by a black Hummer, and another approached from behind. Lydia felt her heart skip and her mouth go dry as at least ten men wearing black body armor and ski masks and carrying large automatic weapons surrounded the car. One of them turned on a spotlight and shone it into the window. Lydia blocked her eyes and leaned against Jeffrey, thinking that he was always right. She hoped she'd have another chance to listen.

chapter thirty-one

The sky was turning a misty gray and on either side of the rocky road were the charred remains of olive trees, their branches black and twisted like witch's fingers. No one had said a word to them, only pulled them firmly, but not violently, from the Mercedes. One of the masked men had leaned into the car and said something to Gabriel in Albanian, handing him a wad of cash. The Hummer pulled out of his way, and he then backed away down the road, not looking at Lydia, making a quick U-turn and spitting up gravel as soon as he had room to turn around. Lydia and Jeffrey had been walked to the leading Hummer, where they were each forced to spread their arms and legs against its hood. The hood was warm and gritty beneath her hands and Lydia worked hard to control her breathing. Her head had started to pound and she could feel her pulse throbbing in her temple. The scene—the masked men in black body armor, the dead trees and slate sky—was surreal and eerily quiet. She could hear only the sound of the wind and the footsteps of their captors.

Normally, Lydia would have immediately started shooting off her mouth, but she kept quiet, unsure of what and of whom they were dealing with. And she was afraid. It was a lot safer to be a loudmouthed smart-ass in the First World, where it generally didn't cost you your life. She endured a vigorous rubdown, which resulted in the loss of her weapon. The man in the ski mask inspected it and made a sound of approval as it disappeared into his pants.

"Take it easy," Lydia finally said to the man, who continued frisking her even after he should have been satisfied that he'd confiscated her only weapon. He ignored her but stopped and pushed her into the leather backseat of the Hummer next to Jeffrey.

"Where are you taking us?" she asked the man in the passenger seat, who turned around to keep Jeffrey's Glock pointed at them.

"Shut the fuck up," the man said in English. She was surprised to note that he was American. She really hated being spoken to that way; a shitty tone of voice and rude language were two more of her serious pet peeves . . . at least when she was on the receiving end. Jeffrey put a hand on her shoulder and pulled her back toward him. He gave her a look that warned her to keep her temper.

The steep road wound through the ruined olive groves, and finally they reached an elaborate, heavy black iron gate hinged to a high stone wall edged with razor wire. Lydia felt her mouth go dry and her heart was beating like a drum. The gate swung open as they approached, then closed behind them with a heavy clang. Lydia reached for Jeffrey's hand. He squeezed it hard and looked into her eyes, which seemed to say, It's okay. We're going to be okay. But she could see in the grim line of his mouth that he knew they were in over their heads—unarmed, taken prisoner by masked men with machine guns.

The house they approached was essentially a stone fortress with huge wooden doors, lanterns burning on either side of the arched entryway, and narrow windows. High towers jutted up from the four corners, and Lydia could see a figure holding a rifle standing at the top of one of them. The SUV limousine they had seen so much of over the last few hours sat next to the entrance of the house. She shuddered. What had she gotten them into? And how was she going to get them out?

She was not comforted by the sight of Sasa Fitore casually approaching the door of the Hummer. "Hello, Ms. Strong," he said with a cold smile as he opened the door. "Funny meeting you here."

"Well, you know, we were in the neighborhood and thought we'd drop by."

Sasa laughed at her joke, but the sound of it filled Lydia with dread.

chapter thirty-two

In the dusk, with the leaves falling from the trees in the newly harsh cold of late autumn, he relished his freedom. The sky was a gunmetal gray against the fall colors, now past their peak, turning from flame to bloodred, from spark to ember. The scent of wood burning in fireplaces carried into his nostrils on the wind coming through the open window, reminding him of the warmth of a home and family he had never known. He inhaled deeply, taking in the aroma. He realized suddenly that he was gripping the wheel of the brand-new Land Rover so hard, his hands were starting to cramp. David Bowie and Bing Crosby sang their rendition of "The Little Drummer Boy" on the easy-listening station he had tuned in, even though Thanksgiving hadn't even arrived.

He pulled down the sun visor, looked at his reflection in the mirror there, and took off his black wool hat. He looked like the monster that he was, his cold blue eyes placid pools in the landscape of his jutting cheekbones and badly shaved head. He ran his large sinewy hands over the top of his head, feeling the rough stubble, the raised scar on his crown from a fight with another inmate. He sighed. He felt angry and used.

Given the things he'd done, Jed McIntyre imagined that he'd be treated with a little more respect. Well, maybe *respect* wasn't the right word. *Trepidation, fear, revulsion* were more like it. He really enjoyed it when people cowered from him, when he saw real terror in their eyes. But people, he noticed, seemed a bit desensitized to murderers these days. It wasn't like back in the days of Son of Sam and Richard Ramirez, when it was enough just to be really fucking insane. People were repulsed but fascinated; those guys had fan clubs, pen pals, even women proposing to them. He hadn't received any of the attention he'd expected.

He blamed Thomas Harris and all those other writers, with their larger-than-life villains. How was a real serial killer supposed to live up to that image of the brilliant, sophisticated Dr. Lecter? It just wasn't realistic, and he resented it. Nothing was ever as cool in real life as it was in books and the movies, not even serial homicide.

On the other hand, it was interesting how in *Hannibal,* it was only when Clarice Starling had lost everything that Lecter was able to have what he had wanted from her all along. That was the only thing that kept Jed in check, even though he'd wanted to strangle R. Alexander Harriman, Esq., or whoever he was today, with his bare hands. A few thousand dollars, some new clothes, and a Land Rover were supposed to turn him into some kind of puppet taking orders from a mystery mogul. Didn't these guys get it? He was a homicidal maniac . . . not some thug, some killer for hire. He had impulses that even *he* couldn't control. What hubris to think that *they* could control him. But he was proud of himself because he had kept his cool. He was smart enough to know that someone powerful enough to get him out of the hospital was powerful enough to put him back. In the meantime, Jed's benefactor was allowing him to travel in style . . . while doing exactly what he would have done anyway—rip the flesh off of Lydia Strong's life, take it right down to the bone, so she'd be nothing but a shell of herself, broken and empty.

Both cars were in the driveway, a black Lincoln Continental and a sporty red BMW, but the lights were low and Jed hadn't seen any activity in the house. It would be hours before he made his move. He reached over to the floor on the passenger side and picked up the bag of Krispy Kreme doughnuts he'd bought on Twenty-third Street before leaving Manhattan on his way up to Sleepy Hollow.

chapter thirty-three

With the fire crackling in the hearth, the dark varnished floor, antique furniture, plush Turkish area rugs scattered throughout the room, it would have been a pleasant and cozy place if they hadn't had to worry about whether or not they were going to be killed. Lydia and Jeffrey sat stiffly but unbound on an overstuffed red velvet sofa. Once they were inside, they were treated like guests, except for the armed men in black ski masks and body armor blocking any potential exit from the posh sitting room. Lydia could see Jeffrey scanning the room and counting men, assessing their options. His face was stony, but she could feel the tension coming off him in waves.

A sophisticated older woman with salt-and-pepper hair styled in a neat bob entered the room on quick, quiet feet. She was dressed in a simple black long-sleeved sheath and was carrying a tray with a teapot and cups, cream and sugar, and a plate of cookies. She didn't look at them at all as she placed the tray on a table before them and then moved quickly from the room.

"How civilized," commented Lydia, wisecracking to manage the fear rising in her belly.

"There's no reason not to be civilized," said Sasa, entering and sitting opposite them. He threw one leg over the arm of the overstuffed chair and touched his fingertips together. "In Albania, there are strict laws of hospitality."

"But there's nothing on the books about selling young women into sexual slavery?" she said, shifting forward on the couch.

Sasa smiled and shrugged. "There are not a lot of ways to make a living in Albania," he said simply, not a trace of shame on his coldly handsome face. She noticed how at ease he was, how sure of himself. And it made her wonder about what it might be like to operate without a moral code, whether somewhere deep inside he knew what a monster he was.

"Why have you brought us here?" asked Lydia.

He laughed. "I did not bring you here. *You* followed *me* here. I have been trying to shake you off for days, but you are like something sticky on my shoe."

"You know what I mean. Why did you bring us here instead of just shooting us out on the road?"

"It wasn't my decision to make. If it were up to me, you would have been dead a long time ago," he answered, anger seeping into his voice and darkening his eyes. As he slid forward in the chair, Lydia shrank back involuntarily.

She had expected him to seem more ghoulish, but now that she was seeing him up close for the first time, he was handsome and well dressed, soft-spoken. It made him all the more horrifying. She imagined that the young women he'd led to the slaughter were charmed by him, seduced by him. That they had looked into his blue eyes and naïvely saw someone they could trust, someone who could make them into models and actresses. It wasn't fair that nature so often played such games. Monsters should be recognizable, but they seldom were.

"So educate me, Sasa," she said, his name feeling dirty on her tongue. "What's going on?"

He looked at her sullenly and got up from his chair as the doors opened. Lydia saw Jeffrey do a double take as Jenna Quinn entered the room—followed by Jacob Hanley. Jacob nodded to the men standing guard at the entrance. When they took off their masks, Lydia recognized Special Agents Bentley and Negron.

"Jesus," said Jeffrey, standing up, "what the fuck is going on?"

"You couldn't have just stayed in New York, right?" said Bentley with a grim smile.

"Shut up, Bentley," snapped Jacob, and the agent's face darkened. He complied but continued to glare at Lydia and Jeffrey.

Jeffrey sank back down onto the couch, staring at Jacob, trying to get his mind around his sudden appearance in this place. Lydia was at a rare loss for words. She regarded Jenna and Jacob with wonder as her mind raced through all the possibilities. Jenna, looking smaller than Lydia remembered her, walked over toward the window and Jacob came to stand in front of them. He wore a pair of loose black pants and a beige cable-knit sweater. She could just make out the outline of the butt of his gun under the sweater. He stood with his hands in his pockets, rocking back and forth on dark brown suede shoes. His expression was some combination of triumph and condescension. As the pieces started to fall together in Lydia's mind, things made more sense than they had in days.

"She's here, isn't she?" asked Lydia finally.

"Yes, she is," replied Jacob, sighing. He leaned against the fireplace mantel and regarded Lydia with something that looked annoyingly like benevolent pity.

"And she has been all along?" asked Lydia with a shake of her head, never taking her eyes from Jacob. She was amazed that this person they thought they knew so well was a complete stranger to her, with an agenda that they had never suspected.

"Yes," he said. "Understand that it had to be this way, Lydia."

She knitted her brows together and rubbed her hands absentmindedly on her thighs as she tried to understand, the pieces slowly coming together. But for all the things that were starting to make sense, there was one thing she couldn't understand. "Why?" she said after a moment.

"Because Tatiana's safety was the only condition acceptable to the person who could help us to bring down Nathan Quinn."

"Who's 'us'?" asked Lydia.

"The FBI," said Jeffrey, looking at Bentley and Negron, then back to Jacob. "Are you working for the FBI, Jacob?" Lydia heard something like hope in Jeffrey's voice, as if he was still searching for something redeeming in the man who used to be his friend.

"More or less," said Jacob with a shrug. "Let's just say that the FBI's interests happened to collude with the interests of another organization that could no longer condone Nathan Quinn's activities."

"The Council," said Lydia.

Another shrug from Jacob and a kind of half nod confirmed Lydia's guess.

"And Jenna Quinn was the only person who could help you?" she asked.

Jenna stood at the window. She couldn't have been more than five four, but there was a hardness to her bearing now that Lydia hadn't seen before. She had her arms folded across her chest and she leaned against the sill. The morning light was gray and dull; it was bad for Jenna, making her look older and washed-out, tired. She hardly looked like she could be the lynchpin in this operation, but it was all starting to make sense now.

"Well, Jenna Quinn and Sasa Fitore," answered Jacob.

"So the FBI got into bed with the Albanian mob in order to arrest Nathan Quinn?" asked Jeffrey. "They must have wanted him pretty bad."

"He's a very bad man. And he needs to be stopped," said Bentley with a passion that surprised Lydia. "By any means necessary."

"So how did the FBI get Jenna Quinn and Sasa Fitore to cooperate?" Lydia asked.

"I married Radovan when I was a child, only fifteen," Jenna said, so softly that Lydia wasn't sure she had heard her right. "It was an arranged marriage, like so many marriages here. Our families were both very powerful in the organized-crime syndicate that existed even when the Communists were in control. I was too young to know any of this then, but he taught me everything . . . over the years. And as I grew older, he treated me as much like a partner as a wife, very unusual for an Albanian man."

She moved away from the window and began pacing in front of the fireplace, her arms folded across her belly, her eyes on the floor.

"When the Communist regime fell, Radovan became even more powerful—the most powerful man in Albania. Even the new government was in his pocket, its officials made rich by their expensive 'ignorance' of Radovan's businesses. He had interests in the trade of guns, heroin, women—everything went through him. But then with all the money coming in from the West, he began to realize that there were even bigger opportunities awaiting us. He started his company, American Equities, supposedly to export tobacco, but, in reality, it was women he was exporting.

"He sought American investors. Nathan Quinn was one of those men. The government wanted their share, of course, so they insisted that the company be open to Albanian investors, as well. Then they encouraged Albanians to invest their meager life savings. Of course, the whole country was in a feeding frenzy; everyone thought they would be rich like Americans, but that money went directly into the hands of the corrupt government. It was all a sham—in a matter of a year, all the money was gone, stolen by government officials; people lost everything. The country, as you know, descended into chaos.

"Radovan was murdered. I was a pariah in this country. Many people would have liked to see me dead, as well. I had no choice but to accept Nathan Quinn's proposal and take Tatiana to America. I had always dreamed that she would be educated there."

Jenna spoke of the murder of her husband and the destruction of her entire country in a quiet monotone, betraying neither emotion nor regret.

"I was grieving and afraid when I first moved to the United States," Jenna went on. Lydia detected the same note of drama that she remembered from Miami. "Sasa, who was Radovan's closest associate, took over the exporting business. But seeing a bigger opportunity, he came to the United States to start American Beauty, the film company. Nathan financed much of the operation, and his business associates became American Beauty's biggest clients. Nathan offered a liaison to a world Sasa never would have been able to enter otherwise."

"So you knew that Sasa Fitore and his men were tricking or abducting young Albanian woman and using them in snuff films? And that Nathan Quinn was profiting from it and providing the clientele?" interjected Lydia, her voice thick with judgment.

"What could I do? I was powerless to stop it," Jenna said, not trying to hide her shame. She took a moment to compose herself and then she continued. "Until now."

Lydia remembered Tatiana's taped indictment of her mother and thought how right she had been.

"Then I finally noticed how Nathan looked at my own daughter. I realized then how truly evil Nathan was, and I became very afraid for her, for us. I knew I had to find a way out. I just wasn't sure how. He is so powerful, I never could have gotten away from him on my own." She turned a pleading gaze on Lydia and Jeffrey, as if begging them with her eyes to understand the predicament in which she had found herself.

Lydia wondered if Jenna considered Nathan to be more or less evil than her first husband, who, by her own admission, was an arms and drug dealer and a pimp, the man responsible for the fall of Albania, or her current lover, who was a producer of snuff films.

"Nathan Quinn was a star in the Council, once," said Jacob.

"Through his brilliant investments and international connections, he made a lot of money for a lot of people."

"Let me guess," Jeffrey said. "There came a time when Nathan Quinn's interests no longer meshed with the interests of the organization. But because of the people he had on the end of his strings, he was untouchable. Some people were making a lot of money . . . but some people weren't. And the decision was made to bring Quinn down. But it turned out to be harder than they thought."

"He has a lot of important people by the balls," said Jacob.

"What do you mean?" asked Jeffrey.

"Because they are clients of American Beauty," said Lydia. "Jesus Christ." Flashing on the images of the DVD, she felt sick. She'd imagined the men she saw to be criminals, maybe mob bosses; she'd never imagined them to be senators and businessmen. She could hardly judge Sasa, who'd grown up surrounded by crime, poverty, and desperation, when these men of privilege were just as morally bankrupt.

"That's right," said Jacob. "Men you wouldn't believe . . . raping and murdering young women for sexual gratification. They were a secret society within the secret society, sexual deviants with ravenous appetites. Quinn was untouchable by law; even the other members of the Council couldn't get near him."

"So it became like a war?" asked Lydia.

"A quiet war. A war they were losing until we realized that the FBI had already begun an investigation into Nathan Quinn and Sasa Fitore. Through their intelligence within the ranks of the Albanian mob, we learned that all of Nathan Quinn's illegal operations—including American Beauty—were in Jenna's name."

"So you threatened to charge her with crimes and send her to prison?"

"We threatened to extradite her to Albania so that she could face the charges pending against her here," said Jacob with a grim smile. "A far more frightening option."

"But she's here now."

"Those charges have been dropped," he said, sitting down in the chair where Sasa had been earlier.

Jenna hadn't moved from the mantel, where she stood staring into the flames, holding her hands to the heat. She seemed not to be listening to their conversation, lost in her own thoughts. She had her back to Lydia, who could see that her shoulders were slumped, and Lydia wondered if the shame she seemed to feel was real. She hoped so. Her eyes drifted to Sasa, who stood sullen and silent in the corner, watching Jenna, an ugly look in his eye.

"How convenient," said Lydia. "And how did you get this piece of shit involved?" she asked, nodding at Sasa. She saw Sasa's face flush and his right hand clench into a fist, and she was glad.

"Through the same FBI investigation. They'd been watching Sasa for over a year, gathering evidence against him on a number of illegal operations. Marianna was a key player in that end of things, even though she never trusted us any more than she trusted her uncle. But addicts are always easy to control. Thanks to her and to Agents Bentley and Negron, we have enough on Mr. Fitore to keep him in prison for most of the next century. It behooves him to cooperate with us."

At this, Sasa let out a little laugh, which Jacob seemed to ignore. Lydia turned to look at him. His face had grown angrier, and his body language brought to mind a pit bull on a chain. Sasa had the arrogance of a man with something to prove, an ego that when challenged would defend itself at all costs. He is a very dangerous man to be relying on, thought Lydia. And she hoped the leash they had him on was strong enough to hold him.

"And what's Jenna providing for you on Quinn?" asked Jeffrey.

"She's providing us with information, security codes, account numbers, habits, names of associates, things that Sasa doesn't have access to. We're gathering evidence against him."

"Gathering evidence? You threw the DVD you had with his

voice on it out the window of the car the other night," said Lydia, remembering that night clearly and wondering how she hadn't realized his motives then.

"Oh," said Jacob with an indulgent laugh, "we'll never get him on that. Too many people, too high up, are involved for that ever to come out. Snuff doesn't even exist, according to the FBI."

"What, then?" she said, trying to quell her rising frustration and anger, as well her sense of helplessness.

"We'll get him on tax evasion . . . something like that," said Jacob with a world-weary sigh.

"And he'll go to federal prison," said Jeffrey. "Where, having lost everything, he'll sadly 'commit suicide.'"

Jacob gave a cryptic smile and crossed his legs. "Well, it would be quite a blow to poor Mr. Quinn."

"They don't want to expose him, or bring him to justice," Jeffrey said, turning to Lydia with a sad smile. She could see her own emotions mirrored in his face. "Because to do so would be to expose the Council and their dirty little secret. They just want to get rid of him."

"Getting rid of him is the only justice we can hope for here, Jeff."

"But what about the rest of them, like those two men on the tape?" asked Lydia. "Who are the rest of these men?"

"I could tell you," said Jacob, smiling, "but then I'd have to kill you." He laughed heartily then and said, "I've always wanted a legitimate reason to say that."

Jeffrey just glared at him.

"We have another copy of that tape," said Lydia pointlessly, hating him so intensely, she could taste bile in her throat. She hated him more than she hated Sasa, because at least Sasa knew what he was. Jacob still considered himself one of the good guys. "We could find out who those two men were."

"I'm sure," said Jacob with an indulgent smile. "It doesn't

matter. There's no law-enforcement or media agency in the world that will touch it. If you try to expose it, you'll be destroyed. You'll go from Pulitzer Prize–winning journalist to conspiracy theorist in no time. One day, you're on the cover of *Time* magazine; the next, you're on the cover of the *National Enquirer*. You, of all people, should know never to underestimate the power of the media. Trust me. You'll never work again."

Lydia stood up, walked over to the fireplace, and looked into the flames. Jenna moved to the other side of the room and stood by the door. Lydia's anger was reaching a crescendo, leaving her suddenly feeling shaky and weak. Hers was the anger of a person who knew she'd lost a battle; she felt small and powerless, beaten. But there were still a thousand questions floating around in her head.

"And what about him?" she said, looking at Sasa, her voice rising. "He just walks away from it all, no justice for the women he has sold, or murdered, or watched murdered in Technicolor? What happens to American Beauty?" asked Lydia.

She looked at Sasa and thought of the girl they had seen murdered on the tape. She remembered how the girl had trusted him at first, then how frightened she had been, and finally how horribly her life had ended. She was nameless and faceless and would never have justice. She wanted Sasa to feel that kind of pain and felt sick that he would walk away from this with no punishment, no remorse. She looked at him, and he looked back at her with a kind of smug, heavy-lidded gaze, his mouth twisted into a condescending sneer. Lydia wanted to beat him with her fists until he felt something, wanted him to know what it meant to hurt, to be helpless and afraid, and then to die alone.

"The terms of our agreement are not your concern," said Jacob.

"Nothing happens, right, Jacob?" said Jeffrey, standing and walking over toward Lydia. "It's business as usual. It never stops."

Bentley and Negron stood stone-faced now. Lydia thought she saw anger in Bentley's eyes, but she couldn't be sure. She didn't know that people who made the rules were playing a game that most people didn't even know about. Maybe this kind of justice was good enough for the FBI, but it wasn't good enough for her.

"We'll stop Nathan Quinn. That's about all I can promise. The rest of it . . . well, it's too complicated," said Jacob. "I know it doesn't seem like it, but we're the good guys here, for Christ's sake."

"It's getting a little hard to tell the difference," said Lydia.

"How did you get involved in this, Jacob?" asked Jeffrey.

"I can't discuss that with you, Jeff."

"Why not, buddy? Aren't we *partners*?" said Jeffrey, his voice tight with angry sarcasm.

"You're better off not knowing," answered Jacob with monklike composure. "Think of it as a freelance project."

"It's just like the George Hewlett case."

"There are similar forces at play," he admitted. "But last time, you listened."

"I didn't have a choice. It disappeared."

"If you'd listened this time," he said, looking at Lydia, "Jed McIntyre would still be behind bars."

Jeffrey rose quickly, and just as quickly Bentley and Negron moved in. "Easy, boys," said Jacob as Jeffrey sat back down, eyes on their guns.

"Did you orchestrate that?"

"Don't be ridiculous. Do you think I'd be in Albania with these assholes," he said, gesturing toward Negron and Bentley, "if I had that kind of power? I already told you that it was Quinn who arranged that. He knew you were close to finding out about American Beauty. It was his way of trying to get you two to back off. All I did was to come up with a body that we pretended was Tatiana. That was really to throw Quinn off. But I thought it would end it for you and Lydia, too. But it didn't. I guess I can take comfort in knowing that no one can stop Lydia, not even Nathan Quinn.

"I'm only a pawn in this game, Jeff," he went on. "I just do what I'm told."

"Why, Jacob? Why play at all?" Jeffrey asked, his tone now some combination of exasperation and sadness.

Jacob looked out the window, as if trying to get a fix on the answer himself. "It's the only game in town."

They were all silent for a long moment. Jenna kept her eyes focused on the window, looking out at the ruined countryside. Negron and Bentley stood near her by the door, their faces expressionless. Lydia walked back over to the couch and sank into it, feeling like she'd lost the strength to stand. Jeffrey stayed by the fireplace and seemed to be in a staring contest with Jacob. Sasa stood behind Jacob, smiling malevolently. They were a motley crew with mixed agendas and conflicting motivations, and Lydia wondered what good could come of all of this.

"What about Valentina and Marianna? Why did they have to die?" she asked, looking at Sasa.

"If it hadn't been for them," Sasa said, "you never would have known about any of this. They betrayed me . . . their own flesh and blood."

Lydia didn't even bother to suppress a laugh at his righteousness, and he turned an ugly stare on her.

"They were innocent," said Jenna bitterly, practically spitting the words at Sasa. "They feared for Tatiana; they never knew she had been hidden by the FBI. Valentina had always been tortured by the knowledge of her brother's activities. When she believed that Tatiana had fallen prey to him, she couldn't bear it. So she contacted you. It was a mistake that cost both of them their lives."

Lydia watched as Sasa and Jenna glared at each other. Trouble in paradise, thought Lydia.

"And the tape?"

"Tatiana was lonely and afraid when we first put the plan into action," said Jenna. "She was in the custody of the FBI. She was angry at me and wanted to talk to the only people she trusted, Valentina and Marianna. She knew she wasn't supposed to call anyone, but she got to a phone before she could be stopped."

"So, what happens now, Jacob?" asked Jeffrey.

"Mom?"

Everyone turned toward the doorway, where Tatiana was standing, her young face pale and wet with tears.

She was lanky and awkward, with the beauty of a foal not yet sure of its legs. Her lustrous hair was pulled back in a thick ponytail. Her blazing green almond-shaped eyes were framed with impossibly long black lashes. She wore a pair of jeans and a simple short white T-shirt. Her nails and toes were painted the same cotton candy pink. She was loveliness personified, and it was clear to see that she would grow into a goddess. But today, she was just a girl, a teenager wrestling away from childhood, not quite ready for adulthood. A girl who in her short life had lost her father and her home . . . twice. Lydia wondered about the things she had seen in her life and what impact it would have on her, what kind of woman she would become after all of the death and horror she had witnessed. Tatiana moved slowly into the room and seemed suddenly shy because everyone was looking at her.

Lydia smiled at her. Because for all the girls that were lost in the world, all the girls that had left on a boat in the middle of the night, hoping for a new life and finding only pain and death, for all the Shawna Foxes who never had a chance, Tatiana was safe. And even one life saved was a victory for good in a battle where the lines had grown vague and the enemy uncertain.

"Is this all true? What they said . . . is it true?" she asked her mother.

Her mother didn't say anything, and for a moment everyone in the room saw themselves through Tatiana's innocent eyes. Even Sasa's smile faded. Jenna walked over toward her daughter and led her out of the room. Lydia heard her whisper something to the girl when they were out of earshot.

"They're *dead*. You lied to me *again*," Tatiana yelled from outside the room, her voice despairing and shrill.

"What happens now, Jacob?" repeated Jeffrey, ignoring the adolescent scene outside the door. He was more concerned with getting Lydia and himself out of Albania alive than he was about Tatiana's psyche.

"You go back to New York and handle Jed McIntyre. Leave Nathan Quinn to us," he said, trying to place a hand on Jeffrey's shoulder, which Jeffrey quickly shrugged off.

"I don't think so," said Sasa. No one had noticed him moving toward the door or that he had drawn a gun with a silencer and was holding it down by his leg. And in the time it took the three of them to look around, Sasa had put a bullet between the eyes of Agents Negron and Bentley. They slumped down against the walls like deflated blow-up dolls, leaving long, dark trails of blood on the walls, both dead instantly. Lydia cried out, feeling panic rise in her chest, and heard a gasp from outside the door. She moved instinctively for Jeffrey. And as she turned, she caught sight of Jenna pulling Tatiana back from the door frame. Jeffrey was on his feet, ready to grab Lydia and move her behind him, by the time she reached him. Jacob rose slowly from his chair and Sasa pointed the gun at him.

Lydia stared at the dead men, stunned at how fast the life had drained from them. She remembered Negron's words: "Is the body count so high everywhere you go, Ms. Strong?" And she grieved that it had to be that way between them.

"What are you doing, Sasa? There's no problem here," said Jacob, narrowing his eyes and slowly raising his hand in response to the weapon Sasa had turned on him. Lydia saw perspiration beaded on Jacob's forehead, a vein throbbing in his throat. Sasa's leash had just snapped, and Jacob knew he was fucked.

"I couldn't agree more," he said, his tone level. "Why don't the three of you lie down on the floor and put your hands behind your heads?"

At this, Sasa started to laugh, "Who's the piece of shit now?"

The three of them hesitated, exchanging a look. They were all thinking that Sasa couldn't kill all of them before one of them got to him. Jeffrey had to assume Jacob was armed. He saw Jacob's right arm twitch.

"Don't even think about it, Jacob," said Sasa calmly. "Reach very slowly for the weapon."

As he spoke, he reached behind him and grabbed Jenna by her hair. He pulled her into the room as she shrieked and clawed at his hands. Lydia saw her draw blood, but Sasa didn't even flinch as he pulled her into a headlock and held the gun to her temple.

"Mom," Tatiana yelled, her voice shrill with panic.

"She's dead if anyone moves," he said quietly. "The gun, Jacob. Slowly. Slide it over here."

Jacob removed the gun from his waist as Lydia scanned the room, looking for a weapon, for a way out for them. She saw the men in masks through the window. One paced and another smoked a cigarette. She wondered whose side they were on and how she could get their attention.

Jacob squatted down to slide the gun across the wood floor.

"All of you, on the floor," Sasa barked. Lydia could hear Jenna whimpering.

"Shut up," he yelled, tightening his hold on her throat. She made a horrible choking sound, and Lydia could see that her face was turning bright red.

Lydia's mind raced as they moved slowly to the floor. She couldn't stand to put her head down, not wanting to turn her eyes away from Sasa, sure if she did that the floorboards would be the last thing she would ever see. She met Jeffrey's eyes and wanted to tell him how sorry she was for never listening to him and dragging them into hell.

"This accomplishes nothing for you, Sasa," said Jacob, trying to keep his voice calm but having trouble controlling the pitch. "If you kill me, you'll get no deal. This house is surrounded by agents, and you've just killed two of their own. You'll be hunted by the FBI *and* by Nathan Quinn, *if* you even make it out of this house alive."

"You're still trying to control me, even though I have the gun, Jacob? You are ignorant of my power. I am not afraid of you or your agents. Those two never had a chance to pull their guns," said Sasa with a smile.

Lydia dropped her eyes from Sasa's face and saw a tiny hand snaking around the doorjamb, reaching for the semiautomatic pistol that was holstered at Bentley's waist. She looked up and met Tatiana's green eyes.

"Do you think I need your fucking little deal, your *protection?*" Sasa went on, his tone becoming angrier. "The terms of this arrangement have changed."

Jacob looked uneasily at Lydia and Jeffrey, then back at Sasa. Lydia could hear the blood rushing in her ears as her eyes locked with Tatiana's.

"We can discuss it," he said quietly.

"We *are* discussing it," Sasa said with a laugh.

Tatiana had managed to withdraw the weapon from the holster and was raising it to Sasa's head. The heavy Glock shook in her grasp as she wrapped both her hands around the grip. Lydia was struck by what a bizarre image it was: Tatiana's tiny arms and her pretty face seemed so incongruous with the murderous intent in her eyes and the gun in her hand. If she'd been in any position to do so, Lydia would have wrested the gun from Tatiana's hand and shot Sasa herself. With everything she'd been through, Tatiana definitely didn't need to be the one to kill her mother's boyfriend. But she seemed more than prepared to do it. And she looked to be their only hope. Lydia watched as Tatiana switched off the safety on the side of the gun like a pro.

Tatiana never moved her eyes from Lydia's, as if seeking strength and approval there. Lydia nodded slightly; as she did, Sasa dropped his eyes to her. Time crystallized into milliseconds as Sasa followed the path of Lydia's gaze. A look of surprise crossed his face, and he spun quickly around, forgetting Jenna and allowing her to fall to the floor. She hit the ground hard, gasping, her hands to her throat, and pushed herself away with her legs. Sasa swung his weapon toward Tatiana but seemed to hesitate when he saw her there.

It was in that moment of hesitation that Tatiana emptied the gun into Sasa's chest and head. The room exploded in gunfire as the mirror that hung over the fireplace shattered and fell to the floor, a lamp exploded into a million pieces, and stuffing burst from the couch and chairs. Jeffrey crawled toward Lydia in an effort to shield her. Jacob lay on the floor, hands over his head. Jeffrey watched as Sasa fell to the floor, his chest open and dark with blood, his face a mass of torn flesh. Jeffrey dove for the semiautomatic weapon that went sailing from Sasa's hand, catching it before it hit the floor. There was a moment of silence, everyone too afraid to move.

Then Tatiana dropped her hands, which still held the gun, her mouth slack and her eyes glassy. She burst into tears, releasing heartbreaking sobs. "Mom," she called, her voice sounding so young and desperate.

Three FBI agents from outside burst in through the front door, cradling machine guns as Tatiana sank to the floor. Jenna rushed to her daughter, removed the gun from her hands, and slid it across the floor. Then she took Tatiana into her arms. Lydia could see them both shaking from across the room.

"Nice work, guys," Jacob said sarcastically to the men as they entered the room too late. Jacob stood and brushed himself off. The agents took off their ski masks and stared at Sasa's dead body. "Make yourselves useful and get rid of that," he said, trying to sound cool and in control, but the quaver in his voice told the tale.

"Jesus," Jeffrey said as he and Jacob knelt next to Bentley and Negron, pointlessly checking for a pulse on both of them.

"They were the good guys," said Jacob, as if it needed clarifying. And maybe it did.

The other FBI agents lifted Sasa's body and carried it out of the room. He wore an expression of stunned surprise, the smug grin permanently removed from his face, his expensive suit soaked in blood. Tatiana's sobs filled the room as Jenna rocked her like an infant. Lydia looked around at the mess, amazed at how the moment she had opened the envelope in her office, she had set a sequence of events into play that had led them all to this. Like a magnet, the darkness had gathered them all together, for different reasons and to different ends, but together nonetheless.

One down, two to go, thought Lydia, walking over to the girl to tell her she had done the right thing. She wanted to tell Tatiana that they were all okay and that everything was going to be all right. Even though she wasn't sure that was the truth.

chapter thirty-four

It had grown dark in the quiet suburban neighborhood. He'd sat there for hours and hadn't seen one person on the street, not one car go by. He'd dozed for a few minutes here and there when the sugar rush had passed, but mostly he'd just watched as one by one the lights in the home of David and Eleanor Strong had gone off. He hadn't seen any movement in the house, no shadows in the windows. But he hadn't wanted to risk walking onto their property and trying to peer inside. He knew enough about these neighborhoods to know that even when you thought people were all snug and sound asleep in their beds, there was always some insomniac watching out the window, waiting for a reason to wake everybody else in the neighborhood. Misery loves company.

He was cold, and he was getting stiff and numb, in spite of his gloves and heavy boots. He couldn't have the engine on all this time; people notice that kind of thing these days, someone sitting in a running car for hours. So he just sat low in the backseat, behind the tinted windows, and waited.

He remembered when he'd sat in front of Marion Strong's house, not far from here. It had been different then. He almost hadn't known what he was doing. He was only aware of a desperate psychic hunger churning within him, a kind of edgy desire. And the knowledge that the act he was about to perpetrate would soothe the ache within him for a time. There had been so much speculation, so many books written on the how and why of killers like him. People were endlessly fascinated by what drove the madman, what made him, what made him *different* from other people. But Jed believed that it wasn't the differences that made him fascinating, but the similarities.

He remembered with clarity the day he'd discovered his passion. He was twelve, living with his uncle Bill and aunt Mary. The year before, almost to the day, he'd watched his father murder his mother in their kitchen. Watched him slit her throat with a cleaver. She died slowly, bleeding out, the wound on her neck bubbling and hissing as she tried to draw breath. Jed had sat beside her in a kind of shock, trying to stop the bleeding by putting his hands on her wounds, one and then another, until she was silent. His father lay on the floor weeping, and Jed cried, too. For the last time.

His father was taken to prison and Jed was sent to live with his uncle Bill and aunt Mary. They were fine; it wasn't one of those sob stories where he'd been molested, on top of everything else. They were just sort of dull blue-collar people without much imagination or emotion. They fed him, clothed him, made sure he did his homework. They treated him like he was made of blown glass, so aware of what he had experienced that they were afraid to look at him cross-eyed. He was pretty sure he had been normal before his mother died. He had been a Boy Scout, played on a Little League team. But maybe not; maybe murder was in his blood, a dominant gene inherited from his father.

He had just stepped off the school bus and was walking up his drive when his next-door neighbor invited him into her garage. "Come look at this, Jed," she'd called. She was a pretty young mother who had a new baby. Her name was Cheryl, and she had blond hair like silk and skin like velvet. The baby slept peacefully against her chest. "Look," she said as he followed her. And he saw in the corner of her garage, nestled under a workbench, a mottled Maine coon cat in a sheepskin bed, surrounded by suckling kittens.

"Isn't that wonderful?" she asked him with a smile. "Cool," he'd answered with typical adolescent reticence. "Maybe Bill and Mary will let you have one."

"Yeah. I'll ask."

The sight had awakened an evil within him. All the rest of the afternoon, he couldn't put the image out of his mind. A burning agitation grew inside him; a deep ache of loneliness, anger, and fear felt like a cancer eating away at him. He went to his room and did not come out when called for dinner. After he did his homework, he tried to sleep, but he couldn't. After tossing for hours, he left his bed in the night, taking a knife from the wood block on the kitchen counter.

He was too young then to put words to the way he felt when he walked in the open side door to his neighbor's garage. He heard the soft mewing of the kittens and watched them, warm and soft, next to their mother. Their eyes were still mostly closed and their little bodies wriggled slowly with oblivious innocence and peace. He hated them, wanted to smash each of them on the floor like tennis balls. The mother issued a low growl. She must have sensed him there. She was a big cat. So Jed reached in quickly with one hand and grabbed her by the scruff of her neck, picked her up, and, with the other hand, slit her throat. He held the body away from him until it stopped moving. Then he put it back in its bed next to the kittens, who continued their soft mewing.

The release could only be compared to orgasm, though it wasn't a sexual pleasure he derived. He just felt . . . better, like a normal boy. He felt like he had when he still lived with his parents, not angry and afraid. Not alone. And for months, he was interested again in baseball and music. Intellectually, he knew what he had done was wrong, but he couldn't help the way he felt.

He had heard her screams before anyone the next morning, had sort of been waiting for them.

"Oh God, Rick!" she yelled, her cries carrying in the quiet, sunny suburban morning. "Who could do such a thing? What kind of monster?"

Only he really knew the answer to that question. Only he really knew what kind of monster he was. But it wasn't that romantic. It wasn't like he had some sick agenda like on *Profiler* or something. He'd just stumbled on something that took the pain away. He was more like an alcoholic or a drug addict than anything else.

Of course, it had escalated from there. Like any addict, he needed more and more, trying to recapture that first high. He didn't have all this intellectual perspective when he'd killed Marion Strong. But he'd matured. He didn't need to kill any longer to feel whole, to feel right. He had forgiven and accepted himself. He could control his impulses now . . . most of them. But that wasn't going to help David and Eleanor Strong.

The neighborhood was dark now, and all the lights were out at the Strong house. He grabbed his backpack and slid out of the car. He didn't shut the door all the way, just enough to make sure the interior lights were out. Then he moved carefully into the trees surrounding the yard.

As he rounded the corner into the backyard, a rather dim amber light over the deck came on, activated by a motion sensor. Jed stood very still, his back pressed against the white aluminum siding, but the sudden light didn't seem to bring any reaction from inside the house. After a moment of holding his breath, he continued toward the back door. The yard was surrounded on all sides by thick, dark trees that he couldn't identify in the night, but they provided excellent cover. The backyard could not be seen from any of the surrounding properties. He walked up three low steps onto the leaf-covered deck and easily picked the lock on the simple doorknob. People who were stupid enough to have such poor security deserved what they got.

The door led him into a small laundry room that smelled strongly of Bounce fabric softener, a scent he recognized and associated with freedom. They hadn't used any fabric softener on the prison hospital uniforms. They had used the cheapest brand of detergent, so the uniforms never seemed clean, were always scratchy, and irritated his sensitive skin. It annoyed him just thinking about it.

The laundry room was connected to the kitchen, which was illuminated by a pink seashell night-light nestled beside a toaster oven. He slid over the green-and-white linoleum floor and sneered at the imitation Tiffany lamp that hung over the dark wood and wrought-iron table in the breakfast nook. The counter was cluttered with ribboned baskets, a hideous wooden duck napkin holder, and a bunch of other country-kitsch crap. Bad taste was another thing he found unspeakably annoying. What inspired such poor decorating decisions? he wondered as he pulled a roll of duct tape and a large sheathed hunting knife from his backpack. Jed McIntyre did not like guns. They were loud and unpredictable, not to mention lazy and sloppy. Anyone could shoot another person. It took skill, speed, and stealth to kill someone with a knife. He took off his parka and laid it next to the backpack on the floor.

The stairs were heavily carpeted, so moving silently to the second level was easier than it might have been on bare wood. He placed the duct tape around his wrist like a bracelet and the knife in the waistband of his pants. There were no more night-lights, a detail of which he was glad, because they created shadows. So he imagined himself a wraith in the darkness, one with the night, and slowly ascended to the master bedroom, which he was guessing was the first room at the top of the stairs. He could hear the softly labored breathing of sleep as he reached the top landing.

When he turned the corner into the bedroom, the digital clock glowed green at 1:33 A.M., casting a strange light over the two sleeping forms, one large and round, one smaller and flatter. He'd need to dispense with David Strong first, so that he could take his time with Eleanor. He unsheathed the hooked, serrated blade of the knife and moved in slowly. Keeping his breathing shallow and footsteps light, he moved toward the bed.

It was too late when he noticed what he should have noticed at the door—that only one of the forms was breathing. As his hand reached out to pull back the bedclothes, a large black form sprang like a panther, and in an instant Jed McIntyre was on his back on the floor, the wind knocked out of him, a knee on his chest, the nose of a gun to his forehead.

A cheerful Australian greeting sounded in the darkness. "Hullo, mate. Can't be having you lurking about in the night. Can we?"

chapter thirty-five

She slept finally, uncomfortably, seeming to want to turn on her side and curl up the way she normally slept at home. In spite of the adrenaline coursing through his veins, the restless, helpless unease he always felt on airplanes, he felt more relaxed now that she was asleep. She looked small and tired; he reached out and touched her forehead, which was cool and dry.

"I'm sorry," he whispered, though he wasn't sure what he was sorry about. He just had the vague feeling in his heart that he had let her down. Tatiana was safe, but they had walked away, leaving countless others to their fates at the hands of demons. Lydia knew they were beaten, standing at the fireplace. There was a look of angry resignation on her face that he had never seen before. And he had grieved a little in that moment for her usual smart-ass defiance, her inability to accept defeat. But there was a clear choice to be made. They could get themselves killed, or live to fight another day. At least Sasa Fitore had gotten what he deserved. And the party wasn't over yet. There were still Nathan Quinn and Jed McIntyre to deal with.

She hadn't said anything really since she'd said good-bye to Tatiana. She'd walked away from Jacob without a word at the airport. But Jeffrey didn't hate him as much as he knew Lydia would now. In his own way, Jeffrey believed, Jacob was still one of the good guys. He was fighting a battle that couldn't be won, choosing lesser evils, making the most of hollow victories. Without his involvement, Jeffrey and Lydia would probably be dead right now. But of course, his and Jacob's partnership would have to end. There were too many secrets, too much going on behind his back. Jeffrey needed to fight his battles on solid ground, needed to be able to distinguish between enemies and allies.

He pressed the button on the seat back and popped the air phone out. He slid his credit card in the slot and dialed.

"Go," answered Dax Chicago.

"What's the status of our situation?" he asked quietly.

"You were dead right, man. He was right where you thought he'd be. And now . . . we're in a holding pattern," he answered, his mouth full of something he was eating.

"As discussed."

"That's right. Piece of cake."

"Don't get relaxed. He's not as stupid as he looks."

"No worries, mate. You always did worry too much."

"You don't worry enough."

"The situation is under control," Dax said calmly.

"I'll be in touch."

He hung up the phone with a sigh, wondering if he had acted too quickly, bringing Dax into an already volatile mix. But in a situation where the law didn't apply, Jeffrey believed you had to ally yourself sometimes with lawless men. Dax certainly qualified. Besides, the game wasn't nearly over. Dax would certainly be valuable when it came to that, no matter how they decided to proceed.

He looked over at Lydia, who was wide awake and staring at him with her big smoky gray eyes. "Jeffrey," she said, suspicion knitting her brow and narrowing her eyes, "what's going on?"

chapter thirty-six

She exploded as soon as the elevator door to their apartment closed behind them. He'd been waiting for it since he told her about Dax on the airplane. Her face had gone pale, her lips pulled into a tight line. He thought she was going to blow right there, but instead, she just crawled over him and went to the bathroom. She looked almost normal when she came back. She sat down next to him again and gave him a cold smile.

"Lydia . . ."

She lifted a hand. "Stop. I don't want to discuss what you've done right now."

Lydia was a brave, strong woman, but he knew that she was reaching the limits of what she could take. He could see it in the tension in her shoulders, in the taut muscles of her face, the dead expression in her eyes. He knew her so well, he could almost feel the tempest rolling within her. Depression setting in over her perceived failure in Albania, Nathan Quinn still to confront, the fear looming in the back of her mind with Jed McIntyre on the loose, now her grandparents being in jeopardy. For the duration of the flight, she sat ramrod-straight, eyes ahead, totally silent. Same deal on the cab ride home. His additional attempts at conversation were rebuffed with a withering stare.

"What the fuck did you think you were doing?" she yelled, blowing off steam as soon as they were safe at home.

"I don't know why you're so upset. You told me yourself to get a handle on him. I did that."

"I didn't tell you to use my grandparents as bait."

"Fuck that," he said, angry now, too, but refusing to raise his voice to her. "I didn't use them as bait, and you bloody well know it. We anticipated his move and headed him off. There was no other way to track him. He's not leaving a fucking trail of bread crumbs."

"And now what? You've got him caged up somewhere with Dax. For what? Why didn't Dax just turn him over to the police for breaking and entering? What are you intending to do with him?"

"Knowing what we know, do you really think it's going to do us any good to turn him over to the police? If Nathan Quinn wants him out, he's out. Don't you see what we're dealing with now? We can't play by the rules here, Lydia. You are in danger. And I am going to do what it takes to protect you . . . whether you like it or not. Christ."

"I'm not a little girl, Jeffrey. I don't need you to protect me. I should have been a part of this decision," she said, lowering her voice and looking at him. She sat down on the couch and put her head in her hands. "I need you on my team, but I need to be a part of the game," she said into her palms.

He wasn't going to argue with her and he had no intention of apologizing for doing what he felt was right and would do again. He sat down beside her.

"What do we do with him now?" she asked, still not looking at him.

"We make him go away."

"What does that mean, Jeffrey?"

"Whatever you want it to mean."

She raised her eyes to him and shook her head slowly. "What happened to your whole 'People Have Rights' speech?"

"Some people don't deserve the rights they have."

"And we're supposed to be in a position to decide who those people are?"

No one would argue Jed McIntyre's right to live in society, particularly not Lydia. He was an evil, twisted human being who had been unjustly released into the world by another arguably more evil and twisted human being, if such a comparison could be made, someone who had the money and the power to bend the rules of law to his will. Lydia recognized that if they played by the rules of morality that they had always followed, they would lose and lose ugly. But in the cosmic scheme of things, who was she to decide anyone's fate? Even Jed McIntyre, who had brought nothing but horror and death to most people with whom he came in contact . . . maybe even his life had meaning, however elusive and incomprehensible that might seem. But how was she to know? Who was she to judge the value of a life? She placed a hand on her belly.

"Before we decide what to do about Jed McIntyre, Jeffrey, there's something I want you to know."

He looked at her, and in his eyes she saw all the things she loved about him. She saw his strength, his compassion, his honor, and his kindness glittering in the flecks of amber and green in his hazel eyes. She felt suddenly horrible for yelling at him, for making him account for loving her and wanting to keep her safe, for needing to take action to protect her. Because these were all the reasons she needed him in her life, and all the reasons why he was going to be a wonderful father.

chapter thirty-seven

"I wanted you to know that you did the right thing, Detective," Lydia said into the receiver as Jeffrey sat across the kitchen table from her, his brow creased with worry.

"I already knew that, Lydia. I did the only thing I could do," said Manny on the other line, his voice serene. He sounded like he'd gotten some rest.

"But I wanted you to know that she's all right."

"Tatiana?"

"Yes, she's safe. I can't tell you any more than that. But she's alive, and we've all been played."

She heard him exhale on the other end of the phone in anger or relief or maybe both.

"You told me to go where the money took me, and it led me straight to her," she went on, glancing at Jeffrey, who nodded.

"Well, she better hope that Nathan Quinn doesn't do the same."

"Who? What do you mean?"

"I mean that Jenna Quinn somehow managed to steal about a hundred million dollars from Quinn over the course of their brief marriage, siphoning money from Quinn Enterprises into a company she owned called American Equities. She has disappeared, and the money with her."

"Really."

"It's funny in a way. A man like that . . . so powerful as to be untouchable. Taken by his own wife," he said, and chuckled as though he was really enjoying it.

"Well, there's even more to it than that. I'll tell you the rest of it the next time I'm in Miami. Not over the phone, though," she said, smiling.

He paused a second before answering. "It's not over yet, right? That's why you're calling to tell me this."

"You're a smart man, Detective."

"And you're a smart woman. So be careful."

"I will be. I understand the choice you made better today than I did, Manny."

He gave a little laugh. "Then be even more careful."

Lydia put down the phone, let her hand rest on the receiver for a second. She looked at Jeffrey, who was watching her with a kind of love combined with awe she hadn't seen in his eyes before. He reached out a hand to touch her, as though she were made of glass.

"I'm not one hundred percent comfortable with this," he said, pulling on his distressed-leather bomber jacket. "There are too many variables."

"I know. But I think it's the only way."

"It's not the only way."

"It's the only way I can live with."

He nodded and held her by the shoulders. "Remember this . . . protect yourself for me. That's your first priority tonight."

She held him tightly around the waist, feeling the stiff Kevlar vest against her chest and the hardness of his gun on the inside of her arm, "Yours, too," she said.

"We'll meet you behind the museum in Van Cortlandt Park at midnight."

They released each other reluctantly and Jeffrey stepped onto the elevator. "Don't forget to put on your vest," he said, tapping his chest as the door closed.

"Shit," she whispered, a twister of anxiety spinning suddenly in her stomach as she wondered if her brilliant plan was so brilliant after all.

Jeffrey jogged to the parking garage where they kept the black Mercedes Kompressor that Lydia used to drive in Santa Fe. Because of the heavy Kevlar and the unusually mild temperature, he was sweating heavily when he got behind the wheel. His mind was racing as the engine hummed to life. He pulled out onto Houston Street and headed for the West Side Highway. The sun was low in the sky, casting the city in a pink-orange glow as he crawled through the usual downtown congestion. The same construction project that had been taking place on the Henry Hudson for the past fifteen years showed no sign of nearing completion. Past Twenty-third Street, the traffic cleared and he sped up toward Dax Chicago's place.

His head was spinning with a tornado of emotions, and he had to suppress the urge to run back to Lydia and tell her to bag the whole plan, say that he couldn't stand the thought of risking her life and the life of the child that could be inside her right now. The thought of having a child with her filled him with a kind of helpless feeling of love and gratitude that he'd never experienced before. And it made him more afraid than he'd ever been in his life. It made him want to lock her in a cushioned room, so that not even the slightest mishap could befall her. But he recognized the impossibility of protecting Lydia: She was too much herself ever to yield to his control, no matter how loving and well-meaning he intended it to be. Their knowledge of each other, their acceptance of each other's flaws and needs, was one of the things that made them so good for each other. And it was one of the things that had caused him the most amount of inner conflict: It was his nature to shelter and protect, and it was her nature to break free. There was no holding her unless she wanted to be held. He'd come to trust that she did. But a baby would add a whole new dimension to that struggle—his need to protect, her need to be independent. It would change everything for both of them. He gripped the wheel as he passed the high stone wall of the Cloisters, hoping they were doing the right thing.

Riverdale was one of the last nice neighborhoods in the Bronx. Past the train yards and up a winding road, Jeffrey entered an enclave of tree-lined streets sheltering mammoth, hugely expensive homes. Wealthy people who had children to raise but still wanted to be near the city lived in Riverdale, sending said children to one of the exclusive private schools in the neighborhood. He wondered how they'd feel if they knew Dax Chicago was one of their neighbors and whom he had as a houseguest.

Dax's house was more isolated than the rest of the homes in the area, and as Jeffrey pulled up the long driveway, the garage door opened for him. He pulled the Kompressor in next to a Land Rover with heavily tinted windows. He got out and stood at the metal door, looking up into the camera. The door buzzed loudly and he pushed it open.

"Dax?"

"In here, mate." But his voice sounded strangled, and Jeffrey drew his weapon, a Magnum Desert Eagle. He rounded the corner, to find Dax in the kitchen, eating a submarine sandwich that was bigger than his arm, which was pretty damn big.

"Jesus," Dax said, glancing up at Jeffrey's enormous gun. "You are fucking paranoid these days. What's with you?"

Jeff breathed a sigh of relief and sat at the kitchen table, placing the gun down in front of him. "I've just got more on the table than I used to."

"It's messy, love and all that shit. It's not for me, I'll tell you."

"Where is he?"

"In the dungeon," Dax said, his green eyes glinting with mischief.

"Is he alive?"

"I dunno. He was yesterday," he said, wiping mustard from his chin. He tapped the mouse on a laptop that sat next to the coffeemaker. A small image appeared in the corner of the screen, and Jeffrey could see Jed McIntyre in a windowless cell, bound onto the same type of table he had seen in execution chambers. The sound was off, but Jed's mouth was open and his head was thrashing as if he was screaming.

"Yeah, he's still alive."

"What's wrong with him?" Jeffrey asked.

"I imagine he's pretty upset. I don't blame him. I could have finished this the other night. He'd be out of your hair and mine. Why are we keeping him on ice?"

"Lydia doesn't want his death on our hands."

"He killed her mother."

"'Two evil acts don't equal a good one,' or something a bit more eloquent than that," Jeffrey said, still not sure if he agreed with her on any of this.

"So, what are we going to do with him? I can't board him permanently, you know. I have other clients."

Jeffrey told Dax what they were planning for midnight in Van Cortlandt Park. Dax lowered his head when Jeffrey was done and paused a second before commenting, "That's the worst plan I ever heard."

chapter thirty-eight

Lydia was sure she had been followed as she stepped off the number 9 train at 242nd Street in the Bronx. There were more people riding the train than you'd expect at midnight, and about thirty or forty other people exited at its final stop. As she walked down from the elevated platform, Van Cortlandt Park yawned deep and black to her left as cars sped by on Broadway to her right. She stood for a second at the bottom of the steps and saw out of the corner of her eye a figure in black stop up at the top. She didn't turn around to look, but walked onto the path that led her into the darkness. She could hear the blood rushing in her ears and felt a flutter deep in her belly.

With her hands in her pockets and her head low, she prayed that she hadn't fucked them all with this plan, but so far, it was working exactly as she'd thought it would. The sound of the heels of her boots on concrete and the street noise fading as she moved deeper into the park were all she could hear. She looked around her and behind her, but she saw no one.

The call to Detective Ignacio had been a lure, Lydia banking on the possibility that either his calls or hers were being monitored by someone who was reporting to Nathan Quinn. The phone rang not five minutes after Jeffrey had left the apartment.

"Let's deal, Ms. Strong," said Nathan Quinn. Lydia had shuddered as she remembered his voice on the DVD.

"I was expecting your thugs to show up in a limo. Something more dramatic than a phone call anyway."

"I think we're beyond that now. Don't you?"

"What do you want?"

"You know what I want. The question is, What do you want?"

"I want you to arrange for Jed McIntyre to be picked up and put behind bars tonight. Forever."

"I don't know where he is," answered Quinn.

"I do."

"If you know where he is, why don't you take care of him yourself?"

"Because I don't want to play God, Quinn. I just want him back where he belongs."

"And you'll tell me where I can find Tatiana."

"And who took her. And why."

"How do I know you'll tell me the truth?"

"You can always arrange to have Jed McIntyre released again if I haven't."

"I guess I was right after all, wasn't I, Ms. Strong?"

"How's that?"

"Everybody wants to get paid sooner or later. I figured out your price."

"I guess you did. But not before I figured out yours."

He laughed, but it sounded fake and evil, like something recorded for a house of horrors.

"When and where?" he asked.

If the call Jeffrey was to make from his cell phone went half as well, you'll be having a regular party tonight, she thought.

Van Cortlandt Park, on 1,122 acres in the ridges and valleys of the northwest Bronx, was New York City's third-largest park. Originally the land of the Weckquaesgeek Indians, it was "sold" to the Dutch

West India Company in 1639. It passed through a couple of hands before being given to Jacobus Van Cortlandt, who would one day be mayor of New York City. In 1748, Jacobus's son Frederick built the Van Cortlandt Mansion, a stately stone home right out of a history textbook, with gaslights outside and the inside furnished in the height of eighteenth- and nineteenth-century home fashion. It stood there still, the oldest building in the Bronx.

Parks in New York City, no matter how nice they looked during the day, were scary at night. All that wide-open darkness in the heart of the Bronx was not a good idea, as far as Lydia was concerned. But it served their purposes tonight.

Lydia walked off the concrete path and approached the Van Cortlandt Mansion from a rocky trail. She noticed that the flood-lighting that usually illuminated the building at night and the lights within were dark. She imagined that Jeffrey and Dax had something to do with this. At least she hoped so. Across the path from the house was a wide staircase with narrow overgrown steps that led to the picnic grounds. If things were going as planned, this was where Dax and Jeffrey were. She wondered if she'd made a mistake. Ideas that she had when she was pissed and scared generally didn't turn out the way she had planned. Maybe she should have just let Jeffrey handle the situation the way he thought best and put it out of her mind forever. She heard footsteps behind her and she knew it was too late.

"What are you doing here, Lydia?" asked Jacob Hanley.

Her breathing came quick and shallow as she turned to face him.

"Jacob . . . you sure do get around," said Lydia, trying to sound surprised. "I could ask you the same question."

"I heard you were about to sell us out to Nathan Quinn. I came to talk you out of it," he said, removing what looked like the Glock his cronies had confiscated from her back in Albania. It was then that she saw on Jacob's right hand the insignia ring she'd seen on

Nathan Quinn and on the men in the snuff film. She blinked as if she might clear the sight from her eyes. Since her conversation with Detective Ignacio, Lydia had been thinking about all that money that Jenna had supposedly stolen. And she remembered the moment back in Albania when Sasa had told Jacob that the terms of their agreement had changed. She remembered the uneasy look Jacob had cast at her and Jeffrey.

"I trusted you to do the right thing for Tatiana," said Jacob, his stare menacing and his lips turned up in slight smile. "That's why we let you go."

"I've never seen that ring before," she said, surprised to hear her own voice quaver slightly.

"I only wear it on special occasions, and this certainly qualifies," he said.

"You're one of them?" she asked.

"Not really. Not a member of the Council, exactly. Obviously, I'd be a much wealthier man if that were the case. But we all come from the same Ivy League fraternity. I just do a little freelance enforcing now and again, if you know what I mean."

"I have no idea what you mean."

"Those against Quinn on the Council needed someone to get his hands dirty with the FBI and Sasa Fitore. Someone who could help them get Nathan Quinn and save Tatiana, as well."

"Right," she said, and laughed. "It was all about Tatiana, right, Jacob? Saving Tatiana and putting Quinn away. How does the one hundred million dollars Jenna stole from Nathan Quinn fit into this? How much of that money belongs to you?"

A cool wind picked up and blew the leaves above their heads, lifted some of the dirt at their feet. Lydia felt a sudden drop in temperature, and a chill moved through her body.

"What are you talking about?" he said, his tone dull and cold.

"I have to admit, you nearly had me convinced back there. You almost had me thinking you were doing the right thing. Or as right a thing as anyone could do under the circumstances. But then I started thinking about what Sasa said before he died, about the terms changing. And tonight, when Detective Ignacio told me about the money, it all made sense. For you, it wasn't just about taking Nathan Quinn down; it was about taking his money. It's all about stealing money.

"Jenna Quinn and Sasa Fitore couldn't kill Nathan Quinn. She couldn't divorce him. Either way, they risked not getting the money. They couldn't just siphon money from Quinn Enterprises into American Equities and run away from him, because she knew he would use his influence and go to the ends of the earth to find Tatiana. There would be no hiding from him. When the FBI approached her, she must have thought it was her lucky day. With their help, with your help, she staged the abduction and murder of Tatiana. She gives the FBI the evidence they need, Quinn winds up in jail and eventually 'commits suicide,' and Jenna Quinn lives happily ever after. Everybody else gets their cut, right, Jacob? And if Marianna and Valentina hadn't contacted me, no one ever would have suspected a thing."

"That's ridiculous," he said. "I always knew you were off your rocker, Lydia. But this is totally out of line." But even in the relative dark, she could see his Adam's apple moving up and down in his throat.

Jeffrey walked up from the darkness and came to stand beside Lydia. "That's why you didn't want me to see the books and why you didn't want to bring Lydia in as partner. How long, Jacob, have your involvements been so fucking dirty?"

As Jeffrey, from his hiding spot on the stairs, had listened to Lydia talk, he realized the truth in her conclusions, a truth he had never considered—or maybe never allowed himself to consider. Though, maybe he had known it since the night in the darkened hotel room years ago. Friendship and loyalty are funny things. You never want to believe the bad things of the people you love; you only want to see them as you hope they are. As maybe they once were, when you first loved them.

"How long, Jacob?" Jeffrey repeated.

Jacob would never have a chance to answer that question. Right before his head exploded in a volcano of blood and brain, there was a look of shame and resignation on his face that Jeffrey would never forget.

In a hail of gunfire, Jeffrey threw himself on top of Lydia. He could hear the bullets hitting trees and the ground around them and then felt them both being dragged away, sliding on their bellies over gravel down the flight of stairs leading to the picnic grounds. Dax, all 250 pounds of him covered head to toe in black body armor, including a hood, pulled them onto the first landing and lay on top of them, acting as a shield. The gunfire continued for what seemed like hours, until a heavy silence fell. Jeffrey could hear Lydia's frightened breathing beside him, and his whole body shook with adrenaline.

In the silence, they all waited. Then after tense moments, Dax rolled off of them and crawled back up the steps, aiming the assault rifle he had slung around his shoulder. There was silence.

"Jesus fucking Christ," whispered Jeffrey, the last moments of Jacob's life burning into his mind. He crawled up behind Dax, Lydia right behind him. "Did you see who it was?"

Dax shook his head. "There was a vehicle without its lights on. A Hummer. It's gone now. Bloody quiet, it was. I'll have to get one of those," he said, his voice muffled by the hood he wore. "Funny thing . . . it was the same vehicle that brought him in."

"But who was it? Who wanted Jacob dead?" asked Jeffrey, shock wearing off and emotion creeping into his voice.

"Maybe Jenna Quinn didn't want to share her hundred million with him?" suggested Lydia. "Or maybe he had served his purpose with the Council and shared more information than they felt comfortable with."

Jeffrey looked at Jacob's body lying in a bleeding pile in the dirt, and he felt a wave of intense sadness, profound loss. But more than anything, he was angry that Jacob had let it come to this for all of them. He thought of Jacob's wife, his children, and the moment when he would have to tell them that Jacob was gone. He put his head down in his hands and felt Lydia's shoulder on his back.

"I'm sorry," she whispered. "There was nothing you could have done."

He nodded, not sure if she was right and not sure it mattered either way. He'd always carry this with him, regardless of where the blame lay.

"What now, then?" asked Dax, seemingly unperturbed by the events.

"I'm meeting Nathan Quinn in Croton Woods in twenty minutes," answered Lydia, still looking at Jeffrey with concern. "It'll take us that long to get there on foot. The entrance is on Two Hundred and Thirty-third Street."

"No worries—I've got the Rover."

"Where's Jed McIntyre?" said Lydia, a question she'd hoped never to ask in her life. And hoped never to ask again after tonight.

"Back in the dungeon."

"I thought you were going to bring him with you."

"No . . . too risky. Can't keep an eye on him and the two of you, now, can I?" He winked and gave a smile totally incongruous to the situation. And Lydia thought he might have a screw loose.

"Go get him and wait for me at Two Hundred and Thirty-third Street," she said with a frown.

"Meet *us* at Two Hundred and Thirty-third Street," Jeffrey said, correcting her as he snapped back into the moment. "I'm going with you."

"Nathan Quinn is not going to hurt me. I'm the only one who knows what happened to Tatiana."

"You know, it always comes to this. We split up and the shit hits the fan. I'm staying with you. Dax can handle McIntyre."

"Pick your psycho," said Dax, with a short, hard laugh.

"What about Jacob?"

"We'll have to come back for him later," said Jeffrey, his voice flat and unemotional as he avoided looking at the body. Lydia looked at Jeffrey. His face was stone, expressionless and cold. Lydia was starting to feel like she was in a video game where everyone who came into her view screen wound up dead in some awful way.

The old Putnam Division railroad track had ceased operation in 1958 and was now the corridor that passed through the wetlands and divided Van Cortlandt Golf Course. It had originally been part of a route that ran between the High Bridge and Brewster, New York. Now a gorgeous and serene nature trail during the day, it was a dark and treacherous trek at night. But this was the path they chose to Croton Woods, rather than the sidewalk that ran along the edge of the park, preferring the darkness to the exposure of the street. The night was cold and alive around them, wind whistling through the oak and maple branches, which had already dropped most of their leaves. She heard something small and four-legged rustle to their left, and it sent a jolt of adrenaline through her. Lydia pulled a small Maglite from her pocket.

"Bad idea," whispered Jeffrey.

She put it back in her pocket without a word.

"Why didn't you tell me what you were thinking?" he asked her quietly.

"Honestly, I didn't even put it together until I started talking."

He frowned at her, which she felt more than saw in the darkness. "Bullshit."

"It's not bullshit. I never hide anything from you," she said, grabbing his arm as they kept walking.

They took the rough path to Old Croton Aqueduct Trail and walked into the woods, which were wedged between the Henry

Hudson and Mosholu parkways and bisected by the Major Deegan Expressway. They could hear the whisper of cars passing on the highways beneath them.

"I'm supposed to meet him there," she said, pointing to a large structure.

The segment of the trail they were on was part of the forty-one-mile aqueduct built in the 1830s as New York City's first extensive water supply. It brought water from Croton Dam into the city. The large stone building they approached was a weir that once existed to maintain the flow of water and control air pressure. It was isolated and abandoned. Not even homeless people or squatters came this far inside the park at night.

"How did you get him to meet you here?"

"He would have met me anywhere I said. He's desperate," she said.

"How's it supposed to go down?"

"He's supposed to have the means for taking Jed McIntyre into custody. And once he does, then I supposedly tell him where to find Tatiana."

Jeffrey reached into his pocket and pulled out his cellular phone, which Lydia had not heard ring. He didn't say anything as he put the phone to his ear.

"Jeff," said Dax, breathless on the other end. "He's gone. I've lost Jed McIntyre."

"What? How?"

"It looks like someone blew him out of here. You two are in fucking trouble. Where are you?"

"We're at the Croton Aqueduct Trail, by the weir," he answered, looking around him. But the line was breaking up, and he wasn't sure whether Dax heard.

"Let's get out of here. We've been set up," Jeffrey said to her, taking the Dessert Eagle out of his waistband. "What are you carrying?"

"The Sig. What's happening?"

"Jed McIntyre's loose. Let's go."

"What?" she said, her brain not willing to accept the information.

"Where are you going, Ms. Strong? I thought you and I had a deal," said Nathan Quinn, emerging out of the darkness like a shadow.

"This park is like a house of horrors tonight, some ghoul always creeping out of the darkness," said Lydia, her flip comment belying that her throat was dry as sand and her legs felt weak underneath her.

"There's no deal, Quinn," said Jeffrey.

"There never was any deal, though, was there, Lydia?" asked Quinn. "You weren't going to tell me where to find Tatiana. You were going to lie, then bank on the FBI getting me before I was able to have him released again."

Lydia shrugged. "You'll never know." She couldn't help but glance around her into the darkness between the trees, wondering if Jed McIntyre was lying in wait for her there. She felt more numb than terrified, the events of the evening taking on a kind of unreality.

"Let's not rush to judgment," said Quinn, walking toward them. He stopped when Jeffrey leveled the Desert Eagle at his head. "I wasn't comfortable playing this game by your rules. I didn't see how I could win. Jed McIntyre was in your custody. If I didn't do what you wanted, all you had to do was kill him. Now, he's in my custody. If you don't tell me what I want to know, then I'll unleash your nightmare, Lydia. The outcome remains the same: You get what you want—your mother's killer behind bars—and I get my Tatiana back. Only now the means are slightly altered."

"What's to stop me from killing you?" asked Jeffrey.

"If you kill me, Jed McIntyre is released into the world. Maybe you'll catch him. Or maybe he'll catch Lydia. Is that a gamble you're willing to take?"

"Why do you want her so badly, Nathan?" Lydia asked suddenly. "You have a million girls at your disposal. Girls you can do anything to—rape, mutilate, murder. We've seen the footage. We know what you are, what you do. . . . But why Tatiana?"

Nathan Quinn sat down on the stone steps leading to the entrance of the weir. He wore a long black wool coat cinched at the waist; the top three buttons were undone, revealing the collar of a white shirt. He was utterly relaxed, not even remotely concerned that Jeffrey had a gun pointed at his head, as if he believed himself to be immortal. He leaned back on his elbows, looking like an older male model in recline, perfectly groomed for a crisp evening stroll in the park. With his immaculately styled hair and square jaw, he could have been in a Ralph Lauren advertisement. The greatest trick that Satan ever played was getting the world to believe he doesn't exist, Lydia thought, remembering the adage as she looked at him, though she couldn't say why.

"Most people learn limits," he said, thoughtful. "The things they cannot have, what they cannot do within society's boundaries. For me, a child of extreme privilege, there were, of course, fewer of those limits. My parents, to be honest, weren't exactly religious or particularly moral people. They, too, were the children of wealthy parents and had grown up valuing material goods, pleasure, and leisure more than, say, ethics. I was handsome and rich, and people wanted to be in my company and in my favor no matter how I acted. There were few, if any, consequences for poor behavior as a child, or illegal behavior as an adolescent and young adult. I came to the conclusion fairly early that conscience is learned, not innate, because it wasn't taught to me, as far as I can remember, and I certainly wasn't born with one.

"I've always loved women. Or I should say, I've always had an appetite for them, a ravenous appetite. And women have always wanted me. When you are handsome and rich and charming, you can get most women to do almost anything for you, sexually and otherwise. At least the women I've encountered. I became bored early with the acceptable boundaries of sexual gratification. I knew there had to be more—places inside myself where normal men were not allowed to go but where I might. Wondering what levels of pleasure existed behind the iron wall of law and morality.

"So I started pushing boundaries. Once you begin, it's never far enough; every climax is an anticlimax. So I kept pushing, until I learned there were no real boundaries, only those imagined by ordinary men with mediocre minds. It wasn't long in my circle before I found men who understood my appetites. I learned that there was a culture of great men before me who fed the hunger, reaching for enlightenment, searching for nirvana. They only found it when they'd walked over the edge of society. It's the interpretation of the average man that Kurtz in *Heart of Darkness* was mad. In fact, the farther into the Congo he went, the more sane he became. It was the rest of the world that had gone mad, slaving for their meager dreams and goals. When all along, true pleasure, the only thing we really seek as humans—whether we call it love or peace or whatever—is within our grasp if we dare to step across the line society draws.

"Tatiana was the first person whose love I had to earn. She didn't care how handsome I was, or how rich. She distrusted me and shunned me, right from the night I married her mother. All the things that had drawn people to me were useless with her. Her love was the last thing on earth that I couldn't buy or steal. I couldn't manipulate her with charm, or Backstreet Boys tickets. Of course, she lived in my house. I could have raped her. I could have stolen her body; I could have eaten her heart. But I could only have her love, her smile, her trust if she gave them to me. Tatiana was the final boundary."

That was his reason. The full impact of his insanity and evil hit Lydia like a battering ram. It was not the fact that he was so bad that really bothered her; it was that he was so okay with it. Here was a monster whose mask was so artfully constructed that he operated in society, successful, admired. It was sick.

"Wow . . . you are extremely fucked-up," said Lydia, her voice shaking a little because she really meant it. Nathan Quinn struck fear in her soul.

"That's the longest, most complicated bad-guy speech I ever heard," said Jeffrey. He'd never once dropped his weapon from its aim at Nathan's head.

A cool Cheshire cat smile split Nathan's face. "So what do you say, Lydia? Do we have a deal?"

"Not on your life."

He stood and smiled at her, removing a cellular phone from his pocket. "How about on yours?"

There was an eternal moment where the three of them stood like stone; each second was a universe in which a thousand different decisions could be made, the future altered by each irrevocably. Then Jeffrey spoke.

"Tatiana was kidnapped by the FBI, in cooperation with your wife and Sasa Fitore, Nathan. When we saw her, she was in Albania, being protected at a kind of fortress in Vlorë."

The look on Lydia's face felt like a bullet in the gut. The disbelief and betrayal were palpable in the air.

"No," she said pointlessly, as if she couldn't find any other words. Her brows knitted together, and her eyes opened wide in sadness.

"I'm sorry, Lydia," Jeffrey said, lowering his gun. "I can't let Jed McIntyre go free. I could never live with myself if anything happened to you."

Nathan Quinn stood and laughed, a deep, guttural laugh.

The laughter seemed to change something inside Lydia. Her face went from broken to hard in under a second. Jeffrey watched her move her hand to her waistband and remove the Sig, and the two feet between them seemed like a canyon as he moved to stop her. Nathan Quinn's face went from smug satisfaction to uncertainty as he stumbled back two steps, toward the trees. Lydia took aim, but before Jeffrey reached her, she dropped her arm to her side. In those seconds, Lydia chose life, her life, her life with Jeffrey, the life of their child. She chose them all over Tatiana.

The silver hunting knife seemed to come disembodied from the branches of trees behind Nathan Quinn. His brow rose in surprise and his head tilted as if jerked back hard. He looked nothing so much as confused. Then the steel blade opened a thick red line on Nathan's neck before he even had a chance to scream. And when his body fell to the ground in a gurgling heap, he writhed there, clutching his throat as Lydia and Jeffrey watched in shock. Jed McIntyre stepped from the darkness and grinned.

"It's good to see you, Lydia," he said, the embodiment of all her darkest, worst fears.

From behind, Dax fired the first round at Jed, a high-pitched piercing of the silence around them, the bullet contacting with the tree just to the right of his head, sending wood chips splaying like shrapnel. But Jed McIntyre had already disappeared into the woods as quickly, as horribly, as he'd come.

chapter thirty-nine

"Services were held earlier this evening for New York City private investigator Jacob Hanley, one of two men discovered dead last week in Riverdale's Van Cortlandt Park," said the perfectly coiffed newscaster in his deep, mournful voice, "the result of an apparent sting operation gone wrong. The police and the FBI identified the second man as Miami multimillionaire entrepreneur Nathan Quinn. Wanted for questioning in their murders is this man, Jed McIntyre, the convicted Sleepy Hollow Killer, recently released from a maximum-security hospital for the criminally insane because of a computer glitch. The murderer of thirteen women, including the mother of bestselling true-crime writer Lydia Strong, McIntyre was serving consecutive life sentences for each of his victims. Strong could not be reached for comment.

"The investigating officers have refused to comment on the situation but warn viewers to be on the lookout for McIntyre, considered to be armed, extremely dangerous, and still at large.

"A former FBI agent and West Point graduate, Hanley's funeral took place in Queens. A memorial service will take place tomorrow evening in Miami for Nathan Quinn.

"In a related story, Jenna Quinn, wife of the late Nathan Quinn and mother of the late Tatiana Quinn, who ran away from her home and was found dead earlier this month, has disappeared. She is alleged to have stolen nearly one hundred million dollars from her husband's company and has allegedly been discovered to have ties to the Albanian mob, particularly reputed mob boss Sasa Fitore, who is also missing. Ms. Quinn is also wanted for questioning in connection with the murders of Nathan Quinn and Jacob Hanley."

Jeffrey got up from the chair where he sat and walked over to the window, still wearing the charcoal gray Armani suit he had worn to Jacob's funeral. Lydia lay on the couch in a simple black sheath dress and smoky gray Nero jacket. They were both spent from comforting Jacob's wife, whom they'd found pale and shaking from grief, on top of the battle she had been waging against lung cancer—a piece of information that Jacob had chosen not to share with Jeffrey, though she'd been diagnosed nearly a year ago.

"Maybe that's why he needed the money," Lydia had suggested in the limo on the way back from the service, trying to salvage some memory of the friend Jeffrey had lost.

"Maybe." Jeffrey had shrugged. "Let's not talk about it right now."

She'd placed a hand on his knee, which he'd covered with his. She let him look out the window at the sea of grave markers that was Woodlawn Cemetery, not trying to comfort him except just by being beside him.

He walked over to her now from the window, and she lifted her head so he could sit; then she lay back on his lap. He absently stroked her hair with one hand as the newscast droned on. He placed the other hand on her belly, looked her in the eyes, and smiled. It was weak and sad, but it was a smile. She smiled back, not trying to hide or wipe away the tear that trailed down her cheek.

"I'm scared," she said.

"Me, too," he answered softly, his voice catching.

"He's out there."

"We'll get him," he said with total confidence. And she believed him.

A thorough examination of the accounting over the last five

years—not from the printout that Jacob had provided, which had been altered, but from the computer files that Jeffrey had never been able to check—revealed that nearly a million dollars had come into the firm from unknown sources. An investigation of Jacob's personal finances, done in secret by Craig, had revealed several large deposits over the last five years, corresponding with the deposits made at the firm, totaling a million more. Lydia, Jeffrey, and Craig agreed to keep that among themselves, not wanting to cause Jacob's wife any more pain.

Craig's job over the next few weeks would be to try to match questionable deposits with invoices. Any funds that couldn't be attributed to clients would be removed from the firm's account and used to establish a grant to aid young women in the escape from sexual slavery. All proceeds from the book she would write and entitle *Tatiana* would go to this fund, as well. It was Lydia's hope that publicizing it would encourage women in trouble in the United States and around the world to seek assistance and would attract the attention of a national forum committed to helping the victims of sexual slavery and snuff films. Of course, she first had to get people to acknowledge that these things existed.

"Will you be able to forgive me someday, Lydia?" Jeffrey asked, so quietly that she almost didn't hear him, she was so deep in thought.

They hadn't spoken at all about the night in Van Cortlandt Park. It was as if she had blown glass around it and those final moments existed in a snow globe, nightmarish but silent. Dax had taken off like a panther through the trees after Jed, moving with impossible speed and agility for a man of his size. They heard three more shots and then in the distance the wail of sirens. A moment later, Dax had appeared through the trees.

"Don't just stand there gape-jawed, you two. Let's get the fuck out of here."

"Did you get him, Dax?" Lydia asked, her voice so small, she almost didn't recognize it.

He looked at her with eyes full of apology. "He got away, Lydia. I'm sorry. I'll get him, though. We'll get him . . . me and Jeff. I promise you that."

The Land Rover was parked on the other side of the narrow, rough path. They cut across the Parade Grounds with their lights off, and the heavy vehicle easily climbed the incline to the street. Dax made a left on Broadway and turned the headlights on. By the time squad cars began rushing past, they were just another vehicle on the road. Lydia sat in the backseat, having a hard time processing the things she knew, almost unable to believe that Jed McIntyre had appeared before her, was free, and that she could still draw air into her lungs. Surely when your worst nightmare enters your waking world, you burst into flames or die from sheer fright. But she was still alive and felt relatively normal, considering the circumstances.

The next day, they'd jumped to action, handling Jacob's affairs for his wife and consulting with the NYPD on the manhunt for Jed McIntyre, playing stupid with the FBI about everything else—just the way the Bureau wanted them, it turned out, stupid and forgetful. They'd learned enough to know it had to be played that way if they wanted to fight the battle another day.

Lydia sat up and looked at Jeffrey now, frowning with concern. "Forgive you for what?"

"For giving up Tatiana to Nathan Quinn," he said, looking as though it had been eating at him since that night and he couldn't believe she didn't know what he was talking about.

"For choosing my life and the life of our baby over a girl you barely know?" she said, putting her hand on his shoulder. "For choosing a life of peace over a life where we spend every day looking over our shoulders, worrying about each other, waiting for Jed McIntyre to appear out of the darkness with a hunting knife? Yes,

Jeffrey, I forgive you for loving me and for loving our life. Don't forget that I made the same choice. I didn't shoot Nathan Quinn when I had the chance."

He leaned in and kissed her on the mouth, his heart flooding with relief.

"I have an idea for the new firm," said Jeffrey, referring to their plans for Lydia to come in as a partner. He took her hand in his.

"Yeah?"

"How about Mark, Mark and Striker?"

"No way. I'm keeping my own name. Anyway, it should be Strong, Mark and Striker. I have more name recognition," she said with a smile.

"Was that a yes?"

"What was the question?" she replied, looking at him with mock innocence.

"Why don't we go upstairs, and I'll see if I can communicate it to you better."

She pressed her body against his and put her mouth on his neck, smelling his cologne and feeling the stubble against her lips. He put his mouth on hers and she felt the familiar jolt of desire, the seductive wash of safety and comfort she knew only in his arms.

"Help me close up first," she said, her smile wavering a bit.

"You bet," he answered. "I think the book for the new security alarm is on the counter."

As Lydia walked over to turn off the television, something on the screen caught her eye. "Look," she said.

The camera had zoomed out a bit and the famous newscaster with salt-and-pepper hair and sparkling blue eyes had his hand folded in front of him as he delivered the rest of the news script. On his right hand, he wore the gold insignia ring Lydia and Jeffrey had come to know so well.

They exchanged a look and turned off the television. They hadn't spent a whole lot of time discussing what they had learned about the way the world worked. And maybe that was because they recognized themselves to be powerless to change it. For the time being anyway. And they had a more present demon to battle than the shadowy, nebulous ones they knew maneuvered behind the scenes. If the Council members were the masterminds of world order, then Jed McIntyre was chaos. A chaos that needed to be chained.

Lydia truly hoped that with Nathan Quinn and Sasa Fitore burning in hell, where they belonged, she'd done significant-enough damage to their evil operation to have saved some of the women who might have met their fates at their hands. She knew they had only scratched the surface and there were many more battles left to fight.

While she went over to get the new manual, Jeffrey closed the security gates they'd had installed on the windows and in front of the elevator door, locking them each with a heavy clang. They walked together to the new touch pad installed that morning by the elevator. Jeffrey pressed the keys as the manual instructed, waiting for the confirming beeps that would assure him he'd set it right. If compromised, the system would sound an alarm and send a signal to the police, to a private security firm, and to Dax. It was only Jeffrey's FBI contacts that allowed them access to the sophisticated system, normally reserved for government officials, diplomats, and heads of state.

Lydia looked at the gates with dismay before turning out the lights. They were harsh and ugly in contrast to the warm and beautiful living room with its carefully chosen colors, lighting, and soft, luxuriant materials.

"I feel like an inmate," she said.

"We'll paint them."

"That won't change what they are or why they're there."

"It's not forever," he said, walking over to her and touching her face. As he took her hand and led her upstairs, she pushed away the black fingers of despair that tugged at her inside, reaching for the hope that forever was a place they'd find together . . . all three of them.

Author's Note

While the circumstances, people, places, and events in this book are entirely a product of my imagination, they do have a basis in reality. My knowledge of Albania, its conflicts and challenges, has been quilted together from extensive research, including news broadcasts, newspaper archives, and several books.

In my research, I obtained a wealth of information from the following Internet resources: the *New York Times* archives (www.nytimes.com); ABCNEWS.com; Albanian.com; BBC News Online (news.bbc.co.uk); the Friends of Van Cortlandt Park Web site (www.vancortlandt.org); The World Sex Guide (www.worldsexguide.org . . . for those of you who are interested); and numerous other sites.

Though *The Darkness Gathers* is, indeed, fictitious, Albania and the Balkans in general are clearly in crisis. The International Committee of the Red Cross (www.helpicrc.org/help) offers relief to this area and troubled areas around the world and is a good place to start if you are wondering how you might get involved. Furthermore, the trafficking of women and girls into sexual slavery is a very real situation and occurs daily around the globe. The Global Fund for Women (www.globalfundforwomen.org) or Amnesty International Women's Pages (www2.amnesty.se/wom.nsf) are both good places to start if you are interested in becoming more involved or informed on women's rights internationally.

It was not my intention to malign or degrade the Albanian population in this country or anywhere in the world in any respect.

All the Albanian characters in this book, good and bad, are entirely fictitious and have absolutely no grounding in reality and were not inspired by any real person.

All mistakes are my own.

Thanks for reading.

Lisa Miscione
www.lisamiscione.com

Acknowledgments

W riters are solitary and work in isolation. But no book is completed or published without the support and encouragement of a vital network of people. And I am truly blessed in that regard. I am most profoundly grateful to:

My wonderful husband, Jeffrey Unger, for his tireless reading of drafts, his unflagging enthusiasm and encouragement, and his seemingly endless supply of patience. I am also thankful for his genius in designing and maintaining my Web site and taking my author photographs. And most of all, I am grateful for his love and support in all things. Without him, I would be only half the person that I am.

My literary agent, Elaine Markson, for her wisdom, optimism, patience, and encouragement. And her assistant, Gary Johnson, who offers all those things with his own brand of personality and humor.

Kelley Ragland, my talented and inspiring editor, for her extraordinary ability to see through the flaws of my manuscripts to something better and lead me there. And everyone at St. Martin's Press, for turning the pages of manuscript into an actual book and getting it out there into the world! And especially the wonderful artists in the art department—their vision puts a face on the body.

My mother and father, Virginia and Joseph Miscione, cocaptains of Team Houston, for their shameless bragging and endless promotion.

My wonderful network of dear friends and family, especially my brother, Joey Miscione, my cousin Frankie Benvenuto, as well as Marion Chartoff, Heather Mikesell, Tara Popick, and Judy Wong, who each offer a crucial and thankfully endless supply of love and support, cheering me through the great days and pulling me through the tough ones.

My friends and neighbors Joan and Carroll Lovett, Marty Donovan, Kimberly Beamer, and JoAnna Siskin, whose day-to-day enthusiasm and support in a thousand different ways help to infuse me with excitement even in those moments when I'm stuck inside my own head.

Special thanks to Pembe Bekiri for her invaluable insight and advice on Albanian culture. She provided a much-appreciated insider's perspective, offering details that turned out to be priceless.

About the Author

Lisa Unger, writing as Lisa Miscione, is an award-winning *New York Times, USA Today,* and international bestselling author. Her novels have been published in more than twenty-six countries around the world. She was born in New Haven, Connecticut (1970), but grew up in the Netherlands, England, and New Jersey. A graduate of the New School for Social Research, Lisa spent many years living and working in New York City. She then left a career in publicity to pursue her dream of becoming a full-time author. She now lives in Florida with her husband and daughter. She is at work on her next novel.

an excerpt from

twice

BY

LISA UNGER, WRITING AS LISA MISCIONE

COMING IN
FEBRUARY 2012

Prologue

It was night when he came back. His return was washed in bright moonlight, accompanied by the crackling whispers of branches bending in harsh cold wind. He stood for a while on the edge of the clearing, making himself one with the barren trees and dry leaves beneath his feet. Standing tall and rigid as the black, dead trunks around him, he watched. It stood like an old war criminal, a crumbling shadow of its past grandeur, the stain of its evil like an aura, the echo of its misdeeds like a heartbeat. It lived still. He couldn't believe that after all this time, it lived. He pulled cold air into his lungs and felt the fear that was alive within him, too. Like the old house, his dread had aged and sagged but would not be defeated by time alone.

He made his way across the once elaborately landscaped and impeccably manicured lawn, now a battlefield of dead grass, weeds, hedges that had grown wild then died from neglect. The branches and thorns pulled at his pant legs like an omen. Everything about the house, even the grand old oak that stood like a sentry beside it, warned him away. But he was a part of that house and it was a part of him. He was all about collecting the lost parts of himself now. It was time.

Memories flickered before his eyes, 8mm film projected on a wall. He could see her dancing and see her smiling, see her running. Her chubby little girl legs, her tiny skirts and little shorts. He could see her blond pigtails, her round blue eyes. As she grew older, grew beautiful, her hair and eyes both darkened, her skin looked and felt like French vanilla ice cream. He could see her in those last moments before everything went bad. He heard her laughter and her screams and both were music to him. His love for her was a ghost pain. Since they had been wrested apart, he felt as though someone had donated his organs to science without waiting for him to die. He lived with a prosthetic heart.

He stood on the porch and felt the old wood groan beneath him, threatening to snap. He heard skittering behind the door, and the branches from the great oak scraped the sides of the house, fingernails on the inside of a coffin. He was the damned in front of the gates of hell. He was terrified but knew in his heart that he was deserving.

The house was a caricature of itself, dilapidated, shedding splinters and shingles, with cracked windows and sagging eaves, every house in every horror movie ever made. As he pushed the door open, it knocked some beer cans and they rattled across the floor. The house seemed to sigh with relief as he stepped into the foyer and he felt its cold breath on his neck. The chandelier, made of a thousand crystal teardrops, blanketed in dust, was the central point for a million spider webs that reached across the grand foyer. The crystal jingled like tiny bells above his head.

The door blew closed behind him. He looked around at the havoc disrepair and neglect had wreaked. He felt a rush of anger. It was to have been maintained; instead it had been vandalized and looted. Sun damage had drained all the colors from the rugs and furniture, the portraits on the walls. Spray-painted obscenities screamed in black and red. He could see in the sitting room that a sofa teetered on three legs. But his anger passed quickly. It was nothing a good cleaning wouldn't fix.

"Or a good exorcism," he said aloud to himself. He was surprised at how old his voice sounded.

A cracked mirror framed in ornate gold-leafed wood hung lopsided on the far wall. Someone had spray-painted *Tracy Loves Justin TL4* on the glass. He startled at his own reflection there. His face was masked by a long full beard and straggling gray hair hanging in limp, dirty dreads. He wore a tattered denim jacket, filthy and stiff over layers of equally rank T-shirts and a once-red sweatshirt. He looked like the kind of man people avoided on the street, the kind people turned away from, holding their breaths against the inevitable stench. He raised a hand to his face and his beard felt gritty and stiff as steel wool. His fingertips were as thick and hard as stones, his nails black with dirt.

He stood mesmerized as the wind hissed through broken windows, rattled cans across the floor, fluttered the heavy drapes that hung in tatters in the study. He couldn't remember the last time he'd seen his own reflection. In his mind's eye, he always saw himself as a young man. Handsome and lean, with ice blue eyes and hair so black it sheened violet in the sunlight. But he was less shocked by what he saw in the mirror today than he used to be. At least now he was as wrecked on the outside as he was on the inside. It used to seem like nature's joke to him that his heart was such a black dead place while his skin flushed with youth and health, while his smile dazzled, electric and charming. The same infected, twisted DNA that made him what he was, that forced upon him his congenital legacy, also had made him exceedingly handsome, like the Venus's fly-trap that attracts insects with its scent and beauty and then snaps them within its jaws. At least now he was recognizable for what he was.

He heard the echo of laughter and he looked behind him at

the sweeping staircase that led into the darkness of the second level. And he heard the house draw and release its foul breath. The bright full moon outside passed behind clouds and the room fell into darkness. He felt his heart rate elevate slightly and his belly fluttered with fear.

"I'm home," he said as he turned and walked up the stairs into the black, knowing as he did that there was no turning back. That the curtain had risen on the final act and that all the players would be pulled inexorably toward their end.

**Also Available
from the Author**

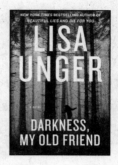

Darkness, My Old Friend
A Novel
$24.00 (Canada: $27.00)
978-0-307-46499-6

Angel Fire
Book One in the Lydia Strong series
$15.00 (Canada: $17.00)
978-0-307-95309-4

AVAILABLE WHEREVER BOOKS ARE SOLD

Want More Lisa Unger?

Use your smartphone to take a photo of the barcode below for exclusive **short stories, sneak peeks,** and **behind-the-scenes** access.

If you do not have a 2D barcode reader on your smartphone, download the software free at LisaUnger.mobi.

Don't have a smartphone? Text GATHERS to 333888.